Lorton Legends

BY

EYONE WILLIAMS

www.dcbookdiva.com

ISBN-10: 0-9846110-6-1
ISBN-13: 978-0-984-6110-6-5
Library of Congress Control Number: 2011933082

Paperback Edition, September 2011

Publisher's Note

This is a work of fiction. Any names historical events, real people, living and dead, or the locales are intended only to give the fiction a setting in historic reality. Other names, characters, places, businesses and incidents are either the product of the author's imagination or are used fictiously, and their resemblance, if any, to real life counterparts is entirely coincidental.

Edited by: Jenell Talley

DC Bookdiva Publications
#245 4401-A Connecticut Ave
NW, Washington, DC 20008
www.dcbookdiva.com
facebook.com/dcbfanpage
twitter.com/dcbookdiva

DC BOOKDIVA PRESENTS

LORTON LEGENDS

EYONE WILLIAMS

This book, Lorton Legends,
is dedicated to my father:
Larry Williams

Chapter 1

The Old D.C. Jail, Thurdsay, December 21, 1974

The sound of a young man struggling against his attacker woke Ronald Mays as the tussle bumped into his bunk late at night. A brute of a man had a smaller and younger man in a menacing headlock, dragging him to the bathroom. Startled, Ronald's eyes shot open as he tightened his grip on the sharpened steel that he slept with. Moments later, it was clear that the young man that had been dragged to the bathroom was being raped; his screams echoed throughout the dorm. Ronald tried to ignore the screams; he tried to push the thought of what was going on out of his mind. The shit was a regular thing where he'd been confined for the last few months of his young life.

Ronald Mays was seventeen-years-old and still had a boyish innocence in his young face that made him appear younger than he really was. He was tall with light-reddish-brown skin that gave him a young Malcolm X type of look. Ronald stood 5' 11" and carried a solid one hundred and seventy five pounds. His small afro made him appear a little taller. Ronald's record had him locked up with much older and harder criminals. He had been arrested for burglary at fourteen and sixteen, and was sent to a juvenile detention center in Laurel, MD called Oak Hill. Oak Hill gave Ronald his first taste of being locked up, and as far as juveniles were concerned it was a rough spot, however, it had nothing on D.C. Jail. In a violent escape, Ronald and a homie of his ran from Oak Hill. Back on the streets of D.C., Ronald lived from one robbery to the next until he boldly went inside a crap house and robbed it for sixteen hundred dollars; however, he ended up shooting a man in the chest. A week later, Ronald was arrested for attempted murder and had been in jail ever since.

Ronald saw the dude that had just raped the young man walk out of the bathroom like nothing was wrong. The dude walked straight to his bunk and lay back down without a care in the world. Ronald slept two beds away from the dude. Looking around, Ronald wondered what the young man that had been raped would do about it. *A nigga gotta kill me if he think he gon' fuck me*, Ronald thought. That was exactly why he slept with his blade. He hated butthole bandits.

"Damn, he must've bust that young nigga's ass open," Blue said, laying on the bunk next to Ronald's. He was watching the young man that had just been raped limp from the bathroom holding his ass. The young man went and laid back in his bunk, a broken soul.

Ronald shook his head. "Ain't no way in the world I could go for some shit like that. Fuck that."

Ronald and Melvin "Blue" Peoples were cool from the time they'd spent down Oak Hill together. They had been at odds before since Ronald grew up around 7th and T Street—Uptown—and Blue was from Valley Green in deep Southeast. Ronald and Blue had rumbled a few times during their time down Oak Hill; both swore that they were the one that came out on top. The fights were that close. Nevertheless, Ronald and Blue respected each other as thorough. Blue was eighteen-years-old and was a gorilla of a young man. Still growing, Blue was 5' 10" and two hundred and twenty pounds with blue-black skin. He was charged with robbing the aid of a U.S. Congressman on Capitol Hill.

"Go back to sleep," Blue said to Ronald. "I'll holla at you in the mornin', brutha."

Ronald didn't fall to sleep until somewhere around two A.M. He had no idea how long he would have to deal with the madness of being in jail in the 70s, when jail was jail.

The Old D.C. Jail, Monday January 16, 1975

The old jail was a massive and ugly building constructed of dull red bricks and sandstone sometime in the late 1800s. It was surrounded by two chain link fences topped with barbed wire and sat between the D.C. General Hospital and the D.C. Armory, right down the street from where the Washington Redskins played football. The old jail was a totally different world; it was filthy, overcrowded, and infested with rats and roaches. Ronald couldn't wait to leave the jail and get down Lorton.

Sitting at an old table, Ronald, Blue, and two other young dudes ate hot dogs and beans while talking about Youth Center I, where they were all headed. All four youths had done time together down Oak Hill. Ronald ended up with a six-year Youth Act and Blue got a ten-year Youth Act. The four youths had heard so many stories about Youth Center I, it was no place to play. One of the youths' older brother was beat to death with a hammer over a bag of heroin down the Center.

"I already know my peoples gon' have a knife for me as soon as I hit the compound," Blue said, stuffing his face. "If a nigga get out of line, bus' his muthfuckin' ass. Ain't shit to it ... shhhiiidd, I ain't doin' my time at a nigga's mercy. Fuck that."

Everybody at the table felt Blue's words. But, not everyone could live up to such words when talking about Youth Center I or any other part of Lorton.

Two C.O.s walked by, keeping an eye on the prisoners as they ate lunch.

"Man, I'm just tryin' to do this little bit of time and get the fuck outta prison," Ronald said.

"We gotta stick together," Frank said. He was the kind of young dude that would do anything on the streets, but was somewhat timid in jail. Dudes used to disrespect him down Oak Hill, but since his brother, Gangsta, was so respected, all that stopped when Blue got down Oak Hill. Gangsta was a Valley Green legend—a Lorton Legend as well; he was murdered with the hammer down the Center over the heroin. Frank was seventeen-years-old and was considered a "pretty nigga." Young and pretty didn't mix in jail. He was 5' 7", one hundred and fifty pounds with light skin, dark curly hair, and could pass for a Puerto Rican. Frank was sitting on a six-year Youth Act for armed robbery. "Shit gon' get serious down the Center." Frank bit into his hot dog.

"Shut your scared ass up, nigga," Blue joked. "I ain't gon' let nodody fuck wit' you." All four youths laughed.

Nate Bailey and Butch Wood walked by, they spoke to Ronald. He knew them through his older brother. Roland knew everybody that was somebody.

"Things ain't never as bad as people make 'em out to be," T-Bone said, speaking for the first time. He was soft spoken, so much so that one would think that he was a scared nigga when he spoke, but he was far from that. At nineteen-years-old, he was the oldest of the group. He also had the most time. He had a ten-year Youth Act for armed robbery and an adult sentence of seven to twenty one for armed robbery as well. Once he was done with his Youth Act, he was going to be sent over Big Lorton on the Hill with the older and hardened convicts. T-Bone had more robberies on his record than he had fingers. It was hard to believe, considering the fact that his mother was one of the biggest heroin traffickers in the D.C. area. T-Bone was far more aggressive than most dudes his age. Seeing his father shot dead before his eyes at five-years-old had changed his life and made him cold. "It really ain't no sense in us talkin' 'bout all this shit. A man gotta be a man wherever he at. The Center a rough

4

joint, but men respect men. I ain't tuckin' my tail for no nigga. That's it, that's all." T-Bone sipped his water. He was 6' 4", two hundred and fifteen pounds, and black as tar; his dark skin and the nasty scar under his right eye made him look menacing. He was the only one out of the four at the table that was from Northeast—8th and H Street.

"Well, one thing for sure," Ronald said, "we gon' be outta this stankin' ass jail in a minute."

Back in the dorm, as most men went on with their daily routine, Ronald and T-Bone sat on T-Bone's bunk talking about the streets. They were both high and nodding a little bit. Ronald had picked up the heroin habit down Oak Hill.

Rubbing his nose, T-Bone spoke with a slight slur. "Our visits should be here in a minute, huh, man?"

"Yeah, it's about that time," Ronald said.

"My peoples should have that boy for me," T-Bone said. He needed a certain amount of dope to keep him going from day to day.

A short while later, dressed in his blue jail outfit and the brown Stacy Adams he was arrested in, Ronald was called for a visit. Stepping into the room for his "special visit", Ronald smiled when he saw Synthia sitting at the table with a Bible. They were allowed the special visit through the chaplain. "How you doin', sexy?" Ronald hugged and kissed Synthia. He had strong feelings for her, even though he didn't know what love felt like. All of Ronald's dealings with females came in short spurts, he never really had time for them considering all the trouble he had with the law as a teenager. As far back as he could remember, since Ronald was old enough to run the streets, he was always trying to find a way to help his sister put food on the table.

Ronald was raised by his older sister, Diane; she was ten years older than him. Both of his parents were dead. His mother died of cancer and his father was shot dead by police in the riots that followed Dr. King's assassination in 1968. D.C. Blacks tore the city up. Ronald's older brother, Roland, was down Big Lorton for armed robbery. Ronald and Roland weren't close at all. Ronald didn't respect his brother because Roland didn't help out after their parents died, at least not the way Ronald felt he should. Roland was too busy getting the monkey off his back. Ronald, on the other hand, had dropped out of school in the fifth grade to help put food on the table. He could barely read because of that.

Sitting side-by-side in the room alone with Synthia, Ronald held her hand and began rubbing her thick thigh. Her long, black skirt fit her just right. Synthia was telling Ronald how hard it was to keep up with the bills since he'd been locked up. While on the run, Ronald met Synthia, who was two years older than him. They never claimed to be a "couple", but they were as tight as two people could be. Synthia was a brick-house, she somewhat looked like the real Foxy Brown—Pam Grier. She had smooth, brown skin, a thick body, and a cute face. Synthia had an attitude to match as well.

"You makin' my pussy wet, Ronnie," Synthia said, her breathing was already heavy. She loved to be able to still feel Ronald's touch. "Let me give you this real quick." She pulled out a small red balloon containing weed and handed it to Ronald. He stuffed it down into his drawers. "Well, what's up, can I get some lovin' now that I done caught the bus all the way over here to see you and bring you some weed?"

Ronald patted the Bible, and said, "I thought you was tryin' to read the Bible," he joked.

"Please." Synthia laughed and kissed Ronald. He slid his hand up her skirt as they stood. "Come on, daddy, fuck me. We don't have all day." She turned around and bent over the table. Pulling up her skirt, she smacked her ass and made it shake like jello.

"That's what I'm talkin' about." Ronald dropped his pants and grabbed her by the waist. He slid inside of her nice and slow, making her moan softly as he inched his way deeper and deeper, in and out. Slowly, he long-dicked the pussy, making it wetter with every stroke until it was gushing and sopping. "Damn, girl ... you so wet ..."

"Ahhh, yeah, daddy. I get so wet for you." She pushed the pussy back at him, and with her hands spread out on the table, she rocked back and forth. The deeper she felt him dig, the greater the fire burned inside of her. "Uh ... uh ... uh, right there, daddy, don't stop." She bit down on her bottom lip and began banging the pussy back at him, loving the dick. "Oh ... oh ... ohhhh ... ahhhh, daddy, I'm ... aahhhh ... it's your pussy, it's your pussy, daddy." Synthia came all over his thrusting dick. Still high, Ronald kept digging up in the pussy for a good fifteen minutes before he came inside her.

After they got themselves together, Synthia looked at Ronald, and said, "I can't get enough of you." She smiled as she sat in the chair, pulling her hair into a ponytail.

"Is that right?" Ronald was fixing his pants.

"You know it."

"You sure gon' have your chance to show me," he cracked slick.

"What's that supposed to mean?" She pursed her lips and rolled her eyes.

"Don't take it like that, baby, I'm just sayin', I got this time to do now. You gon' be in my corner?"

"Am I in your corner now?" Synthia shot back with attitude.

"Yeah."

"Then, don't ask me no shit like that."

"Calm down, sweetheart." He patted her thigh.

"You tell me what you want from me." She turned a little in her seat to face him.

"It's like this, I've never done adult time before. I really don't know what I'm in store for..." Ronald paused for a second, getting his thoughts together. Rubbing his forehead, he continued. "For the little bit of time that we've been dealin' wit' each other it's been good ... real good ... what I'm tryin' to say is, just be real wit' me. Don't sell me no dreams or make me no promises you can't keep, you dig?"

"I understand. You don't have to worry about that wit' me." Synthia kissed him on the lips.

The Old D.C. Jail, Wednesday, January 25, 1975

In the open shower area in the back of the dorm, Frank was alone, letting the hot water run down his back. The jail wine he, Ronald, Blue, and T-Bone had drank last night had given him a vicious hangover; his head was killing him.

Lustful eyes gazed at his ass, but Frank didn't know it, he was slippin'. A known butthole bandit crept in the bathroom behind Frank when he saw him separate from his little crew. The butthole bandit had been watching Frank for days and felt that he was the weakest link in his crew. After being on boys—faggots—for years down Big Lorton, the bandit loved pretty, young, red niggas. He also loved making fuck boys by breaking in weak niggas and making them take the dick. *This is going to be too easy*, the bandit thought as he watched Frank. He felt himself growing hard. With all his clothes on, the bandit stepped in the shower area and stole Frank in the back of the head with a punch that could have dropped a mule. Frank fell to the wet floor like a sack of bricks, but he didn't go out. Frank didn't know what hit him, the pain was the only thing keeping him from going out. Frank looked up and saw the huge, older dude standing over him. The sound of the water hitting the floor and the voices coming from the dorm were the only sounds until the bandit spoke. "You know what time it is, youngster. You can make it quick or long and painful."

Dazed, naked, and wet, Frank was scared to death as he looked up at the huge man towering above him. He didn't know what to do, but he wasn't giving up the ass. For sure! That much he knew; he would die first.

"So, how we gon' do this, youngster?" the bandit said, glaring down at Frank. Standing 6' 2", two hundred and fifteen pounds rock solid, the bandit knew Frank had no win. The youngster was just a boy to him.

"Fuck you, nigga!" Frank kicked the bandit in the nuts and tried to make a run for it. The bandit doubled over in pain, but recovered quickly and grabbed Frank, slamming him back to the wet ground, falling on top of him. The bandit had Frank in a powerful headlock, laying on top of him. Frank was on his stomach trying with all he had to loosen the deadly grip around his neck; he struggled to breathe, but felt himself losing consciousness. Frank could smell the nicotine on the bandit's breath. Nevertheless, Frank refused to give up, he knew what that would mean.

Nodding off the dope he'd just blown about twenty minutes ago, Ronald strolled into the bathroom feeling like he had to spit up. "What the fuck?" Ronald rushed the bandit, landing two heavy blows to his head. "Get the fuck off him!"

The bandit jumped up and rushed Ronald, throwing serious blows; it was clear that he knew how to use his hands. Ronald and the bandit exploded into a thunderous clutch of bone-crushing hooks and upper-cuts. Although the bandit was much bigger and his blows were doing more damage, Ronald was holding his ground against the more seasoned fighter. Slowly, Frank got himself together and joined the fight, attacking the bandit from behind. Together, Ronald and Frank began to punish the butthole bandit, fucking him up.

Somehow, a C.O. got wind of the situation and called a code. In seconds, nine C.O.s rushed the bathroom and broke up the situation. Ronald, Frank, and the butthole bandit were dragged out of the dorm and to the hole. Ronald's face was a mess, he looked like he'd gone ten rounds with Sonny Listen. The bandit had a black eye and a busted nose. Frank, who was dragged out the dorm ass-naked, only suffered from embarrassment, but his manhood was still intact.

Later on, Blue and T-Bone sat on T-Bone's bunk talking about what had went down. They were fucked up! Ronald and Frank were part of their crew. Blue was even more so fucked up because Frank was his homie from the streets—Valley Green.

"We should break that knife off in one of them old freak niggas," Blue said in a hushed tone as he eyed one of the butthole bandit's partners that slept a few beds down. "We gotta make an example out of one of them old Lorton niggas."

T-Bone said nothing for a second. He thought about what Blue wanted to do. T-Bone understood jail a little bit better than Blue; he knew that the butthole bandit that tried Frank was well respected in the system, he was also a Lorton Legend that had paid his dues down Big Lorton and Youth Center I. Consequences of a violent form would come with fucking with the butthole bandit and his partners. "If we stab one of them niggas we gon' take a serious beef down the Center wit' us, you know that, right?"

"Yeah, I'm hip, so what. We gotta set the tone and let niggas know we ain't goin' for that bullshit," Blue said.

T-Bone took a deep breath and raised his eyebrows, looking around the dorm. No one seemed to be paying him and Blue any attention. "You got your knife on you?"

"Yeah." Blue patted his waist.

"Let me go get my knife. I'll be right back." T-Bone went to get his knife from the stash spot and returned. "Let's do it."

Laying on his bunk smoking a KOOL, another butthole bandit was unaware of the danger in the dorm. He had been down Big Lorton twice and had never had any problems at all. In fact, he was much more respected in prison than he was on the streets. Blue and T-Bone, still teenagers, slid up on the older man and started stabbing the living shit out of him, not cutting him, not scratching him, but slamming their blades into the screaming victim as if they were trying to force the blades through to the hilt. Their bold assault was so quick and aggressive that it shocked the other men in the dorm. As Blue and T-Bone punished the older man, all eyes were on them. Moments later, countless C.O.s rushed the dorm and put an end to the bloodshed. Blue and T-Bone were taken to the hole as well.

The Old D.C. Jail, Monday, January 30, 1975

Frank sat on the floor in his cell, his pride crushed. He, Ronald, Blue, and T-Bone were all locked down on the same range along with other prisoners, including the butthole bandit that tried Frank. The small, one-man cell that Frank was locked in was cold, dark, and dirty. The smell of shit and piss was thick in the air. There were no toilets in the cells on that range. There was nothing in the cells; no bed, no nothing except the man locked inside. All Frank had on was drawers and a T-shirt. He had to shit and piss in a hole in the floor.

The four youngsters had made a statement; Fuck with one, you fuck with all. They had formed a bond out of necessity and when one was violated, they all responded, violently. Their environment called for such action. Their environment was schooling them to the laws of the land in a brutal world.

"Hey, Frank!" Blue called out from three cells down. "You okay down there? Why you so quiet?"

"Just thinkin'," Frank said. On the real, he was doubting himself; his manhood had been tried in the worst way. What would have happened if Ronald didn't come to his aid? What would happen if he was tried again, and he was alone? Frank knew that he was the weak link in their circle. It had always been like that, and he hated it. Growing up under his big brother, Gangsta, had never allowed Frank to fight his own battles. That hurt him in the long run. Now, in the lion's den, Frank was going to have to toughen up.

"I know you ain't trippin' off that shit like that," Blue said, knowing what was on Frank's mind. "Fuck that shit! You ain't no less of a man. You fought for yours, man."

"I ain't trippin' off that, I'm just thinkin' about how shit gon' be down the Center." Frank could still feel the butthole bandit's weight

11

on top of his naked body, choking the life out of him.

"Ay, Frank!" Ronald called out from down the range. "Look here, man, we lettin' it be known we ain't goin' for shit. From here on out, if a nigga get in our way we bus' his ass. Fuck who he supposed to be. Fuck that Lorton Legend shit." Ronald knew there were a lot of listening ears on the range, and he wanted them to hear him as well.

T-Bone was laying on the cold floor of his cell listening to the different conversations that were going on up and down the range. He didn't have too much to say; he didn't like talking up and down the range. After all, his actions spoke louder than words when he and Blue put that knife work in. T-Bone and the other three youths would be heading for Youth Center I any day now, that was all T-Bone was waiting for. He knew that once they hit the compound down the Center that it would be on. The butthole bandit that he and Blue stabbed suffered a punctured lung as well as a number of other wounds, his name was Joseph Hall. He was known for the Lorton riot of the 60s where he was accused of stabbing a captain to death with a butcher knife out of the kitchen—he beat the charge. T-Bone was thinking about who he would have to see for stabbing Joe, as Joseph Hall was called.

"T-Bone, what's up wit' you down there?" Blue called out.

"I'm layin' back, you know I don't do all that yellin' up and down the range," T-Bone said. "I'm just waitin' for that bus to roll in." T-Bone resigned to his thoughts and let Blue and Ronald continue to shoot the breeze.

Chapter 2

Youth Center I, Tuesday, February 7, 1975

Youth Center I—the Center—was just like the projects, the only exception was the fence, gun towers, and masses of convicts that made the prison the violent and overly aggressive world that it was. The Center was a little piece of Washington, D.C. scooped out of the nation's capital and dumped onto a chunk of land in Fairfax, VA. Dorms 1, 2, 3, and 4 along with the Max, 3 Tower, and Admission housed hundreds of convicts roughly between the ages of seventeen and twenty six.

Ronald, Blue, Frank, and T-Bone, along with a bus-load of other convicts, hit the compound on a bitterly cold afternoon as snow fell in huge, thick chunks. The four youngsters wore their game faces all the way down I-95 in chains and shackles. The system was turning them over to the wolves. On the outside, they were ready for whatever, but on the inside, butterflies of uncertainty plagued their stomachs. They knew how fast news traveled. Word of who they were and what they'd done up the jail made its way down Lorton less than twenty four hours after it went down. All four youngsters stepped off the prison bus into an atmosphere of uncertain danger, just like U.S. soldiers of World War II in the 1940s as they attacked Germany.

The youngsters were processed and sent to the Max in the far right corner of the compound because they were sent down early for acts of violence up the jail. In so many words, they were starting their time in prison in the hole. Locked down!

Ronald and Frank were put in the same cell toward the end of the range. Blue and T-Bone were sent on the other range. Ronald and Frank couldn't see Blue and T-Bone, but they could yell over to them through the vent in the back of their cell.

Laying on the top bunk under the old, rough, wool blanket with his hands behind his head, Ronald kicked it with Frank. He liked Frank. Even though Frank wasn't a "rough" dude, he was real and very loyal. Ronald loved that about him. When Ronald escaped from Oak Hill, it was Frank that provided the wire cutters.

Looking around the dirty cell, Frank said, "My brother used to talk about this joint all the time when he came home the first time." Flipping through the pages of an old cowboy book but not really reading it, Frank was more interested in the writing on the walls of the cell. On the wall in the back of the cell, in black ink, was some handwriting that read, *Gangstas live and die with honor, I carried the Valley on my back—1969; Valley Green Gangsta.* Frank's brother had written the words on one of his many trips to the Max before he was murdered. "He was a legend in his time," Frank said, out of the blue.

"Who?" Ronald asked.

Frank pointed to the writing on the wall and told Ronald that his brother wrote it.

"Who killed your brother?" Ronald asked. He knew that Frank and a lot of other Valley Green niggas looked up to Gangsta.

"Some dude name Ricky Horton. He ended up goin' to the feds after he killed Gangsta. I got a uncle in the feds name John-John, they say he strangled the nigga to death in Leavenworth."

"Your uncle wasn't playin' no games, huh?"

"Not about family." Frank lit a KOOL. "I was fucked up

14

about that shit. That shit drew a whole lot of lines on the south side, niggas picked sides all the way around the board. A lot of niggas still don't fuck wit' each other behind that shit." Frank blew smoke into the air and handed Ronald the cigarette. "The shit spilled over into the streets and everything, man."

"Yeah, I heard about that shit," Ronald said.

Frank told Ronald a few stories that he'd heard from Gangsta about the Center.

After talking for a few hours, Ronald said, "I'm 'bout to get some rest. I'll catch you in the mornin'." Ronald drifted off to sleep with the old Youth Center I stories still on his mind. His young world would never be the same.

Youth Center I, Friday, February 10, 1975

"Ay, Blue!" Frank yelled through the vent in the back of his cell. He and Ronald were being sent to general population. Frank's heart was pounding with apprehension of what awaited them on the compound. It was time to face the music. "Ay, Blue, get in the vent, nigga!"

"What's up?" Blue yelled back.

"They 'bout to send us to the pound," Frank yelled.

"Oh yeah?"

"Yeah, they just came to see us."

"Me and T-Bone gon' be in here for 'bout another week or so. Y'all stay on point out there," Blue yelled.

Ronald got in the vent. "Ay, Blue, remember what we talked about, man." They had vowed to never let the Northwest/Southeast bullshit come between them.

"You know that, bro," Blue confirmed.

"Tell T-Bone to get in the vent."

"Aaaaayyyy," T-Bone yelled through the vent.

"I'ma see y'all when they let y'all hit the pound."

"Be safe, Ronnie."

"I'ma do that if I don't do nothin' else." Ronald could hear .

15

the C.O.'s keys coming down the range over the loud talking of other convicts. "I talked to Synthia, she should be hookin' up wit' your girl."

"Okay, man. I'll holla at you when we get on the pound. I'm 'bout to get out this vent," T-Bone said.

Ronald and Frank stepped into the unknown world of the Center. Ronald was assigned to 3 Dorm. Frank felt those familiar butterflies in his stomach when he was assigned to 2 Dorm without Ronald. As Frank and Ronald crossed the compound, they saw people everywhere, just like in the hood. They saw a few people they knew from the streets and from down Oak Hill. Some dudes they hadn't seen in years. One of Frank's homies that ran the streets with Gangsta, a dude by the name of G-Train, pulled up on Frank and Ronald.

"Damn, what's up, baby boy?" G-Train hugged Frank. "What dorm they got you in?"

"2 Dorm," Frank said, pleased to see a homie of his.

"You over there wit' me," G-Train said, looking at Ronald like, *Who the fuck is you?* Ronald looked back at G-Train the same way.

"This my man, Ronald," Frank said, sensing the vibe.

G-Train and Ronald exchanged nods, nothing more.

"Come on, I'ma walk you over to the dorm," G-Train said to Frank.

Frank gave Ronald five and a hug. "I'ma catch you after I get my shit together."

"Cool. Be safe," Ronald said. He then headed to his dorm.

Inside 3 Dorm, Ronald ran into a partner of his brother's, a dude by the name of Fray. He had some juice with the female C.O. that ran the block; she was a bad-ass sister with a sexy body. Fray got Ronald moved on the wing with him and a few other Uptown dudes.

Going on twenty three, Fray was well respected and already established down the Center. He had always looked at Ronald like a little brother and had watched him grow up.

16

Ronald had a lot of respect for Fray; it was Fray that gave him his first .32 revolver at thirteen.

"So, what's up wit' this beef you got wit' the dude Keith Henderson?" Fray asked as he and Ronald sat in his cell smoking a KOOL. "You know how word travels."

"That nigga violated, Mike." Ronald said, addressing Fray by his government name. He went on to explain how Keith Henderson tried to rape Frank.

Fray nodded. "Y'all did what y'all was supposed to do." Fray respected the fact that Ronald and his little crew were coming through the door standing up as men. There was no other way to be respected down Lorton.

"Who all fuck wit' the dude down here?" Ronald asked, knowing that he had to deal with the dude's peoples. Not to mention, the people that fucked with the dude Joseph Hall— the dude T-Bone and Blue stabbed.

"Most of the dudes that fuck wit' them dudes over Big Lorton, but the dude Keith got a brother in this dorm on the other wing--"

"In this dorm?" Ronald cut Fray off. His antennas went up.

"Yeah, but he ain't that type of dude, he don't want no trouble. He ain't nothin' like his brother."

Ronald was already shaking his head no. "We can't sleep in the same dorm, that's out, Mike. If the nigga don't want no trouble, then he gotta go. Matter fact, we can't be on the same compound."

Fray laughed a little. "Let me holla at the dude. He from Northwest, so let me talk to him real quick."

"Mike, I fucks wit' you and everything, but it's nothin' to talk about. He gotta go or I'ma put the knife in him." Ronald's mind was made up.

Fray tried to talk Ronald out of it, but it made no difference. "Okay, I see you got your mind made up, so I got your back. At the same time, the dude Joseph got a cousin over 2 Dorm, he pull a little weight down here. He from Southeast.

17

You know we gon' have to deal wit' that, too."

"You don't gotta get into this shit. I got it on my end, man. All I need is a knife," Ronald said.

"Hell nah, I fucks wit' your brother and you like family to me. I can't let you go out there like that."

Moments later, Fray had armed Ronald with a lawn mower blade that could decapitate a bull. Fray also pulled up on a few of his comrades and let them know what was going on. Wookie, Larry Williams, and Greg Royster backed Fray's call to back Ronald. Eddie Mathis and Fly were on board as well. In a huge green army coat, Ronald walked down the wing followed by Fray and his comrades. Convicts standing out on the tier looked on, knowing something was about to go down. Seeing who was backing Ronald, the convicts knew that the youngster was not some young off brand.

Pulling up on Kenny Henderson, Ronald found him talking to another convict and cut into their conversation. "Main man, let me holla at you real quick."

Kenny could tell that Ronald was strapped, the huge coat said so. Kenny also knew that Fray and his crew were backing the youngster. "I don't want no trouble, youngster."

"I'm tryin' to holla at you alone," Ronald said with authority.

Kenny's buddie spoke up. "You can speak to him right here."

Wookie spoke up and addressed Kenny's buddie. "You want some work?"

The dude sighed. "Y'all know Kenny ain't wit' no beefin'."

"Fuck all that. Do you want some work?" Wookie got up in the dude's face.

"Nah, man." The dude left Kenny for dead.

"Look, man," Ronald said to Kenny. "We can't both sleep in this dorm. One of us gotta go and it ain't gon' be me ..."

"I ain't wit' that shit my brother tried. I know y'all did what y'all had to do."

Ronald thought about what Kenny said, but he wasn't taking any chances. He refused to be rocked to sleep. "Look here," Ronald pulled out the lawn mower blade, "I said one of us gotta go. Either you start steppin' or shit gon' go to another level." In a way, Ronald felt fucked up knowing the dude had no win, but it was what it was.

"You got it, youngster." Kenny eased by, heading for Protective Custody. "I'm goin' in."

Meanwhile, in 2 Dorm, Frank and G-Train were suited up as well. Frank was hiding in G-Train's cell with a ten inch blade, his palms were sweaty and he could feel himself trembling. G-Train told him that he would go get Joseph Hall's cousin and tell him that they wanted to squash the beef. It was game. G-Train was rockin' the joker to sleep. He had told Frank to stab the joker right in the neck with no talking as soon as he walked him in the cell. Frank was having second thoughts as he impatiently waited for G-Train to lure the joker to the cell.

"Yeah, man, that shit ain't for us," G-Train said to Freddie Hall as he walked him to the cell. "My man ain't tryin' to beef wit' you. Frank just comin' in, he really don't know how this shit go."

With his chest out haughty and cocky, Freddie said, "Yeah, I hope so, cause I'd hate for us to fall out over this shit here." Freddie was twenty five, he'd been down the Center for seven years and had been known to be a thorough dude. He respected G-Train, but saw him as a young nigga that was still coming into his own. As far as Freddie was concerned, G-Train had a long way to go before he could even think about getting in his business.

This nigga just don't know, G-Train thought, *we gon' bus' his ass*. G-Train was nineteen, and he'd been down the Center for three years at that point. During that time, he'd already gotten away with a murder and countless serious assaults. He couldn't believe that Freddie was acting like he didn't pull weight.

As soon as G-Train opened the cell door, Frank struck like an angry diamondback rattlesnake, stabbing Freddie right under his Adam's apple. G-Train whipped out his joint at the same time and hit Freddie in the back.

"Aaahhrrggg!" Freddie screamed, making a gagging sound as he grabbed his neck and forced his way backward, getting stabbed over and over again. Frank became possessed, stabbing Freddie in the face, neck, and chest. Freddie got unnaturally strong and ran down the wing trying to get away. Frank and G-Train were right on his ass like piranhas. They chased him and stabbed him all the way into the TV room where he collapsed, a bloody mess.

"Come on, let's go." G-Train grabbed Frank's shirt, pulling him along.

Youth Center I, Saturday, February 11, 1975

The visiting hall was jammed packed like a black church on Sunday morning. Aside from family members, the convicts had some of the baddest black sisters around up in the spot. Synthia was among the top five at least, that had made the short trip down I-95 to the Center. She and Ronald sat face-to-face, holding hands as they enjoyed being close to one another. She could talk to him about anything, he knew how to listen. She loved that.

"It's hard right now, money is real low. I just had to give your sister some money for her electric bill," Synthia said.

Rubbing her small, soft hand, Ronald listened to what she was going through on the streets. She and his sister were hard working black women with no man out there to help them. Ronald desired to extend his hand and help as he was doing when he was home. Being a provider ran in his blood. Now in prison with nothing to give or bring to the table, he felt like less of a man. It bothered him. "How much did you have to give her for the bill?"

20

"Eighty dollars. She needed a few other things so since I had some extra money from doin' hair, I gave it to her."

"I'ma get that back to you."

"You don't have to do that, baby."

"Shh ..." Ronald placed a finger to her soft sexy lips, hushing her. "That's my sister, it's my job to make sure she's taken care of. That's how it goes."

"Where are you gonna get eighty dollars from?"

"Let me worry about that, okay?"

"I don't want your money, Ronald, and I don't want you gettin' in no trouble." She really cared about Ronald. "All you need to worry about is going to school and making parole. I seen brothers come home from down here in a year to eighteen months, and they had the same kind of time you got."

"I got this, sweetheart. Don't worry your sexy self." He rubbed her chin softly, making her blush. Planting a soft kiss on her lips, he said, "I'm focused on comin' home as fast as I can, okay?"

"Okay, you just be careful down here."

They talked, touched, and kissed for the rest of the visit until it was time to take pictures. After that, their visiting time was up.

"I'll try to come see you next week, if I can. I'm 'bout to start a second job, so I'ma be kinda busy, okay?" Synthia said, locked in Ronald's embrace.

"I'ma miss you, baby." He kissed her and squeezed her plump ass. "Just take care of yourself. Don't work yourself to death."

"Call me."

After his visit, Ronald was walking the pound with Frank; they both were strapped with steel. They roamed the pound as if they were walking through the ghetto. All of the same elements were present; hustling, getting high, drinking wine, robbery, murder, even females—in that case they were female C.O.s, but some of them were down for whatever as well.

21

"I'm tellin you, we punished that nigga," Frank told Ronald with hot steam coming out of his mouth as he spoke in the cold air. They were on their way to buy some dope. Frank and G-Train got away with the stabbing. For Frank, it was big shit. He was proving to himself that he wasn't a pushover; he wasn't a weak link. He vowed to himself that he wasn't going to do his time running scared. If aggressive was what he had to be to survive down the Center, that was what he was going to be. In fact, he told himself that he was going to stab the shit out of anybody that got in his business in any shape, form, or fashion. "I'm tellin' you, Ronald, I ain't goin' for that bullshit down here."

"I hear you." Ronald laughed as they walked by a group of convicts. The look that the convicts gave them was one of acknowledgment, they respected the way Ronald and Frank hit the compound—playing no games.

One of the convicts, Eddie Mathis, a friend of Gangsta's, spoke to Frank. "Keep ya head up, youngster."

"Bet," Frank said, and kept stepping.

"One thing for sure, we let it be known that we ain't goin' for nothin'," Ronald said. He and Frank copped two bags of dope and went back to Ronald's dorm to blow.

Chapter 3

Youth Center I, Monday, February 20, 1975

Ronald sat on his bed smoking a cigarette, looking at pictures of Synthia. *Damn, she a bad muthafucka*, he thought. Synthia wrote him almost everyday; Ronald began looking forward to her letters. They made his day and always smelled so damn good. After getting mail from her, his whole cell smelled like her.

A knock at the cell door grabbed Ronald's attention. He looked up and saw the brother that slept next door standing outside the cell. "What's up?" Ronald nodded, putting the pictures up.

"What's up, brother? Can I come in?"

"Yeah." Ronald wondered what the dude wanted.

"My name's Harrison-EL. I'm a good friend of your brother's." Harrison-EL extended his hand. Ronald shook it with a firm grip. "Fray was just tellin' me that you and Roland are brothers."

"Yeah, that's my older brother."

"I didn't know that and you been sleepin' next door for almost two weeks now." Harrison-EL nodded at the chair against the wall as if to ask if he could have a seat. Ronald gave an approving nod. "I ain't seen Roland since the riot up the jail.

How's he doin'?"

"We don't really keep in touch," Ronald said.

"Oh yeah?" Harrison-EL gave Ronald a funny look, but didn't try to get in his business. "Hell of a man, your brother. One of the thoroughest brothers I ever met. Ain't never back down from nothin'."

Harrison-EL, Roland, and a few other men took over the jail in October of 1972. The armed prisoners turned the jail into an arena of life and death conflict between them and D.C. officials. D.C. Department of Corrections head, Kenneth L. Hardy, and close to a dozen C.O.s were held hostage for close to twenty four hours. The prisoners demanded an extraordinary court hearing where they voiced their grievances. Congresswoman Shirley Chisholm, Walter E. Fountroy, D.C. school board president, Marion Barry, and aids of Mayor Walter E. Washington acted as intermediaries. Julian Tepper, a negotiator during the Attica prison riot, was also involved.

After Harrison-EL told Ronald a little about the riot, he got up and shook his hand again. "I just wanted to introduce myself. Let me know if you need anything."

"Okay," Ronald said.

Ronald headed over to T-Bone's wing. T-Bone and Blue were out of Max now. As Ronald walked down the range, he passed a bad-ass C.O. broad by the name of Ms. Goodall. Everytime Ronald crossed her path, she looked at him like she wanted to fuck him. He would always give her a smile and keep stepping.

Ms. Goodall looked him up and down, winked, and said, "Hi you doin', Mays?" She sounded so sexy.

"I'm okay. How 'bout you, good-lookin'?"

"I'm holdin' on, could be doin' a little better." Her tone was provocative as she kept stepping herself that time. Her dark-blue pants were so tight that her panty line could be seen. She threw an extra twist into her walk, making her phat ass shake as she continued down the range. Peeking over her shoulder, she saw that Ronald had stopped in his tracks and was looking at her ass like he wanted to tear her clothes off. She smiled to herself and walked off the wing.

Ronald shook his head. "Damn," he said out loud in a low voice as he walked in T-Bone's cell. He could tell that T-Bone was high because of the slight nod his man was in. "What's up, T?"

Rubbing his nose slowly, T-Bone said, "What's up, Ronnie?"

"I see you got right already." Ronald sat on the bed.

"The dude Bulldozer got that shit. I told him give me a couple bags until my visit get here." T-Bone handed Ronald a small jail bag of dope. Ronald carefully opened the paper and took a one-on-one to get right for the Valentine's Day dance that was about to start in the gym. Chuck Brown and The Soul Searchers along with Trouble Funk were coming down the Center to bring the go-go sound to the convicts of their home town. Ronald and T-Bone had their girls coming down.

"What your peoples gon' send us?" Ronald asked, feeling the euphoric effect of the heroin.

"Somethin' small ... a spoon or two. Moms wanna make sure I ain't gon' blow it all. I told her I wanted to make some money. We gon' be alright in a minute." T-Bone lit a cigarette. He and Ronald were planning to start selling dope on the pound, even though Fray told Ronald it was a bad move for them to make, being as though they were still new down the Center. They really needed to feel the joint out a little bit more. However, Ronald and T-Bone had their minds made up.

A knock at the cell door grabbed their attention. It was a dude by the name of Tommy; he and T-Bone placed bets on sports. "What's up, Tommy?" T-Bone smiled, knowing the Bullets had beat the 76ers.

"Here you go." Tommy handed T-Bone a twenty-dollar bill. "I'll catch you later on. Who you like in that L.A./Boston game?"

25

"L.A."

"You givin' up the seven?"

"Yeah."

"Bet forty."

"Bet." T-Bone gave Tommy five. Tommy left.

"That nigga sweet as candy," T-Bone said as he stood up. "You ready to hit the gym?"

Ronald stood up. "Yeah, let's go."

They met up with Frank and Blue, and hit the gym.

Inside the gym, Chuck Brown was on the mic talking shit while his band, the Soul Searchers, tested the sound system. A few visitors were already in the gym. A few sisters brought friends along to meet some dudes at the dance. A few convicts were sure to get lucky.

Southeast dudes had a spot up front, Northwest dudes were up in the bleachers as well as by the door, Northeast dudes were against the far wall, and a few Southwest dudes were at the other end of the bleachers. A few dudes from all over were mixing on the gym floor, talking to each other about business and rapping to honeys.

"I got a few jays," Blue said as he, Frank, Ronald, and T-Bone stepped in the gym. "Let's fire 'em up before the show start."

"Let's hit the bathroom," Frank said, watching two bad-ass honeys walk by; they flashed inviting smiles at him and his crew. The whole scene inside the gym was just like being at a go-go spot on the streets at the Northwest Gardens or the Masonic Temple, go-go spots that all four youngsters played tough. Blue led the way to the bathroom.

After smoking a few jays in the bathroom, the youngsters headed back into the gym area as the go-go band began to crank up. Visitors were now pouring into gym. Too many beautiful sisters to count. While everyone else was checking out the honeys, T-Bone had his face twisted into a mask of anger. He saw a nigga talking to his woman, a cold-blooded violation that could get a lot of iron in a nigga's diet down Lorton. T-Bone rushed over to his woman, followed by his men, and put his arm around her. "You know this nigga?" he questioned his woman, looking the joker up and down like, *Who the fuck is you?*

"No, he was just askin' who I came to see," Cristal said, not knowing that her words could get the joker murdered.

"If you don't see me, don't say shit to none of these niggas." T-Bone checked his woman harshly in front of everybody. He then turned his attention to the tall, brown-skinned joker that stood in front of him, and said, "You retarded or somethin'?" The anger in T-Bone's voice made Cristal worry. She knew him well and knew that he was a real laid back dude, but when mad, he was a live wire. "Look here, shortie..." the joker began, but was cut off.

"Fuck you callin' shortie?" Frank got in the joker's face. "You think a nigga playin' wit' your bitch-ass?" Frank was on a tip where he was ready to fuck any nigga over that got out of line even a little. He and G-Train didn't kill Freddie Hall, but they put enough holes in him to make him wish he was dead. Frank was itching to put that knife in a motherfucker.

From across the gym, Fray saw what was going on and quickly intervened before the youngsters put an end to the go-go before it even got in full swing. After cooling the situation off, Fray said, "Y'all can iron that shit out later on. Niggas tryin' to make moves and shit. Alright?"

The youngsters agreed.

A short while later, Ronald, Frank, and T-Bone were dancing with their girls on the crowded gym floor along with everyone else. The dancing looked more like dry-fucking than anything else. Chuck Brown and The Soul Searchers had the energy at an all time high. Grinding on Synthia from behind had Ronald so hard that he thought he was about to cum in his pants. It was time to slide under the bleachers and get up in that pussy. "Let's take a break real quick, baby." Ronald yelled into Synthia's ear. She looked over her shoulder with a sexy smile, knowing what time it was. They headed for the bleachers.

Frank was grinding against his girl's ass to the sound of the go-go beat when a dude by the name of Charlie Dickerson walked up and asked him if he'd seen his girl. "Nah, I ain't seen her, Charlie," Frank yelled over the music. He knew Charlie from down Oak Hill.

With no visit, G-Train was roaming the gym rapping to different broads. He pulled a few and even gotten some head under the bleachers. Now, it was time for a one-on-one as he headed to the bathroom to blow some boy that he'd just gotten from Bulldozer. A homie of G-Train's was standing in front of the bathroom door when he got there. His homie looked like he was standing guard or something. "What's up, Tank?" G-Train said.

"Everything cool," Tank said. Blue had him watching the door while he got some pussy in the bathroom. Tank wasn't supposed to let anybody in, however, he wasn't going to tell G-Train that he couldn't go inside. G-Train made his own rules, always had. Tank told G-Train what was going on in the bathroom.

"Oh yeah?" G-Train smiled and thumbed his nose as he walked right pass Tank. As soon as he opened the door, he saw Blue fucking the shit out of a bad-ass redbone from the back; he had the redbone bent over the sink with her pants around her ankles. Blue was slamming into the pussy. The redbone looked over her shoulder with a lustful look on her face as she threw the pussy back at Blue. Seeing G-Train only turned her on more.

"This bitch a monster," Blue said, pulling her to him by the waist as he dug deep into the pussy.

"Aaaahhh ... you want next?" the redbone asked G-Train between moans and grunts. "I ... aaaaahhh ... uh, uh, uh ... ooooohh shit. I, I got enough to go around."

G-Train grew hard instantly. "Hell yeah." While Blue finished up, G-Train stepped into the stall and blew the dope he had. He was going to burn the pussy up off the dope dick.

Blue came all over the redbone's ass. "Damn, you got some good pussy."

"I know you tell all the girls that after you finish wit' them," the redbone said, cum slowly slid down her ass and thighs. She wiped it off with her hand, ready for G-Train, who was already dropping his pants. The redbone loved the Lorton functions; that was when she could really let her hair down. "Come on, daddy," she said to G-Train. He picked her up and sat her on the sink, facing him. She locked her legs around him, feeling him dig deep inside her pussy. "Sssssssshit, daddy! When the last time you had some pussy?" she gasped.

"The other day." G-Train had his arms around her, squeezing her soft ass as he plunged in and out of her tight, wet pussy. It made all kinds of sopping sounds.

Blue slid out the bathroom door as G-Train got down to business.

"Aaaaahhh, daddy! You too big, you too big! Ow, ow, ow, ow! Daddy you hurtin' me!" She wanted him to stop, she really couldn't take it any more. "Daddy!" she yelled like she was really in pain. "Daddy! For real! You hurtin' me! I can't take it! Stop! Stop!"

"Shut up, bitch!" G-Train fucked her harder.

"Ahhhhh ..." she yelled and began to squirm with a look of anguish on her cute face.

"Shut up, bitch!" G-Train covered her mouth, plunging into the pussy with speed and force as she scratched his face trying to get him to stop. She felt like her pussy was being ripped open. "Damn, bitch!" G-Train grabbed her hands, still fucking the shit out of her.

"Come on, daddy, put it in my mouth. Let me suck your dick, please. It's too big." The redbone was about to cry. "Please!"

G-Train pulled out. "Okay." Redbone got on her knees and put him in her mouth. Deep throat action. She was a pro. Almost gagging, she went up and down on his dick while looking up into his glossy eyes. G-Train put both hands on the back of her head and let her do her thing at her pace.

Coming up for air, Redbone said, "You so big, daddy." She gave his dick one long lick and went back to work.

Blue came back into the bathroom with two other Valley Green niggas. With a mouthful of dick, Redbone looked up and knew what time it was. She was going to have to fuck her way out of the bathroom. "That's it, no more, okay?" she pleaded, on her knees with G-Train's dick in her hand. "My man gon' be lookin' for me."

Blue laughed. "I got you. Get my men and you can go, baby."

Redbone licked G-Train's dick again and went back to work.

Outside the bathroom, Big Floyd had taken Tank's place watching the door—Tank was now in the bathroom waiting his turn to hit the redbone. Charlie Dickerson walked up, still looking for his girl; she'd been missing for a good twenty minutes. Putting his hand on Charlie's chest to stop him, Big Floyd said, "Can't nobody go in there right now."

"Why?"

"'Cause I said so, niggas taken care of business." Big Floyd was known to knock niggas out cold with one blow. "Keep it movin'."

That's just what Charlie did.

Ronald and Synthia were just coming from under the bleachers; Ronald had hit that thing from the back like never before. It was one big orgy under the bleachers. As Chuck Brown kept the go-go moving, Ronald and Synthia slid over to the chairs and took a seat.

"I meant to give you this when you first came in." Ronald handed Synthia one hundred and fifty dollars.

"I told you I don't want no money from you." Synthia wouldn't accept the money.

"Just hold it for me, baby."

"You don't quit, do you?" She took the money.

He kissed her. "Thank you."

"You are somethin' else, boy." Synthia smiled, still feeling the sensation of Ronald inside her.

Blue and G-Train were leaning against the back wall of the gym, smoking cigarettes as they watched the go-go and nodded to the beat. They saw some wild shit, Charlie and Redbone were hugged up, tongue-kissing on the dance floor. Blue and G-Train looked at each other and doubled over in loud laughter. "Daaaaamnl" they said together. After they got all their laughs out, Blue told G-Train about the dude that was talking to T Bone's woman and what the plan was for later.

"Man, look here," G-Train yelled over the music. "You fuck wit' all them bammas, if they ain't from the Valley I don't fuck wit' em."

"Nah, T-Bone a good nigga. I fucks wit' him." Blue had told G-Train how T-Bone rolled with him up the jail when they stabbed the nigga Joseph Hall. "That's my man."

"That's right, that's your man. I ain't got shit to do wit' that. I don't like them Northeast niggas, they snakes. Them Uptown niggas punks. If you fuckin wit' them you on your own wit' that, Blue." G-Train had felt such a way since his Oak Hill days.

Blue gave G-Train a fucked up look. "G, I fuck wit' a few good men from Northeast and Uptown. If they get into somethin' I'm rollin' 'wit' em."

"What if they get into it wit' the Valley?"

"That's different."

"Remember that. We Valley Green niggas, always will be. Sides already been picked way before we came along. Don't get confused."

After the go-go, in 3 Dorm, T-Bone, Ronald, Frank, and Blue met up in T-Bone's cell; all four of them were armed with deadly weapons. It was nothing to talk about, they were going up in 4 Dorm slinging steel. Frank was determined to kill something.

Larry Williams came in the cell and addressed T-Bone and his comrades. "The dude Cedric just sent word over here sayin' that if you got somethin' you wanna get off your chest, y'all can go knife-to-knife so don't nobody else gotta get caught up."

Ronald looked at T-Bone to see what his man thought. Ronald really didn't like the idea, he wanted to be beside his man every step of the way.

"Fuck all that," Frank blurted out.

"Hold up." T-Bone put a hand up to cut Frank off. "I respect that, yeah, we can do that so niggas don't have to pick sides. We can knife fight."

Larry respected the young nigga. He was thorough. "That's what you wanna do?"

"Yeah, I can hold my own," T-Bone said.

Fray and Wookie stepped in the cell. Fray said, "The nigga Cedric Staples out front."

"Cool." T-Bone headed out the cell door. Everyone followed behind him. Stepping out the front door, they saw Cedric and a few of his men standing in front of the dorm in army coats.

"What's up? You tryin' to see me head-up or what?" Cedric addressed T-Bone.

Before anyone could say anything, Frank pulled his lawn mower blade and went dead at Cedric, igniting an explosion of bloody violence right on the walk, in front of C.O.s and other convicts that were moving about the compound. The mayhem was like a scene out of a barbarian movie. Knives were slinging, hammers and hatchets were swinging, and blood was everywhere as niggas went for the kill. Frank was going all out with the lawn mower blade; he'd tried to hit Cedric in the head, but ended up chopping into his shoulder. Cedric was trying just as hard to hit Frank with a fatal blow from his knife as he stabbed through the thick army coat that Frank wore. Finally, Frank got a clean blow and opened up the side of Cedric's head to the white meat. Gruesome. Cedric was still swinging his knife as he fell. Frank went in for the kill, but was stabbed in the back out of the blue. He turned and went after his attacker with the bloody lawn mower blade. A monster had been unleashed.

Swarms of C.O.s rushed the scene, many of them in football helmets and carrying ax handles. Lieutenant Jones was dragging at the end of the pack. Still waring, convicts fought amongst themselves and against the C.O.s. After a while, the convicts that could get away made a run for it in different directions.

Cedric Staples was dead from blows to the head from a lawn mower blade and an ice pick through the heart.

Ronald and Blue got away. The C.O.s really didn't know them like that, so when dudes were rounded up they were left behind. Most of the known cut-ups were locked down. Tim Holiday, Fray, Wookie, and Larry Williams were locked down under 3 Tower where convicts were sent when the administration was sick of their shit. Under 3 Tower convicts weren't fed real food, instead, they were given a protein drink called Metrical for every meals.

One of Cedric Staples' men got away as well. However, Ronald and Blue caught him the very next morning on the way to breakfast and stabbed the shit out him, chasing him all the way into the chow hall. They were caught and sent to the Max. Their victim didn't tell; he was cut from that kind of cloth.

After Frank had opened up Cedric's head with the lawn mower blade, T-Bone found him on the ground and plunged an ice pick through his heart, finishing the job.

In the end, no charges were filed.

It was kill or be killed.

Chapter 4

Youth Center I, Sunday, August 29, 1975

The heat was in the high 80s and it wasn't even noon yet. The sun was beaming, there wasn't a cloud in the sky. Convicts were everywhere, doing everything, just like in the streets. Ronald and T-Bone were behind 3 Dorm smoking weed, waiting for Frank to come over. Dudes were playing basketball, running full court, while others were sectioned off into cliques.

Ronald, T-Bone, Frank, and Blue all got out of Max in early August; their six months in the hole flew by in no time. They were funning in the hole for real. Most of the older dudes that got locked down with them had been sent to the Wall— Maximum Security. The four youngsters were allowed back on the compound only because they weren't seen as trouble makers. Back on the compound, they found that older convicts took them serious. The demonstration they laid down back in February showed that they would down a nigga, for real. The Center was shaping and molding them.

"Let me hit that," Frank said as he stepped on the scene wearing a fresh white tank top, gray shorts, and black boots. The ice pick he carried in his pocket was unseen.

Ronald passed him the jay. "Where Blue at?"

Hitting the jay, Frank rubbed his hands through his curly

34

hair, and said, "Him and G-Train on a caper. A nigga got fifteen hundred dollars over 4 Dorm, they goin' to get that." Frank blew smoke in the air and glanced around the basketball court at all that was going on. It reminded him of the Valley in the summer time.

"Fifteen hundred, huh?" T-Bone said with his arms folded, leaning against the red brick wall of the dorm in the shade. He didn't trust G-Train nor did he like him. Blue had been hanging real tough with G-Train since they all got out of Max; he was getting high with him and robbing niggas with him every time T-Bone turned around.

A bad-ass C.O. broad walked up, switching. Her name was Ms. Baker. "Y'all just going to smoke that out here like ain't nothin' wrong wit' it?" she asked in her little girl voice.

"Baby, we got this under control," T-Bone said in a smooth voice.

She looked up at the smooth, tall, dark-skinned brother and smiled. *Damn, he fine*, she thought. "Y'all better be careful." Ms. Baker walked off, still switching like she was walking the track on 14th Street somewhere. T-Bone watched her until she bent the corner.

"I'ma fuck her," T-Bone said.

"Nigga, you say that about all these C.O. bitches," Frank joked.

"Watch," T-Bone said.

Meanwhile, in 4 Dorm, Blue and G-Train had a nigga hemmed up in a cell at knife point. They had already gotten the fifteen hundred dollars, but wanted the heroin the dude had as well. Hitting the dude with a crushing blow to the body like heavyweight boxer George Foreman, Blue watched him double over in pain and fall to his knees. Blue stood over the dude, and hissed, "If you don't give that shit up I'm goin' in ya ass to get it myself."

"I told you..." The dude tried to speak through the pain in his stomach, but he could barely breathe. "I don't got no dope."

"Get up, nigga!" G-Train cocked his knife back and snatched the dude to his feet. Looking at Blue, G-Train said, "Grab that shampoo." Blue handed him the shampoo. G-Train smacked the taste out of the dude's mouth. "Open your muthafuckin' mouth, nigga!"

"Man..."

G-Train poked the dude in the arm with the razor sharp knife, letting him know that he was serious. "Open your fuckin' mouth before I put this knife in your ass for real!" he hissed. "This the last time I'ma tell your bitch ass."

G-Train made the dude swallow the shampoo, and then had Blue beat his body like a punching bag until the dude spit up all over the cell floor. Sure enough, in the vomit, there was a fat red balloon. G-Train picked the balloon up, and said, "Nice doin' business wit' your bitch ass."

Back in 2 Dorm, G-Train and Blue split up the money and dope in G-Train's cell.

"Make sure you keep your eyes open," G-Train said. "That nigga a coward, but still be on point."

"Bet." Blue was counting his share of the money. "Don't worry, I'm on point."

"Don't be walkin' around high and shit, either. I'ma holla at you when I get back. I gotta run around the school building real quick." G-Train looked in the mirror to make sure his waves were flowing.

Blue smiled. "Catch you when you get back." He knew G-Train was going to get some pussy.

Knowing what Blue was smiling about, G-Train said, "You know me. Just watch your back, nigga."

G-Train left the dorm and stepped outside, the sun was so bright that it hurt his eyes. He slid on his shades. The smell of freshly cut grass filled his nose as he crossed the compound. Adjusting his knife, G-Train strolled the compound like he owned it.

"G-Train!" Tommy called out.

G-Train saw Tommy jogging up behind him. He loaned Tommy money to gamble with from time to time. "What's up, Tommy?" He gave him five.

"You know me, chasin' this money," Tommy said, killing a cigarette "They got a big crap game goin' on down the gym, I just lost three hundred, but I know I can sting them niggas. Loan me a hundred dollars, I'll give you back one fifty, cool?"

G-Train pulled the money out of his pocket and handed it to Tommy. "I don't want no sad story when I come get my money."

"Don't worry, man. I got you." Tommy took off jogging for the gym.

G-Train continued on his way. Approaching the school building, he saw a nigga talking to Ms. Goodall. G-Train felt like niggas knew she was off limits. After all, he had punished two niggas over her already, put the knife in both of them. That should have let niggas know, he thought. As he got closer, he saw that it was Ronald that had Ms. Goodall smiling and laughing. *This bitch-ass nigga*, G-Train thought as he walked up. He was heated. "Main man!" G-Train called Ronald. Ms. Goodall sensed danger, she knew what kind of reputation G-Train had. It turned her on. She wanted to see how Ronald dealt with the situation. If a nigga wasn't thorough, she wasn't giving him no play.

"What's up?" Ronald said with a daring look on his face. He saw the look on G-Train's face and wanted him to know that he didn't give a fuck about him, for real.

"Let me holla at you real quick."

Ronald and G-Train took a few steps down the walk, leaving Ms. Goodall behind. As other convicts walked past, G-Train said, "You know that's my peoples, right?"

With a confused look on his face, Ronald said, "You steppin' to me about that?!" His confused look turned into one of disbelief and irritation.

Not feeling Ronald, G-Train said, "Yeah, I stepped to you

about that." He had that 'and what' look on his face.

"Look, man, I ain't know that was your peoples, but we can kill all that other shit." Ronald stepped closer to G-Train.

Stepping even closer to Ronald, G-Train said, "All what other shit?!" The two of them were so close they could almost kiss.

Frank and another Valley Green homie of his bent the corner and saw Ronald and G-Train having words. "Hold up, hold up." Frank got between Ronald and G-Train with his hands on their chest. "What's up wit' you niggas?"

Ronald really didn't want to get into it with G-Train, knowing what kind of position it would put Frank and Blue in. Nevertheless, Ronald wasn't going for shit with G-Train. "Your man think I'm tryin' to holla the broad Ms. Goodall and it ain't even like that. I ain't steppin' on nobody toes, but I ain't gon' let a nigga talk to me any kind of way. I'm a man." Ronald was looking G-Train right in the eyes.

"Man, what you tryin' to do nigga?" G-Train said, trying to push Frank out of his way.

"Whatever you wanna do, nigga," Ronald shot back.

"Nah, man, I ain't gon' let y'all do that," Frank said.

Ms. Goodall looked on, impressed that Ronald wasn't trippin' off G-Train.

"Come on y'all, go 'head wit' that bullshit," Frank said.

Lieutenant Jones and his fat ass flunky, Sharp Eye, bent the corner as well.

"You better check your man, Frank." G-Train stepped off, he couldn't afford to get hemmed up by Lieutenant Jones and Sharp Eye, not with a knife on him and a few hundred dollars. He went in the school building behind Ms. Goodall.

Walking with Ronald, Frank tried to smooth things out, but it was clear that Ronald and G-Train would never get along. They couldn't stand each other.

Later on in 3 Dorm, Ronald was telling T-Bone about his run-in with G-Train while they cut and bagged dope in T-

Bone's cell. They had a nigga outside the cell watching their back for the law. T-Bone had a C.O. by the name of Turner that was bringing in the dope for him and Ronald. Turner and T-Bone lived on the same block in Northeast. Turner would get the dope from one of T-Bone's mother's workers and bring it down the Center, for a small fee.

"I don't like that nigga G-Train, anyway. He one of them niggas you gotta put that knife in," T-Bone said, sitting in front of a small pile of heroin, about three spoons worth. "You wanna see that nigga?" he asked Ronald, who was bagging the dope.

"I really don't wanna make Frank and Blue pick sides, so I'ma just stay out the nigga's way, but if he come at me wrong again I'ma put that knife in his ass."

"I'm wit' you, just let me know," T-Bone said.

There was a knock at the door. A brown-skinned dude stuck his head in the cell, and said, "That police broad Ms. Baker comin' down the tier."

"Okay," T-Bone said, cleaning up a little bit. He looked at Ronald, and said, "I got that bitch. I been layin' it down real strong, too. She biting. Be comin' to holla at me and everything."

"You fucked her?" Ronald asked.

"Not yet, you know I woulda told you." T-Bone lit a cigarette.

Ms. Baker opened the cell and stepped inside, looking good as always. She could tell that T-Bone and Ronald were up to something. "I see you busy, I'll come back later." She smiled.

"Where you workin' at?" T-Bone asked.

"They got me in the school building right now," Ms.Baker said.

"Good spot for you." T-Bone smirked.

"Whatever." She playfully rolled her eyes and turned around inside the cell so all could see what she was working with. She was phat to death. Switching, she strolled out of the cell. "Stop by and see me over the school building," she said over her shoulder.

"Wouldn't miss it for the world." T-Bone smiled. Once Ms. Baker was out of earshot, he looked at Ronald, and said, "I got her, man."

"You want all the C.O. Broads," Ronald said. "What's up wit' the broad Mrs. Jones?"

"She cool, but she really ain't goin' for nothin'. For real, I think she like you. I see the way she be lookin' at you."

"Cut the jokes out."

"For real."

Ronald looked at his watch. It was almost eight P.M. "It's time for you to go holla at Turner." He handed T-Bone a hundred dollars.

"Yeah, I'm 'bout to go do that now, and then slide up the school building," T-Bone said.

Youth Center I, Wednesday, September 15, 1975

The visiting hall was packed. Countless conversations and laughter all mixed together was the sound. Ronald and Synthia were in a conversation about his sister being hurt at work a week ago. She was okay, but was out of work. The five hundred dollars a week that Ronald was sending home was helping out a lot. Now, he would need to step it up some. Bills were sure to pile up with his sister out of work.

"Tell my sister I said don't worry about nothin'." Ronald rubbed Synthia's hand. "I'll make sure everything is okay." Synthia nodded. She no longer questioned Ronald about anything. Whatever he said was gold. If he said he was going to do something, it always got done. He was a man of his word. At that time, he was paying his sister's rent as well as Synthia's.

"Oh yeah, your brotha will be home in a few months," Synthia said.

"Whatever that means." Ronald seemed unconcerned. He felt that his brother wasn't going to do shit on the streets. Damn sure wasn't going to help him or their sister out.

Synthia knew Ronald and his brother weren't close, but she didn't know why. "What's up wit' you and Roland?"

"That's my brotha, we just don't see eye to eye. Ain't nothin' up. We family. Sometimes family disagree." Ronald wasn't going to talk bad about his brother. "We'll work things out one day."

Roaming the visiting hall with a watchful eye, Lieutenant Jones walked by Ronald and Synthia, trying to hear what they were talking about. He did the same thing to everyone that he walked by. Lieutenant Jones was the kind of cop that went out of his way to make a convict's bid as hard as possible. He had worked down the Center for close to fifteen years. He'd seen a lot and been through more than his fair share of drama. In a huge fight in the gym a few years back, he was blind-sided and knocked out. Ever since then, he'd been an asshole. He was in his early forties with a little gray in his hair. He also had one of the baddest women that worked down the Center as his wife— Mrs. Jones.

Ronald gave Lieutenant Jones a vicious look as he walked by and continued his conversation with Synthia.

"You promised me you would get into school. Did you get on top of that yet?" Synthia asked, she wanted Ronald to get his G.E.D. and make early parole. Things would be much better with him on the streets.

"I'ma get on top of it. I been rippin' and runnin', you know how it go," Ronald said. On the real, he didn't want to be bothered with school because he hated the fact that he could barely read or write. "I really been focused on makin' a little money. I'll get on top of it, baby."

"Please, do that. I want you to hurry up and come home."

"I promise." He kissed her. "Now, let's go take some pictures."

When it was time to go, Ronald hugged and kissed Synthia like it was the last time he would ever see her. He always did that.

"I can't wait to get some more of this." Synthia discreetly rubbed his dick.

"I can't wait, either, baby." He smiled.

"Me and Cristal gon' get somethin' to eat when we leave here, after that we gon' go mail off the packages for you and T-Bone," Synthia said. She and T-Bone's woman were getting close, they clicked like sisters.

"That's good, y'all be safe," Ronald said.

After being strip searched, Ronald and T-Bone headed back to their dorms. T-Bone had to go collect some money, so he broke off and headed over to 2 Dorm. Ronald strolled across the compound alone. It was a clear, bright day, still warm outside, too. Close to sixty five degrees. Groups of convicts were hanging out in front   dorms and all over the walk. Mrs. Jones walked by and smiled at Ronald, looking good as ever. "How you doin'?" he spoke.

"Fine, thank you." She kept walking.

Ronald had to take a look at that ass. "Damn." He shook his head at the sweet sight.

As he approached 3 Dorm he felt an uneasy feeling in his gut. Cautiously looking around, he saw G-Train and Blue standing off to the side of the dorm. They looked like they were up to no good, but that was nothing new. Since their run-in, Ronald and G-Train had exchanged hard glares, nothing more. Ronald knew that G-Train and Blue were always strapped. That made Ronald watch them. Not to mention the fact that Blue and G-Train were together all the time now. Coming off a visit, Ronald had no knife on him and he knew it was a perfect time for G-Train to bring him a move. *Damn, would Blue cross me like that?* Ronald asked himself. On point, watching Blue and G-Train like a hawk, Ronald walked by. Blue spoke and asked Ronald to let him holla at him.

"What's up, Blue?" Ronald gave him five and kept his eye on G-Train. "What you up to?"

"Waitin' on the nigga Bulldozer to come off his visit," Blue said. He and G-Train were on another caper; they knew Bulldozer was coming off with some dope and they were going to take it.

"You need to slow down, Blue, you in everything but a casket," Ronald warned his man.

"Yeah, I know, but I'm livin' off the land right now. You know how that go."

"Yeah, I know. Be safe. I gotta piss bad as shit. I'll catch you later." Ronald gave G-Train a quick look, and they exchanged a cold glare before Ronald went inside the dorm.

A good fifteen minutes later, Bulldozer walked into his cell. WAM! WAM! He was hit in the head with a lead pipe and fell to the floor, but didn't go out. Dazed and seeing stars with a deep gash on the top of his head, he looked up and saw Blue and G-Train; they had climbed through his cell window and were waiting for him. Bulldozer tried to get up, but G-Train cracked him in the head with the pipe again, forcing the big man to stay on the floor. "Stay down, big man. Don't get fucked up for real!" G-Train said, standing over him.

"Where that pack at?" Blue had a lawn mower blade in his hand.

"Fuck you, nigga!" Bulldozer lunged at Blue. Blue caught him on the chin with a short and powerful left hook that knocked Bulldozer out cold. G-Train stuck his hand down Bulldozer's pants and checked his asshole. He pulled out a green balloon full of dope.

"Let's go," G-Train said. He and Blue climbed back out the window so no one would see them leaving the cell.

Ronald and T-Bone were sitting in Ronald's cell with the door open when Bulldozer sluggishly limped by, bloody and dazed.

"Damn, they punished big boy," T-Bone said, smoking a cigarette. Ronald told him what Blue and G-Train were up to.

"Blue gon' get caught up fuckin' wit' that nigga G-Train,"

Ronald said. "I been tryin' to tell him to slow the fuck down."

"I know one thing for sure, they gon' have to see that big nigga about that shit." T-Bone shook his head.

Later on inside 2 Dorm, a group of convicts crowded around the black and white TV watching a re-airing of the June 30, 1975 Muhammad Ali/Joe Bugner heavyweight title fight. The TV area was loud and live, as if the fight was live.

Blue, nodding off the dope, left the TV area and went out back to get some fresh air. It was dark outside, like a back alley in the ghetto. Only two other dudes were out back, they were smoking weed at the other end of the basketball court. Blue slowly blinked and nodded. Then, he spit up and stayed doubled over for a second. *Damn, this some good shit*, he thought. Wiping his mouth, he stood straight up. The dudes at the other end of the court were leaving. The only sound in the air was the chirp of crickets.

Out of the shadows came three dudes, one had a hammer and the other two had knives. Blue didn't even see them coming he was so high. The hammer smashed into the back of Blue's skull like it was a watermelon, he fell to the ground, never knowing what happened next. Bulldozer got his man. Holding the bloody hammer, Bulldozer stepped back as his comrades butchered Blue until he was no longer breathing.

At nineteen-years-old, Blue was gone. He didn't last a year down the Center.

Chapter 5

Maximum Security, Thursday, January 15, 1976

An old, beat-up prison van navigated the rural roads of Lorton, VA heading for Maximum Security—the Wall. Hot ass Sharp Eye was behind the wheel talking a bunch of shit that Frank wasn't trying to hear. A bunch of shit about how convicts behind the Wall were much older, real killers, and were on ass hard. Sharp Eye thought he was scaring Frank. He wasn't. Frank no longer cared about anything Lorton had to offer; he was ready for whatever came his way. Pushing steel was an art he'd learned to use for his survival.

Sitting in the back of the van handcuffed and shackled, Frank said, "Sharp Eye, I ain't tryin' to hear that bullshit you talkin'."

Sharp Eye laughed. "Yeah, I know you think you rough now. You twenty years old, you stabbed a few guys over the Center, got away with a murder, maybe two, for real, and you think you ready for the Wall. You in for a rude awakening." Sharp Eye smiled and shook his head. "See, what you youngsters don't understand is that there's always a nigga rougher and tougher than you. The shit you and your boys were doing over the Center ain't shit to what you gon' see behind the Wall. Trust me. I've driven a thousand tough youngsters from the Center to the Wall after they'd worn out their welcome over the Center. You wouldn't believe how many of them were taking dick in less than a week."

"Shut the fuck up. A nigga ain't tryin' to hear that shit you talkin'." Frank snapped. Sharp Eye had him fucked up. "Nigga, you takin' me to the Wall 'cause I push that steel. Don't forget that. If a nigga get out of line you gon' hear about me pushin' that steel again."

Frank wasn't just talking. He was dead serious. After Blue was murdered, it was a bloodbath over the Center. Frank, G-Train, and four other Valley Green niggas stormed 3 Dorm and stabbed every nigga that ran with Bulldozer. Out of the seven niggas that they hit, two of them had taken part in Blue's murder. Bulldozer was already locked down for Blue's murder, so he was lucky as far as Frank was concerned. However, no one died when the Valley Green niggas stormed 3 Dorm that morning. They were all locked down and sent to the Max. Their Youth Center I days were over. They sat in the Max waiting to be sent to the Wall. They had left their mark on the Center for good. Convicts were still talking about how they had stormed 3 Dorm and butchered shit. Among the C.O.s, the incident was dubbed The Valley Green Massacre.

While in the Max waiting to go to the Wall, Frank put a murderous plan into effect. He got C.O. Turner to let him out while Bulldozer was in the shower. Frank caught Bulldozer off guard while he was washing his hair and stabbed him in the eye with a six-inch blade. It felt like a knife sliding into a piece of steak. After that blow, it was all she wrote. Frank stabbed Bulldozer five more times, all neck shots. When his work was done, he slid back into his cell and Turner locked him back in. Turner swore to the captain that he didn't know who stabbed Bulldozer or how another convict got out of their cell to do it. An investigation began that was focused on Frank. When it was all said and done, Fairfax VA didn't feel as though there was enough evidence to charge Frank with murder. He ducked a bullet. There was no turning back for him. All problems would be solved with steel from there on out. It was the law of the land, Frank thought. The Center had turned him out.

"Well, we're here," Sharp Eye said as he drove through the gate that separated the Hill from the Wall. He pulled up outside of R-N-D. Frank looked up at the 30-foot red brick wall that would now confine him and felt a sense of awe. He was now behind the Wall. There were no time for games. At least he could bank on G-Train having a knife for him. G-Train was sent behind the Wall just over a month ago. "You ready, Thompson?" Sharp Eye asked, looking back at Frank.

"As long as my time still runnin' I don't give a fuck where they send me," Frank said, looking out, the window. He could see convicts outside cleaning up and doing other details.

"You gotta lotta spunk, son. Word to the wise. if you fuck up back here and kill somebody, your next stop is the feds."

Youth Center I, Thursday, Janury 15, 1976

Ronald returned to his dorm aftcr a scrious work out at the gym. He'd joined the boxing team a few months ago and got to leave the Center to box at other Lorton institutions as well as at some gyms on the streets. The boxing team also fought at a skating rink not far from where Ronald had grown up. Every time he left the Center with the team and went to the skating rink, Synthia would be there to see him. In fact, the reason he joined the boxing team was because he learned that they got to leave the prison. Now, he was in love with boxing. Ronald patterned his style after "The Greatest" --Muhammad Ali. Harrison-EL was training Ronald. He even told Ronald that he had the natural speed and grace of a young Ali, although Ronald still had a lot to learn. Boxing and street fighting were two different things. Ronald's name was kicking on the boxing tip, as far as Lorton boxers. He, Larry Pringle, and Wilbert Cook had all put on big shows at their last fights. Boxing also helped Ronald in different ways: It helped him shake his heroin habit. So far, Ronald had a record of eleven and two with six knockouts. His two loses came by way of much bigger boxers, both loses were by decision. However, Ronald was working on getting bigger. He had already added twenty pounds of solid muscle to his 5' 11" frame and now weighed in at one hundred and ninety five pounds with a punch that had stopping power that often went unnoticed when an opponent looked at his slim, but cut up, frame.

As Ronald got ready for his shower, T-Bone walked in the cell smoking a cigarette. "What's up?" He gave Ronald five.

"Tired, 'bout to take a shower and lay back for a minute."

"You know they sent Frank to the Wall today, right?" T-Bone asked.

"Yeah, I'm hip."

"He gon' be alright. This prison shit done turned him into a man."

"More like a monster," Ronald joked.

T-Bone laughed. "No bullshit, he love that knife."

"I just hope he don't get caught up behind the Wall fuckin' wit' that nigga G-Train," Ronald said.

"You know Frank could always think for himself. He far from a dummy." T-Bone took a long drag on his cigarette. "I see you 'bout to get in the shower, I ain't gon' hold you up. I was just comin' to give you your break down, I'll hold it for you until you get out the shower." T-Bone was talking about Ronald's share of their drug money.

Ronald and T-Bone were making a killing off the dope over the Center. Ronald was sending home almost $2,500 a week. T-Bone would have been able to do the same thing, but he was still getting high and that took money out of his pocket. Nevertheless, they were selling heroin over Youth Center I. They had a few problems, but nothing major thus far. They were putting the dope in the hands of others to keep the law off of them. All they had to do was govern the product and collect the money. So far, the game plan was working.

"I'll catch you when I get out the shower," Ronald said.

Walking down the range with his towel wrapped around him, Ronald passed Mrs. Jones. She spoke and couldn't help but to stare at his body, especially his abs. Ronald smiled, rubbed his stomach muscles, and said, "Hard work."

Mrs. Jones flashed an embarrassed smile and diverted her eyes from Ronald's body. "Mmmph, I see." She kept walking.

Ronald took a look at that ass and headed for the shower with a smile on his face.

After his hot shower, Ronald sat in his cell getting dressed, thinking about his upcoming fight. The next day he would be outside of the prison gates again, back in D.C., boxing. Maybe even getting some pussy after the fight, depending on how much time he had after the fight. He felt a little anxiety, his opponent was the same dude that gave him his first loss.

"What's up, Ronald?" Harrison-EL walked in the cell.

"Just got out the shower, 'bout to lay back for a minute."

Ronald and Harrison-EL had gotten close since Harrison-EL started training him. Harrison-EL was extremely intelligent. His only downfall in life was that he was a criminal at heart and couldn't stay out of prison. He was ten years older than Ronald at twenty nine. After trying to give Ronald a few things to read, Harrison-EL learned that Ronald could barely read. He then began to work with Ronald on his reading; he also began to enlighten him on other things like religion, Black history, Black Power, the struggle of George Jackson, and why he was murdered in San Quentin State Prison. He was schooling Ronald on different levels.

"You got somethin' else for me to read?" Ronald asked, putting on lotion. "I finished that other literature."

"What you want?" Harrison-EL smiled, the young brother was hungry.

"Give me somethin' else on the Black Panthers and somethin' on the Nile Valley."

"Good subjects." Harrison-EL rubbed his chin and nodded approvingly. "What you know about the Nile Valley?"

Ronald thought about what he'd read the night before. "Well ... I know that people from there were no doubt Black and that they were contributors to the Cradle of Civilization. Civilization started in the river valleys of Africa and Asia in the Fertile Crescent."

"You on top of your game," Harrison-EL said.

"I'm gettin' there."

"I'm gonna get you somethin' to read, I'll be right back."

Later on in the bathroom of the school buidling, C.O. Turner gave T-Bone four balloons containing five grams of heroin each. T-Bone slid the balloons in his pocket, and said, "Good lookin' out." He then handed Turner one hundred dollars.

"T, do somethin' wit' me. I got that monkey on my back," Turner said. "I need somethin' to hold me 'til I get off."

"I don't got nothin' on me right now. Go tell Ronnie I said hit you off for me."

"Thanks, man." Turner left the bathroom headed for 3 Dorm, he needed a fix bad.

T-Bone headed down the hall to the last class room. He looked inside and the lights were out, but with the light coming from the hallway, he could see Ms. Baker sitting in the back of the class room waiting for him. T-Bone smiled, looked up and down the hallway to make sure no one was paying him any attention, and slid inside the class room. By that time he'd been fucking her for months. The pussy was on one thousand. He was feeling Ms. Baker, but nowhere near as much as she was feeling him. Her feelings were starting to get caught up.

Short and sexy, Ms. Baker was 5" 4" with thick thighs and an ass that made all of her pants look too small. Her smooth, dark-brown skin always had a beautiful glow to it that made her look like she could be from the Caribbean. She had pretty, dark brown eyes that T-Bone loved. Her succulent lips always had a gloss to them. T-Bone made it his business to suck on them every time he kissed her. Ms. Baker wore her hair in tiny little braids that hung to her shoulders. She was thirty one-years-old and single. Her last relationship had been an abusive one that she tried not to think about. As T-Bone laid his rap game down on her, over time she couldn't help but fall for him. He was smooth and knew what to say to a woman.

"How you doin', sweetheart?" T-Bone hugged and kissed Ms. Baker, sucking her bottom lip a little bit. That made her wet instantly. As she wrapped her arms around his neck, he rubbed his hands down her back and rested them on her ass. Squeezing it, he said, "Damn, you smell good, baby."

Ms. Baker blushed. T-Bone always had that kind of effect on her. "Thank you." She kissed his lips. "I couldn't wait to see you."

"Me too." He continued squeezing and rubbing her ass. "I got a surprise for you."

"A surprise? What?" She smiled.

T-Bone let her go and went in his pocket. He pulled out a gold chain with a gold heart hanging from it with a diamond in the middle. He'd bought it on the compound for a bag of dope. Holding it in front of her face, he said, "You like it?"

Reaching up to touch it, Ms. Baker said, "It's beautiful."

She was all smiles. *Damn, this young boy is smooth*, she thought. "You got this for me?"

"It's the least I could do for someone I care about." T-Bone put the chain around her neck and kissed her lips again. He then slid his tongue inside her mouth and played with hers as he gripped her ass. She felt him grow hard against her leg and loved how big he felt.

"Is Turner watchin' your back?" Ms. Baker asked, knowing that T-Bone had Turner on his team.

"Yeah, he gon' make sure we alright, don't worry about that. He ran down to the dorm real quick, but he'll be right back." T-Bone began to suck on her neck as his hands explored her body. Her hands did the same and ended up in his pants, stroking his manhood. He felt so big in her soft, small hand. T-Bone slid one hand inside her shirt and began squeezing her right breast, playing with her hard nipple with his fingers. She began to moan and breathe hard. She purred like a cat and tingled between her legs. T-Bone opened her shirt and pulled both of her breasts out of her bra. He took one in his mouth and sucked her nipple. Her hand was still inside his pants, stroking his huge manhood. She wanted him so bad. *Damn, I wish I could take his ass home with me,* she thought.

"You're so big, Ty," she whispered.

Sucking her breast and slowly sliding his long fingers in and out of her wet pussy, T-Bone said, "You get so wet."

"I want to taste you," she said.

"I'm all yours."

She got down on her knees and pulled out his manhood. She kissed the head as she looked up into T-Bone's eyes, licked the sides, licked underneath, and then put him in her mouth. "Aaahhh." T-Bone closed his eyes. She pulled him out of her mouth, stroked him, and teased him with her tongue. He put a hand on the back of her head, encouraging her to keep it in her mouth. He tasted too good to her, too good to be true. It had been a long time since she enjoyed having a mouth full of dick.

She came up, and said, "I want you inside me, Ty."

"Whatever you want, baby," T-Bone said.

Ms. Baker let her pants fall to her ankles and bent over an old wooden table. T-Bone dropped his pants, rubbed his dick against her smooth ass cheeks, and slapped her plump ass. "Ssssss, owww." She looked over her shoulder. "Put it in, daddy." She reached back and grabbed him, pulling him toward her wet pussy. She needed and wanted penetration bad. Couldn't wait any more. T-Bone slipped right inside. Deep inside. Felt her tight walls grip him like a squeezing fist. With every stroke, she got wetter. The sound was a turn on alone. "Aaaahhh ..." she gripped the sides of the table and rocked back and forth with every deep stroke as her eyes rolled back in her head. She didn't care that she was at work, didn't care that she could lose her job if caught. All she cared about at the time was what T-Bone was doing to her. Doing so right. He slapped her ass again. "Sssssss ..." At least ten inches inside her, T-Bone hit her spot over and over again. As he continued to stroke her, it felt like he was getting deeper. "Ooohh, Ty, I'm cummin'""she panted as she tried to keep up with his strokes that were turning into pounding stabs. But, they were oh so good. "Fuck me." She couldn't believe T-Bone was twenty and knew how to work her over like he was doing. "Don't cum inside me, Ty."

Holding her small waist, T-Bone pulled her to him as he thrusted up inside of her with quick powerful strokes. It was too late to talk about not cumming inside of her. "Aaaaahhh ..." he exploded inside of her. She felt the explosion, but didn't even care. It was worth it.

Youth Center I, Sunday, January 18, 1976

The visiting hall was packed like a Baptist church on a Sunday afternoon. Loving family members and friends came to see convicts that the system saw as nothing more than numbers. Synthia and Ronald's sister, Diane, came to see him.

Diane was twenty nine and looked just like her deceased mother. She stood six-feet even, was slim with a sexy body, silky black hair, and reddish-brown skin. She had full lips and light-brown eyes, they were features that she shared with Ronald.

Diane was talking about a recent article that had been written about Ronald in *The Washington Post*. The sports writer spoke highly of the positive effects that prison boxing could have on the lives of youths that had made mistakes. He highlighted the Youth Center I boxing program and made special mention of Ronald Mays, who he'd seen knockout a semi-pro boxer at the Kalarama skating rink. After being knocked down early in the first round, the reporter saw Diane go up to Ronald's corner and tell him to stop acting scared and fight like a man. That did the trick. When Ronald answered the bell for round two, the reporter saw a flash of potential that he hadn't seen since he first saw a young Joe Louis fight. Ronald made quick work of the semi-pro boxer late in the second round with a combination of quick blows that he wrapped-up with a neck-snapping uppercut that ended the fight. The Youth Center I team didn't lose a fight all evening.

"The reporter said that you could really do somethin' wit' your skills when you get out if you keep working on it," Diane said. "He talked to me for a good hour after the fight, said he loved your left hook."

"What you know about a left hook?" Ronald laughed at his sister.

"I know where you got your left hook from." Diane pursed her -lips and rolled eyes playfully. She used to beat Ronald's ass when they were younger; in fact, she was the one that taught him how to fight—not box. "Maybe you can get paid for that left hook when you come home."

"You think he could go pro for real?" Synthia asked, looking good as always, even being two months pregnant by Ronald. They had a Lorton baby on the way.

"Ronald can do anything he put his mind to. He been like that since he was a baby. The lil' nigga was walkin' at nine months. I caught his ass walkin' to the dining room table, goin' for Roland .s beer." Diane laughed at that memory. Ronald and Synthia had to laugh, too.

On the other side of the visiting room, T-Bone held Crystal's hand as they talked about the news she had just dropped on him, she was pregnant. T-Bone was pleased. It was the best news he'd heard all year.

Standing at the visiting hall door with tears in her eyes as she rubbed the heart on the chain that T-Bone had given her, Ms. Baker was jealous. She hated the sight of T-Bone sitting all up in Cristal's face. At first it didn't bother her when she would see T-Bone with Cristal, but lately, it tore her heart out to see the shit. Made her sick to her stomach. Snatching the chain off her neck and slinging it to the floor, Ms. Baker ran back to the school building.

"What's up wit' Roland?" Ronald asked. Since he made parole, Roland had been living with Diane. He was working for Metro, was drug-free, and he was helping out with the bills.

"He doin' pretty good," Diane said. "When he's not gettin' high, Roland always does good for himself."

"He wrote me. He said he wanna come see me, but he had some problems with his ID the last time he tried to come," Ronald said.

"Yeah, he told me. He got that straight now. He should be down here soon," Diane said.

The C.O. walked over and told Ronald that his visit was up. Ronald hugged his sister and told her he'd see her next time. "I love you, you take care."

"You do the same, boy." Diane kissed his cheek.

Giving Synthia a big hug and a wet kiss as he squeezed her ass, Ronald said, "I love you, too, baby. Drive safely."

"I will. Keep your head up," Synthia said. "I just took some more pictures for you,too. You gon' really like these ones." She smiled.

Walking across the compound in the cold heading for the lieutenant's office, Mrs. Jones was on her lunch break and needed a few dollars, so she decided to get it from her husband. When she walked into his office, she gasped and covered her mouth. "Oh my God." She couldn't believe her eyes. "Bastard!" She ran in the opposite direction with that vivid mental picture etched across her mind. When she stepped in the office, she saw Ms. Goodall down on her knees sucking Lieutenant Jones' dick. Mrs. Jones was sick of her husband fucking every young bitch that got a job down the Center. Tears ran down her beautiful face as she rushed back to 3 Dorm in the cold. A hand grabbed her shoulder. She snatched away. "Get off me, you bastard!" She glared at her husband with hate in her eyes.

"I'm sorry, baby," Lieutenant Jones said.

"That's what you always say, fuck you!" She tried to hold her tears back, but they were running down her face like wild horses. She took off in a quick sprint to get away from her husband. She couldn't stand to look into his lying eyes.

A short while later, almost all of the 3 Dorm convicts were watching the Super Bowl. Pittsburgh and Dallas were just getting started. T-Bone had five hundred dollars riding on the Steelers.

"This sweet money here," T-Bone said to Ronald, smoking a KOOL. "Everybody know the Cowboys can't fuck wit' the Steel Curtain."

Ronald laughed. His team was the Washington Redskins; he wanted the Cowboys to lose, anyway. "For five hundred dollars, Pittsburgh better gut the Cowboys."

During half time, Ronald went to use the bathroom. On his way back to the TV area, he passed Mrs. Jones. She was walking down the range with her head down. It was clear that something was wrong with her and that she'd been crying.

"What's wrong, Mrs. Jones? You okay?" Ronald asked with concern.

"I'm okay, Ronald," she said with her arms folded. Her head was still down, eyes to the floor.

Ronald gently put his finger under her chin and lifted her head so that he could look into her eyes. She didn't try to stop him from touching her. "You don't look okay. You can't even look me in the eyes. How you gon' tell me you okay? I can tell something's wrong wit' you. Ray Charles can see that."

Mrs. Jones smiled at that.

Ronald rubbed her arm. It comforted her. He could tell that she was hiding her pain. His concern eased her pain and began to tear down her protective walls. "Talk to me, what's wrong?"

Wiping away a lone tear, Mrs. Jones said, "I caught Ms. Goodall sucking my husband's dick." She paused and looked around, making sure no one could hear them. "I'm sick of his shit ..." She began to vent her frustration and anger. She needed to get it out or she would blow. Smoothly, Ronald listened, nodding in agreement here and there. He let her get it all out. She then let out a low laugh of self-pity, and said, "Look at me, I don't mean to bore you with all my problems."

"You're not borin' me. We're talkin', that's all. I'm glad that I could lend you an ear." Ronald flashed her a smile and rubbed her cheek with the back of his hand. "You'll be okay. A strong sister like you can always do better."

She blushed and wiped some of her hair out of her face. "You're so sweet. Let me go."

"You take care." Ronald headed back for the TV area, taking a look over his shoulder at her ass as she continued down the range.

The Steelers beat the Cowboys 21-17. T-Bone was up five hundred dollars, a good come-up. While T-Bone went to get his money, Ronald went to his cell and laid back. He wanted to do a little reading about Huey Newton, Bobby Seale, and the Black Panthers. Fifteen minutes into his studies he was interrupted by a huffing and puffing T-Bone.

"Let me see your joint!" T-Bone said with a busted lip.

"What's up?" Ronald jumped out of bed wondering why T-Bone wanted his knife.

T-Bone told Ronald that he went to get the five hundred dollars he won on the Super Bowl from Tommy and they got into an argument about the money. Tommy felt like T-Bone was pressing him about the money. T-Bone didn't give a fuck how Tommy felt about the situation. It was his money he was checking on, T-Bone thought. The two traded a few harsh words until T-Bone got tired of talking about what belonged to him and punched Tommy in the mouth. They clutched, each landing good blows until a dude that was cool with them both broke it up.

Ronald pulled his knife from under his pillow and handed it to T-Bone. "Come on, we gotta go get that other joint, too," Ronald said. They went and got another knife from their stash spot before sliding over to Tommy's wing. They headed straight for Tommy's cell and found him wrapping a shred of torn sheet around a flat piece of steel-with a monster point. He was making a handle for his knife. No doubt about it, he was thinking the same thing T-Bone was thinking.

"It's too late for that, nigga!" T-Bone said as he and Ronald rushed Tommy. They were all over him in seconds, stabbing him in the neck and chest. Tommy fought back for a second, even scratched T-Bone in the chest and arm a few times. Ronald grabbed him by his shirt and began stabbing him in the stomach. Tommy got super hero strong and bolted out of the cell like an NFL running back. Blood was all over the place. T-Bone went after Tommy, stabbing him in the back once more before Ronald pulled him back, letting Tommy get away.

"Let him go." Ronald knew Tommy was hit bad. It was time to think about getting away with the stabbing. "He through, we gotta get out of these bloody clothes."

They ran down the range and into an empty cell where they threw their bloody clothes out the window. In their underclothes with their knives at their sides just in case, they slid back over to their wing of the dorm. Ronald and Mrs. Jones made eye contact along the way. He could tell she knew what was up. Tommy was passed out in a pool of blood in front of 3 Dorm. Ronald and T-Bone stashed their knives and got dressed, making sure they appeared to have nothing to do with the vicious assault that had just taken place.

Moments later, Lieutenant Jones, Sharp Eye, and about six other C.O.s came in the dorm looking for the aggressors. Lieutenant Jones questioned Mrs. Jones about the stabbing. She said she had no idea who did it, even though she had a feeling that Ronald and T-Bone were behind the assault. Lieutenant Jones and the rest of the C.O.s then walked around the dorm checking things out. It was as if nothing had went down. Sharp Eye asked a few questions, but everybody's response was the same, "I ain't see nothing."

Ronald was laying in the bed pretending to be sleep when Lieutenant Jones opened his cell door. Sharp Eye was standing right behind him. Ronald's heart was pounding as if he was in a speeding car that was about crash. He just knew that Mrs. Jones had put the law on him. He knew he was on his way to the max.

If Tommy was to die, Ronald would be facing murder charges and would be on his way behind the Wall.

"Everything okay in here, Mays?" Lieutenant Jones asked, looking around the cell.

Faking like he was just waking up, Ronald spoke in a groggy voice. "What's up, Jones?"

"You seen anything?"

"Nah, man, I'm tryin' to get some sleep." Ronald rolled back over and pulled the covers over his head, hoping Lieutenant Jones went for the move. He did. Ronald heard the door close.

Just as Lieutenant Jones and the C.O.s left Ronald's cell, he could hear the helicopter landing outside on the compound. It was so loud that it seemed like it was right outside of his window. Tommy was being rushed to the hospital by helicopter. Ronald wondered if Tommy would live.

About an hour later, things were back to normal. T-Bone and a few other convicts were in the cell next to T-Bone's cell shooting dice. Mrs. Jones walked by and didn't say a word, even though she saw cash money all over the cell floor. She stopped at Ronald's cell and knocked on the door. He opened the door in nothing but his boxers. Mrs. Jones' eyes fell to his abs and down lower with a mind of their own. She had to struggle to bring them back up. After seeing the print in his boxers, she knew what Ronald was working with. *Nice,* she thought.

"What's up, Mrs. Jones?" Ronald smiled. Earth, Wind & Fire's hit song, *Shining Star,* could be heard coming from a radio down the wing.

Leaning forward, Mrs. Jones whispered, "You better behave yourself, boy. Y'all almost killed that boy."

Tommy was in bad shape, but he survived the assault.

Ronald nodded. "I knew you saw us. You ain't give us up, huh?" He knew that she had taken a liking to him. He smiled and folded his arms, making them look much bigger.

"Nah, I ain't say nothin'. Tommy had that coming. But anyway, I just wanted to say thank you for listening to me earlier. I really needed someone to talk to and you understood me."

"Anytime, think nothin' of it."

"See you tomorrow."

"Drive safely."

Mrs. Jones walked away. Ronald watched her ass the whole way down the range. "Damn." he said to himself, nodding his head. "That's a whole lotta of woman."

Chapter 6

Youth Center I, Monday, April 6, 1976

Ronald had a big day ahead of him. Some pro boxers from Pennsylvania were coming inside the prison to spar with the Youth Center team. Among the pro boxers was a well known boxing trainer by the name of Wilfred Walker who ran a gym in Easton, PA; he was also the trainer of heavyweight boxer James Holmes. Holmes was working his way up in the rankings, in search of a title fight. Ronald was hyped about being able to get in the ring with Holmes. It would test his young skills against a former Olympic gold medalist. Although it would be Ronald's first time in the ring with a pro that had a name for himself, it was not the first time that a pro boxer had graced the Center. Pro boxers came to all parts of Lorton to check out the hype behind the Lorton boxing teams.

Ronald walked into Harrison-EL's cell and found him reading *The Washington Post*. An incense was burning by the window making the cell smell like frankincense. A small radio sat on the floor with sounds of Marvin Gaye coming from it—*Let's Get It On.*

"What's up, Harrison-EL?" Ronald took a seat in the wooden chair beside the small metal desk Harrison-EL had in the back of the cell.

"Just readin' the paper." Harrison-EL sat the paper down. "What you think about that information I gave you last night?" He'd given Ronald some information about the U.S. Supreme Court decision of 1857 that made America's feelings about Blacks clear: No Black could be a U.S. citizen and Black people had no rights in America that White people were bound to respect. It was all right in black and white in the case of Dred Scott.

"I couldn't believe that shit," Ronald said. "They just out right put it out there like, Fuck us ... we ain't even human, in so many words." The more Ronald learned about the history of his people, the more he found himself growing a deep hatred for White people. To add to that, when he looked around all he saw were Black convicts, maybe one or two whites out of hundreds of Blacks. Blacks couldn't be the only ones in D.C. breaking the law.

"Always remember that, young brotha. The Europeans that run this racist country gon' always feel that way. They don't put it out there like that no more, but the conscious man will always be able to read between the lines." Harrison-EL pointed to his head, alluding to the power of thinking. "I never allow myself to forget what's really goin' down. My views might be extreme ...but that's how the world is, man. I was just reading the paper and it's right there, in between the lines. This government hate us. They launched a war on crime that's really a war on Blacks and poor people. Ain't no different than what President Johnson did wit' his punk-ass Crime Commission. That was the beginnin' of this war on crime. Anybody who knows anything about politics knows that the Crime Commission was some bullshit. In my eyes, only two things came from it was a bunch of new task forces and the Safe Streets Act of '68. All in all, they was just settin' the stage to lock more of us up."

Harrison-EL and Ronald continued their conversation as they crossed the compound. Along the way, they stopped and spoke with Nate Bailey. Ronald also saw T-Bone standing by the school building talking to Ms. Baker; Ronald smiled, T-Bone had his hands full with Ms. Baker.

Inside the gym, dudes were everywhere. The convicts were waiting to see the action, they had to support the Youth Center team. The ring was already set up and two Youth Center boxers were sparring, Others were getting loose, throwing punches at the mitts their trainers were holding. A few C.O.s were hanging around to see the action as well. Even Ms. Goodall and a few other C.O. broads were in the gym. Ronald wasted no time, he began warming up with Harrison-EL.

Will Johnson walked by, and said, "Lookin' good." He kept it moving.

A short while later, the pro boxers came through the door. Everyone continued what they were doing while checking out the pros at the same time. After a few formalities, the sparring began.

An unranked pro middleweight boxer sparred with a Youth Center boxer. They mixed it up and put on a nice show.

Pointing at the Youth Center boxer from ring-side, Harrison-EL looked at Ronald, and said, "Watch his left hand. Everytime he pop the jab, he drops his hand."

"Yeah, I see." Ronald was paying close attention, taking mental notes on both fighting styles in the ring. Sure enough, the pro fighter landed a powerful right hand to the eye of the Youth Center fighter, staggering him.

"I bet you he'll keep his hands up now," Harrison-EL said. "That pretty shit gets you knocked out.

Meanwhile, the school building was damn near empty because most of the convicts were in the gym. T-Bone now worked in the school building. Inside an empty class room, he and Ms. Baker were in a heated argument, like two lovers. She was beefin' hard. Her period was late and the only man she'd been with in the last few months was T-Bone. She knew he had a woman, but she was growing closer to him with every passing day. Her mind was made up, she was going to have his baby and there was nothing anyone could say to her about it.

"I'm good enough for you to cum all inside me, but I'm not good enough to have your baby, is that what you're tellin' me, Ty?" Ms. Baker snapped, tears in her eyes. "That's some foul shit!"

T-Bone felt her pain, but Cristal was his baby, his heart, and more. Ms. Baker was just pussy as far as he was concerned. "It ain't like that, Tonya, but you can't have this baby ..."

"Fuck you!" She pushed him and stormed out of the room crying. T-Bone let her go, he needed time to think. As he left the school building he passed Ms. Goodall, who licked her lips and winked at him on her way to the Lieutenant's office. T-Bone winked back with a smile and headed for the gym.

Inside the gym, a few dudes were waiting for T-Bone at the door. They needed their fix. T-Bone put them on hold until he passed the heroin off to one of his runners. After T-Bone took care of his business and took a seat in the bleachers with a few of his homies, James Holmes was in the ring with Wilbert Cruise—a Youth Center heavyweight. They had sparred for two rounds already. At twenty six, two hundred and nine pounds, and in great shape, Holmes had already went three rounds with another boxer and was still fresh. T-Bone looked over at Greg Williams, and asked, "Did Ronald spar yet?"

"Nah, he next," Greg said.

When it was Ronald's turn to spar with Holmes, Harrison-EL gave him a pat on the back and said, "Watch the left hand, he got one of the best jabs in the business."

"I'm on it." Ronald nodded. He was a little nervous getting in the ring with Holmes, who hadn't lost a fight his whole career and was chasing a title fight with Muhammad Ali. As the sparring began, Ronald was very careful at first, just popping his jab and throwing a few basic combinations to see how hard Holmes could hit. Holmes threw a powerful left jab, doubled it up, and followed it with a big right hand, blasting Ronald right in the mouth. Nevertheless, Ronald stood his ground and fired back with a combination of his own, hard and fast. The crowd went off like it was a prize fight.

"Rumble that nigga!" T-Bone yelled along with other encouraging shouts from fellow convicts.

Shaking his head at Ronald teasingly, Holmes said, "They want you to fight. Let me see what you got." He caught Ronald with another loud and stinging jab before dancing out of reach.

Ronald tried to cut the ring off on Holmes as they traded punches. Ronald caught Holmes with a crushing body shot that appeared to hurt him. Ronald didn't know he'd stung Holmes until Harrison-EL yelled at him, telling him so. "Go at him!" Harrison-EL yelled. Holmes was too skilled, he threw a quick flurry of punches that ended the round and allowed him to get himself together.

By round two, Ronald was in a zone. Holmes' punches didn't seem to be landing as hard as they did at first. Holmes was getting tired. In a vicious clutch toward the end of the round, Ronald unloaded a sweet five piece combination that went from the body to the head of Holmes; Ronald ended the combination with a thunderous left hook that knocked beads of sweat from Holmes' head. The gym went off with cheers as Holmes staggered. However, well seasoned, Holmes answered Ronald's attack with one of his own. Side-stepping Ronald, Holmes popped two text book jabs and followed them up with an uppercut that rocked Ronald. Ronald took the punch well, but went on the defensive until the round was over. He, too, needed to get himself together. Round three got exciting, both fighters showed signs of greatness. Ronald caught Holmes with a mean left hook.

"I like that, youngster." Holmes popped his jab and slammed a shotgun of a punch to Ronald's body, making the younger fighter grunt in pain. Relentlessly, Ronald fought back, throwing another combination that ended with two left hooks from the body to the head, making Holmes dance away. Ronald knew that his left hook was his best shot, he always used it to try to take control of his fights. The bell rang and the sparring match was over.

Out of breath, Ronald regrouped as Harrison-EL took his gloves off for him, telling him how good he looked in the ring. Moments later, Holmes walked over and shook Ronald's hand, saying, "You got that fire in you, youngster."

Ronald smiled. Thanks, I was tryin'."

"You got some thunder with you." Holmes was still breathing hard. "You caught me with a nice body shot, but you ain't know it ... you gotta pay attention to your opponent. Learn to understand the damage your punches do. You gotta strong left hook. Find a punch to follow it up with and that'll be your knockout punch."

Ronald took the wisdom in stride. A few months away from nineteen, he knew he still had a lot to learn. "I'ma do that."

Holmes shook his hand again. "Keep your head up."

After Holmes stepped off, Harrison-EL and Ronald stepped out of the ring and hung out at ring side as two fresh fighters took the ring. "You earned Holmes' respect, he ain't set nobody else's props out."

As Ronald and Harrison-EL talked, an old white man walked up and introduced himself as Wilfred Walker, James Holmes' trainer. Walker liked what Ronald had displayed in the ring. "How old are you, son?" Walker asked.

Not liking white people, Ronald gave Walker a funny look. Harrison-EL poked Ronald with his elbow. "I'm eighteen."

"You're a natural, son." Walker rubbed his balding, gray hair backward. "I haven't seen such raw talent since Sonny Liston, although you have far more finesse in your fight game than Liston's intimidating, bully style. But nevertheless, I see something in you, kid. How long have you been boxing?"

"'Bout six months."

"Six months?" Walker was shocked. "Who taught you to move like that? That kind of foot work takes time."

Ronald pointed at Harrison-EL. Walker and Harrison-EL spoke for a second. Walker found out that Harrison-EL had fought in a few pro fights before he came to prison.

"So, how long do you have to do in this place?" Walker asked Ronald as the gym exploded in a roar of cheers. Larry Pringle had just sat one of the pro boxers on his ass with a big right hand.

"I see the parole board this summer. Last time I saw them I was in the hole. If I get my G.E.D. by then, I might have a chance to get out of here," Ronald said.

"Stay in touch with me." Walker gave Ronald his card. "I'm about to donate some money to the boxing program down here. I want you to take advantage of it. You got good hands, kid." Walker laughed and placed a mock punch on Ronald's chin. "And, a good chin, too. You took some blows today that I've seen James put men to sleep with." Walker extended his hand and Ronald shook it. "Take care, and stay in the gym. You got a future, kid."

As soon as Walker stepped off, Harrison-EL pulled Ronald's coat, letting him know that not all white people were bad people. Harrison-EL told him that he wasn't sharing knowledge with him to make him hate white people, he was sharing knowledge with him to make him aware of his true self and to hip him to what the real world was all about. Without a true knowledge of history, one would repeat it. "That man, white or not, sees somethin' in you. You gotta know when somebody's tryin' to help you or harm you."

"I dig it." Ronald nodded his head.

Youth Center I, Wednesday, May 13, 1976

Laying in the bed reading *The Ring* magazine while waiting on a visit, Ronald played with the idea of one day being a pro boxer. It could be done. T-Bone walked in the cell dressed for a visit as well. The nigga had on a pair of black gators with his prison gear. "You got that money on you?" T-Bone asked Ronald.

"Yeah." Ronald handed him eleven hundred and fifty dollars to give to C.O. Turner who would pass the money off to Cristal in the parking lot. It was safer than passing the bank off in the visiting hall. "I just gave the dude Charlie the last ten bags a few minutes ago, so that's everything."

"Cool, we'll be back on tonight." T-Bone left the cell.

Ten minutes later, Mrs. Jones came to the door and told Ronald he had a visit. "Thanks," he said as he headed for T-Bone's cell. "They just called me for a visit."

"Oh yeah?" T-Bone looked at his gold watch and wondered why he hadn't been called for a visit; he and Ronald were always called at the same time. "I'll see you when I get up there."

Inside the visiting hall, Ronald spoke to a few good men as he made his way over to Synthia. "What's up, baby?" Ronald gave her a hug and kiss. "You look damn good to be six months pregnant."

Synthia smiled, but it was forced. She had an attitude.

"What's wrong, sweetheart?" Ronald asked as he sat down and looked around for Cristal, not seeing her.

"Some C.O. bitch outside talkin' 'bout she pregnant by Ty." Synthia pursed her lips and rolled her eyes. "The bitch got all up in Cristal's face talkin' 'bout how Ty be fuckin' her and that she pregnant, and he actin' like he don't want nothin' to do wit' the situation no more. Cristal punched the bitch in the face." Synthia looked at her watch. "A whole bunch of C.O.s had to break the shit up. They was about to have Cristal arrested, but decided to not let her in."

Shit had hit the fan like Ronald knew it would. He'd been telling T-Bone so. T-Bone had a mess on his hands. As loyal as Cristal was to him, she was going to feel played. Being pregnant was only going to add to her pain. "Is Cristal okay?" Ronald asked.

"Is she okay?" Synthia asked sarcastically and rolled her eyes. "Like you care. How do you think she is? She sittin' in the car waitin' on me. She pissed off at Ty's triflin' ass."

"Hold up," Ronald waved his hand with a serious look on his face. "Who you talkin' to like that? You act like I done somethin'."

"Is he fuckin' that bitch?!"

"Huh?"

"You heard me, is he fuckin' that lil' bitch? Don't lie, either. I know that's your man."

"Look here, I don't like your fuckin' attitude." Ronald poinyed his finger in her face and hissed. "Don't question' me 'bout another man's business, and don't be gettin' slick out the mouth wit' me 'bout some shit I ain't got nothin' to do wit'."

"You niggas ain't shit.."

"Fuck you mean, 'you niaggas'?"

"You heard what the fuck I said, we be out there doin' what we supposed to do for you niggas and. y'all up in here fuckin' these nothin' ass C.O. bitches!"

"I ain't fuckin' nobody!" Ronald snapped. "You better watch your fuckin' mouth."

They got into a heated argument, a vicious one. They began to make a scene. Getting fed up, Ronald cut everything off and stood up. "Take your ass home." He pointed at the door.

"You niggas ain't shit!" Synthia rolled her eyes. "Fuck that! I'm gone!" She stormed out of the visiting hall, crying herself. Other visitors shook their heads and whispered about what had just happened as Ronald left.

Back in the dorm, Ronald told T-Bone what had went down with Cristal and Ms. Baker. He also told him how he sent Synthia's ass home behind it. T-Bone was stressed out about the situation. He knew he had to do something to try to clean the mess up.

"I can't believe that bitch did some shit like that." T-Bone took a hard pull on his cigarette. He had a long history with Cristal and believed that would help him fix the situation. At least he hoped it would help. He felt dumb as shit for risking his relationship with

Cristal for some in-house pussy while locked up. "Shit!" T-Bone said out loud. He plucked the cigarette out of his cell window into the cool spring air. "Fuck it, ain't shit I can do about it right now. I'll try to call her later." He looked at his watch, it was seven ten P.M., he had to go meet Turner to get the balloons of heroin.

"You got a whole lot of smoothin' out to do." Ronald shook his head, feeling bad about how he'd carried Synthia. She didn't deserve that, but she was way out of place and he had to check her.

"You got some smoothin' out to do your damn self."

"Synthia gon' be alright once she get home. She gon' think about it and know she was wrong. I ain't do nothin' for her to be goin' off on me about," Ronald said.

"I'll catch you in a minute." T-Bone gave Ronald five and lit another cigarette as he left.

Heading for the school building to holla at Turner, all T-Bone could do was shake his head. He knew he'd fucked up. There was no one to blame but himself. As he crossed the compound, T-Bone stopped to holla at a few convicts about business. He kept his eyes open and watched everything. The compound was alive and moving fast, just like the streets. T-Bone could feel some tension in the air that made him feel uneasy, but he chalked that up to the stress he was feeling concerning the situation with Cristal. By the time T-Bone made it to the school building, countless C.O.s were running toward the gym. Something was going down. His senses were on point. He went on about his business, whatever was going down in the gym had nothing to do with him.

"T-Bone!" a voice called out.

T-Bone turned and saw Sharp Eye coming his way. T-Bone sighed. He wasn't in the mood to deal with Sharp Eye. "What's up, man?" T-Bone said.

"Come here," Sharp Eye said. "I know you got somethin' on you."

T-Bone laughed. "You think I'd let your fat ass catch me

dirty? Please!" T-Bone turned around and raised his arms so Sharp Eye could pat him down and get the fuck on about his business.

Sharp Eye began patting him down. "Ummm, what do we have here?" he said, feeling a knot in T-Bone's pocket.

With all that T-Bone had on his mind he forgot that he had eight hundred dollars in his pocket. T-Bone thought about the money in his pocket and snatched away from Sharp Eye.

"Let me get that," Sharp Eye said with a smile, extending his hand.

"I ain't givin' you shit," T-Bone hissed.

"Don't make me get on the radio." Sharp Eye reached for his walkie-talkie. T-Bone knew he was on his way to the Max one way or another. He reacted quickly and fired two blows right down the pipe, tagging Sharp Eye's chin. Sharp Eye went straight to sleep, out cold, stretched out in the middle of the walk. T-Bone took off running across the compound, heading back to the dorm to put the money up.

Inside the dorm, T-Bone gave Ronald the money and told him what had just went down. "I know they on they way to get me," T-Bone said.

A few moments later, Lieutenant Jones, Sharp Eye, and a good fifteen C.O.s came inside the dorm looking for T-Bone. They stopped dead in their tracks as they entered the wing. What they saw made them think twice before rushing onto the wing. Twenty convicts, maybe more, were crowded up in the back of the range. They had surrounded T-Bone.

"Go to your cells!" Lieutenant Jones barked. Nobody moved, only glared at him and the other C.O.s with mean looks. "Now! Go to your cells or it's gonna get ugly!"

"We ain't goin' no muthafuckin' where!" a deep voice yelled back.

"We only want Wilson!" Lieutenant Jones said, sensing where things were going.

"Fuck that!" Sharp Eye tried to force his way past

Lieutenant Jones like he was going to tear some shit up. Yeah, right."

"Are you crazy?!" Lieutenant Jones grabbed Sharp Eye. "What is your fuckin' problem? You tryin' to start a fuckin' riot?"

"You gon' let him get away with that?" Sharp Eye asked.

"Let me do this," Lieutenant Jones said. He then sent two C.O.s to get more officers. The staff was spread thin dealing with the gym stabbing and now this. "Make sure they get suited up, too. We might have a problem here." Lieutenant Jones sent a few C.O.s to secure the other wings of the dorm. "Look here," Lieutenant Jones addressed the convicts that surrounded T-Bone. "We ain't gon' jump on Wilson..."

"You damn right!" a convict cut Lieutenant Jones off.

"All Wilson gotta do is cuff up and walk to the Max ... no one gets hurt," Lieutenant Jones offered.

The convicts' only objective was to make sure that T-Bone didn't get jumped and dogged out by the C.O.s. Harrison-EL spoke for the whole group. "Don't be bullshittin'!" Ronald stood to his left and T-Bone to his right.

"Y'all got my word," Lieutenant Jones said. He knew all too well how fast a riot could break out; he'd seen many down the Center. "We ain't gon' lay a hand on him."

While Lieutenant Jones negotiated with the convicts, twenty C.O.s came in the dorm in riot gear. Not only was there a problem on T-Bone's wing, the other wings refused to lock down as well. Tension was building.

"I'ma go 'head and go," T-Bone said. He didn't want his comrades to get caught up. "They ain't gon' fuck wit' me. I'm sure! They scared to death."

"If they do, we gon' tear this muthafucka up," Ronald said.

"Yeah, if they try to jump on you we gon' shut this muthafucka down," Harrison-EL said.

"I'ma go over the Max, but I ain't cuffin' up," T-Bone said as he walked toward Lieutenant Jones and the C.O.s.

"Fair enough," Lieutenant Jones said. He walked T-Bone

to the Max personally and made sure no one laid a hand on him.
Unity.

Youth Center I, Monday, May 25, 1976

Ronald hadn't seen Synthia since their big argument in the visiting hall. He decided to call her.

"Hello?" she answered the phone.

"How you doin', baby?" Ronald tried to feel her out.

Synthia was silent for a while, she was still hurt by the way Ronald carried her. She'd been nothing but good to him. For him to just send her home like she wasn't shit really hurt her. On top of that, she pregnant with his child.

"Hello?" Ronald said.

"I'm here."

Ronald could hear his sister in the background, she was asking if it was him on the phone.

"Hello?" Diane got on the phone.

"What's up?" Ronald said with a smile on his face, knowing what was coming.

"What the hell is wrong wit' you, boy?" Diane asked.

"Huh?"

"If you can huh you can hear, nigga! You heard what I said." Diane got right in his shit. "You don't be treatin' her like that. Have you lost your damn mind? That girl is pregnant, comin' down there to see your ungrateful ass..."

"Hold up, Dee..."

"Hold up my ass! I ain't scared of your little ass. You my LITTLE brotha, I used to change your shitty diapers, nigga! You gon' apologize to Synthia. She been cryin' like a baby."

Ronald let Diane get her thing off. He had too much respect for her to do anything else. "Okay, Dee, you right. Put Synthia on the phone."

"Hello," Synthia said in a low, shy voice.

"What's up, baby?" Ronald, said.

"You know what's up. You took me bad for no reason."

"You right, baby, I'm sorry." Ronald was rolling with the punches; he wanted to smooth things out. "I apologize. But, from here on out, our business is our business. We was sittin' up in the visitin' hall arguing about somebody else's business."

"You right, baby. I was wrong about that, but you didn't have to treat me like that. I thought you love me."

"I do love you, you know that. Don't worry, that'll never happen again."

"Cristal said she ain't comin' down there no more."

"Baby."

"Huh?"

"That's Cristal and T-Bone's business."

Synthia giggled. "You right."

Later on as Ronald sat in his cell reading, there was a knock at the door. He looked up and saw Mrs. Jones; he flashed a smile and unlocked the door from the inside. "What's up, sweetheart?"

"I brought this for you." Mrs. Jones handed Ronald two fish and cheese subs wrapped in tinfoil.

"Thanks."

"I took T-Bone one down to the Max. He told me to tell you to send his mother the money you got for him."

"Okay, I'll take care of that. Thanks. What about you, you need anything?" Ronald asked.

"I'm fine."

"Treat yourself." He handed her a one-hundred-dollar bill.

"I can't."

"Yes, you can." He stuffed it in her hand and closed her fingers around it. "That's a birthday gift."

"It's not my birthday." She smiled.

"It is now."

Chapter 7

Central Facility, Tuesday, May 25, 1977

Central Facility, better known as the Hill, was like a small city as far as prisons were concerned. A small city surrounded by a fence and gun towers. Convicts called it Big Lorton or the Hill. The Hill was "real" prison, everything under the sun went on inside the fence—everything! Murders, rapes, robberies, kidnappings, drug dealing, drug use, gambling, drinking, and anything else one could think of. Amongst countless red brick structures, a few roads that cut through the compound and twenty-some open dormitories that housed close to eighty convicts resided some of D.C.'s most vicious criminals.

Convicts covered the compound on the bright spring afternoon, they were engaged in their day-to-day dealings. One group of convicts stood right outside of R-N-D waiting on the new arrivals that were coming from the Wall, which was right behind the Hill.

With his property in two green army duffel bags over his shoulders, the first of the new arrivals stepped out into the bright sun light and warm air of the May afternoon. It was good to be on the Hill after being stuck behind the Wall for sixteen months. During that time, the young convict had seen some serious things as well as been through some serious things. He'd been in two bloody knife-fights and took part in a riot that left two C.O.s in the hospital. The young convict had come a long way since he first came to prison; prison had hardened him in many ways.

G-Train dropped his bags and embraced his homies that were waiting for him outside. Frank and four other Valley Green dudes awaited G-Train. The group of young convicts joked around for a second and then headed to 18 Dorm, which was located in a section of the Hill known as the Hollow—the center of most of the action on the compound. Everything came through the Hollow. A convict had to know where his ass was at to live in the Hollow. Simple as that. At that time, it was up to the new arrivals to find some place to live. G-Train didn't have to worry about that, he'd already paid his dues. Niggas knew him. Frank, who had earned plenty of respect by then, got G-Train a bunk right next to his along the wall in the back. It was a good spot where they could see everything that was going on in the open dorm. All the bunks along the back wall belonged to men that were cool with Frank. He was cool with all the thorough convicts in the dorm, men like David Ford, Pearl Early, Flick, Homicide, Butch Wood, and others.

Smoking a joint of weed, Frank and G-Train sat on G-Train's bunk as Frank gave him the rundown about what was going on on the compound.

"I heard you crushed the nigga Keith Henderson," G-Train said in a low tone as he looked around the dorm, taking in the scenery. Most of the convicts were outside somewhere on the pound.

"I told you I ain't playin' wit' none of these niggas," Frank said.

Cadillac walked by and spoke to Frank. He was another thorough dude that Frank had gotten cool with during his time behind the Wall.

"Yeah, that nigga violated," Frank said to G-Train, talking about the nigga that tried to rape him up the jail.

Frank had only been on the Hill two weeks when Keith Henderson came on the compound. Wasting no time, Frank got his knife and went to take care of business. When he caught Keith, Keith was getting his dick sucked by a boy in the bathroom stall. Frank had literally caught the nigga with his pants down. He butchered Keith right in the bathroom, gutting him with the butcher knife that had been stolen out of the kitchen. The boy that was sucking Keith's dick got the fuck out of dodge and never said a word when Keith's body was discovered at count time. The next morning, Frank and two of his homies ran down on two of Keith's comrades and stabbed the shit out of them in their bunks just before dawn. From that point on, Frank had no problems on the Hill.

"That's what you was supposed to do." G-Train smiled, he couldn't believe how violent Lorton had made Frank in such a short amount of time. G-Train still remembered Frank as the timid, little pretty boy that was Gangsta's little brother.

After they finished smoking the joint of weed, Frank and G-Train hit the compound. G-Train wanted some dope, so Frank took him to get a few bags. As they walked the compound, they passed convicts dressed in street clothes that lined the streets and walks as if they were hanging out on street corners back home in D.C. Vans with C.O.s in them patrolled the compound like police. Alley cats were all over the place and were treated like royalty in some cases. Frank and G-Train copped the dope in front of 7 Dorm and headed back to theirs, stopping along the way to holla at Billy Howard and Ho Bo.

Youth Center I, Monday, May 31, 1977

Ronald, T-Bone, and a few other convicts were returning to the dorm after watching *Cooley High* in the school building. As soon as T-Bone got back in the dorm, he went right to his cell and blew some dope to get the monkey off his back, just as he always did before he went to see his case worker. After fucking up with Cristal and finding out that she wouldn't forgive him, T-Bone realized just how much she meant to him. He was crushed behind the lost, even though he kept his head up and rolled with the punches. Only Ronald really knew that T-Bone was hurting inside. Heroin was the only thing that helped him ease the pain. On top of all of that, Cristal had his son on August 10, 1976 and named the boy Chris Mayo. T-Bone hadn't seen his son yet, although Cristal told T-Bone's mother that she would allow her to take the baby to see him. Deep in his heart, T-Bone knew everything was his fault. Nevertheless, he still loved Cristal with all his heart, even though he tried to make himself hate her to ease the pain.

As far as Ms. Baker, she quit her job down the Center. T-Bone had no idea where she was or what she was up to. Ms. Goodall told him that Ms. Baker had a baby boy and moved out Maryland somewhere. T-Bone wondered what his other son's name was.

Checking his gold watch, T-Bone looked in the mirror to make sure he was looking good. It was eleven thirty A.M., time to go holla at his case worker. Headed across the compound and selling a few bags of dope along the way, T-Bone pocketed a quick seventy dollars. When he got to Mrs. Mitchell's office, Lieutenant Jones was on his way out. Lieutenant Jones was chasing Mrs. Mitchell, but couldn't get in her pants.

"Stayin' out of trouble, Wilson?" Lieutenant Jones asked.

"Yeah, you know me, Jones, if it ain't no blood on the scene, I ain't do it," T-Bone joked. Ever since the incident where he knocked Sharp Eye out, Lieutenant Jones respected T-Bone and even turned a blind eye to some of the small rules that T-Bone broke. Lieutenant Jones let the young, twenty one year old stretch his legs as long as he didn't get too out of control or get into any knife play.

"What's up with Mays? What's he going to do this evening?" Lieutenant Jones asked about Ronald's upcoming fight on the Hill; the Youth Center team was taking a trip to

Central. "I got a hundred dollars on Mays. Captain Jennings on the Hill say the guy he's fighting is going to stop him."

"You know the Center run that boxin' shit. Ronald the man on the heavyweight tip, all them niggas over Big Lorton know he can't be fucked wit'. The whole pound know Ronald gon' lay fire to his man."

"We'll see." Lieutenant Jones stepped off.

T-Bone stepped into Mrs. Mitchell office and shut the door behind him. "How you doin'?" he said.

"Fine." Mrs. Mitchell was sitting behind her desk doing paper work. She was a small but sexy woman at 5' 5" and one hundred and ten pounds. She didn't have a whole lot going on bodywise, but the way she walked, talked, looked into a man's eyes, and licked her lips was enough to drive a nigga crazy with his dick hard. She was also very attractive and down-to-earth. What really turned T-Bone on was the fact that Mrs. Mitchell had blond hair and blue eyes that reminded him of the nasty-ass white bitches in the fuck magazines that were floating around the compound. When T-Bone first set out to pull Mrs. Mitchell, he'd taken a huge risk by accidentally touching the white woman on her ass. But, to his surprise, she didn't trip. She turned around and smiled, only asking him was he crazy. T-Bone then laid it on thick, seeing that the white woman would go for something. Within the next week, Mrs. Mitchell willingly kissed T-Bone and gave him a hand job right in her office. It was curtains from then on. Once Mrs. Mitchell got a taste of Mandingo inside her blue-blooded, white, American pussy, she was on it like a drug. T-Bone was giving her as much as she could take. If Mrs. Mitchell's racist father knew that she was fucking a young "nigger" convict, he would die of a heart attack. However, Mrs. Mitchell didn't care. T-Bone was a fantasy of hers that did things to her that her push-over husband couldn't dream of.

"I see you're high again," Mrs. Mitchell said, knowing how T-Bone nodded in spots when he had heroin in his system. She also knew he always fucked the shit out of her when he was high. T-Bone had her wearing a loose skirt to work everyday so he could hit it when he felt like it.

"Yeah, I got a little buzz. I had to get right before I came to see you." T-Bone was already hard as a rock.

"I want you to uh ... uh ..." She got up and locked the door. "I wanna show you something, Ty."

"Somethin' like what?"

Mrs. Mitchell gave up a shy smile, like a school girl about to give her first kiss. "Don't laugh."

"What's up?" T-Bone asked with a puzzled look on his face. "What you up to?"

In a bashful tone, she said, "I ... I want to give you a blow job."

T-Bone wanted to die laughing right in her face, but he kept his game face on. "Okay, cool." He softly grabbed her hand and pulled her close to him. Looking down at the stiff print in his pants, he said, "You seem like you not too sure."

"Because I've never done it. My husband keeps pressuring me to do it, but I can't stomach the idea of putting his dick in my mouth. I had a dream about giving you a blow job last night and I want to try it. I want you to ... uh ... show me how to do it." Mrs. Mitchell had T-Bone's big, black dick on her mind ever since the dream; she'd awaken and found her pussy soaking wet.

"Come on," he smiled, "I'll show you." He sat down in the chair and undid his pants, watching Mrs. Mitchell's eyes light up at the size of his hard dick. "Get down on your knees, sweetheart." Mrs. Mitchell eased down to her knees. T-Bone rubbed her hair backward and said, "Lick it up and down, get it wet." He watched her grab it with her tiny hand and begin to lick it like ice cream. She licked all around the head, down the sides, down the bottom, all the way down to his balls. Licking his balls, she came all the way back up and licked circles around the head. "That's right." T-Bone looked down at her with thoughts of cumming all over her face. "Put it in your mouth, just use your lips and your tongue, watch your teeth ... Ouch, be easy, baby."

"Sorry." She slowed down and began sucking on his dick, taking as much as she could inside her mouth. "Is that better?" she looked up into his eyes, licking the head.

"Yeah, that's much better." T-Bone put a hand behind her head. "Just take it easy." Mrs. Mitchell took him back in her mouth like she was trying to suck the life out of him. Her head went up and down as her hair fell into T-Bone's lap. All he could see was blond hair bobbing up and down until he heard her gag a little. "Relax, it's okay. Open your throat and let it just slide in and out, let it sit there until you get used to it." T-Bone looked down into her deep blue eyes while she was down on her knees, looking back up at him, deep-throating his dick, just holding it in her throat. "You got it. Now slide it in and out." Mrs. Mitchell caught on quickly.

After about four or five minutes, she came up for air, jerking him off while she said, "Am I doing it right?"

"Hell yeah, you got the hang of it, like a pro." He smiled.

She smiled and went back to work, taking him deep in her mouth and throat. "Are you going to cum in my mouth?"

"You want me to?"

"I don't know, I don't know what you like, daddy."

"I like it in your mouth or all over your face."

Mrs. Mitchell smiled. "Yeah, cum in my mouth."

"You gon' swallow it?"

"Yeah."

Five minutes later, T-Bone was cumming in her mouth as he held the back of her head with both hands. She closed her eyes and struggled to swallow his load without choking or letting any semen get on her clothes. "Swallow it," T-Bone said.

"You like that?" She smiled when she was done, still tasting his nut in her mouth.

"Hell yeah, did you like it?" T-Bone asked, still sitting in the chair with his dick out, standing tall like the Washington Monuument.

"Yeah, I loved it," she said, still on her knees between his legs. "I like the way you taste. When I'm with you I feel so ... free ... you know?"

Fixing his pants, T-Bone smiled. *This bitch is mean,* he thought. He helped her up. "I should run, we been in here for a while."

"Okay, come see me again before I get off."

"I will." He hugged her and squeezed her ass. "You got them balloons for me?"

"Yeah." Mrs. Mitchell got two red balloons out of her purse and gave them to him. She knew they contained heroin. She'd picked the balloons up herself from 8th and H Street, Northeast.

"Take this to my mother for me." T-Bone gave her twenty five hundred dollars. "I'll have two-hundred for you when I come back." He kissed her on the forehead and left.

If T-Bone couldn't do anything, he could pull a broad.

Central Facility, Monday, May 31, 1977

The gym was so packed that one would think Muhammad Ali was in the house. Convicts, C.O.s, and guest from the streets were all packed in the humid gym. Even though a few boxers from the streets were going to get in the ring, the main event was the heavyweight fight: Ronald Mays vs. Tony Jackson. The fight had been hyped up all over Lorton, even a few people from the streets were talking about it and had come to see it. Tony's name was kicking all over Lorton and on the streets of D.C., on the boxing tip and on the stick-up tip. Tony was favored to win, he hadn't lost a fight yet and had been knocking shit out cold! On the Hill, talk had it that the two hundred and ten pound Tony Jackson was telling people that he was going to put Ronald to sleep in the first round. Ronald was fucked up about that, but kept his thoughts to himself with the exception of telling T-Bone that he was going to knock Tony out for talking shit. At two hundred and five pounds packing a mean left hook, Ronald had the tools to put Tony to sleep; the only question was did he have the skill to put the older fighter to sleep.

Standing ringside with Harrison-EL, Ronald listened to old man Wilfred Walker spit boxing game. The gym was loud as a football arena, so Ronald had to listen closely. He'd taken a liking to the old white man, they'd become close over the last year. Wilfred Walker was cool peoples. Although Ronald didn't make parole, he had gotten his G.E.D. and Wilfred Walker had gotten a lot of letters written in support of Ronald's parole. Wilfred felt strongly about Ronald's future in boxing; he often made trips to the Center to check on Ronald and watch him spar.

"How's the family?" Wilfred asked.

"Holdin' on. You got them thinkin' I'm the next Ali or somethin'." Ronald smiled.

Wilfred rubbed Ronald's shoulder, and said, "Ali was only twenty-two when he shocked the world and took the crown from a bigger Liston. You're not even twenty yet, kid. You got a bright future ahead of you if you stay focused."

A young Ray Leonard walked in the gym, fresh off a gold medal performance in the '76 Olympics, he'd just turned pro. He walked over and spoke to Wilfred. Wilfred introduced Leonard to Ronald and Harrison-EL.

"Like I was saying," Wilfred continued after Leonard stepped off. "I seen a lotta of great fighters come out of prisons and go pro. Don't be content with being a jailhouse legend. Whatever you do in life, do it to the limit. You can box for real, kid."

Ronald thought about what Wilfred was saying. He hoped that boxing would open up some doors for him. He damn sure needed a break, Diane and Synthia needed his help bad. Ronald thought that his brother would be able to help out, but Roland was strung out on heroin again. The money Ronald was sending home was helping out a lot, but his people were still struggling out there. Ronald was now a father, boxing could be a way for him to take care of his son and his family. Synthia gave birth to Ronald Mays Jr. on August 25, 1976. At nineteen, Ronald knew he had a lot of responsibilities. He welcomed them and understood that boxing could be his meal ticket.

Frank and G-Train came through the door like super stars; they were getting money on the Hill on the dope tip. Frank and Ronald stayed in touch through the mail; they had a bond that would last a life time. They were brothers from a another mother.

G-Train couldn't stand Ronald and had bet two hundred dollars on Tony Jackson, so when Frank went to holla at Ronald, G-Train went to holla at Big Naughty as the first fight began between a boxer from the Hill and a boxer from the streets.

"What's up?" Frank hugged Ronald. He spoke to Harrison-EL and gave him five. "What you gon' do today?"

"I can show you better than I can tell you," Ronald, said as the gym went–off.   The boxer from the streets had sat the boxer from the Hill on his ass. Slowly the Hill fighter got up and shook it off.

"I got two hundred dollars on you," Frank said.

"Your money safe, man." Ronald winked. "Trust me."

T-Bone walked up on them, he'd made the trip to the Hill with the boxing team as he always did. T-Bone ran around the compound on the Hill like he was doing time there. He knew a lot of good men on the Hill. "These niggas crazy as shit," T-Bone said. "They talkin' 'bout Tony Jackson gon' knock you out." He looked at Ronald. "I done bet 'bout four more niggas, I got eight hundred dollars on you."

"I ain't payin' these niggas no attention," Ronald said.

Harrison-EL cut in. "Come on, Ronnie, let's get ready."

As time passed, all the fights were action-packed. A

Youth Center fighter knocked a Hill fighter out right before it was time for Ronald to get in the ring. The sounds of Stevie Wonder's *Isn't She Lovely* filled the gym as Ronald climbed in the ring.

Moments later, Ronald and Tony Jackson were ready to mix it up. Shouts of support for Tony was all Ronald could hear, but he blocked that out and stayed focused, staring Tony down and sizing him up. Tony was a huge looking man with thick sideburns that made him look like former heavyweight champ, Joe Frazier. At 5' 10", two hundred and ten pounds with a killer right hand that came with paralyzing power, Tony Jackson had patterned his fight game after big George Foreman. Tony was a pressure fighter who rarely took a backward step in the ring. He unloaded tremendous punches to take the fight out of his opponent and to take control of the ring. Harrison-EL had already schooled Ronald to Tony's fight game and what to do about it.

"Remember whose arms are longer," Harrison-EL whispered in Ronald's ear. "Don't feed into the hype. Win the fight. Dance and land punches. That's all you gotta do. You got the heart, you got the skills, and you got the tools to do the job. All you gotta do is want it."

"I want it." Ronald was focused.

Like clockwork, Tony came out punching as soon as the fight started. Ronald felt the thunder behind the blows, but answered with well timed and placed blows of his own behind his long jab, frustrating Tony. With a head fake, Ronald acted like he was throwing a right hand and blasted Tony with a crushing left hook that sounded off like a car crash. The gym went off. "Keep rushin' me," Ronald warn Tony as he backpedaled like Ali. Pissed off and a little dazed, Tony rushed Ronald, cutting off the ring and trapping him in the corner while unloading relentless blows. Ronald didn't panic at all, he just covered up perfectly and took the blows. The body shots were enough to make a man piss blood. Just before the round was over, Ronald pushed Tony off of him and fired a quick flurry of colorful punches to end the round. "You like that?" Ronald winked at Tony. "It's a lot more of that comin'."

"I'ma knock your young ass out." Tony headed for his corner.

In his corner breathing hard, Ronald looked up at Harrison-EL, and said, "He gon' gas out, I know it. He ain't got no gas."

"Make him chase you," Harrison-EL said.

Ronald went out and did just that, jabbing Tony to death with his long reach. He blasted Tony with countless right hands after the long jab. Tony weaved a wide hook and leaped in hard and fast with a left hook of his own that knocked Ronald's mouthpiece across the ring and caused him to fly into the ropes. Ronald hit the canvas. The gym went off again in support of Tony. Ronald was delirious. For all Ronald knew, by the sound of the crowd he could have been on the canvas in Madison Square Garden. He wasn't, he was laying on his back in a Lorton gym being counted out until he heard Tony's voice. "Get up and take it like a man, young nigga!" Tony screamed. Ronald's pride and courage pulled him up off the canvas at the nine count. He was still dazed, but the round was over.

"Get it together, Ronnie!" Ronald heard someone yell from the crowd. He looked over his shoulder and saw Fray standing next to Moose and Tony Harris. "Show me somethin'!"

Ronald gave Fray a quick nod.

Harrison-EL grabbed Ronald's face. "You okay?" he asked, checking out Ronald's swelling right eye.

With blurred vision, Ronald gathered his senses, and said, "I'ma knock this nigga out."

Round three began. With his hands up, Ronald tried to adjust to seeing out of his left eye only. He was still a little dazed and his right eye was killing him. Tony came at him full steam with everything he had. Ronald fought back like a wounded mongoose, going toe-to-toe with Tony. Mixed in with a handful of other crushing blows, Tony threw his knockout punch, a paralyzing straight right hand. He missed. Ronald had seen it coming and side-stepped it; Ronald countered it and rung Tony's bell with a lethal left hook and a heart-stopping uppercut that floored him. Ronald stood over Tony for a second and glared into his glassy eyes as the gym went off. "Get up! Get up!" Ronald shouted before he was rushed to his corner by the ref. Tony was out cold. The fight was over. A number of convicts left the gym pissed off and out of a few hundred dollars.

"Where everybody goin'?" T-Bone yelled from his seat, joking. Frank and Fray laughed.

Moments later, Ronald stood next to Harrison-EL and a few other Youth Center boxers. Ray Leonard came over and shook Ronald's hand. "You showed a lot of heart and skill today. A lot of courage." Leonard smiled. "Getting up off that canvas ain't easy to do. You did it and found enough desire to finish your man off. Stick wit' it." Leonard stepped off.

Wilfred Walker patted Ronald on the back, and said, "That was the best I've seen you fight as of yet."

Ronald really couldn't see why, he was fucked up about being knocked silly. "What makes you say that?"

"Simple, that was the toughest fight you've had and you went down hard, but fought back with the heart of a lion. That's what champs are made of, " Wilfred said.

Ronald's victory over Tony Jackson put him on a totally different level among Lorton boxers.

Central Facility, Friday, July 23, 1977

G-Train hid in a blind spot behind the chapel waiting for his victim. He had on a ski mask so no one could identify him. He'd found out that a female C.O. was bringing in heroin for another convict and that she always met the convict in the chapel around that time. G-Train planned to intercept the transaction.

A cute, brown-skinned young woman bent the corner in a pair of tight pants. Before she knew what was going on, G-Train had her in a strangling headlock dragging her back into the blind spot. Ms. Thomas tried to scream but G-Train covered her mouth, and hissed, "Shut up, bitch, unless you want me to put this knife in your ass. Now, where that shit at?"

"I don't know what you talkin' 'bout," she said after G-Train uncovered her mouth. She looked up into the fearsome eyes behind the ski mask, and said, "Please, don't hurt me."

POW! G-Train smacked the shit out of her and placed the knife against her neck. "I don't have no problem leavin' you back here butchered. Now, give me the shit! I know you got it." He searched her, sticking his hand, inside her pants. "I thought you ain't know what I was talkin' 'bout, bitch." He slapped her again. He'd pulled an ounce of heroin from her panties along with some Dilaudid pills. Dilaudid pills moved just as fast as heroin, sometimes faster; crushed up and fired like dope, some say it was better than a heroin high. G-Train pulled a pair of handcuffs from his pocket and cuffed Ms. Thomas. "You be good now, you hear?" G-Train said as he stepped off.

Back in his dorm, G-Train stashed the goods or, better yet, had his boy to stash the goods in his asshole. G-Train was on butt now and had one of the so-called premier homosexuals on the Hill. G-Train's open dealings with punks had created a slight rift in his bond with Frank. However, G-Train didn't give a fuck about what another nigga thought. His boy, Tina Turner, had the best head and asshole that he'd ever had. G-Train had already stabbed a nigga about Tina Turner, so niggas knew he was serious about the punk. Frank couldn't believe how G-Train was carrying it about a punk.

In the bathroom with Tina Turner—the boy looked just like Tina Turner—G-Train told him that he'd be back and that he'd give him some dope later.

"Come on, daddy," Tina said. "I need a fix now. Please."

"Bitch, what I just say?!" G-Train snapped.

"I'm sorry, okay, daddy. I'll see you when you get back." Tina stepped off, he knew G-Train would beat him down to the concrete.

G-Train left the dorm on another mission. It was visiting hours on the Hill. A pimp by the name of Prince had snuck one of his hoes onto the compound and had her hid under a bunk in 7 Dorm, selling pussy. He was charging twenty dollars a nut.

G-Train stepped inside 7 Dorm. He saw Prince's man, Norman, a known killer. Norman watched over the hoe while Prince was on a visit with his woman. It was also Norman's job to get the hoe back to the visiting hall before visits were over. "What's up, Norman?" G-Train gave him five and slid him twenty. Just because G-Train was on boys didn't mean he didn't like pussy.

"You next," Norman said in his deep voice. "Go 'head to the back." Norman pointed toward the back of the dorm were his comrade was watching over the operation. They had a bunk jacked up about four-feet in the air with blankets draped over it like curtains. Under the bunk was a mattress where the hoe took care of her business, sucking and fucking.

Under the bunk, the hoe sucked and jerked a convict. He exploded inside her mouth. She milked him until he was done and then spit out his semen in a cup she had beside her. The convict left, satisfied. G-Train slid under the blanket next. He was shocked when he laid eyes on the hoe. She was young with brown skin and short hair, very cute. Her name was Sarah, she and G-Train went to school together back in the day. Ass naked and laying on her back with her legs wide open, Sarah was shocked to see G-Train as well.

"Damn ... Sarah?" G-Train asked, sitting in the dark.

Embarrassed, but used to the feeling, Sarah said, "Yeah, it's me." All she cared about was getting high. Heroin had taken everything from her, all pride and self-respect.

"Damn," G-Train said again. He couldn't believe his eyes. He used to be attracted to the twenty two-year-old Sarah. "What the fuck you doin' up in here ... doin' this?"

She shrugged. "I'm doin' bad." she said, unable to look G-Train in the eyes.

"Doin' bad?" G-Train, as heartless as he was, felt sorry for her. He felt her pain. He couldn't fuck her. He couldn't take advantage of her situation. "How much you make doin' this?"

"Not much." She rubbed her nose and scratched her arm like a fiend.

"I understand. I can't judge you." G-Train pulled two hundred dollars from his pocket and gave it to her. "Keep that for yourself, don't let nobody know you got it. Okay?"

"Thank you, Germaine," Sarah said with tears in her eyes.

"Don't worry about it." G-Train left.

On the way back to his dorm, G-Train thought about Sarah. She was a bad-ass broad at one time. He couldn't believe what life had done to her.

"G-Train!" Frank called out, running up behind G-Train.

"What's up?"

"What's up wit' you?" Frank said.

"Takin' it slow."

"Man, guess what."

"What?"

"A nigga robbed the broad Ms. Thomas over the chapel, she was toutin' for the nigga Convict."

G-Train smiled. "I heard." He kept the caper to himself, even though he hit Frank off with ten grams of dope later on that he claimed he got from a smaller robbery.

Chapter 8

Youth Center I, Wednesday, August 11, 1977

Watching a re-aring of the May 16, 1977 title fight between Muhammad Ali and Alfredo Evangelista, Ronald, T-Bone, and few other convicts were checking out an aging Ali work his famous rope-a-dope and punish his opponent with big right hands. Ronald studied Ali's every move, every punch, every bob of the head, everything. He wanted to be the best, so he studied the best and trained to be the best. While watching the fight, Ronald and T-Bone also discussed business. T-Bone's mother, Carole, hadn't sent them any dope in almost two weeks. Her New York connect was having problems stemming from the legal issues of Nicky Barns. Ronald and T-Bone weren't the only dudes having problems getting dope at the time. The whole compound was dry, with the exception of one dude that had some dope that was stepped on so many times, a baby could blow a gram and would have no idea what it was. T-Bone was selling Bam pills in the meantime.

"Shit should be back on track by Friday," T-Bone said, sweating and drinking ice-water from his Redskins jug. With no AC in the dorm, it felt like a sauna that afternoon. The fans only blew hot air.

"Your mother found a new connect?" Ronald asked.

"Yeah, she took a trip up to Harlem herself and hooked up wit' some peoples that she had dealings wit' once before. She said shit gon' be much better than it was before, she cuttin' the middle man out."

"That's a big move there," Ronald said.

"Yeah so we'll be back in action." T-Bone looked at his watch. "I gotta go holla at my white girl." He gave Ronald five. "Catch you when I get back."

Ronald just shook his head and smiled.

"What can I say, the pussy good. Plus, she do anything I say." I got the bitch wide open, she take it anywhere." T-Bone smiled.

"You gon' have her pregnant in a minute, too," Ronald joked.

T-Bone waved Ronald off and laughed as he stepped off.

Ronald finished watching the Ali fight and went to his cell to get ready to go for a run. He threw on an Adidas sweat suit and a pair of Ponys and hit the track in the blazing sun.

Hours later, Ronald and T-Bone were both in the visiting hall. Synthia had came down with Lil' Ronald. T-Bone's mother had came to see him.

T-Bone's mother, Carole Mathis, was thirty six- years-old, dark, and lovely, She was 5' 9", one hundred and forty sexy pounds with rich and smooth blueberry skin, silky jet-black hair, and bright white teeth. No one ever thought she was T-Bone's mother being as though she was so young. She had T-Bone when she was fourteen; her relationship with her son was like that of a brother and sister. Aside from her good looks, Carole had a mean reputation in the streets that had earned her the name, The Black Widow. She and her brother, Carl, ran a heroin operation out of their Northeast neighborhood that controlled most of the market in the area. Carole was known to order vicious beatings of all those who fucked up the money and murders for any who crossed the family. In 1971, the year her brother was murdered, Carole unleashed her goons and ordered them to take no prisoners while retaliating for Carl's murder. Bodies dropped like flies all over the city for the whole summer. Carl's close friend and business associate, Frank Matthews, had to come to D.C. to end the bloodshed. When the smoke cleared, The Black Widow was a name that carried weight; she was one of the first female gangsters to ever walk the streets of D.C. The Black Widow ran things with an iron-fist and a close crew of loyal hustlers and killers.

"I'll send you somethin' nice tomorrow," Carole said.

"Okay, I'll send the white broad to get it," T-Bone said.

Carole laughed. "Boy, you just like your daddy, got a way wit' women."

"I gotta do what I gotta do."

"Yeah, I understand. If you would've listened to me on the streets and had a little patience, you would've been able to get some real money, but you wanted to run around robbing and shit.

Now you in prison and you wanna hustle." Carole shook her head and smiled. "A hard head make a soft ass."

"You right," T-Bone agreed.

"Now, you gotta leave that boy alone if you really want to get some money." Carole got reports about T-Bone using dope heavy. "I been hearin' about you. That's how my brother got killed, he got sloppy gettin' high. You need to decide what you wanna do."

T-Bone had nothing to say, he knew his mother was right. He couldn't deny the fact that he was blowing dope real heavy; he knew his mother had eyes everywhere. "Okay, I'ma slow down, but you know how it is."

"You right, I do know how it is. I got tired of firin' that shit in my arm. I decided that I wanted to use it to make a better life for us, not to keep me noddin' all damn day."

A few seats away, Ronald was talking business with Synthia. "I want you to give fifteen hundred of that money to Diane," Ronald said, slap-boxing with Lil' Ronald, who was on his lap. "Keep the rest."

"Okay, baby." Synthia saw the picture line getting smaller. "You ready to take pictures?"

"Yeah, we can do that now."

Ronald, Synthia, and their son took pictures. T-Bone and Carole took a few pictures with them also.

"How are you doin'?" Carole asked Ronald.

"I'm holdin' on."

"You still workin' on that hook?" Carole threw a mock left hook to his body. She liked Ronald.

"Always workin' on it." Ronald smiled and blocked the punch she threw with his elbow, off of instinct.

Carole nodded toward T-Bone, and said, "Make sure you keep my baby out of trouble."

Ronald laughed. "I will."

Carole looked at Synthia, and said, "You make sure you keep Ronald in line, too. We got the next heavyweight champion of the world right here." She patted Ronald on the back.

Youth Center I, Saturday, August 14, 1977

The compound was flooded with convicts and their visitors the hot summer afternoon. The sun was bright and beaming down on the fair. There was live music provided by Trouble Funk, and Chuck Brown and The Soul Searchers; the sound of go-go music covered the whole compound. Everybody was dancing and having a good time, even old people. There was food and drinks. A miniature carnival set up for the kids. All kinds of fun and games. Over on the football field the Youth Center team was practicing; they had a game coming up later on against No.3, who was coming down from D.C. to scrimmage. Over in the gym, there was one-on-one basketball games for prizes. For a moment, the convicts weren't locked up, in a sense.

Ronald was on a mission. He left his son with T-Bone at the pony ride while he and Synthia snuck back to the dorm. Not everybody could sneak their woman back to the dorm, a nigga had to be strong and respected. Ronald had seen another convict try the same thing, the convict ended up getting his woman gang-raped by three other convicts. Not only was his woman raped, he was raped as well when he tried to buck.

C.O. Turner was working the dorm. Ronald slid him a few dollars to watch his back while he and Synthia went to his cell. Synthia looked around Ronald's cell, and said, "So this is how you live, huh?"

"Yeah," Ronald said as he locked the door behind them and put a piece of paper over the window so no one could see inside the cell. He covered the outside window as well.

Still looking around the cell, Synthia said, "This doesn't even look like a prison cell." She sat on his bed. "It's like a bedroom."

"I gotta live here for minute, don't I?" Ronald smiled.

A wooden dresser with a huge mirror lined the wall with pictures of Ronald's loved ones around the edges. The top of the dresser was covered with cosmetics. A fish tank sat on a stand beside the dresser with goldfish inside.

"You got a fish tank in here, you doin' big things, ain't you?" Synthia said.

"I'm gon' be here for a minute, I gotta' be comfortable, you know?"

Synthia opened his closet-like cabinet and saw jeans, dress slacks, sweats, silk shirts, and other street clothes. "You got a whole wardrobe, huh?"

Ronald pulled his blanket back and exposed silk sheets. "I got these just for today, just for you."

Synthia shook her head and laughed, wiping sweat from her head. It was hot as shit in the cell. "You got everything in here but AC, don't you?"

"I got a fan." He turned the fan on. "AC ain't gon' make a

difference for what we came to do." He smiled.

"Is that right?" Synthia hugged and kissed him. She sucked on his tongue, squeezing him tight. She missed him and hadn't felt him inside of her in a good while. For some reason, she was turned on by being in Ronald's cell with him. "Where's the baby-makin' music?" Synthia joked. "We can't do it to Chuck." Chuck Brown's go-go sound could still be heard booming across the compound.

"I'm on top of it." Ronald pulled out his radio and put on Al Green's I'm Still in Love With You. He looked at Synthia, who was undressing, and got hard seeing her sexy body laying on his bed. Ronald began to undress as well. Synthia smiled when she saw his tattoo with her name across his arm.

Mocking the song, Synthia said, "You in love wit' me, baby?"

"Like never before." Ronald climbed on top of her, kissing her passionately. He rubbed all over her body as he licked down to her neck nice and slow. Wetness crept between her legs. He squeezed her breast as he sucked on her nipples, making her moan softly. "You like that?" Ronald asked. Synthia moaned her approval as she rubbed his back. He continued licking down her stomach all the way down to her sweet wetness. He licked around her fat, pink lips. By the way she moaned and moved, Ronald knew he was taking care of business. He licked her clit as he slid his finger inside her.

Grabbing the back of his head, Synthia's eyes rolled back in her head. "Sssssss...oh yeah, daddy... ssssss... aaaaaahhhh..."

She wrapped her legs around him. Pushing her soaking wet pussy up into Ronald's face, she continued to moan. "Oooohh, daddy, don't stop! Aaah, aaah ... oooh, sssshhhiitt." Synthia came so hard that she began to shake. "Aaahh, yeah, I'm cummin'...oooh...yeah, I'm...I'm...yeah, yeah, yeah, I'm cummin'."

After making her cum, Ronald slid back up, licking up her body until he got to her neck. He slipped inside her pussy nice and slow. Inch after inch. "Aaah, yeah, baby, you like that?" he asked as he began stroking her.

"Oh yeah, daddy," Synthia moaned. After a few more strokes, she said, "Let me put it in my mouth, daddy."

Ronald agreed. Synthia got on her hands and knees between his legs and without the use of her hands, she took his whole manhood in her mouth while looking him in the eyes. She went all the way down on him until her lips touched the base of his dick. She held him there for a second and then began working her mouth, her lips and her tongue in such a way that made Ronald close his eyes and rub her head while she took him where he needed to be. Her warm mouth and throat was too much, Ronald couldn't hold it anymore. He came all inside her mouth. She swallowed it and licked all over his dick.

Naked, they both sat on the bed for a few moments, smoking a joint of weed. "We can just sit in here and smoke weed and the C.O. ain't gon' do nothin' about it?" Synthia asked as she blew smoke in the air. Marvin Gaye's *What's Going On* was playing on the radio.

"I got the police in my pocket." Ronald smiled.

After smoking the joint, they had to go another round. Ronald bent Synthia over the bed and fucked her hard from the back, holding her by her waist. With her hands grabbing handfuls of the silk sheets, Synthia moaned and moaned, loving the pounding she was getting. Ronald was giving her something to take home with her. Looking over her shoulder, Synthia moaned, "Smack my ass, daddy, you know how I like it." Ronald did as she asked. "Ssss, yeah, do it again. Owch, owch, owch, sssssss, yeah, daddy, treat me like a whore, fuck me, fuck me harder, daddy." Synthia bit down on her bottom lip, her ass was stinging, but she loved it. "Oh yeah, daddy, oh shit ... I'm cummin' again."

Ronald came seconds later and slow stroked Synthia until he was spent.

"I love you so much, baby," Synthia said as Ronald continued to slow stroke her from the back.

"I love you, too, baby."

Central Facility, Thursday, September 31, 1977

Frank pulled up and shot a pretty jumper over the dude, checking him. All net. At 5" 8" and one hundred and fifty pounds, Frank was still small at twenty-years-old, but was one of the best point guards on the Hill. He'd dropped sixty five points in his last game while high. "Thirteen up!" Frank stated, backpedaling to the other end of the court. The gym was somewhat packed that evening. Pick-up games were a passtime for Frank, but every now and then he would bet on the games. He had money on the game he was now playing. The game was very rough and physical, like most prison sports. With money on the line, the game had turned into Lorton-ball as soon as Frank bet Chew one hundred dollars that his team would win.

At the other end of the court, Chew faked left and drove hard to the basket, and made an easy lay-up for his team. "Thirteen-Fourteen!" Chew said, glaring at Frank. Frank waved him off like he was nothing.

Looking at one of his teammates that he felt was playing scared, Frank said, "Play like you got some heart, nigga. Check that nigga, he ain't nothin'." Frank got the ball and dribbled down court, dripping with sweat. "Play these niggas hard, like they playin' us!" Frank passed the ball off to his big man, who tied the game at fourteen. "That's right!" Frank rushed back on defense. Quickly, both teams scored and the game was tied at fifteen; both teams had already agreed that the game would only go to sixteen. "Play D! No lay-ups! Make 'em earn it!" Frank yelled, playing his man tight as if it was game seven of the NBA finals.

"You can't stop me," Chew said as he went left on Frank and shot a jumper. The shot hit the rim and bounced out. Frank took off down court at top speed. His big man rebounded the ball and slung it down court. Frank caught the pass in stride and, without dribbling, took two long steps to the basket; he jumped high in the air but before he could lay the ball up and end the game, Chew came out of nowhere and shoved Frank out of the air. Frank hit the ground hard. The whole gym was silent except for the sound of the bouncing ball. Everyone was waiting to see what would go down next.

Much smaller than Chew, Frank jumped to his feet like a raging bull. He swung and cracked Chew on the chin, dazing him. Other convicts tried to break it up as Frank and Chew traded blows.

"Leave 'em alone!" Cadillac said. "Let 'em fight." Niggas did just that as Cadillac said. Even the C.O. that stepped in the gym didn't interfere, he knew the convicts had things under control. The C.O. left the gym.

Frank and Chew went at it, hard, both landing big punches. Taking too many blows to the head, Chew grabbed Frank and started wrestling him.

"Don't grab him!" Cadillac pulled Chew off of Frank. "Fight him, nigga."

Frank was dead on Chew's ass as soon as Cadillac pulled them apart. Frank threw nonstop blows. Chew seemed to have had enough. Cadillac broke it up. "You took care of your business," he said to Frank, putting his arm around Frank's shoulder, trying to walk him out of the gym to calm him down. "Sometimes, you gotta punch these niggas in the mouth to put 'em in they place, they'll come around after that. I know Chew, he ain't 'bout nothin'."

"Fuck that, he fuckin' wit' the right nigga," Frank said as they passed a crowd on the corner in front of laundy. Gray Top called Cadillac. Cadillac told Frank he'd be right back. "I'll catch you in the dorm." Frank kept stepping, he had something on his mind. He continued down the walk, past a group of punks that were dressed like hookers, out selling ass.

Minutes later, Chew was stabbed in the neck behind 18 Dorm. Still hanging on the strip, Cadillac walked toward the Hollow and into 18 Dorm to check on Frank. Frank was sitting on his bunk listening to The Quiet Storm on WHUR. Cadillac sat on Frank's bunk, and said, "I turn my back for a second and you just disappear on me like that?"

"My mind was already made up." Frank lit a cigarette. "Fuck that nigga."

Cadillac smiled. "Was it worth it?"

"Yeah."

"Why?"

"'Cause the nigga violated," Frank said as G-Train walked by with Tina Turner.

"What's up wit' you and G-Train." Cadillac picked up on the vibe. He'd noticed that Frank and G-Train weren't hanging tough like they used to. In fact, they weren't even speaking.

"I don't know what's up wit' that nigga, G-Train. I guess he think I'm supposed to kiss his ass or somethin'. Fuck that," Frank said. He and G-Train had had some words after G-Train came and got him about a beef he had with a dude in another dorm. Being the loyal nigga that he was, Frank didn't ask no questions, he got his knife and went to see what was up. He had his man's back and they put that work in, stabbing the nigga seventeen times. After getting away with the assault, Frank found out that the dude they had stabbed was trying to fuck Tina Turner. Frank was fucked up G-Train came to get him about some shit dealing with a boy, he hated punks. He and G-Train got into a heated argument that almost led to blows being thrown. "That nigga been walkin' by me like he don't know me since then, so fuck 'em," Frank said to Cadillac.

"Nah, man, you can't carry it like that, that's your man," Cadillac said. "Men don't do that. Women stop speakin', men address shit. If that's your man, don't let pride come between a bond y'all done had since the streets."

Frank thought about what Cadillac was saying. If Gangsta was alive, he wouldn't approve of the way Frank and G-Train were carrying things. "You know what?" Frank said, watching Big Mack and Eggie come through the door, they were coming in the dorm to holla at Fray and Tony Harris. "You right, but G got this thing in his head where he still think I'm the little kid I was when he left the streets, like I'm under him or somethin'. It ain't like that, it ain't that kind of party at all, Cadillac. I'ma man, just like him. If he can't respect that, fuck 'em, it might be best that we stay away from each other. I respect man all the way around the board, and I ain't lettin' nobody disrespect me, and I ain't gettin' caught up about no fuckin' punks. G-Train fuckin' wit' that nasty-ass punk, knowin' how much shit come wit' them."

"I see where you comin' from," Cadillac said.

Youth Center I, Monday, December 13, 1977

Snow covered the compound as convicts walked around in huge green army coats. It was just after seven P.M. and it was already dark outside. Some convicts were going around R-N-D to pick up packages they had been sent from home. Other convicts were lurking in the dark waiting to rob niggas of their packages.

Ms. Goodall, who was now Sgt. Goodall, was passing out the packages. As always, she was looking good with her thick, redbone self. She was behind the counter with her hair in a bun. Quickly, not really checking the contents of the boxes, she got three convicts out of the way and saw Ronald. "Come on, Mays, wit' your fine-ass." She winked at Ronald. "You ain't got no drugs in your box, do you?" she joked as she opened his box in front of him.

Ronald smiled. "You know better than that." His eyes were bloodshot red from smoking weed. Sgt. Goodall was looking extra good to him at the moment. "But, if I did have some drugs in there, what would you do?"

She whispered, "I might blackmail you to see what you workin' wit' down there." She nodded toward his crotch.

Ronald smiled but didn't have time for her, she had too much shit with her. He played along, got his package, and left. Outside with his package in his hands, Ronald headed for the dorm. The wolves were out and waiting for their prey, right outside the door of R-N-D. With no problems, Ronald made it back to the dorm. The dude that came after him was robbed for his whole package.

Inside the dorm, a few convicts were watching the movie *Roots*.

Ronald went to holla at Harrison-EL. He found Harrison-EL sitting at his wooden desk studying. The whole cell was a think-tank. Against the wall in the back of the cell was a wooden bookshelf that was packed with books of all kinds. *The Souls of Black Folks* by W.E.B. DuBois, *Up From Slavery* by Booker T. Washington, and *Out of Africa* by Isak Dinesen were just a few books on the shelf. "What's up?" Ronald said, taking a seat.

"You popped up just in time, I was just thinkin' about you. Your timin' is always on the money." Harrison-EL sat his book down. He'd been reading *Ideas and Opinions* by Albert Einstein. "Let me ask you a question." He paused. "You go home in what ... two months or so, right?"

"Yeah, seven weeks," Ronald said.

"So ... uh, I guess you think you gon' sell dope while you train to go pro, huh?" Harrison-EL looked him in the eyes.

"I don't plan to, but if I have to that's what I'ma do." Harrison-EL folded his arms. "So, sellin' dope is your plan B?"

"I got a family out there. I gotta put food on the table, by any means."

"I'ma be frank wit' you, only because I care about you, Ronnie." Harrison-EL rubbed his chin. "You can be a great fighter, but if you don't give yourself a real chance, you gon' end up back in here... I know what I'm talkin' 'bout. From me to you, get a nice little job and focus on fighting. I advise you to go up there wit' the dude Wilfred and stay in the gym. If you stay in D.C., you settin' yourself up."

Ronald nodded in agreement.

"I know you done established some strong bonds in here, but remember this here, you gotta focus on Ronald first. Once Ronald is straight, then you can make sure everybody else is straight. Look at what I'm sayin' like this." Harrison-EL searched for the right words. "Look at it like this here, strengthen your foundation—your home, your family—and focus only on that at first, make sure it's taken care of. Once your house is in order, it's like a fortified kingdom, secure against attack from the outside, you dig? The game plan must always be, first things first. Don't forget that."

"I dig."

"It's like this ... men, in general, if they are stand-up men, are always loyal. However, loyalty can be a man's downfall if it ain't put in the proper perspective. On the strength of our loyalty, we tend to place ourselves under obligations to those we are close to. Everything in life has an extreme and a bare minimum. The best thing a man can do is find a firm course in the middle and hold fast to it. You dig?" Harrison-EL looked Ronald in the eyes.

"Yeah, I dig it." Ronald felt every word.

"On another tip, remember this, Ali was twenty two when he took the title from Liston. Don't throw your chance away. Do it for your family, by any means."

"You right." Ronald nodded.

"Put your mind to it and don't let nothin' come between you and your dreams, don't let nothin' or nobody take your dreams away from you. Never," Harrison-EL said.

Chapter 9

Washington, D.C. Wednesday, April 14, 1978

Tate's gym, located in Northeast, D.C., was closing for the night, but the lone sound of powerful blows slamming into the heavy bag was a clear sign that Ronald was hard at work. He'd just finished jumping rope for forty five minutes, so he was soaking wet when Buck Tate came out of his office. Buck smiled when he saw Ronald hard at work. *That kid's gonna be something*, Buck thought.

Buck Tate was an old black man in his early sixties with gray hair, a big belly, and the frame of a former heavyweight boxer. Buck and Wilfred Walker were good friends; Wilfred asked Buck to give Ronald a job and take him under his wing. Buck had no problem with it, in no time he'd taken a liking to Ronald and saw great potential in him. Buck knew the boxing game like the back of his hand. He began to work with Ronald just as Harrison-EL used to. Buck had had a nice professional career as a heavyweight from 1934 to 1952. His record stood at 89-21-3 with forty eight wins by knockout. He'd fought some of the greats. In 1946, at thirty one-years-old, Buck fought the first heavyweight title fight to follow World War II. He lost a split decision to the great Joe Louis. Buck didn't get a rematch due to politics. However, he got another shot at the title in June of 1950 but was knocked out by the champ, Ezzard Charles, a fighter who Buck had knocked out back in 1943. Among other big names, Buck had fought the only heavyweight champion to retire undefeated—Rocky Marciano. Marciano stopped Buck in the eighth round. Now, as an old man, Buck got joy out of teaching the ghetto youth how to box. It was what he lived for.

"Make sure you lock up when you get done, Ronnie. I'm leavin'," Buck said, admiring the razor sharp combinations Ronald was blasting the heavy bag with.

Taking a pause, Ronald said, "Okay, Mr. Tate." He wiped sweat from his forehead with his forearm. "I'll see you tomorrow."

"Bright an early," Buck yelled over his shoulder, going out the door. "We goin' runnin' first thing smokin'. Gotta keep you in shape for that Johnson boy." Buck disappeared through the door.

Ronald went back to blasting the heavy bag with all kinds of blows. His mind was filled with visions of his first pro fight. Although Wilfred was busy preparing James Holmes for the upcoming title fight against Ken Norton, he still managed to get Ronald a pro fight against a boxer by the name of Cleveland Johnson. The money was next to nothing, but in a city like Philly Ronald was sure get a lot of attention once he showed the world his skills. Buck was walking him through his first fight, but Wilfred was going to focus on Ronald as soon as the Holmes title fight was over with. With Muhammad Ali aging and coming off a lost by split decision to a young Leon Spinks, the heavyweight division was somewhat up for grabs and Wilfred felt that Holmes was the champ to fill Ali's void. Ronald knew that if he stayed focused, he could go somewhere with his fight game.

Ronald finished working out and locked up the gym.

Outside, he walked down the street in the dark heading for his old Chevy. He saw someone leaning against his car. As he got closer, he saw that it was Roland leaning against his car smoking a cigarette.

"What's up, Ronnie?" Roland said, looking nice and clean, like he'd just taken a shower and jumped into some new clothes.

"I'm holdin' on, what's up wit' you?" Ronald said, checking his brother out. He hadn't seen him in a while. "Where you been?"

"I checked into a drug program, I didn't tell nobody, I just wanted to do it for me and make a change. You know what I mean?" Roland plucked his cigarette into the street and blew smoke in the air. "I know you fucked up at me."

"It ain't about bein' fucked up at you, it's about bein' family," Ronald said. "We family, we supposed to always be there for one another, ain't that how we was taught?"

Roland nodded in agreement. "You right, Ronnie. I can't get around that. I won't try. All I can say is that when that boy get ahold of your soul, like it had me, all you can think about is where that next fix gon' come from. You know how that go. It had that hold on me. But now, I'm in control, I shook that monkey off my back. I'm tryin' to stay clean, tryin' to stay away from everything and everybody that can take me back in that direction. I got a lotta wrongs to right. I gotta make right wit' you and Diane, I hope you can understand where I'm comin' from and be open to my struggle. I want us to clear the air, Ronnie."

Ronald said nothing for a second, just looked at Roland. He then gave him five, and said, "We family. I'm always there for you."

Roland smiled. "Thanks, Ronnie."

"We brothers, that's more important than anything else." Ronald looked up and down the dark street. "You seen Diane?"

"Not yet, I heard that you be up here all the time. I wanted to see you first. I needed to talk to you."

"We brothers, that's it, that's all. I'm here for you," Ronald said.

Roland smiled, his little brother was thorough. "So, you stickin' wit' the boxin' thing, huh?"

"Yeah, I got to carry it like this. It's all I got goin' for me right now."

"I respect that, but look here, I ain't gon' hold you up. I just wanted to talk to you for a few minutes. I'ma be on my way."

"Where you goin'? Where you stayin' at?"

"I'm stayin' wit' this girl I met in the program, she got a spot over Southeast. I'm stayin' there until I get my shit together."

"Well, let me give you a ride over there," Ronald said.

"Thanks, but I'm 'bout to go see Diane."

"I'll drop you off there then," Ronald said, pulling out his keys. The two brothers hopped in the car and headed for Diane's.

When Ronald got home, he found Synthia on the sofa in the living room of their Southeast apartment. She looked frustrated.

"What's wrong, baby?" Ronald shut the door behind him and sat beside her, putting his arm around her.

She took a deep breath, and said, "I got laid off today." She'd been working two jobs and was bringing in the most money. Although they had a small stash of money they'd put aside from when Ronald was sending money home from prison, they were still struggling, only because Ronald made a vow to himself that he would not involve himself in crime. "I don't know what we gon' do now," Synthia said, shaking her head.

Ronald kissed her cheek. "Don't worry yourself about that." Synthia knew that Ronald was trying his best to stay focused and keep his hands clean. She was worried that he would turn to drug dealing if he felt they needed the money.

"I'll get another job, we cool. Money gon' come, we ain't gon' starve," Ronald said, rubbing her thigh, feeling her smooth skin; all she had on was a long T-shirt and a pair of cut off jean shorts. "As long as I'm here, you ain't gotta worry about nothin'."

"How you gonna train if you workin' two jobs?"

"I'm young." He kissed her again. "I'll be okay. Let me take care of this here."

Central Facility, Saturday, April 24, 1978

Behind 18 Dorm, there was a nice size crap game going on. G-Train was shooting the dice and had the hot hand at the time. He was picking up money on almost every roll. Out of the blue, a convict came out of the dorm and told G-Train that he had a visit. "Me?" G-Train asked, shaking the dice. He didn't get visits. The convict assured him that he had a visit. G-Train cut the crap game short and went in the dorm to freshen up. He then headed straight to the visiting hall.

The visiting hall was crowded when G-Train stepped inside. He looked around from face to face, and saw no one that he knew. He asked the C.O. who had came to see him. The C.O. directed him to an attractive young woman in the back. "You sure she here to see me?" G-Train asked the C.O., he was sure there was a mistake.

"You're Germaine Wilson, right?" the C.O. said.

"Yeah."

"That's your visit. If you don't want to see her, I'm sure there's a whole lotta other brothers that wouldn't mind seein' her fine ass," the C.O. joked.

G-Train gave the C.O. a vicious look and headed toward the back. He passed Frank along the way; they didn't acknowledge each other. Ronald came to visit Frank and brought Lil' Ronald along. Frank and G-Train didn't fuck with each other at all. G-Train had began to envy Frank; he really didn't know why, but he did. As G-Train walked up on the young woman in the tight blue jeans and gray windbreaker with the fresh hairdo, he still had no idea who she was for a second.

"You seen a ghost or somethin'?" The sexy young woman smiled.

Boom, it hit him. "Damn, girl!" G-Train hugged the young womman. "You look good." He let her go and looked her up and down.

"I had to make some changes in my life," Sarah said as they sat down. She'd come a long way since G-Train had ran into her selling her body in a Lorton dorm and strung out on heroin.

"I see, you lookin' damn good." G-Train rubbed her knee. "Look like you made some good changes, too."

"I got sick and tired of bein' sick and tired. I had to look in the mirror every mornin' and hate myself." She shook her head, still hating that stage of her life. "That ain't no life, you know where I'm comin' from?"

"Yeah... I do." G-Train nodded.

"I know you wonderin' what I'm doin' comin' down here to see you."

"It crossed my mind." G-Train raised his eyebrows. "But, I don't have no complaints. I'm happy to see you, but yeah, to what do I owe this honor?"

"You remember when I saw you under that bed that day? When I was on it and whatnot?" Sarah spoke with no shame.

"Yeah."

"Do you know that in two whole years you were the only person that treated me like a person, a real person and didn't take advantage of me." Sarah looked G-Train in the eyes and held his hand. "Really. That night when I got home, I took the money you gave me and bought a bus ticket to North Carolina. I went into rehab down there. You sparked somethin' inside of me that made me look at myself. Like I said, I didn't like what I saw in the mirror, I hated what I saw. I had to fix it. I told myself that once I got myself together that I was goin' to pay you a visit and show you that whatever you saw in me was still alive." Sarah took a sip of her 7-Up. "I want to thank you, Germaine, thank you for bein' a friend."

"You ain't gotta thank me, girl. I was crazy about you when we were comin' up..."

"Please, nigga. I couldn't tell."

"I was, serious business. But, you gotta keep in mind that I stayed locked up all the time as a juvenile. I never had a real relationship wit' a female out there because of that. Since I was uh ... ten or eleven, I don't think I been on the streets more than two months at a time."

"Ummh." Sarah gave up a grimace of sympathy. She could remember the first time she saw the police arrest someone. She was in the fourth grade and the police came to her school and arrested another fourth grader. The scene was scary for her because she was always told that when the police arrest a person that they took the person straight to prison, no matter what the age was. The fourth grader, she later learned, was charged with burglary. He had broken into a grocery store and stole more than fifty pounds of steak. That fourth grader was little Germaine Wilson a.k.a. G-Train. "You been in and out of jail your whole life, Germaine. How old are you now?"

"I just turned twenty three last month."

"How long have you been down here?"

"I been in on this case goin' on six years."

"Damn, you been down here since you was seventeen?"

"I been locked up since I was seventeen, but I stayed over Youth Center for a while."

"When do you get out?"

"I should be home next year," G-Train said.

Across the visiting hall, while G-Train and Sarah were catching up on old times, Ronald and Frank were talking about Ronald's adjustment to the streets. In the two months that

Ronald had been on the streets, he had been down to visit Frank and T-Bone twice. Both times he went to see T-Bone, he took his son; Cristal let Ronald pick the boy up any time he wanted to. Ronald's son and T-Bone's son got along like brothers. Ronald had also been to see Harrison-EL twice.

"Right now, I'm tryin' to find a second job. I think I'ma get this security job downtown at one of them office buildings. They say they ain't got no problem wit' my record." Ronald gave his son some change for the soda machine. "I gotta work the graveyard shift, though, which really ain't no thing. It's a nice gym in the basement. I can work out while I'm there, go home, take a nap, and go down Tate's at four in the afternoon. I can make it work. Plus, T-Bone's mother loaned me ten Gs until I get myself together. I'll be okay."

Frank listened to Ronald and admired his partners dedication to his goals, he respected Ronald's drive to succeed. "So, when do you fight the Johnson dude?"

"May 21st," Ronald said as he cut his eyes at G-Train, who was looking his way. They locked eyes for a second, the animosity was still mutual. "I'm ready as ever. This is my big shot and I'ma take it."

"That's right, you gotta make it happen. You know how it go." Frank smiled. While Frank was talking, one of his comrades came up to him and slid him a knot of cash in a rubber band and kept stepping.

"I see you still makin' it happen," Ronald said.

"I got to, everybody can't bank on knockin' a nigga out," Frank said, keeping an eye on the C.O. as he flipped through the knot of tens, twenties, and fifties. It had to be a good twenty five hundred dollars. "Here, this for you." Frank handed Ronald the cash. "I know it's hard when you tryin' to do the right thing out there. I wanna see you come up. If you come up, I come up. Whatever you do, you ain't gotta break the law. I got you."

"Thanks, man. This takes a hell of a load off my shoulders." Ronald had no pride issues nor moral issues about accepting the money. T-Bone had given him two thousand dollars the last time he went to visit him.

Ronald's comrades wanted him to accomplish what he'd set out to do, they wanted him to obtain all of his goals. In essence, if Ronald was to succeed, they would all be a part of that success. That was what was really important. At the same time, Ronald had a responsibility to his family and his comrades: He had to stay focused and bring everything to reality. Ronald accepted that responsibility.

Frank gave Ronald five. "You know how shit go, you my peoples." Frank was making a nice piece of change on the Hill, close to two thousand dollars every three or four days. He and his crew kept heroin moving all over the compound. They ran everything from the Hollow. Frank was plugged in with T-Bone's mother, so he was getting grade-one dope twice a week. "Anytime you need somethin' out there just let me know, you hear?"

"Yeah, I hear you." Ronald laughed. "You gettin' it like that, huh?"

"I'm killin' 'em down here. My stash got popped two weeks ago, lost 'bout eighty five hundred dollars, that was just gamblin' money. Since I started fuckin' wit' The Black Widow's peoples, I been takin' this shit to another level. I'm tellin' you, Ronnie."

"Oh yeah?"

"No bullshit. That's who I'm gon' fuck wit' when I get out," Frank said, handing Lil' Ronald some candy as he came back from the soda machine.

Meanwhile, G-Train and Sarah were real comfortable together. G-Train had her smiling, laughing, and blushing, and feeling real good about herself. As their visit came to an end, they hugged and kissed on the lips. "I'll come see you again real soon, okay?"

"Don't be too long, I'll be missin' you."

"Please." Sarah blushed. "You just be good."

"You know I'ma do that." G-Train smiled.

Ronald hugged Frank as their visit came to an end. "I love you, man. Keep your head up."

"Always, you do the same out there. Stay focused," Frank said, rubbing Lil' Ronald on the head. "You be good lil' man." Lil Ronald punched Frank in the leg. Frank laughed and looked at Ronald. "He like usin' his hands already.""

Ronald laughed. "Like father, like son. You know how them Lorton babies is."

Frank and Ronald laughed, giving each other five.

Youth Center I, Tuesday, May 17, 1978

Alone in her office, Mrs. Mitchell kept having mental visions of the way her husband had been beating her at home. The night before, he smacked her across the bedroom and to the floor, accusing her of having an affair as he'd been doing for a few months now. He kept screaming that her pussy was getting looser and looser every time they made love. Not to mention how she just laid there, not into the act at all, she just let her husband hump away until he was done. T-Bone was the only thing on her mind all day long, he had her sprung. Mrs. Mitchell wanted out of her marriage so bad that it hurt. If it was up to her, she would never go home from work.

Feeling depressed, Mrs. Mitchell locked her door and pulled one of the heroin-filled balloons from her purse. She tried to open it, but it popped. Heroin went everywhere, it was all over her desk and her clothes. She stood up and dusted herself off. Looking to her left, she gazed at a picture of her and her husband on their honeymoon in Martha's Vineyard. The memory disgusted her, and she knocked the frame face down on the desk. With no idea about what she was doing, she reluctantly rubbed her index finger into a small pile of the beige powder on her desk. She had no idea what the drug would do, but if it made T-Bone feel good, she was sure it'd do the same for her. She sniffed the heroin that was on her fingertip and braced herself for what was to come. Everything seemed to slow down as her eyes slowly rolled back in her head as she took a seat. The

113

feeling was better than sex, she thought, it was the most euphoric sensation she'd ever had. Leaning her head back in the chair, she slowly rubbed her face, and then her arm as she drifted into a nod.

Moments later, Mrs. Mitchell came out of her nod, still in her euphoric state. She sluggishly cleaned up the mess she'd made and gathered the dope on her desk into a piece of paper. She folded the paper up tightly and went to put it back in her purse, but the unstoppable urge to vomit sent her rushing to the trash can in the corner of the office. She spit up everything in her stomach as she hovered over the trashcan like it was a toilet. It scared the shit out of her at first. She then wiped her mouth and slowly stood up. Feeling even better, she took a seat. After nodding a few more times, she went to the bathroom to freshen up. When she got back to her office she just sat behind her desk, slowly blinking, until there was a knock at her door that scared her. She jumped a little. Opening the door, she saw that it was T-Bone.

"What's up?" T-Bone said as he shut the door behind him. Off the break he could tell something was up with Mrs. Mitchell. "What's wrong wit' you?" he asked as he sat down.

"Please, don't be mad at me," she said as sat back down.

"Mad at you for what?"

Mrs. Mitchell explained everything to T-Bone, praying that he would understand. At first, T-Bone was pissed off. He wanted to get up and smack the motherfucking shit out of the white bitch, but he kept his cool. He was good at that. Sometimes! Mrs. Mitchell could still be good for something. He assured her that everything was okay. "Don't worry about it," T-Bone said.

"You sure?" she asked, her speech was somewhat slow.

"Yeah, don't trip off it, baby," T-Bone said. "But, I don't want you playing wit' this stuff. Let me get the rest of it." She gave him the rest of the dope and he put it in his pocket. Mrs. Mitchell turned her back to put her purse back up. T-Bone hugged her from the back and rubbed his dick against her ass.

She responded by grinding against his dick. T-Bone knew that she wanted some dick. "That shit got your pussy on fire, don't it?"

"Yeah," she moaned as she closed her eyes, still grinding against his hard dick. *Damn, I want him inside me so bad*, she thought,

T-Bone stuck his hand under her skirt and rubbed her smooth leg all the way up to her panties. "How you want it?" He rubbed her ass with one hand and her breast with the other while grinding against her ass, setting her insides ablaze. "You want it from the back?"

She reached behind her and pulled up her skirt. "Put it in my ass, daddy." She knew that T-Bone loved being called daddy. She was his perfect whore.

T-Bone pulled her panties down and undid his pants, and then bent her over the desk and began rubbing her pussy with his fingers. He then rubbed her cream between her ass-cheeks and around her asshhole, making her moan.

"Just put it in, daddy." she said, pushing her ass back at him. "Fuck me like a whore, T-Bone!" She looked over her shoulder with her glowing blue eyes. "Ahhhh, yeah, owwww ..." She felt him slide inside her ass. Deep. "Yeah, daddy." She pushed her ass back at him with every stroke. "Fuck me harder."

T-Bone gave her what she asked for, he fucked the shit out of her. He pulled her blond hair as he dug deep inside her asshole. "You like that, bitch?" T-Bone smacked her ass with a loud pop. He left a handprint on her pink ass.

"Oh, yeah, smack my ass again, ow, ow, ow, just like that. Uh, uh, uh, uh, oh yeah, fuck this ass." Mrs. Mitchell was in another world as T-Bone dug deeper inside her asshole. "Oh God, I love it, I'm cummin. I'm cummin', T-Bone, I'm cummin'. Don't stop. I love you!"

T-Bone almost laughed, but he kept fucking the shit out of her instead.

"I love it in my ass," Mrs. Mitchell said as her legs began to shake from the backbreaking orgasm that rocked her body, complimenting her dope high. She was in love.

Philadelphia, PA, Saturday, May 21, 1978

The Blue Horizon was packed; it was no Caesars Palace or Madison Square Garden, but some big names had fought in the spot. Back in his locker room with Buck, Roland, and a few other members of his boxing crew, Ronald was anxious to get in the ring and do his thing. He'd watched some of the first fight and felt the energy from the crowd as the two boxers put on a show. Ronald planned to put on a show of his own. He was fighting right before the main event, which was Richard Dunn v. Mike Weaver.

Wilfred Walker walked into the locker room and sat down beside Ronald while Roland was wrapping Ronald's hands. "This is your night, kid," Wilfred said. "I'm banking on you. Buck told me that he's been working you real hard down there. I know you're ready."

"I'm ready as I'll ever be," Ronald said.

"Make the best of this fight, let them see what you're made of." Wilfred gave Ronald some advice, and then went back to his ring side seat.

"Ronnie, this is what you train so hard for, just put the game plan in effect," Roland said, rubbing Ronald's shoulders to loosen him up. Roland was now helping Ronald train.

"I got this, I'm focused," Ronald said.

A short while later it was fight time for Ronald. He and his crew marched to the ring with Marvin Gaye's *If I Should Die Tonight* playing. In his black robe with the hood over his head, Ronald was in a zone as he headed for the ring. He felt butterflies in his stomach, but he blocked that out, he had work to do. Looking around at all the faces in the crowd, he knew the world was watching.

Ronald's opponent had been in five pro fights already and

116

ended two of them with knockouts. Early. Ronald and his opponent were both two hundred and five pounds and each stood 5' 11". It was a pretty even matchup. In the ring, Ronald studied Cleveland Johnson as they were introduced. Brown-skinned and lean but muscular with a bald head, Johnson reminded Ronald of a heavyweight version of Marvelous Marvin Hagler. Just like Hagler, Johnson was a hard hitting southpaw with fight-stopping power in his left hand.

In his corner after introductions, Ronald listened to every word Buck said. Putting Ronald's mouthpiece in, Buck said, "This is the beginnin' of it all, son." Buck's voice was deep and raspy. "In this game, your record is your reputation. It's what gives you power, it's what gets you paid and what gets you bigger fights. This Johnson boy is tryin' to build his reputation on his left hand and his stopping power. He wants to end the fight early. Take that away from him, show these people you can punch holes in his reputation."

Ronald shook his head. The bell rang and the fight was on. The two fighters met each other at center ring with their hands up, shaking their heads slightly from side to side. For a second, Ronald was uneasy fighting the southpaw. They traded a few punches, getting a feel for each other. Johnson caught Ronald with a sweet right hand and followed it with a powerful uppercut. Ronald had a good chin, he took the blow and countered with a four piece combination that got a roar out of the crowd. The fighters danced around, attacking like pit bulls when an opening appeared. For the first three rounds, they both put on a great show, they were even neck and neck on the scorecards. In the middle of the fourth round, Johnson landed his wicked left hand in the form of a hook, the punch opened a cut over Ronald's right eye. With blood in his eye, Ronald sidestepped Johnson and fired his long jab, following it with his mean left hook and hammering uppercut that staggered Johnson and sent him to the canvas. The crowd went off.

"That's right, nigga!" Roland screamed. "Put 'em together,

Ronnie!"

Johnson got up quickly and finished the round.

After the bell, Ronald sat in his corner with Roland working on his cut. Roland was a great cut man, a skill he'd picked up down Lorton, on the Hill.

"He ain't got no chin!" Buck said. "You got 'em! Your left hook got 'em runnin' scared, it got 'em shakin' at the knees every time you land it. Work his body, make him drop his hands and then go upstairs! You know what you gotta do!"

In rounds five and six, Johnson came on strong, re-opening the cut over Ronald's eye. The bleeding wouldn't stop. Nevertheless, Ronald's body attack was killing Johnson, he grunted in pain every time Ronald went to the body with his shotgun hook. Before round seven began, the ref told Buck that he was going to stop the fight if something wasn't done to stop the bleeding over Ronald's eye. Roland assured the ref that he'd stop the bleeding, and he did.

Johnson floored Ronald with a big left hand late in the eighth round. However, Ronald was up before the five count and back at it. The ninth round belonged to Ronald, thanks to his crushing body attack. The two fighters let it all hang out, going toe-to-toe. With a left to the body and head of Johnson, Ronald sensed something. Stepping back as if he was running, Ronald danced a little bit. Just as he thought, Johnson rushed him. Ronald weaved two blows that went wide and then blasted Johnson with a crushing over-hand right followed by a left hook that he threw his whole body into. The hook knocked Johnson to the canvas, again. As the ref began counting, Ronald headed to his corner, bleeding, with his hands raised in triumph; he knew the fight was over when the hook landed and knocked Johnson's chin past his shoulder, knocking his mouthpiece out.

After Johnson had been counted out and the ring began to fill with people, Johnson was still out cold. The doc was working on him. Ronald was 1-0 in his professional career. He felt his own potential, he was now a pro fighter. A promising one at that.

Back in the locker room, Wilfred sat with Ronald, Buck, and Roland. He looked at Ronald, and said, "You gave the people what they came to see. I knew you had it in you."

Ronald smiled. He was feeling real good about the fight. "I got the right people in my corner." Ronald looked at Buck and Roland. They seemed to be real pleased about the fight.

"Things are going to start looking up, kid," Wilfred said. He'd known since the first time he'd seen Ronald spar down Youth Center I that the young man had what it took to be a pro boxer. "I saw the signs of greatness in you out there tonight. When will you be ready to fight again?"

"I can do this everyday," Ronald said. That got a laugh out of everybody. "Line 'em up, whoever."

"I know we didn't get you much for the fight..." Wilfred began.

"It's two thousand dollars of legal money, it's a start. I'm grateful," Ronald said, rubbing the stitches over his eye.

"You got a lot of attention tonight, people are talking. That'll make it easy for me to get you a better fight, for more money. Give me to July. I give you my word, I'll have a better fight for you." Wilfred pulled one thousand dollars out of his pocket. "Here, this is for you ... a little something extra."

"Thanks, man." Ronald nodded.

Later on in his hotel room, Ronald laid in the bed thinking about the last five years of his life. He thought about Synthia and his son. They made all that he was trying to do worth it. He thought about being an ex-con. He'd been through a lot, but he was blessed to be able to change it all with his hands. He thought about Wilfred's other fighter, James Holmes, a boxer that he'd sparred down the Center. Holmes was about to fight for a title. Ronald knew that could be him if he stayed focused.

Washington, D.C., Wednesday, May 25, 1978

On his day off, Ronald and Diane cruised down 14th Street,

Northwest in his Chevy Nova. Ronald had just taken her grocery shopping, and was taking her home to put the food up and then to get her hair done.

As they crossed U Street, Diane looked at Ronald, and said, "Don't you need a manager or somethin' now that you done went pro?"

Ronald laughed. "Why you ask me somethin' like that out the blue?"

"I was just thinkin'. I heard that pro fighters need a manager and stuff like that."

"Wilfred gon' work all that out for me. Right now I'm focused on fightin' and stayin' in shape."

"Don't get me wrong, Ronald, I know that Wilfred has done a lot for you, but you can't trust nobody one hundred percent, just check on it. Ask Buck about it." Diane rolled her window down and let the warm May air in. "I was always taught that nothin' in the world is free, you gotta always be on top of things."

"You right." Ronald nodded with a smile. "What made you think about that?"

"Just thinkin' about your best interest, you know?"

"Yeah, I dig it. I'ma get on top of it."

Ronald hung out with Diane until four P.M. and then dropped her off at home. From there, he went to pick Synthia and Lil' Ronald up from Synthia's mother's house.

After picking up his family, Ronald let Lil' Ronald sit on his lap and hold the wheel as they headed home.

"Daddy, make us go fast!" Lil Ronald said all smiles, holding the wheel with both hands as if he was really driving the car.

Ronald laughed and sped up a little bit. "You need a race car, little man."

"You gon' get pulled over, boy, slow down," Synthia said as they cruised down Southern Avenue, Southeast, headed for their Condon Terrace apartment.

"I got this, baby." Ronald rubbed Synthia's head. "You wanna eat out?"

"Yeah, we can do that." Synthia turned the radio to WHUR. Earth, Wind & Fire's *Reasons* was on. "I forgot to tell you that Cristal called me today, she said that you can come get Chris tonight if you gon' take him to see T-Bone."

"Okay, I'll call her when we get in the house."

Ronald took the family to Gino's and got them chicken dinners. After eating, they headed home.

Youth Center I, Thursday, May 26, 1978

The visiting hall was packed, Ronald had brought his and T-Bone's son down the Center to see T-Bone. The two boys loved being together, they were like brothers. Before getting on the highway, Ronald had stopped and bought the boys some small boxing gloves, The boys had them on in the visiting hall and were putting on a show for T-Bone. Had him dying laughing. Ronald had to get a picture of that.

After the boys calmed down and went to play with a few other kids in the visiting hall, T-Bone said, "You know your man Harrison-EL went to the hole."

"Oh yeah, what happened?" Ronald asked.

T-Bone told Ronald that a dude had robbed one of the Moors for the treasury of the Moorish Science Temple of America. The Moors were one of the strongest religious groups in the prison system. Harrison-EL and a few other Moors stormed the chow hall and stabbed seven dudes that had something to do with the robbery. They were all locked down.

"I guess they gon' send Harrison-EL to the Wall this time around, huh?" Ronald asked, watching Lil' Ronald chase a little girl around the visiting hall.

"Yeah, I think he goin' to the Wall this time around. They punished shit."

"He'll be alright."

"You know that," T-Bone said before changing the subject. "So, when you fight again?"

"I ain't sure, it should be some time in July. I'm just stayin' in shape right now." Ronald saw Mrs. Jones come in the visiting hall looking good and phat to death. She came over and spoke to him for a second.

"You bein' good out there?" Mrs. Jones asked with a smile.

"You know me. I'm keepin' my nose clean." Ronald smiled.

"I read about you in the *Post*. I'm proud of you, keep doing right, it'll pay off."

"I will."

"Take care of yourself out there, and don't come back."

"Don't worry about that. I don't plan on bein' back in here," Ronald said.

"I hear that." Mrs. Jones stepped off.

Ronald and T-Bone took quick glances at her ass. They had to.

"Yeah, she still dig you." T-Bone smiled. "I think you been up in that and ain't tell me about it."

Ronald laughed. "Nah, man, it ain't nothin' like that. Me and Mrs. Jones just cool. That's all."

"Yeah, whatever, tell me anything. But anyway, you gotta send me some flicks from Vegas," T-Bone said.

Ronald had free tickets to the James Holmes vs. Kevin Norton fight in Las Vegas. It was a title fight. Ronald was taking Synthia and his son. Roland and Buck also had free tickets; Wilfred Walker made sure of it.

"You know I'ma send you pictures," Ronald said.

"Let me ask you somethin'." T-Bone rubbed his chin. "This chump that Cristal mess wit' ... he from Uptown, right? You hip to him?"

"I don't really know him like that, his name ringin' in the streets. He on stick-up time. When I go over to pick up Chris he don't really be around though. What's up?"

"The nigga be actin' funny when I call, little shit like that. You know? I don't want the nigga around my son."

122

"Yeah, I see where you comin' from on that. But, Cristal ain't crazy. She don't be havin' the nigga around Chris like that. Like I said, I don't even be seein' the nigga like that," Ronald said.

"Keep an eye on the situation for me," T-Bone said.

"You don't even have to ask me no shit like that, comrade." Ronald gave T-Bone five.

Ronald left the Center and headed back to D.C. Before taking Chris home, he stopped to get the boys some ice cream. Pulling up in front of Cristal's Maryland Avenue apartment in Northeast, Ronald parked and got out with the boys. It was a cool evening. A few honeys were hanging out on the steps. They were checking Ronald out, one even spoke. Ronald spoke, but kept stepping. He and the boys went inside the building and headed up the steps to Cristal's apartment. Ronald knocked on the door.

Cristal opened the door in a white T-Shirt and a pair of tight blue jeans. She always looked good. "How you doin' Ronald? Come in."

"I'm okay." Ronald stepped inside. The small apartment was nice and clean. Looked real good. Chris and Lil' Ronald ran to Chris' room.

"Was Chris good?" Cristal asked as she sat on the sofa.

"Yeah, shorty don't give me no trouble. That's my little man," Ronald said.

"I see you bought the boys some boxin' gloves. You tryin' to turn them into boxers?" She laughed.

Ronald shrugged. "Might be somethin' in it for them, you know?"

"I hear that."

Ronald pulled one thousand dollars out of his pocket and handed it to Cristal. "T told me to give that to you for Chris. He said he'll send some more next week."

"Thank you." Cristal took the money. No matter what she felt about T-Bone, she had to admit that he took damn good care of his son. From prison at that.

Ronald always noticed a glow in her eyes when he spoke of T-Bone. "You know he still love you, right?"

Cristal looked at the floor and said nothing for a second. "He shoulda thought about that before he got that funny lookin' little bitch pregnant."

"You can't hold that against him forever. Everybody makes mistakes, Cristal."

"Don't start, Ronald. You always try to justify what Ty did. He was wrong and you know he was wrong."

"I ain't tryin' to justify nothin', Cristal. T know he was wrong, he never tried to act like he wasn't. At the same time, you two got history together. Can't nothin' change that. No matter how mad you want to be at him, you still love him, too. You can't hide that." Ronald paused for a second. He could tell that his words were getting to Cristal. "I'm not goin' to get all in your business, I'ma leave it alone. But, I will say that T loves you, and that's sayin' a lot for him. He don't open up his heart for nobody."

Cristal had no response. She knew Ronald spoke the truth.

However, her pain was deep.

Las Vegas, NV, Wednesday, June 9, 1978

Caesars Palace was packed with people from all over the world. James Holmes and Kevin Norton were in the ring mixing it up. The crowd was already into the fight. Holmes was showing the world why he deserved to be a champion. On the other hand, Norton wasn't buying into that idea. In his mind, he was the better of the two fighters. Ronald, Synthia, Lil Ronald, Roland, and Buck all sat on the tenth row.

"Which one is the champ?" Synthia leaned over and spoke into Ronald's ear.

"The WBC recognizes Norton as the champ since Spinks ain't want to fight him. Spinks wanted to see Ali first, for their rematch," Ronald explained. Synthia was very interested in boxing now that

Ronald was pro.

"Who you think gon' win?" she asked.

"Holmes gon' pull it off. At least I think so, anyway." Ronald laughed. If Holmes was to win it would put Wilfred Walker in a good position with the WBC; that would help Ronald's career in untold ways.

As the fight moved forward, Holmes began to take control, clearly. His long left jab began to open up opportunities that allowed him to land his big blows. Ronald watched carefully, taking mental notes. He remembered sparring Holmes down the Center the day he first met Wilfred.

The fight was worth the money, but there was no knockout. Holmes won a split decision after fifteen rounds of slugging. He was now the WBC heavyweight champion.

Shortly after the fight, Ronald and Wilfred were heading down to the private ballroom to celebrate with the Holmes camp.

"Things are going to start looking up," Wilfred said. "I can get you some nice fights now that James has the title."

Ronald smiled. "Sounds good to me."

"With Buck as your manager and trainer, I'm sure you'll be ready for whatever fight we may be able to get."

"Don't worry about that. You get the fight and you can bet I'ma be ready. This is what I train for. It's my meal ticket."

Wilfred smiled and patted Ronald on the back. "You have my word, you'll be on the next undercard for the WBC championship fight."

"My man." Ronald shook Wilfred's hand.

"Don't mention it, kid." Wilfred pulled a Cuban cigar from his blazer pocket and handed it to Ronald. "Don't smoke it."

Ronald laughed. "Why you give it to me then?"

"Because it's classy, we're celebrating, remember?" Wilfred smiled as they walked into the ballroom. "This is only the beginning, kid."

Chapter 10

Maximum Security, Monday, June 19, 1979

In his small one-man cell on the bottom right tier of 4 Block, Frank was down on the floor doing push-ups. He was covered with sweat after doing three hundred and fifty reps in sets of fifties. Erank was on work out time hard now; he wanted to put on a few pounds. Being behind the Wall had such an effect on men.

Seven months ago on the Hill, shit hit the fan when one of Frank's runners was robbed for a package of dope. The runner was also stabbed in the neck in the process. Frank took the robbery as direct disrespect; everybody knew the dope was his. After a little checking around, Frank found out that G-Train was the one that robbed the runner. That was the last straw. Frank got his knife and went looking for G-Train. He caught G-Train and Tina Turner coming out of 11 Dorm. With no questions asked, Frank pulled his knife and went right at G-Train, stabbing him in the neck with the first swing. Blood gushed from the wound as G-Train stumbled, trying to pull his knife. "Bitch ass nigga!" G-Train spit, holding his neck as he got his knife out.

"Nigga, I'ma kill your muhfuckin' ass." Frank rushed G-Train, stabbing him in the chest.

Tina Turner took off running.

Other convicts saw the knife fight and got the fuck out the way.

Frank was all over G-Train. The neck shot that G-Train suffered began to slow him down. Frank slammed G-Train to the ground as they stabbed each other. Getting on top of G-Train, Frank repeatedly plunged his knife into G-Train's chest with an underhanded grip.

A van with four C.O.s inside pulled up, the C.O.s jumped out and rushed to contain the situation. By the time the C.O.s pulled Frank and G-Train apart, they were both covered with blood like something out of a horror flick. G-Train passed out before they got him to the hospital. He'd lost too much blood. Frank was hit pretty bad also, he took a few bad shots to the side, one of which punctured his lung. When it was all said and done, Frank was patched up and sent to the Wall after two days in a local hospital. G-Train had to undergo a painful surgery that left a zipper-like scar from his navel up his abdomen to his chest. He also had three bullet-sized wounds on his neck. G-Train was also sent to the Wall where he was placed on involuntary protective custody.

The cell doors popped open and Frank stepped out on the tier looking up and down, checking things out. Convicts came out their cells moving up and down the tier. Frank stepped back inside his cell, threw on a T-shirt, and slid his knife between his waistband. He never left his cell without his knife.

"What's up, youngster?"

Frank saw old man Stony standing in front of his cell. "What's up, Stony?"

Stony was an old timer that'd done time with Frank's father down Lorton and in the feds.

"You got a cigarette, Frank?" Stony asked.

Frank pulled a fresh pack out of his locker and gave it to Stony. "Here you go. You okay?" Frank asked, he always made sure Stony was okay. Stony didn't have anybody on the streets that looked out for him. He lived off the land in so many words.

"I'm okay now, Frank, thanks, man." Stony popped the pack and got a smoke out. "You got a light?"

"Yeah." Frank tossed Stony a lighter. "You can keep that."

"Thanks, man. You just like your old man, always lookin' out for a brutha that's down on his luck." Stony lit the cigarette and took a deep pull.

Frank didn't really know his father like that. He was always interested when Stony told him stories about his pops. The only memories Frank had of his father were of a man that had spent most of his life in prison and who was now a dope fiend on the streets.

"Me and ole Fred go way back," Stony said. "We were two of the few D.C. dudes that did time in Alcatraz." Stony had a flashback of the dark months he and Fred had done in D Block on the Rock.

"I remember when we got sent to D Block." He sighed, shaking his head as he blew smoke in the air. "That was the disciplinary block. The hole. We did time in total darkness. That was hard time, real hard time. Them pigs that ran the joint used to support the crackers against us in anyway they could. I'm tellin' you, I saw it wit' my own eyes. We had to watch the pigs and the crackers. One time, I saw one of them pigs give a cracker a knife to hit me. Your father saw the move and knocked the pig out cold while I fought the cracker off. I got hit real bad, almost died. I got hit twenty some times." Stony shook his head thinking about those times. "The pigs almost killed Fred, they beat him like a runaway slave, broke his ribs and his jaw. They wanted us to die, they left us there bleeding for close to thirty minutes before medical came. Shit was crazy, like nothin' I'd ever seen before." Stony went on to tell Frank many admirable things about his father. "I don't care what nobody say about ole Fred, don't you ever believe that your father was anything but a man. A thorough man, a man that stood for somethin' no matter what the odds were, you hear me? He may be on it now, but until a muthafucka go through the shit we went through in the system as black men in America in fifties and sixties, they don't know shit about hard times."

"Yeah, I can dig it." Frank nodded. "How long did y'all do out there?"

"Five fuckin' years, five long ass years. Five years out there was like twenty years down here. That was the real Rock, right out in the San Francisco Bay. All we had was a rec yard and a little library. All that commissary shit was unheard of; if you had some money you could get three packs of cigarettes a week. We had to do the best we could wit' what we had, you know?" Stony killed his cigarette and lit another. "We ain't even know what was goin' on out in the world. We were cut all the way off from the world like we were on another planet. No newspapers, no TVs, no radio, or nothin'. At one time, anyway. They damn near cut us off from our families. We could only send out one letter a week and we could only get three.

"Them cracka muthafuckas would send your peoples shit back. All that writing them little hookers, that was out." Stony was on a roll. "If it wasn't family, you couldn't write 'em. On top of that, you could only write about family matters. Dig that. Go through five years of that shit and you might need a fix your damn self." Stony shook his head in disgust. He'd been in prison twenty three years and had just turned forty five. To add to that, he had seventeen more to do. "I was just thinkin' about somethin' George Jackson said, he said that black men born in the U.S. that are fortunate enough to live past the age of eighteen are conditioned to accept the inevitability of prison. George said that prison looms as the next phase in a sequence of humiliations." Stony blew smoke in the air. "Tell me that ain't somethin' to think about. Look at how your father did time, now you doin' time. Tell me it ain't a plan of the highest order."

Washington, D.C., Wednesday, August 9, 1979

Tate's gym was alive with action. Sparring, working out, boxers hitting the speed bags and heavy bags, some jumping rope or training with the mits. Earth, Wind & Fire was coming out of the big speakers Ronald had set up in the back by the heavy bags. Lil' Ronald and Chris were running around without a care in the world; Ronald kept them at the gym with him. Ronald was in the ring sparring with Roland. Roland was a good sparring partner, his fight game was strong and it kept Ronald thinking on his feet.

Popping his jab at Ronald's head as he stepped to the left to see how Ronald would react, Roland said, "You gotta always control the fight, Ronnie."

Ronald went under Roland's jab and went to his body.

"That's right." Roland said. "Work the body."

Buck came out of his office and watched Ronald and Roland spar for a second. He nodded his approval. *Roland knows what he's doing*, Buck thought. "Ronald!" Buck called out.

Ronald stopped sparring and walked to the ropes. "What's up, big man?"

"Come see me when you get a chance," Buck said as Lil' Ronald and Chris ran by.

"I'll be right in," Ronald said. He then looked at Roland. "Good work out. Let me go see what Buck talkin' 'bout."

"Cool." Roland began climbing out of the ring.

Ronald walked into Buck's office and shut the door behind him. The office was so much cooler than the rest of the gym. "What's up, Buck?" Ronald took a seat in an old beat up leather chair across from Buck's desk. Buck was now his manager and trainer, so Ronald was all ears.

"I just got off the phone with Wilfred," Buck said, smoking a pipe, letting it hang from his lips as he spoke. "He said we need to come up there and sign the paper work for the fight."

"When?" Ronald smiled.

"Friday. Before eight. It's gonna be a press conference for Holmes, so he wants us to be there for that, too. Give us a little limelight."

"Sounds good to me." Ronald winked.

Ronald was on the come up, his name was kicking in all kinds of boxing circles. In the streets of D.C. he was becoming a home town celebrity. At 7-0, all by knockout, Ronald stayed in the sports section of *The Washington Post*. Three of his fights were on TV. His biggest fight was one in which he knocked his man out in the second round; the fight was fought in Las Vegas on the undercard of the James Holmes vs. Fernando Evangelista WBC title bout where Holmes knocked Evangelista out in the seventh round. That fight earned Ronald his biggest pay date, ten thousand dollars. Now, he was on his way to Las Vegas again, thanks to Wilfred Walker and James Holmes. That time around, Ronald would walk away with fifteen thousand dollars.

"You doing real good, kid," Buck said. "All you gotta do is keep your nose clean and stay focused."

"You know I'ma do that, Buck."

"Yeah, I know, but reminding you ain't gon' hurt none, either."

Later on, Ronald laid in the bed with Synthia watching TV. She laid her head on his chest as he rubbed his hand through her hair. He was telling her about the press conference with Wilfred and James Holmes. He was excited about it, like a little kid before Christmas.

"I'm proud of you, you know that?" Synthia said, looking into his eyes as she rubbed his chest.

Ronald smiled. "Is that right?"

"Yeah, I am. You're a real man. You came home and put your mind to what you wanted to do and did it."

"That's what it's all about, ain't it? Gettin' the job done."

"Yeah, but a whole lotta brothers don't do that, baby."

"I ain't a whole lotta brothers, though."

"You got that right." Synthia kissed him and got on top of him. "That's why I love you so much and want you all to myself."

Feeling her wetness rubbing against his manhood, Ronald began growing hard. He rubbed his hands down her smooth back and rested them on her ass. She leaned down and kissed him again, deep inside his mouth. "I love you so much, baby," she said.

"I love you, too." He lifted her up and slid her down onto his manhood, nice and slow, making her moan.

"Ssssss, ooohhhh, daddy." Synthia closed her eyes and let him fill her insides until he had every inch inside her. She put her hands on his chest and began to ride him, going up and down nice and slow. With his hands around her waist he helped her. "Ahhhh, daddy. I love you so much. I love you so much. I'll do anything for you, daddy ... mmmmmmmmm ... anything."

Ronald felt her walls squeezing him as she went up and down, getting wetter with every stroke. "Say my name."

"Ronnie, Ronnie, Ronnie, Ronnie ... Ronnie ... Ronnie, oh yeah, Ronnie. You so deep inside me. Don't stop, daddy, don't stop." Synthia began to bounce up and down on him as she grew closer and closer to her climax. "I'm 'bout to cum, daddy." She bit down on her bottom lip. "Mmmmmmmmm, mh, mh, mh, mh, mh, mh." She began to slam the pussy down on him.

"Damn, baby. Ah, ah, ah, ahhhh." Ronald felt her gush and cream all over his dick as he pushed up inside her deeper and faster. "I love you, baby."

"Say it again."

"I love you, baby."

"Oh yeah, I'm cummin', I'm cummin', daddy ..."

Youth Center I, Saturday, August 12, 1979

Under the baking sun drinking an ice tea dressed in a white

Nike short set, Ronald stood in line with Lil' Ronald and Chris at the pony ride. They'd came down for the fair. Like always, the fair had the compound swarming with people. Marvin Gaye came through that go round. The go-go band, E.U., had the party in full swing. While Ronald stood in line with the boys, honeys were trying to holla at him left and right. With his gold chain, gold watch, and diamond pinky ring, Ronald had that getting money look. He played it smooth, but he had no time for the honeys. He had all he needed at home. A few convicts that he was cool with showed him plenty of love; Ronald hit some of them off with a few dollars. Always playing fair. Always down with the struggle. It wasn't that long ago when he was doing time. He could never forget the name of the game. Everyone was proud of him for going home and doing something with his talent. Ronald was proud himself, he felt damn good about his accomplishments. Mrs. Jones made sure she gave Ronald a hug and told him how proud she was of him.

After the pony ride, Ronald and the boys went to catch up with T-Bone, who'd stepped off to get his dope pack.

"Daddy!" Lil' Ronald said, eating a big piece of watermelon. "Let's play football!" He'd seen two other little boys throwing a football.

"Yeah, let's play football." Chris was always excited about football.

"Cool, come on." Ronald said. He got the little boys together and made teams of two, but as soon as he did it a few other little boys came out of nowhere and wanted to play. He had two teams of five now.

"Hold up, man." T-Bone stepped on the scene. "I'm tryin' to play. I"ma quarterback for them." He pointed at the team that was playing defense.

"You gon' lose!" Lil' Ronald shouted with a smile on his face. He and Chris were on the team that was playing offense.

"No, he not!" Chris took up for his father. "I'm goin' on his team!"

"Nah, lil man." T-Bone stopped his son. "It's just fun, don't cross your man like that. You always stand wit' your man to the end. Lil' Ronald's your partner, never go against him."

"Okay, daddy." Chris fell in line. He didn't really understand the lesson, but went with whatever his father told him. His father was his hero.

"Let's play ball," Ronald said.

Like two kids, Ronald and T-Bone played football with the boys. They even drew a little crowd. When the game was over, the score was 28-28.

Walking the compound with their sons by their sides, Ronald and T-Bone discussed a number of things. T-Bone was done with his Youth Act and was waiting to be sent over Big Lorton to finish his adult sentence. He was ready for Big Lorton. As far as he was concerned, there was more money to be made on the Hill. His little arrangement with Mrs. Mitchell had come to an end. Her husband discovered her heroin addiction and had her committed to a mental hospital. T-Bone would have to work on another broad once he got on the Hill. It wasn't like it would be hard to do. Not for him, anyway.

Changing the subject, Ronald said, "I opened up them bank accounts for Chris and Lil' Ronald, so we can start savin' some money up for their future, make sure they alright, you know?"

"Yeah, no doubt. That was a good idea you came up wit'.

"I told my mother about it. She said that she gon' start slidin' you some money every week to put in the bank for the boys."

"That's cool, I'll holla at her when I get back home," Ronald said.

Las Vegas, NV, Wednesday, September 28, 1979

Ronald made sure Diane made the trip to Vegas for the fight. She was talking about being scared to fly, so he played the big shot role and paid for a private limo to drive her all the way from D.C. to Las Vegas. It meant a lot to him to have his sister at his fights. T-

Bone's mother and a few of her people made the trip to Vegas for the fight as well.

The sounds of Marvin Gaye filled the rented Benz 320 SEL as Ronald and Synthia pulled up in front of the Las Vegas Hilton. They were returning from shopping. Synthia was pleased to be able to spend some time with him. Ronald had been training so hard that he and Synthia hadn't had much time together in the last few weeks. He'd been training like he had a title fight coming up. Every fight was a title fight for him. That was his mind set and what kept him focused. Ronald was fighting a dude by the name of Thomas Booker. Booker was ranked number six by the WBA and number four by the WBC. Booker was knocking everything out that got in the ring with him; he was chasing a title shot like a starving lion.

Ronald and Synthia got out of the car and let the valet park it. They entered the hotel like stars, looking like a million bucks. After taking the shopping bags to their suite, Ronald told Synthia he'd be back, he had to go see Diane for a second.

Down the hall, Ronald knocked on Diane's door. She opened it in a thick white robe with her hair wrapped in a towel. "What's goin' on, baby?" Diane smiled.

"Just checking on you." Ronald stepped inside. "What you up to?"

"Just got out the shower. I'm about to get dressed for the fight," Diane said as she shut the door.

"I got a gift for you."

"What is it?" She smiled.

"Close your eyes."

Diane closed her eyes, and felt Ronald grab her arm and lead her toward the bedroom. "Don't open your eyes until I say so," he said. She felt him placing something around her neck. It had a nice weight to it. "Okay, you can open your eyes now."

Diane opened her eyes and found herself standing in front of the mirror. When she saw what Ronald had placed around her neck, she gasped and covered her mouth in amazement. It was a diamond necklace. Diamonds were all over it, sitting in white gold. It was beautiful. "Oh my God, Ronnie. I love it." Diane turned around and hugged her baby brother so tight.

"I'm glad you like it, now don't kill me. I gotta fight tonight, okay?" Ronald laughed. "Let me go. I need to take care of a few things before it gets late."

"I love you, boy." Diane kissed his forehead. "You better get a knockout tonight."

Ronald kissed his left fist, and said, "I'ma do my best, you know that, baby girl."

Later on in his locker room flanked by Buck and Roland, Ronald was focused. He had a job to do.

"You ready, baby boy?" Roland asked, wrapping Ronald's hands.

"Like never before. Believe that, bro."

"That's right. Just stick to the game plan," Buck said. "I can see that look in your eyes, that hunger. I want you to keep that hunger. The first time you lose that hunger this ain't for you no more. You got that, kid?"

Ronald nodded. "I got it."

"Ah, Buck." Roland said. "Who was the hardest hitter you ever fought?"

"Archie Moore, by far. Joe Louis had a shotgun, but Archie Moore could really ring your bell in any round, even when he was hurt."

Ronald laughed. "You take him serious, huh?"

"Damn right, he got more knockouts than anybody in the history of the game ... he holds the record for knockouts, plus, he's one of the only men to drop Marciano. On top of that, he was never a real heavyweight. He wasn't a giant. When I fought him he was like one hundred and eighty eight or one hundred and eighty nine, somethin' like that," Buck said. He had a lot of respect for Archie Moore. "Anyway, back to you, Ronnie. I want you to go out there and do what you do best. Mix it up and stay aggressive."

An hour later, Ronald and his crew made their way to the ring to the sounds of Marvin Gaye's *Let's Get It On*. Ronald was ready to get it on. His opponent was a big, black, intimidating fighter who had awesome punching power. Thomas Booker was the Sonny Liston type of fighter, a grizzly bear of a man. Booker stood 6' 4", weighing in at two hundred and thirty five pounds. He was twenty nine-years-old, but looked much older due to years in the ring; he'd been a pro fighter for twelve years. By that time, Ronald stood 5' 11" and had put on some extra muscle to get up to two hundred and ten pounds.

After introductions, Ronald stood in his corner in a zone. He'd blocked out the crowd and everything else except for Buck, who was going over the game plan again, stick and move but stay aggressive

"I'm on it," Ronald said through his mouthpiece.

The bell rang and Ronald came out on his toes, bouncing. Booker came out stalking. Ronald started off popping his long left jab back-to-back, and followed it with a quick combination of speed and power. Booker was impressed by the power, but shook off the blows like they were bee stings. He then threw a deadly and powerful left hook. Ronald weaved to his right like a young Ali, dipped, slid back to his left, and fired a right uppercut followed by his crushing left hook, knocking spit out of Booker's mouth. The crowd went off. Buck was screaming for Ronald to stay aggressive and turn it up. Ronald did just that, but found out that Booker hit too hard for a toe-to-toe fight. Booker's body blows came with so much fire behind them that they literally moved Ronald from side-to-side whenever Ronald stood in the same place too long.

For the first five rounds, Ronald showed what speed and power could do and had Booker's nose bleeding. Booker, who could knockout opponents out with either hand showed tremendous punching power, but seemed more focused on knocking Ronald out than boxing or scoring points. In the middle of round six, Booker blasted Ronald with an uppercut that looked like a punch that would end the fight. It rocked Ronald to his core, but Ronald took the blow, tucked his chin, and unloaded his left hook twice from the body to the head of Booker. They mixed it up, trading heavy blows. The crowd was going crazy. Ronald and Booker battled through the next three rounds, packing a year's worth of excitement into nine minutes. In a fearsome tenth round, as both fighters tore into one another, Ronald took the edge. He weaved a wild hook and floored Booker with his left hook, followed by his shotgun uppercut. As Booker struggled to beat the count, Buck was barking instructions at Ronald, telling him to finish Booker as soon as he got up. Seconds later, Booker was back on his feet. His eyes were glassy. That told Ronald that he was hurt. As soon as the ref gave the green light, Ronald began his assault. With all the power he had left, Ronald began head-hunting, banging Booker out with lefts and rights, ups and overs, hooks and hooks. Booker refused to go down, though, out of sheer pride, but he was through. Taking too many head blows, the ref stepped in and stopped the fight, saving Booker. Ronald raised his hands, and bathed in the sweet glory and roar of the crowd. His corner, as well as Synthia and Lil' Ronald, rushed the ring. The press took pictures. Ronald was on top of the world, but he still had his eyes on the prize—the title.

"That was beautiful, kid!" Buck hugged a sweaty Ronald. "That was power and determination!"

"You looked good, baby boy, real good!" Roland hugged Ronald.

Ronald smiled and looked at Synthia, tapping her on the chin with his gloved hand. Diane climbed in the ring and rushed to hug Ronald. He kissed his sister, and said, "Got you that knockout, didn't I?"

Diane laughed. "Yeah, you did that, Ronnie."

The night went on. James Holmes got in the ring and defended his title, defeating Earnie Shavers by TKO in the eleventh round. Ronald took notes, he was stalking Holmes and knew in his heart that he could beat the champ. All Ronald needed was a shot at the title. He was now going to be ranked somewhere in the top ten by the WBC. His shot was coming.

Soon.

Washington, D.C., Monday, October 16, 1979

It was nothing but love for Ronald back home. He felt like the man. The streets were buzzing about his Vegas fight. *The Washington Post* was doing big articles about his rise from an ex-con to being ranked number seven by the WBC. Ronald got a kick out of reading about himself in the newspapers. But, nothing was like fighting in front of the world on the undercard for a title fight. Ronald's next fight was to be in Landover, MD, it was sure to bring the home town crowd. Things were coming together.

Pulling up in front of Cristal's apartment in his black Cadillac, Ronald parked and got out into the cool fall evening air. As always, the block was alive. A group of dudes were right in front of the doorway. They all knew who Ronald was; some spoke. Some gritted on him, hating to see a man doing his thing and on the come up because they weren't doing shit with their life.

Inside the building on the second floor, Ronald knocked on Cristal's door. He had a Ralph Lauren winter coat for Chris. Cristal opened the door and let Ronald in. She was wearing a pair of tight blue jeans, a white T-shirt, and a scarf around her head. With her dark skin, pretty brown eyes, and thick sexy body, she could tempt even the best husband to cheat on his wife. "How you doin'?" Cristal said.

"I'm good," Ronald said.

Chris came running from his bedroom. "Ronald! Ronald! Is that for me?" He smiled.

"Yeah, little man. Try it on. I got you and Lil' Ronald the same coat. Y'all can be like twins." Ronald smiled and rubbed Chris on the top of the head. At the same time, he noticed that something was wrong with Cristal, she had an attitude. "You like it, Chris?"

"Yeah, I like it."

"Go hang your coat up, little man," Ronald said. When Chris left the room, Ronald looked at Cristal, who was sitting on the sofa, and said, "What's wrong wit' you?"

"Nothin'." she said, watching *The Jeffersons* on TV.

"What you mean, nothin'?" Ronald asked.

The front door swung open and slammed into the wall. Jimmy, Cristal's boyfriend, stepped inside and slammed the door behind him, causing a picture of Chris to fall off the wall and crash to the floor. "You called this nigga over here, bitch?!" Jimmy shouted at Cristal.

"I ain't call no muthafuckin' body, nigga!" Cristal stood up.

Chris came running back in the room when he heard the screaming.

"Get the fuck out my house, bitch!" Cristal headed for the kitchen to get a knife.

"Hold up, main man," Ronald said to Jimmy, putting a hand on his chest to stop him from following behind Cristal. "Don't you see her son right here?"

"So what!" Jimmy pulled a .38 revolver from his waistband and put it in Ronald's face. "Don't you ever put you muthafuckin' hands on me, nigga!" Jimmy hissed. He couldn't stand Ronald and hated how he was always showing up bringing Chris stuff. He also thought Ronald was fucking Cristal on the sneak tip.

"Go to your room, lil' man," Ronald said to Chris, trying to remain as calm as a man could with a gun in his face.

"What? You his daddy now?" Jimmy said, looking Ronald up and down with contempt.

"Leave him alone, Jimmy," Cristal pleaded, fearing for Ronald's life.

"Shut up, bitch!" Jimmy said. "I know your whore-ass fuckin' this nigga." Jimmy addressed Cristal, but was looking Ronald in the eyes. "You think you big shit, don't you, Ronald?"

"Calm down, man," Ronald said, trying to reason with Jimmy. Ronald was boiling with anger.

"I'll blow your brains out in this muthafucka!" Jimmy hissed, cocking the hammer of his pistol.

"Stop, Jimmy! Stop, don't!" Cristal screamed with tears in her eyes.

BOOM! The gun went off like a bomb in the small apartment.

Cristal froze in shock, covering her mouth.

Jimmy fell and hit his head against the coffee table, smoking gun still in hand. Ronald's hands were like a flash of light when he threw the two piece that knocked Jimmy out right before the gun went off. Instinctively, Ronald snatched the gun out of Jimmy's hand and looked at Cristal. "What the fuck is goin" on?"

"We had a fight right before you came over. He think we fuckin'" Cristal said, looking down at Jimmy who was sprawled out on the floor, out cold.

"Fuckin'?" Ronald looked confused.

"Yeah, fuckin'. Here, give me the gun. You need to leave before somebody call the police. I'll be okay. I don't want you to get in no trouble." Cristal took the gun.

"I ain't leavin' you and Chris in here. Get Chris, I'm takin' y'all over my house," Ronald said.

"What about him?" Cristal pointed at Jimmy.

"He'll find his way out when he wake up, I just want to get you and Chris out of here right now, okay?" Ronald said.

"Okay." Cristal got Chris and they all left.

Inside Ronald's living room a short while later, Cristal was telling Synthia what had went down. Synthia began to worry about what would come of the situation. She feared that Jimmy would come looking for Ronald, and if he did, she feared what Ronald would do.

"Maybe we should call the police," Synthia said. She couldn't think of anything else.

"Nah, I don't want to bring the police into the situation," Cristal said. She then looked at Ronald, and said, "What do you think?"

Ronald was standing in the middle of the living room with his arms folded, rubbing his chin, in deep thought. "Nah, we ain't callin' no cops."

"What we gon' do then? What if this nigga come lookin' for you, Ronnie?" Synthia asked.

"I'll take care of it." Ronald got on the phone. He was calling The Black Widow.

A knock on the door grabbed everybody's attention. Synthia went to see who it was, fearing that it would be Jimmy. Her heart almost jumped out of her chest when she looked out of the peephole.

"Who is it?" Cristal asked, seeing the look on Synthia"s face.

"It's the police," she whispered.

"The police?" Ronald asked, holding the phone to his ear.

"Yeah."

Ronald got off the phone and went to check out the situation. He opened the door and before he could say anything, five police officers rushed inside and threw him against the wall.

"Which one of you is Cristal Mayo?" an officer asked as the other officers handcuffed Ronald.

"I'm Cristal, what's goin' on?"

"Turn around." The officer grabbed her by the arm. "You're under arrest."

"What the fuck is goin' on?" Ronald said.

"You'll find out at the station," an officer said as Ronald was dragged out of the apartment.

"What the hell is goin' on, you muthafuckas better tell me somethin'!" Synthia yelled, causing Lil' Ronald and Chris to come running out of the back room just in time to see the police taking Ronald and Cristal away.

"Where they takin' my daddy?" Lil' Ronald asked Synthia.

"Mommy! Mommy!" Chris tried to run after his mother, but Synthia grabbed him by the arm.

"You two go back in the room," Synthia ordered. The boys did as they were told.

"What the fuck is goin' on?" Synthia asked the officer again.

"Mr. Mays and Ms. Mayo are under arrest for murder," the officer said.

Chapter 11

D.C. Jail Thursday, October 19, 1979

Would-be champ charged with murder. That was the headline on the front page of *The Washington Post* the day after Ronald and Cristal were arrested for Jimmy's murder. All the news channels covered the story, they even aired footage of Ronald being led into the courtroom for his arraignment.

Jimmy died somewhere between the blows Ronald knocked him out with and the fall to the floor where he hit his head on the coffee table. Residents told police that they'd heard a gunshot inside Cristal's apartment and saw Ronald, Cristal, and Chris leave afterwards. Inside, the police found Jimmy dead.

Word spread quickly of Ronald's arrest. Everybody was crushed. Diane, Roland, Buck, Wilfred, and Synthia rushed to put a defense together for Ronald. The Black Widow was also in Ronald's corner, she put up the money for Ronald's and Cristal's lawyer.

Cristal could have been released from the police station, but she refused to answer any questions without speaking to a lawyer. She knew how the game was played. Anything she said would be used against her.

In a conference room with her lawyer, Cristal sat in her

jail jumpsuit and listened as the Jew lawyer told her where things stood on her charges. She and Ronald were being charged with second degree murder. The police knew a gun was involved in the crime, but didn't know how since it was never recovered.

"I'm on your side, Ms. Mayo," Mr. Felson said. He was an old, white man in a cheap gray suit. "You can talk to me openly. Ms. Mathis has already informed me that you don't trust many people. I understand that ... I assure you that everything you say to me stays with me."

"I know how it goes," Cristal said, sitting in the chair with her arms folded. She was pissed off that she was caught up in a murder case, however, she felt like she was the cause of Ronald being locked up and that had her feeling like shit. Her worries were countless. If she was to go to prison for murder, what would happen to Chris? "Can you get me out?" she asked the lawyer.

Mr. Felson smiled. "That's what I'm good at. I get people out, that's why Ms. Mathis hired me." He flipped through a few papers. "I see that you have a few other charges, so it will take me a few days, but you should be out on bond in a week or two. However, we need to talk about what really happened inside your apartment.

"The guy I was seein' tried to kill Ronald. Ronald defended himself, he defended me and my son, too. He wasn't tryin' to kill Jimmy." Cristal explained the whole situation.

"Your story is the same as what Mr. Mays told his lawyer." Mr. Felson took notes. "It would have been so much better if you two would have left the gun alone and called the police, or uh..."

"People where I live don't call the cops, besides, they never come when you need them. Aside from that, I told you we didn't know Jimmy was dead."

"I understand, I was just thinking like a lawyer. Nevertheless, Mr. Mays has a lot of people supporting him, that'll help out a lot." Mr. Felson closed his folder. "We'll work this out, I'll get on top of bond. We should have you out shortly." He shook Cristal's hand.

Meanwhile, Ronald was laying on the bed in his cell. He couldn't believe that he was back in jail. The cells in the cell block were open and the inmates were out and about, going through the motions. Ronald's mind was still replaying the events that led to his predicament. He had so much on the line. He asked himself if there was anything he could have done to change the outcome of the situation. The answer was no every time. Nevertheless, he was still shit out of luck and back in jail. On top of all the bullshit, Jimmy had a cousin over the jail that was supposed to be "somebody" in the streets. His name was Kevin Holt. Kevin had a number of flunkies that were more than willing to do his bidding. That was the least of Ronald's worries at the time; the only thing he was concerned with at the time was making bond. He was trying to stay on the up-and-up and think about all the people that he had in his corner, but there was no getting around the fact that his situation was a mess.

Ronald had told his lawyer to tell Cristal to use the "real" story about what happened to get out of jail. He didn't want her to feel like she was telling on him to do so. After all, his defense was based on the "real" story since he was standing on the fact that he was defending himself.

"Bro, I gotta take a shit," Bennie said, coming in the cell. He was Ronald's nineteen-year-old cellie.

"Cool." Ronald stepped outside the cell and took a walk down the tier. The new D.C. Jail was nothing like the old one that he'd been in a few years back. The new jail didn't have any dorms, just cell blocks. The sight of so many black men roaming the cell block made Ronald sick to his stomach. He'd sworn to himself that he'd never go back to jail, but there he was, among the masses. Again. He shook his head and sighed, frustrated.

"Mays!" a C.O. yelled from downstairs by the bubble where the C.O.s watched the inmates from behind a protective glass.

"You got a visit."

When Ronald got to the visiting hall, he saw Diane and Synthia sitting on the other side of the glass. They both looked like the world was coming to an end. Ronald tried to smile to ease the tension as he sat down and put the phone to his ear. "How you doin', baby?" he asked Synthia, who was holding the phone on the other side.

"I'm holdin' on, how about you. You keepin' your head up?" Synthia asked.

"You know me, I'm holdin' on, bein' strong, but I'd be lyin' if I said that I wasn't stressin'." Ronald rubbed his chin and nodded at his sister, who was sitting right beside Synthia.

"Baby, don't you worry, we're goin' to get all of this shit cleared up, you hear me?"

"I know, baby, I know."

"We just came from seein' your lawyer, he should have you out on bond in a week or so. Just hold on."

"I will. How are you doin'?"

"I'm stressin', just like you, but like you said, we gotta be strong. We've been through worse, right?"

"That's right, baby." Ronald winked at her. "That's right, baby, be strong and this will pass. How's Lil' Ronald holdin' up?"

"He's crushed, he can't understand why the police took you and Cristal away. I told him that it was a mistake and it'll be cleared up soon. He don't want to hear that, he wants his daddy right now. Chris is the same way. That's all they talk about, all day. They cried all day after the police took y'all away."

Ronald sighed and shook his head. "Make sure you let them know that everything is goin' to be alright, okay?"

"I will."

Synthia told Ronald how Buck and Wilfred were talking to the press about his situation, getting supporters together to stand behind him in case the government tried to play hardball. So far, all the articles in *The Washington Post* painted a picture of Ronald in a good light.

Diane got on the phone. "You keepin' your head up, boy?"

Ronald gave up a short laugh. "You know I am. I still feel like I let everybody down, like I fucked up, you know?"

"Stop talkin' crazy, Ronnie. You ain't do nothin' wrong. That nigga was gon' kill you, maybe Cristal, too. We gon' get all this stuff cleared up and everything's gonna go back to the way you had it. Okay?"

"Okay." Ronald nodded. He wanted to believe Diane.

D.C. Jail, Wednesday, December 2, 1979

"I'm so sorry, Ronald, this is all my fault." Cristal sat on the other side of the glass in the visiting hall. The murder charge against her was dropped. The government only wanted Ronald. The judge didn't care what he was doing with his boxing career and saw Ronald as a violent ex-con that went out on parole and killed a man. He ordered him held without bond.

"Don't blame yourself, Cristal. Jimmy created this whole situation. The only thing you did wrong was start messin' around wit' a bamma like that." Ronald cracked a hard smiled. He was trying to take it easy and let fate play itself out, hoping that it would take a turn in his favor.

"That's not funny, Ronald." Cristal smiled. "Look, I want you to know that I'm here for you, whatever you need me to do just let me know, okay?"

"Cristal, I already know that, but now that you say that, I just want to remind you that you're a huge part of my defense. I'm goin' to need you to help me prove that I was defendin' myself if this thing goes to trial."

"You don't even have to ask me to do that. I'll get on the stand for you and all that, that's not even in the talk."

"You might have to paint a picture of Jimmy as a violent dude, stuff like that."

"I can do that. Whatever you need, Ronald."

"One more thing."

"What's up?"

"I don't really like the idea, but my lawyer said that we might need Chris to come to court and tell a jury what he saw that day, just in case."

"I don't have a problem wit' that."

"I'm glad to hear that, thanks, but I need you to holla at T-Bone and see how he feels about it. I don't want to involve his son in this mess without his say so."

"That's your partner, he won't mind."

"That's not the point, Cristal. It's a respect thing. As a man, it's somethin' *I* gotta do, I gotta run it by him. Okay?"

Cristal nodded in agreement, although she was hesitant at first.

"I need you to handle that for me as soon as possible."

"I'll get on top of it tomorrow," Cristal said.

"Thanks."

After his visit with Cristal, Ronald walked through the long hallway headed back to his block. A C.O. stopped him along the way and asked for an autograph. Ronald smiled and gave it to him. It wasn't the first time that a C.O. had asked for his autograph since he'd been in the jail. Ronald continued down the hallway. As he bent the corner to enter his block, a slim, dark-skinned dude in a jail jumper came out of the cut and swung an ice pick at Ronald's neck. The blow could've killed him if he didn't weave it just in time. "What the fuck!" Ronald took a step backward and threw up his fists. His attacker lunged at him again. Ronald blocked the ice pick with his left forearm and smashed the nigga in the face with a big right hand that sent him to the floor like a ton of bricks. Ronald looked down at his attacker who was out cold, bleeding from the mouth. "Bitch ass nigga!" Ronald kicked the nigga in the face. Everything happened so fast, it was over in seconds. Ronald looked at his forearm and saw the ice pick plunged deep into his muscle. "Damn." He tried to pull it out, but it was too deep and the pain got worse as he tried to remove it. Looking around, he saw two C.O.s running his way. They'd seen the whole thing.

"Get against the wall, Mays," one of the C.O.s said. "Are you okay?"

"What it look like?" Ronald said as he got against the wall.

"This guy's out cold," the other C.O. said.

"Let's get them to the infirmary," said the C.O. that was patting Ronald down.

Roanld was patched up in the infirmary and then questioned. He didn't want to press any charges and he didn't fear for his life, so there was nothing much to talk about. The Lieutenant that was working knew Ronald from Youth Center I and let him go back to his block after Ronald signed some papers stating that he didn't fear for his life. It was no secret that Ronald could take care of himself. His attacker was sent to the hole. Come to find out, his attacker was one of Kevin Holt's flunkies. First blood had been drawn.

Washington, D.C., Saturday, January 23, 1980

Riding down Alabama Avenue, Southeast in a dark-blue '76 Pontiac Catalina, the driver took in the sights of the snow-covered streets as darkness fell. His mind was on business. It was a new year, a new decade, and it was time to get money. All the pieces were in place, all he had to do was put his plan into effect. As he headed toward Northeast, the driver of the Catalina smoked a Newport and listened to Marvin Gaye on the radio. Minutes later, he pulled up in front of Carole's Lounge on 8th and H Street where he parked and went inside.

Inside the lounge, cigarette smoke and the sounds of James Brown filled the air. The driver headed to the bar, keeping an eye on the older dudes that were sitting around smoking and drinking at the tables in the back. They had the look of black gangsters from the sixties and seventies with their suits, cigars, and gangster hats.

"I'm here to see Carole," the driver said to the bartender.

The bartender looked the young man up and down, wondering what he wanted with The Black Widow. "What's your name, youngster?"

"Frank."

"I'll be right back." The bartender went into the back and returned shortly. "She waitin' for you, Frank. Go on back."

Frank stepped into Carole's office and found her sitting on the black leather sofa talking on the telephone. She put up a finger to tell Frank to hold on, and then nodded for the chair next to her for him to have a seat. A few moments later, she hung up the phone, and said, "Sorry about that, that was Ty. He told me to tell you to keep your eyes open out here and take it slow."

Frank smiled his pretty boy smile, and said, "I'ma do that."

"So, how you doin', baby?" Carole lit a Newport and crossed her legs. She wore a black skirt that stopped at the knees, an expensive black sweater of some kind, and a pair of black heels. Her silky hair was pulled back into a tight ponytail. "You look good, I see your takin' care of yourself."

"Just tryin' to get used to bein' out here," Frank said. He'd only been home for two weeks and was still in a halfway house. Nevertheless, it was time to put things in motion.

"So, for starters, you need a job, right?" Carole blew smoke into the air.

"Yeah."

"I have a few apartments Uptown, we'll make you the resident manager. How's that sound?"

"It'll sound great on paper and get me out of the halfway house."

"That's simple." Carole plucked ashes into the tray. "Now, as far as business, I normally don't deal wit' youngsters, but you seem to be different. I hear nothin' but thorough things about you from down Lorton." She got up and walked over to the huge wooden desk in the corner and sat behind it. "You sure you ready for this? This ain't prison, this is the real world. It's a dog eat dog world out here."

"Ms. Mathis..."

"Please, call me Carole. Ms. Mathis makes me feel old."

Frank smiled. "Carole, I'm ready as I'll ever be. I already got my game plan laid out. Trust me."

Carole leaned forward and put her elbows on the desk,

looking Frank in the eyes. He still looked to be about eighteen or nineteen. "I think you should take a few weeks to really get a feel of the streets before you jump right into things."

"I thought about that, but I got a little cousin that already has some things goin' on. I can step right in and take things to another level."

"Okay, you know what's best for you. I'll have what you need later on tonight. You'll be able to go pick up around ten. And, Frank ... keep this in mind, *I* run a tight ship. I'm old school. A word of wisdom from me to you, stay on top of your game."

"Say no more." Frank shook The Black Widow's hand and left.

Pulling up in a dark parking lot behind his mother's Valley Green apartment, Frank parked and got out.

"Frank!" a voiced called out.

When Frank turned around, he saw a dope fiend leaning against a car on the other side of the parking lot under the street light.

"Pops?"

"Yeah, it's me."

D.C. Jail Wednesday, January 27, 1980

"These people playin' hardball wit' me, Frank," Ronald said, sitting behind the glass in the visiting hall. "They talkin' 'bout ten or fifteen years. I'ma have to fight it in trial."

"You know them crackers hate to see the black man doin' somethin' wit' himself," Frank said, shaking his head.

"My lawyer talkin' real good, though. I should walk on this shit. They know damn well it was self-defense."

"Wit' Cristal and little Chris on your side, you should be able to beat the shit."

"That's what I'm bankin' on." Ronald rubbed his chin and sighed. "Enough about me, what's up wit' you out there? You takin' it slow?"

"As slow as I can. I'm settin' up shop. I'm 'bout to get me

some serious money out here. My cousin, Baby Face, got a lil' crew around the Valley, they makin' a little change movin' boy. I"ma take that to another level without even getting my hands dirty. The way I see it, I won't even have to touch the shit."

"Be careful out there, man," Ronald said. "You been away for a while. The streets change."

"I can dig it, man. But I'm on top of it." Frank watched a bad ass honey walk by. He took a quick look and turned back to Ronald. "I ain't tell you I been talkin' to my pops, did I?"

"Nah, I thought you ain't deal wit' him."

"I changed my mind about the way I look at that situation. After doin' time, I understand him and what he been through." Frank told Ronald about all the conversations he'd had with Stony and other older convicts behind the Wall that knew his father.

"That's alright, man. I respect that. If I was in your shoes, I'd do the same thing. We only get one father. I heard a lot of things about your pops, they say he was a legend back in the days."

"One of the best bank robbers to ever come outta the Valley," Frank said with pride. "I'm tryin' to clean him up."

"That's right."

"I'm goin' down Lorton tomorrow, I gotta go holla at Cadillac. I'ma take Cristal down there wit' me. She wanna see T-Bone."

Ronald smiled. He knew what he was doing when he asked her to go see T-Bone. They still loved each other, that never changed. One thing was for certain, if T-Bone couldn't do anything right, he damn sure knew how to sweet talk a woman. "T-Bone ain't gon' let her get away from him again."

Frank laughed. "Man, that nigga had me takin' flowers and shit over there the other day."

Frank and Ronald got a laugh off of that one.

"Tough ass nigga!" Ronald joked.

Frank smiled. "Tell me about it."

After his visit with Frank, Ronald headed back to the cell

block. When he walked in his cell, he saw Bennie sitting on the top bunk, nodding. "Damn, you fuck wit' boy?" Ronald asked. He'd only seen Bennie smoke weed. Heroin was a different thing. After Blue's murder, Ronald swore he would never fuck around with boy again.

"Nah, it just ain't no weed in the block," Bennie said, sounding sleepy.

"So, you just wanna get high so bad you gon' fuck around wit' anything?"

Bennie shrugged.

"Check this out. I like you, you a real thorough young dude from what I see, and I ain't judgin' you. I used to blow myself. I don't knock what another man do to get by, but jail ain't the place to be pickin' up no new habits. I started blowin' down Oak Hill and it took me years to shake it. You don't want that monkey on your back. You facin' a lotta time. You need to be focused on your case." Bennie had a first degree felony murder beef.

"I dig what you sayin', but I was stressin'."

"I'm tellin' you what I know, you don't wanna start playin' around wit' that boy, it ain't no joke." Ronald told Bennie about how Blue was murdered.

"I dig what you sayin'," Bennie said.

D.C. Jail, Monday, March 6, 1980

Ronald's lawyer was doing all he could to clear Ronald's name and get him out of the jam he was in. Back and forth, his lawyer had meetings with the prosecutor, but for some reason the prosecutor had it out for Ronald because of his past, as if he hadn't changed his life. The best that the prosecutor would offer was ten to thirty years for manslaughter. Ronald would have to do at least five years on a sentence like that, if he took the deal. Ronald didn't like the deal at all, he was ready to go to trial.

"Whatever you decide to do, you know I'm goin' to stand by you as long as I live," Synthia said, sitting on the other side of the glass with the phone to her ear. She was looking good, too, fresh hairdo and all. "I know how serious this situation is, you know what's best. I'd walk to the ends of the earth wit' you. You know that, baby."

Ronald smiled. "That's why I love you so much." He knew he had a strong black sister, as loyal as they get. "I'm not sure what I want to do right now. I need some time to think this over. I don't want to play games wit' them peoples, they already want to wash me up. I"ma see if I can get that ten to thirty down some more." Ronald sighed and shook his head. He hated the thought of having to go back down Lorton for even a weekend.

Changing the subject, Ronald said, "How's Buck doin'?"

Buck had been sick over the past few weeks, in and out of the hospital.

"He's been holdin' on, but he's gettin" old, Ronnie. Roland looks after him, though, takes good care of him and runs the gym for him while he gets himself better."

"Tell him I asked about him, tell him I'll be out of this mess soon," Ronald said.

"I will."

"You seen Frank?"

Synthia smiled and shook her head. "I don't know what Frank call himself doin' but he better slow down, he movin' too fast. Everybody talkin' about him. He ridin' around in this big ole Cadillac, a 1980, too. Every time he come over he got on all that designer stuff, diamonds, and gold. You'd think he been out there high rollin' for years. I can't believe he only been home two months and some change."

Ronald shook his head. He was worried about Frank, but Frank was a grown man, he was going to do what he wanted to do. It was his time to shine. "Frank gon' milk the streets for all they worth. I just hope he don't come back to jail, or get himself killed out there."

"He gave Cristal that car he was drivin' when he first came home."

"She need it, don't she?" Ronald joked, thinking about how

Cristal and T-Bone were tight again, as they should be.

"Yeah." Synthia laughed. "Cristal be goin' down there to see T-Bone every visitin' day."

"It was only a matter of time."

"Oh yeah, T-Bone gave Cristal two thousand dollars for me, he said it was to help out while you were away."

"I respect that, that's my man."

Washington, D.C., Friday, March 10, 1980

It was dark and windy outside on the tree-lined street. A few people walked up and down the street, but none of them paid attention to the two men in the old Buick. Frank sat behind the wheel and his teenage cousin, Baby Face, sat in the passenger seat. Baby Face was a young gunslinger that was known throughout Southeast to be a mean armed robber that had no picks. He once told another armed robber, "I done robbed half the city wit' no mask, I might've robbed you." Frank was trying to help his cousin get some real money and talk him into leaving stick ups behind. At the same time, he knew Baby Face had no problem pulling the trigger, and that was why Frank had brought him along for the mission.

"Here he come right now." Frank pulled his ski mask over his face and cocked the hammer of the .44 revolver in his hand.

Baby Face cocked the hammer of his .357 magnum and took a look at the nigga they were there to hit. "Let's do it."

Frank and Baby Face slid out of the car without a sound and began to creep across the street in the direction of the halfway house. All of a sudden, their target pulled a gun of his own and fired three shots form his position on the front steps of the halfway house. He was on point. Frank ducked as the shots crashed into a parked car beside him. Frank and Baby Face fired back and gunshots tore through evening air. Their target fired two more shots and ran back into the halfway house. Frank and Baby Face took off after him, running into the halfway house. When they got inside, they saw their target jumping out of a side window. They ran by a screaming woman that worked there and shot at their fleeing target out of the window. It was no use, he was gone. Frank and Baby Face ran back to the Buick and took off flying down the street. They'd missed.

Headed back to Valley Green, Frank looked at Baby Face, and said, "That nigga was ready."

"No bullshit. I thought they check you for weapons when you go inside a halfway house." Baby Face was checking the mirror for the police.

"You know how shit go, a nigga can get around all that shit," Frank said. He knew G-Train would be ready, but he didn't think he would be coming out the halfway house door with a gun on him. He was wrong. G-Train had already paid the man at the door to let him in and out with the gun on him. Sarah had brought him the .38 the first night he got to the halfway house.

Now, two dangerous young killers were in the streets at the same time. The city wasn't big enough for them both. Somebody had to die.

Frank and Baby Face pulled up in a parking lot in Valley Green. Frank's father was outside watching over the dope operation Frank had set up. He put his father in charge because he knew the old timer knew what it took to run it the right way. Frank told his father what had just happened.

"That ain't how you operate, man." Fred shook his head as he and Frank got back in the car to talk while Baby Face got rid of the guns. "When you do shit like that, you gotta make it count, youngster." Fred spit some old school gangster shit at Frank that made him fill as if he'd moved too fast.

"I shoulda ran it by you," Frank said. As soon as he got the phone call that G-Train was in the halfway house, he got Baby Face and they went to handle business without thinking the move all the way through.

"No one seen your faces, right?" Fred asked.

"Nah, we had on masks."

"We need to take care of this situation as quick as possible."

"Yeah, I know," Frank said.

Eyone Williams

Washington, D.C., Sunday, March 12, 1980

Frank got up early and went down Lorton to see T-Bone; he took him twenty grams of dope himself. That was how he was carrying it. He told T-Bone all about the situation with G-Train, even though T-Bone had heard about most of it through the grapevine. The halfway house shooting had been in the paper for the last few days as well as on the news. The police had no leads. They were looking for G-Train to question him about it. G-Train was on the run, he didn't think twice about going back to the halfway house. He knew, without a doubt, that it was Frank that came to kill him. During the visit with T-Bone, T-Bone warned Frank not to take G-Train lightly. Frank assured T-Bone that he was on top of the situation.

Frank left Lorton and went back to D.C., he had to collect some money over Southeast from Baby Face's crew. He still had no leads on G-Train and had even put some money up for information of his whereabouts. No one had seen the nigga.

After collecting the money, Frank went to drop fifty thousand dollars off at one of The Black Widow's spots in Northeast. He had the dope sent to the Valley. Then, Frank went around 8th and H Street to see The Black Widow herself, she wanted to talk to him.

Inside The Black Widow's office, Carole questioned Frank about how he was dealing with the G-Train situation. Word in the streets was that Frank had tried to hit G-Train and missed, and that G-Train had took a bullet to the leg and was laying low until he was in a position to strike back.

"Who told you he got shot?" Frank asked, sitting on the sofa sipping a glass of Remy. He hadn't even heard that G-Train took a bullet to the leg.

"I know things that not everybody else knows." Carole was sitting on her desk smoking a Newport.

"You know where he at?" Frank asked. "I'll go take care of it right now."

"My people are workin' on it. I may be able to let you know somethin' in a day or two."

"You got eyes and ears everywhere, huh?" Frank asked, impressed.

"I been around for a long time in these streets."

"Let me know if you hear anything."

"I will." She put the cigarette out. "I don't mean to get all in your business, but I like you, baby, plus, we're doin' business together. What affects you will somehow affects me. Get the idea?"

Frank nodded, he understood perfectly.

"You came home wit' a plan to get some money, but now you have a problem that demands your attention. A problem that has followed you from Lorton. You can't focus completely on gettin' money until you take care of this problem. See where I'm comin' from?"

"I see where you comin' from, Carole. I got it under control."

"I hear you, but I still think you should put things on hold until you clean up your backyard. You came home first, it's no reason you shouldn't have come out on top. You let the advantage slip away. Now, the other guy has the ups and you don't know when he's goin' to strike."

Frank nodded. His father had told him the same thing in so many words.

"You're just like Ty. All you youngsters act alike, you act first and think second. If you gon' get money and stay alive out here in this game, you gotta be firm, you gotta be seen that way as well. What I mean by that is that you want these niggas to know that you ain't playin' wit' they asses. You want them to know that when they fuckin' wit' you that death is always the price they gon' pay."

Frank had never heard Carole speak along those lines. He understood why she was called The Black Widow.

"Once they know that death is the price, they think twice

before they cross you." Carole lit another Newport. "I don't ever have to do shit in these streets, after all, I'm a woman. But, muthafuckers know this black bitch ain't playin' wit' they asses. They know I'll have they asses touched, quick. They fear that. Remember that, Frank." The Black Widow stood up and walked toward the door. "Follow me, Frank." She led him down a dark hallway and up a set stairs. They entered a plush den of sorts. Carole opened a walk-in closet and pulled out a small machine gun. She handed it to Frank.

Frank had only seen such a weapon on TV. Holding the machine gun with both hands, he smiled. "This one of them Cleopatra Jones pieces," he said, pulling the long clip out.

"It's a Uzi." Carole handed him two heavy clips filled with 9mm bullets. "I give all my people what they need to survive. It's not a lot of muthafuckas walkin' the streets wit' one of those. I just started gettin" them from New York. Your enemy should never get away when you come wit' one of these. In the game of life, we live only once. We gotta always be ready. You gotta be ready for war. Death can always be around the corner." Carole handed Frank a bulletproof vest. "It's no comparison between a man that's ready and a man that's not."

Frank respected the fact that The Black Widow was schooling him. With an Uzi, two twenty-shot clips, and a bulletproof vest, Frank was ready for war. "Thanks, I'm ready for war," he joked.

"You be safe," Carole said before Frank left.

Maximum Security, Thursday, March 16, 1980

It was another day at the office for the convicts of 4 Block, behind the Wall. Kevin Holt walked by Larry Williams' cell, they exchanged nods. Kevin continued down the tier, passing Fly and Brodus. Bending the corner by the showers he heard someone call his name. He turned around and looked down the long, narrow tier. A convict was calling him back down the tier. It was a set up. Like a leopard in dense brush, T-Bone, with a brown stocking cap over his face, jumped out of the shower and wrapped his arm around Kevin's neck in a choking headlock. "You done fucked wit' the wrong nigga!" T-Bone hissed as he dragged Kevin into the shower. Kevin struggled, but T-Bone was too strong. The other convicts on the tier kept it moving, minding their business. T-Bone stabbed Kevin in the chest repeatedly inside the shower; he then slammed him to the wet floor and savagely plunged the knife into his heart and held it there with brute force while applying pressure. Looking into Kevin's dying eyes, T-Bone hissed, "Die, muthafucka!" After watching Kevin take his last breath, T-Bone twisted the knife, yanked the bloody blade from his chest, left the cell block, and headed for the kitchen to mix in with the lunch crowd.

T-Bone knew that Kevin had sent a nigga to stab Ronald, it was no way he was going to let a nigga get away with that.

Washington, D.C., Friday, March 17, 1980

The Howard Theater was packed. Rare Essence had the crowd moving and grooving to the go-go sounds. It was five thirteen A.M. and the go-go was still going strong. Frank and Baby Face were in the spot with their crew from the Valley. The honeys were all over them, they were the new niggas on the scene getting money. A number of movers and shakers were in the spot, Fray, Wookie, and Eggie were looking like millionaires. Eddie Mathis and a few of his men were in the spot. It was dark and humid in the club and the music was deafening, but the Howard Theater was still the place to be. Frank ran into a lot of dudes he knew from down Lorton and before he went to prison. Niggas were hearing about him and what he was doing on the south side. The beef with G-Train was big talk as well. G-Train was still missing in action. His family hadn't seen him since the halfway house shooting.

Grinding against the ass of a bad ass redbone in a short skirt, Frank rubbed his hands up her skirt and discovered that she had on no panties. She looked back, and yelled over the music, "I don't wear drawers!"

"I see," Frank yelled. He continued grinding to the music, growing rock hard as she rubbed her ass against him like they were fucking. She could feel his dick through his thin Armani slacks. Minutes later, Frank had had enough. He was so hard it was becoming painful. Still grooving to the beat in the dark, he pulled out and slid right in the pussy from the back. The redbone jerked away a little bit out of shock, but got with the program. She bent over right on the dance floor while Frank held her by the waist, fucking the shit out her. He stroked the pussy hard and fast, cumming inside her.

After the go-go, scores of people poured out of the Howard as the sun began to come up. Frank and his crew headed for their cars, stopping to speak to a few people along the way.

BOOM! BOOM! BOOM!

Shotgun blasts exploded. Everybody began to scatter toward T Street. "Watch out!" Baby Face yelled at Frank as two masked gunmen crossed the street blasting pump shotguns. Two of Baby Face's partners were blown off their feet in the middle of the street. Shotgun blasting, screams, car tires burning rubber, and breaking glass was all one could hear for blocks. Two more masked gunmen appeared firing automatic pistols. It was a hit. The gunmen were trying to take Frank out. Baby Face got to the Cadillac and grabbed his .357 magnum, dropping one of the shotgunners. Frank made it to the car as bullets flew by his head. He got to the Uzi and came out spraying the fully automatic, clearing the street. He ran after the gunmen and dropped two of them. Spraying bullets at the last gunman, Frank heard police sirens. Baby Face pulled up in the car beside him. Frank jumped in the Cadillac with the smoking Uzi in hand. Baby Face took them flying down the street along with other fleeing cars.

Speeding back to the south side, Frank and Baby Face talked about what had just went down. It had to be G-Train. He'd missed, too. Frank knew he had no business hanging out partying while G-Train was still alive somewhere, planning his murder. Frank made up his mind that he was going to focus on nothing but G-Train until he was in a box.

"Muthafuckas gotta pay!" Baby Face said, driving down Valley Avenue. "They hit Sam and Brother, they can't get away wit' that shit, man."

"They won't," Frank said.

"We need to kidnap that nigga's peoples, that'll get his ass out in the open."

Frank nodded in agreement. "That's just what we gon' do."

D.C. Jail, Wednesday, May 23, 1980

When Ronald returned to the jail from court, he found that he was the top story on the evening news. He'd just taken a cop to manslaughter and expected ten to thirty with a mandatory three years before a parole hearing. Three years was nothing, he could do it standing on his head. However, with all he had going for himself, one day back in prison was a huge setback. Going on twenty three-years-old, Ronald was still young and could do a lot with the time he had left. He wondered if he would still be able to box when he got out. He would only be twenty six if he got out in three years. But, would he get out in three years? That was the question. Ronald understood prison well, he knew that once a man walked into the deadly maze of the injustice system that nothing was guaranteed. Nothing at all. Nevertheless, Ronald sucked it up. He was a trooper and was used to hardships in life.

Ronald went straight to his cell and went to sleep.

Later on, Synthia went to see Ronald. She was dealing with the situation very well. In her mind, the system was going to make Ronald do some more time no matter what he was doing with his life on the streets. Synthia agreed with the cop, at least he had a chance to get out in three years instead of ten or fifteen. However, it really didn't matter to Synthia, she was committed to her man and would stand by him until the end of time.

During the visit, Synthia could see the frustration in Ronald's eyes. He looked like he had been dealt a bad hand in a game of life and death. Synthia felt helpless. There was nothing she could do as she sat behind the scratched up glass with the phone to her ear. "Baby, you been through worse than this. Three years gon' fly by in no time. We gon' be fine. You know that, right?"

Ronald sighed. "Yeah, I know, but it ain't even the time that's really gettin' to me, I can do the time ..." he paused for a second. "It ain't even the boxin' or the money ..."

"What is it then, baby?"

"It's you, it's Lil' Ronald, Diane, Roland ... everybody that was countin' on me to make things right. My family, my future. I had plans on makin' things right for us all and now that's been taken away from me."

"Baby, you have made everything right, you laid a foundation for us all. You didn't let us down. We are proud of you, Ronald, don't ever think otherwise. We can't change what happened, all we can do is be strong. Ain't that what you taught me?"

Ronald nodded.

"What don't kill us can only make us stronger."

"You right, baby." Ronald cracked a weak smile.

Washington, D.C., Tuesday, June 11, 1980

It was all out war in the D.C. streets. Bodies were

dropping like flies, but, according to homicide detectives, the murders were occurring in the Valley Green area of Southeast and the Green Leaf Gardens area of Southwest only. Sides had been taken. Frank had the whole Valley behind him. G-Train had family in the Green Leaf Gardens and they were standing behind him. The few relatives that G-Train had in Valley Green moved to Green Leaf Gardens after Baby Face and one of his partners kidnapped G-Train's aunt to find him. They ended up shooting her in the head and dumping her body in Oxon Hill when they couldn't locate G-Train by holding her hostage. From that point on, it was open season on anybody connected with both sides. However, amongst all the murder and bloodshed, Frank and G-Train couldn't get close enough to one another to end the madness. Frank's crew was doing the most damage in the street battles being as though The Black Widow had armed them with Uzis and bulletproof vests. Uzis were rare in D.C. street battles, almost unheard of at the time.

All the bloodshed that Frank and G-Train were causing in the streets was angering a lot of older drug figures in the city. Behind closed doors, they'd had talks about killing Frank and G-Train to kill the heat that was coming down behind their beef. The Black Widow got wind of the talks and made it clear that Frank was under her protection. To comfort the ego of the others that she respected, she gave her word to have the street war ended, on her own terms. The others agreed. They knew she meant business.

The Black Widow sent word for Frank to meet her at the Lounge. When Frank arrived, she told him that the heat that he and G-Train were causing was angering a lot of old timers and that they weren't pleased.

"Carole, no disrespect to you, but I don't give a fuck about what them old muthafuckas gotta say," Frank said, sitting on the sofa in Carole's office. "How do you feel? Do you feel the same way?"

"Yes, Frank. I think enough is enough. I'm goin' to take

care of the situation for you and put a stop to this madness. It's bad for business." Carole sat behind her desk smoking a Newport.

"You know how I feel about you. I'm all for whatever you say, you've been nothin' but good to me."

Carole smiled. She liked Frank, he listened to her. He knew not to bite the hand that fed him.

Outside of Carole's Lounge, it was a beautiful summer day. People were out and about all up and down H Street. However, danger was near. Laying in the back seat of an old brown Chevy Nova with a pump shotgun, G-Train was ready to tear shit up. He'd gotten word that Frank was inside the lounge. Behind the wheel of the Nova that was parked half a block away from the lounge was Sarah; her wig and makeup made her look like a totally different person. "Somebody comin' out now," she said to G-Train as she watched two of Carole's men step outside and light cigarettes. "It ain't Frank, though."

With a ski mask on his face, G-Train said, "He's in there, he'll come out, baby girl. Mock my words."

"Okay, daddy."

Forty-five minutes later, Sarah said, "Here he come, he wit' a lot of people, though, baby."

"I don't give fuck, just be ready."

"They comin' this way." Sarah started the car.

Frank and Carole walked down the sidewalk surrounded by five of Carole's men. Baby Face and one of his partners was trailing.

G-Train jumped out of the Nova with the pump and took everybody by surprise. Everything seemed to slow down instantly although only seconds passed. G-Train let the shotgun blast four times, back-to-back, spraying buckshots. Frank shoved Carole to the ground and pulled his .45 automatic, firing it like a marksman into G-Train's chest. Baby Face, his man, and Carole's men pulled their pistols and began firing. A

166

load of buckshot from the pump hit Frank in the left shin and crumbled it like bamboo, causing him to fall forward, still firing his pistol. Sarah got out of the car and fired a .357 over the roof at Carole's men. Another blast from the pump sent loads of buckshot into Frank's right side, sliding him across the sidewalk like raked leaves. He didn't fire another shot. G-Train made it back to the Nova, taking five bullets to the back as he jumped inside. Sarah sped away. The Nova took fire as it bent the corner at the end of H Street.

Blocks away, two police cars began chasing the Nova. G-Train took off his bulletproof vest and reloaded the pump. Sarah handled the big Nova like the Dukes of Hazard. At top speed, Sarah raced along Benning Road, weaving in and out of traffic dangerously. G-Train reloaded her .357 and fired out the window at the police, causing one of the cars to swerve into a parked car. One down and one to go. Sarah took them flying over the Anacostia River across the Benning Bridge. Her heart was pounding with fear, but she kept going. She was going to get away. Looking over her shoulder, she saw that she was pulling away from the police. Swinging the flying tank onto Kenilworth Avenue, Sarah floored it. At the corner of East Capitol Street a police car smashed into the front of the Nova, causing a loud collision that violently ejected Sarah through the windshield. Her body flew more than thirty yards before smacking a parked car and falling to the street. The two cops in the police car died on impact. G-Train was knocked out by the collision; he laid stretched out and bleeding on the back seat of the wrecked Nova.

Countless police were on the scene in seconds. Sarah's body was taken away in a meat wagon. G-Train was taken away in an ambulance, under arrest for murder.

Chapter 12

Washington, D.C., Wednesday, June 19, 1980

Tears ran down T-Bone's cheeks as he stood chained and shackled, looking down into his mother's casket. He was flanked by two C.O.s inside Horton's Funeral Home on Kennedy Street, Northwest. Rage boiled inside him. He swore that somebody would pay.

"It's time to go, Wilson," one of the C.O.s said.

The Department of Corrections had allowed T-Bone to be escorted to his mother's wake. She'd died from a shotgun blast to the chest. Frank survived the hit, but was arrested and charged with the Howard Theater murders. He didn't even know he was wanted for the murders. G-Train was in jail, charged with murder as well. He had made a lot of enemies by killing The Black Widow. Frank's vest saved his life, he had to have reconstructive surgery on his leg and was still in the hospital.

In the back of the prison van on the way back down I-95, T-Bone shed no more tears. The only thing he would be shedding was blood. He was going to make everybody pay that had something to do with his mother's murder.

Back behind the Wall, T-Bone blew some dope and sat in his cell for hours. He didn't want to be bothered. The only thing that made him feel better was the mail he got from Cristal.

D.C. Jail, Monday, June 24, 1980

A lot of people picked sides in the beef between Frank and G-Train. The beef spilled over into the jail. An older dude loyal to The Black Widow tried to stab G-Train as soon as he got in the jail. G-Train ended up getting the best of the older dude, stabbing him seven times; G-Train was now in the hole. However, it was clear that the beef between Frank and G-Train would have long lasting effects

Frank was just getting out of the hospital and was being rolled into cell block NW-3. Tension was in the air as soon as the C.O. rolled him through the gate. Ronald and Bennie were right on the scene to help Frank to his cell. Bennie knew that Frank was Ronald's man, so he was down with whatever came with that. He and Ronald were real cool now. After Ronald introduced Frank and Bennie, Bennie left and let Ronald and Frank have some time alone. Sitting in the wheelchair with his leg propped up in a cast with metal pins in it,

Frank explained everything to Ronald, everything that concerned The Black Widow's murder. Frank blamed himself for Carole's murder. He knew that G-Train had come for him. Frank swore to go beyond all bounds to put G-Train in the dirt.

Ronald shook his head. "You ain't stay on the streets six months."

"I know." Frank sighed. "Shit got hectic."

"I see." Ronald had been hearing about the Howard Theater shootings on the news; they'd been big news for weeks. The shooting was the worst single shooting of the year. Frank was charged with two counts of murder and Baby Face was on the run for murder.

"You know how shit be when you first touch down in them streets, everything be movin' so fast. Then, this shit wit' me and G-Train got all outta control. Carole was about to step in and get the shit taken care of the same day G-Train made his move." Frank struggled to the bed with Ronald's help.

"You went out there wit' that Lorton shit ... I told you to take your time."

"I know, but ain't shit I can do about that now." Frank was getting a little irritated. If it was anyone other than Ronald, he would have snapped. "I tried to handle shit as it came, but I couldn't catch that nigga G-Train. Everytime we tried to get him he had four or five niggaz wit' him. We'd end up in a shoot out, that's how so many bodies start droppin'."

Ronald just shook his head. Frank and G-Train single-handedly fucked the streets up in less than six months. They were directly responsible for at least twenty some murders, even though they didn't pull the trigger at times.

"You really ain't in no shape for war right now," Ronald said, checking Frank out.

"I know." Frank looked down at his leg. He would be fine in due time. "But, once I get on my feet, niggas gon' bleed like hogs, that's my word."

"I hear you."

"Ronald, let me holla at you." Bennie stepped in the cell.

"What's up, Bennie?" Ronald asked, becoming alert.

"Them Southwest niggas up to somethin", I think they 'bout to move on your man."

Ronald got up and looked out onto the tier. Sure enough, the Southwest niggas in the block were gathered up at the end of the tier. One of them was walking toward Ronald.

"What the fuck is up?" Frank asked helplessly from the bed.

"Ay, Ronald..." said the dude walking toward Ronald.

Ronald cut his words short with a flashing left hook that put the the dude to sleep. The other Southwest dudes at the end of the tier rushed Ronald, knives out. Ronald braced himself and floored the first one. Bennie stepped out of the cell and went to work by Ronald's side. A few of Bennie's comrades joined the drama. Ronald felt a knife slam into his side from the back as he fought off an attacker; he turned around and blasted the nigga that stabbed him with a mean right hand that knocked the nigga out cold. Ronald grabbed the knife and went at another Southwest nigga. Southwest niggas were coming from everywhere. The C.O.s that were working in the block panicked and ran inside the bubble to call for help. At least a good twenty-five prisoners were going to war in front of Frank's cell; they were fighting and pushing steel.

Moments later, the ERT officers rushed the block. While still warring with one another, the prisoners went to war with the ERT squad as well. The ERT was dressed in riot gear, swinging thick oak clubs. An ERT officer smacked Ronald over the head with a club, splitting his head wide open. Not knowing who'd hit him in the head, Ronald spent around and stabbed the ERT officer in the chest, but the blade dug deep into the padded vest the officer wore. Bennie was going hard, he'd taken a club from an ERT officer and was bashing the officer in the head with it—the officer had lost his helmet in the melee.

The jailhouse brawl lasted for more than ten minutes, after that, tear gas bombs were used. Everyone, officers and all, were bloody, choking, and gagging. When things were finally under control, there were broken bones, stab wounds, missing teeth, and busted heads. Even Frank was fucked up by the ERT.

Ronald suffered two stab wounds, broken ribs, and stitches across the top of his head. After returning to the jail from the hospital, he was sent to the hole along with many others. Words couldn't explain the pain he was in.

Jail life. It's a motherfucker!

D.C. Jail, Saturday, June 29, 1980

In the segregation cage handcuffed behind the visitation glass, bruised, battered, and scarred, Ronald explained to Synthia what had happened when the Southwest niggas tried to move on Frank. She was appalled by the look of her man and what he'd went through. Ronald had to calm her down and make her understand that he'd be okay. Such things came with doing time.

"How's this goin' to look when you go for sentencing?" Synthia was praying that Ronald would get no more than the mandatory three years.

"Don't worry about it, it's nothin' I can do about it now."

"What the hell do you mean, don't worry about it?! What the hell does that mean?"

"Synthia, calm down. You gotta understand somethin' ... in here, survivin' comes first before anything else. You know this. I gotta stand firm in here. I can't control what comes my way." Ronald explained the politics to her again, knowing she already knew how things went on the inside.

Synthia sighed and shook her head. "I don't see how you deal wit' bein' in here. It would drive me crazy."

"I feel the same way at times, like I'm goin' crazy. But, after a while a man has to get used to it. The madness becomes normal in a way. I have to deal wit' it."

"I understand. I just wish I could get you outta here."

"I know, baby."

Ronald and Synthia spoke about Buck, who wasn't getting any better and was still in and out of the hospital. Ronald had grown a real love for Buck; the old man taught him a lot, not only about boxing, but about life as a whole.

"They say he got lung cancer."

"You gotta bring him to see me if you can."

"I'll see what I can do, he's not doin' too well."

Maximum Security Saturday, August 27, 1980

Walking along the dirt track around the big field, Ronald and T-Bone discussed T-Bone's feelings toward Frank. As they walked in the summer heat sweating, T-Bone expressed how fucked up he was with Frank about the murder of his mother. He felt that Frank was on the streets bullshitting with G-Train. He felt that Frank shouldn't have been around his mother until G-Train was dead.

Ronald wiped sweat from his face as the sun continued to beam down on them. He understood where T-Bone was coming from. Nevertheless, Ronald said, "T, you know good and well that Frank would never put your mother in danger on purpose."

"Yeah, but he still brought danger to her doorstep, he know better, he know niggas play for keeps. You know that." T-Bone lit a Newport.

"Yeah, I agree wit' you on that, but I wouldn't hold no ill feelings toward Frank about that. I wouldn't blame him for what G-Train did. Frank's family, that's our man, T," Ronald said as he and T-Bone walked by Fly and James-BEY. They spoke to the other convicts and kept stepping.

"Frank is our man, he family, but that don't mean he wasn't bullshittin', and his bullshittin' got my mother killed. Ain't no gettin' around that, Ronald."

"You sound like you wanna move on Frank," Ronald said, just throwing it out there.

T-Bone said nothing for a second, didn't even look at Ronald. "Nah, I don't wanna move on Frank, I ain't gon' go against the grain. I'ma move on G-Train and whoever wit' him first chance I get. But, that don't mean I ain't fucked up at Frank."

Later on, Ronald was laying in the bed in his small one-man cell thinking about everything that was going on in his life. He'd been behind the Wall for almost a month now. He was sentenced to ten to thirty and had to do five years before seeing the parole board. His lawyer fought for less, but Ronald's record was mean on paper. However, time would fly, that was what he kept telling himself. His boxing dreams seemed so remote. Buck had died of cancer; that crushed Ronald. It was like losing a father. Wilfred kept in touch, although he was busy with the career of James Holmes. Aside from what was going on in the streets, Ronald had to deal with the beef he'd gotten himself in with the Southwest niggas. It was going to be an issue down the road, but most of them were sent to Youth Center I.

The cell doors popped and Ronald stepped out onto the tier. He checked things out, always on point. He believed that men had to keep their eyes open at all times if they wanted to stay alive in prison. Down the tier, he saw Brodus in another convict's face; the two of them were in a heated conversation. Brodus was pressing the other convict about something. Ronald could tell that much from the looks of things. All of a sudden, Brodus hauled off and smacked the taste out of the convict's mouth. Ronald shook his head, he couldn't believe that a man would let another man disrespect him like that, no matter who it was. Come to find out, Brodus had slapped the nigga about moving the fan that was pointed toward his cell. With twenty-four cells on the tier and only four fans to provide a little comfort in the smoldering summer heat, there was always some drama behind the fans, even murder.

With his knife on him, Ronald made his way down the tier to holla at Harrison-EL, who'd been behind the Wall for months now.

Ronald found Harrison-EL in his cell doing legal work. Legal books and papers were all over the bed like a desk. "What's up, Moor?" Ronald said, standing in the doorway.

Harrison-EL looked up and smiled. "Drawin' up that lawsuit I was tellin' you about."

The Department of Corrections was playing a lot of

games with religious services behind the Wall. The Moors and the Nation of Islam were having problems with the warden, who was taking the stand that some of their services were becoming revolutionary in character and presenting threats to security.

"I'm tryin' to file this before things get out of hand." Harrison-EL took a sip of his ice water. "If these peoples keep playin' games, it's gon' get real ugly. A lot of times you gotta file that paper work to get things in order." Harrison-EL told Ronald about the Fulwood vs. Clemmer case where D.C. convicts filed suit in the sixties on the right to practice their faith as members of the Nation of Islam. The system wasn't respecting or recognizing them as a religion; the system wasn't allowing them to obtain literature or to wear their religious medals. They called them Black Muslims. The convicts won a federal court decision in 1962, followed by subsequent cases, that retained constitutional protection for all so-called Black Muslims across the country. However, at certain times, the system would buck on the law. Nevertheless, Fulwood vs. Clemmer, 206 F. Supp. 307 (D.C. Cir. 1962) was the leading case for religious expression in American prisons. Lorton convicts put that work in.

"Damn, I ain't know that, man," Ronald said. He wasn't the type to file law suits, he was the type that believed that if the system was wrong, that convicts were obligated to take a stand physically.

"Yeah, brother, the pen is mightier than the sword a lot of times. It's a time to fight and it's a time to file that paper work." Harrison-EL took another sip of water. "When dudes talk about prison conditions, they always talk about Attica brothers up in New York or Comrade George out Cali at San Quentin, but Lorton brothers put in a lot of work, too. In Lorton and the feds. But anyway, if I don't get this paper work filed, this joint is goin' to blow up, mark my words, Ronnie."

D.C. Jail, Thursday, September 2, 1980

Frank was back on his feet but walking with a cane; his leg looked deformed from the shotgun blast. Frank and Bennie had gotten tight, Frank respected how Bennie went to work when the Southwest niggas tried to move on him. Besides, Bennie was Frank's kind of nigga Wild and didn't give a fuck. They had their cell block fortified. Frank had Southeast on his side and Bennie had Uptown on his side, it was a hell of an alliance that joined killers from all across town. Their crew damn near "ran" the jail. They controlled, or had their hand in, all the drugs that came through the jail. Frank understood the fact that his name carried weight at that point and he used that power well. He also understood the power of fear and how he could use it to make people bend to his will. He was a much better leader in jail than he was on the streets, due in part to the fact that he understood jailhouse politics better than he understood the politics of the streets.

As far as G-Train was concerned, he knew he was outnumbered. He didn't give a fuck. Everyone knew he was fearless, the kind of nigga that one would have to kill. He didn't respect anything else. G-Train had made it to population twice, but every time he hit the block he stabbed a nigga within the hour. The administration was sick of his shit, G-Train was sent to the hole and placed on special-handling status. That meant he would only come out by himself. The plan was to keep him on special-handling until he left the jail. He and Frank had separations, so they would never be put in the same block.

Frank's case was looking real good. His father was on top of business for him, using his criminal mind to instruct Baby Face and the rest of the crew on Frank's behalf. Baby Face and two of his closest comrades had annihilated the government witnesses with Mafia-precision. There was no doubt that Frank's murder charges were going to be dismissed. He'd be back in the streets in no time.

G-Train's case was a mess. He was charged with The Black Widow's murder, Frank's shooting, and the murder of the police officers that died in the car crash. G-Train had his hands full and was looking at life in prison.

In the visiting hall with his father, Frank and the old man discussed everything that was going on with the case and in the streets His father was dressed in one of Frank's black Adidas sweat suits, sitting on the other side of the scratched-up glass. Fred was an older, dope fiend version of Frank. They looked just alike.

"Don't you worry about nothin', youngsta. I'ma make sure all your business is taken care of." Fred was high, but on top of his game at the same time. Being high was normal to him, he functioned at full capacity when he'd had his fix.

"So, Baby Face gon' turn himself in now?" Frank asked.

"Yeah, he might as well. There's no witnesses against him. They gon' have to drop the case." Fred winked. "Let me run this ship, you'll be home in a minute and then you can take the wheel."

"Yeah, okay." Frank laughed.

Maximum Security Sunday, September 5, 1980

Cristal and Synthia brought their sons down Lorton to see T-Bone and Ronald. Cristal was pissed off and she wasn't hiding it. Before she met up with Synthia to hit the highway, Cristal went by Carole's Lounge to holla at Big Teddy, he now ran The Black Widow's crew. Big Teddy made Cristal wait, as if she was nobody, out in the lounge area where one of his men was trying to holla at her. Cold blooded disrespect to T-Bone. T-Bone was fired up when Cristal told him what had went down. After Big Teddy made her wait for half an hour, he didn't even have enough respect to see her himself. He sent one of his men to see her with some short shit for her to take to T-

Bone. Big Teddy had been playing a lot of games with T-Bone since The Black Widow's murder. She'd never allow such a thing. Big Teddy knew that heroin was T-Bone's livelihood down Lorton. T-Bone felt like Big Teddy was saying fuck him. On top of all the bullshit Cristal had to go through to get the little bit of dope she did get, when she got down Lorton, the C.O. that processed her for visitation had harassed both her and Synthia, but he had touched Cristal in a way that made her feel uncomfortable. By the end of the visit, T-Bone was nice and steamed, ready to knock a C.O. out. The Wall was already boiling with tension between convicts and C.O.s.

After their visits, Ronald and T-Bone headed back to the block. T-Bone knew the C.O. that had harassed Cristal and Synthia. "I'ma knock that nigga out as soon as I catch his ass tomorrow," T-Bone said as he puffed on a Newport.

"These punk ass police think a nigga gon' keep goin' for that bullshit," Ronald said.

Inside the block, Ronald and Harrison-EL discussed the conditions behind the Wall.

T-Bone was down the tier talking to Brodus about the C.O. that harassed Cristal. He and Brodus had gotten real cool. Brodus respected real men like T-Bone, although he took a lot of suckers for bad. Brodus had seen T-Bone kill Kevin Holt in the back of the block and knew that T-Bone was more than talk. "I'ma knock that nigga Davis out cold first chance I get, watch."

"That's right," Brodus said. "That's how you gotta do these punk ass cops. I don't care about none of them. Niggas around filin' all that damn paper work, they need to be fuckin' these cops up. After you knock one of they asses out, they'll act like they got some sense. It's time to split a few heads around this muthafucka."

"No bullshit," T-Bone said, leaning against the bars of his cell. Cadillac walked up and asked what was going on, he knew something was up. T-Bone and Brodus put Cadillac on

178

point.

"Niggas talkin" 'bout tearin' this muthafucka up in the. Morin'," Cadillac said. "The Moors just had a run-in wit' the cops about our meetin'." Cadillac was also known as Smith EL.

"It's about time, I was wonderin' when these niggas was gon' figure out enough is enough," Brodus said.

Maximum Security, Monday, September 6, 1980

The cells popped for breakfast bright and early. A crowd of convicts headed for the kitchen. Coming through the door, Brodus knocked out the first C.O. he saw, breaking his jaw in the process. Other convicts followed suit, attacking any C.O. in sight. T-Bone caught the very C.O. that had harassed Cristal and Synthia. He was a big, black three hundred pounder. T-Bone knocked his ass out cold and then stomped him out. Anarchy and chaos ensued and exploded in a violent onslaught as convicts bumrushed the stewards and C.O.s in the back of the kitchen. Convicts quickly got their hands on every knife and every piece of metal that could be used as weapons. In a state of panic, the C.O.s that were able to escape the onslaught ran for the control center and the gun towers. Some barricaded themselves in the empty cell blocks. Rats ran for their lives right behind the C.O.s, all the way to the captain's office. For hours, close to two-hundred convicts held the whole Wall hostage and there was nothing that the C.O.s could do about it. The news media got wind of the situation around one P.M., right around the time the phone in the kitchen started ringing. "Yeah." Harrison-EL answered the phone.

"Who am I speaking to?" Major Smith asked. He was a huge, fat, nasty, sloppy white man.

"Call me Justice," Harrison-EL said, surrounded by Ronald, T-Bone, Fly, Cadillac, Brodus, Lil' Caesar, and other fed up convicts that were willing to go all the way. They had hostages tied up and sitting on the floor by the door. They had set a few rules amongst themselves, no raping the females. Their goal was to demonstrate and demand better overall treatment behind the Wall. Enough was enough. If blood had to spill and lives had to be lost, then so be it!

"Well, Mr. Justice, this is Major Smith. Let's work this out so no one else gets hurt."

"Yeah right. You don't call the shots right now, we do. You get the warden on the phone, then we can talk." Harrison-EL hung up on the Major. He then addressed his fellow convicts like a young Huey Newton. "We all know it's no turnin' back now. We gon' put our demands on the table and stand on them. Everybody cool wit' them?" All the convicts were in accord. "What all do we want?"

"You good wit' talkin'," Cadillac said, "you know what the deal is." Cadillac spoke for everyone. It was a group struggle. One for all, all for one. "The religious services, the food, programs, medical, the whole nine. We want it all."

Negotiations began. The convicts had ten C.O.s and twelve kitchen workers held hostage, and they swore to kill the hostages if their demands weren't met. While the negotiations went on, convicts that were in the kitchen were eating like kings, they'd broken into everything possible.

The phone rang again. That time, Harrison-EL was out on the field with a mob of other convicts that weren't down with the group struggle, they were just rebels without a cause. Harrison-EL was trying to get them on board with the demonstration. Carl Kelley handed the phone to Ronald. "Yeah," Ronald said.

"This is Warden Jackson..."

'Bout time," Ronald cut the warden off. The warden tried to speak again, but Ronald cut him off again, and said, "It's time for you to listen. We doin' all the talkin" right now. We done already let it be known what the deal is. The ball is in your court now."

"You guys have made your point."

"You wrong, we ain't even got started yet."

"It would be best for whoever is in charge to tell everyone to return to their cell blocks. We can work this out from there. Nothing will be accomplished with all of this violence."

"That's where you wrong, house nigger. You gon' work this shit out right now or we gon' tear this muthafucka up. Killin' hostages and all. Make it light on yourself. Call back when you ready to take care of business." Ronald hung up and informed the other convicts about the conversation. At the time, Ronald's mind was far away from ever going home. He was frustrated with the system, angry about his setbacks and the way his dreams were taken away from him by "the man."

A short while later, Harrison-EL and Homicide brought three more hostages in the kitchen at knife point. Convicts had forced their way into protective custody cell blocks and taken more C.O.s hostages. Two well known rats were stabbed to death for their role in the prosecution of other convicts that were now in the feds for jailhouse murders.

As convicts spread across the compound destroying government property and searching for more hostages, Ronald and T-Bone were on a mission. They knew that the D.O.C. would get fed up with the revolt and try to launch an assault on the convicts to take the Wall back and punish anybody that stood in their way. Ronald and T-Bone broke into R-N-D to get boxes of prison coats and riot gear that was reserved for the ERT.

Inside R-N-D, they found all that they were looking for and began loading the prison van they had taken with the goods. In the background, black smoke covered the sky, it looked like the whole prison was on fire. Once Ronald and T-Bone got all that they would need, their plan was to drive it all back to the kitchen. When they thought they had all there was to get, Ronald found some more riot gear, some cans of mace, electric shields, and garden tools. While T-Bone carried two big plastic electric shields to the van, Ronald went back into the storage room to grab some more helmets.

BANG!

An iron pipe came down on the back of Ronald's head, almost knocking him out. Defensively, Ronald spun around with great speed and saw a huge black C.O. that had been hiding in R-N-D. The C.O. swung the pipe again. Ronald weaved it. The C.O. swung it again, almost taking Ronald's head off. On the next swing, Ronald grabbed the pipe and tried to wrestle it a away from the C.O.; the C.O. was stronger than Ronald had thought. Ronald began punching him in the face as they continued to wrestle for the pipe. "I'ma kill your muthafuckin' ass, nigga!" the C.O. hissed, slamming Ronald to the ground and falling on top of him. The three hundred pounds knocked the air out of Ronald, but he kept fighting. They both wrestled for the pipe as if their lives depended on it. Ronald got loose and smashed the C.O. in the head with a riot helmet.

"What the fuck!" T-Bone stepped on the scene with a butcher knife in hand. As Ronald beat the C.O. with the helmet, T-Bone stepped in and slammed the butcher knife deep into the C.O.'s chest. When the knife sunk into his chest, it sounded like a powerful punch that knocked the wind out of the C.O. Ronald kicked the C.O. in the head as the C.O. held his chest, taking his last breaths. T-Bone and Ronald watched the dying C.O. squirm as he held his chest and gushing wound while gurgling blood. "He finished," T-Bone said. "Let's go." Ronald took one last look at the C.O. and followed T-Bone out the door.

The two convicts jumped in the van and drove around the corner back to the kitchen with all the riot gear. Ronald thought about what he and T-Bone had just done. In his mind, he told himself that he'd never go home again. He was sure of it. Looking at T-Bone, Ronald said, "T."

"What's up?" T-Bone was pulling into a crowd of

convicts beside the kitchen.

"I don't gotta tell you that that stays between us, right?"

"No doubt." T-Bone jumped out the van like what they'd just done was nothing to him. Opening the back doors of the van, T-Bone allowed the convicts to grab what they wanted from the riot gear collection. Ronald and T-Bone suited up as well. In helmets and padded vest along with gas masks, the mob of convicts headed inside the kitchen where another mob of convicts were. Ronald broke off from the crowd to go to the bathroom.

On the phone with the warden, Harrison-EL drew the final line in the convicts' stand against the system. The final demands were drawn up like a contract by Larry Williams; the demands included a general liberalization of prison life, provisions for more adequate food, religious freedoms, realistic rehabilitation programs, better education and drug treatment programs, and real legal assistance services. The biggest demand was amnesty for all actions taken by the convicts during the riot.

"I'll work on it," the warden pleaded. "But, amnesty is out of my hands. There will be consequences for any officers that've been hurt. You know that."

"Our demands stand." Harrison-EL hung up. The convicts were ready to get down to business.

Inside the office of Warden Jackson, he wiped sweat from his forehead. The build up of a riot had been on the horizon for months. For the last two years there had been smaller convict uprisings behind the Wall. I knew this shit was coming, the warden told himself. The events of February 1, 1980 were still fresh in the warden's mind. On that day, the gruesome New Mexico State Prison riot took place. Nearly a thousand convicts seized the prison and took fifteen C.O.s as hostages. The convicts also threatened to kill all hostages if their prison conditions were not improved. When the smoke cleared, thirty three convicts were murdered. During the short riot, a seven-man convict execution squad tore through the prison killing rats—one was beheaded, another was found with a metal rod driven through his head, several others had arms and legs cut off or their eyes gouged out, and some were charred by blowtorches. The New Mexico riot was the worst in American prison history and unmatched in savagery in terms of convict violence. Thinking of that riot, Warden Jackson looked over at Major Smith, and said, "Call in the National Guard and the state police. We're not going to have another New Mexico or Attica on our hands. We're putting an end to this shit right now!"

Meanwhile, in the kitchen bathroom, Ronald, dressed in riot gear, discovered something very distasteful to him. A convict had one of the female C.O.s that had been taken hostage on the nasty floor with her pants down. She was already gagged, so she couldn't scream. The convict was trying to force himself on her. It was already understood that there would be no taking pussy. Not only was the convict trying to rape the female C.O., he'd already raped a male C.O. and had him laying in the corner of the bathroom, knocked out. Ronald kicked the convict in the back as if he was kicking in a door. He knocked the convict to the floor.

"What the fuck you doin', Ronald?!" said the convict, looking up at Ronald with a frown on his face.

Ronald looked the convict in the eyes, he knew him from Youth Center I. The convict was a known butthole bandit. "You know we ain't takin' no pussy."

"What?!" the convict tried to stand up. "You the police now?" He got to his feet and got in Ronald's face.

The crying female C.O. hadn't been raped yet, but she'd been forced to watch the convict rape the male C.O. She was so grateful that Ronald had showed up in the bathroom.

In a flash, Ronald threw four bone crushing blows that all landed on the convict's chin. He went straight to sleep, falling to the floor and sliding under the stall. Ronald helped the female C.O. to her feet. Her hands were still cuffed behind her. Ronald fixed her clothes and took her back where the other hostages were. He then told Harrison-EL about what had went down in the bathroom. Harrison-EL was pissed off that a convict was on a mission other than the one that the collective whole had set out to accomplish. He put another man on guard to watch the hostages, and then went in the bathroom. Inside the bathroom, Harrison-EL woke up the knocked out convict and then butchered him like a hog. Coming out of the bathroom, he jumped up on a table and got the attention of the convicts in the kitchen. "Check this out, men!" He looked some of them in the eyes. "Let's get this clear, we are buckin' the system! We ain't riskin' our lives to be takin' no pussy or no ass! If that's what's on your mind, then you need to get your shit in order. Anybody that ain't wit' us is against us. If you against us, then we gon' deal wit' you in accord! Pass the word. It's about to get real ugly shortly, we need to stay focused! Some of us may die here today! If we die, at least we can die standin' for somethin'! Like men!" Harrison-EL jumped down off the table and went into the back of the kitchen were he and a few others were watching the riot coverage on the news, in real time. It was on all stations for the last few hours. Some reporters and camera crews were right on the other side of the thirty foot wall.

Thirty minutes later, Cadillac, Nate Bailey, and Big Terry came inside the back door of the kitchen. Nate Bailey looked at Harrison-EL, and said, "The National Guard and the state police comin' through the back gate. It's about to go down."

"They deep as shit, too." Cadillac said. Brodus came in behind them dressed in riot gear.

"We need a united front," Harrison-EL said. Nate Bailey agreed.

"Let's do it," T-Bone said, heading out the door with Brodus and Cadillac. They began to mobilize the other convicts that were outside. In about ten minutes, more than

185

three hundred convicts were in front of the kitchen, some were in riot gear, some were in Lorton armor— metal food trays and thick magazines wrapped around their bodies like battle armor. All were armed with weapons. Some had the electric shields. At the front of the pack stood Harrison-EL, Ronald, T-Bone, Brodus, Cadillac, and Fly. A few other convicts surrounded them. They watched the National Guard and the state police march in about fifty yards away. A short while later, the warden got on the bullhorn and told the convicts that he had done all he could do and that change would take time; he then told the convicts that it was their last chance to go back to their cell blocks. Tension was at an all time high, danger was thick in the air. Slowly and reluctantly, some of the convicts gave in and broke off from the pack, heading back to the cell blocks. Other convicts began to attack them, but Harrison-EL stopped them and told them to let those that wanted to go leave in peace. After that, more warnings were given, but the remaining two hundred or so convicts stood their ground. The National Guard began firing tear gas into the crowd of convicts and the battle began. In the middle of the field, the scene looked like a scene out of a civil rights riot of the sixties. Without question, the National Guard was cracking heads, they outnumbered the convicts at least three to one. The clash raged on for more than thirty minutes. Blood, sweat, and tears were always a by-product of sacrifice and struggle.

By eight P.M., the National Guard had taken the Wall back. A lot of blood was shed, but no one died in the struggle on the field. All hostages were now safe; four convicts were found stabbed to death in different parts of the Wall; one C.O. was found stabbed to death in R-N-D. By Eleven forty five P.M., the prison buses were loaded up and pulling out. All convicts that were accused of being ringleaders were being shipped to the federal prison system. Among the convicts that were being shipped to the feds were Harrison-EL, Cadillac, Big Terry, Brodus, T-Bone, Lil' Caesar, Nate Bailey, Greg

Williams, Bump, and countless others. They were first sent up to D.C. Jail were they were locked down for a day, and then they were sent out to different United States Penitentiaries, most were sent to Marion and Leavenworth.

Ronald was banged up real bad, but he escaped the fed loads.

Chapter 13

Washington, D.C., Monday, February 6, 1981

Cristal and Synthia moved to Mayfair Mansions, a large housing complex in Northeast D.C. They lived right next door to one another. The relationship between them was a sisterly one; they helped one another deal with the stress of having a man in prison. They also helped one another raise the two boys whose fathers were not around. The two strong black sisters were making it work as best as they could. Synthia worked more than forty hours a week. Cristal went back to her first hustle—boosting. She was one of the best boosters in the city. Cristal hit all the malls and shops in the area, and tore them off for all top of the line gear, jewelry, and furs.

For Cristal, doing time was different now. There was no doubt about it, she was doing time. As long as T-Bone was locked up, she was doing time. Her man was now in the feds, confined at United States Penitentiary Leavenworth, Kansas along with other Lorton convicts that had stood side-by-side in the riot behind the Wall. Cristal had only been to see T-Bone twice since he was sent to Leavenworth; she traveled both times by bus with Chris and took a nice amount of heroin with her. She had no idea that T-Bone was now shooting dope being as, though he still looked good, was in tip-top shape, and was still sending home hundreds of dollars a month. Cristal never questioned him, she loved him and nothing else mattered.

"Lil' Ronald!" Cristal yelled at the top of her lungs. Lil' Ronald was playing with matches. "Get your bad ass over here!" Cristal glared at him as if she was going to kill him. Lil' Ronald dropped the matches in the sink and watched the fire go out before walking over to Cristal, smiling. Cristal always had her hands full when she watched both boys while Synthia was at work. She grabbed Lil' Ronald by his shirt and began smacking him on the ass. "Didn't ... I ... tell ... your ... little ... ass ... to ... stop ... playin' ... wit' ... them ... damn ... matches?!" She popped him hard between every word. "Now, go outside and play before I get my belt." Cristal gave him a light shove toward the door.

With a pout on his face and no tears, Lil' Ronald threw on his coat, hat, and gloves, and stomped out the door into the cold where Chris was throwing snowballs at passing cars and buses.

Lil' Ronald and Chris were going on five years old. They were brothers by all means of the word. They were also partners in crime and did everything together. They also got ass whippings together. If Chris did something and got caught for it not only would he get his little ass beat, but it also meant Lil' Ronald had an ass whipping coming as well. Cristal and Synthia knew the boys did everything together.

Lil' Ronald hooked up with Chris and they ran around outside throwing snowballs at cars and buses until they got bored with it. They then spotted at little girl by the name of Keyona that lived in their building. She liked Chris, but Chris didn't like girls.

"There go your girlfriend," Lil Ronald joked with Chris, knowing Chris didn't like it when he called Keyona his girlfriend.

"That ain't my girlfriend, I told you that!" Chris frowned.

Lil Ronald laughed, sitting on top of Cristal's car. "She

comin' over here to see you."

"No, she not."

"Yes, she is, look." Lil' Ronald pointed at Keyona, who was coming their way.

"Watch this." Chris made a snowball and hid it behind his back.

"Hi, Chris." Keyona smiled as she walked up.

POW!

Chris hit her right in the face with the snowball, making her cry. Laughing, he and Lil' Ronald took off running.

On the other side of the complex, the two boys were still laughing at Keyona. "You shouldna did that, Chris," Lil Ronald said.

Chris sucked his teeth, and said, "Forget her, I told her to leave me alone." Chris pulled some change out of his pocket and continued, "Let's go get some candy."

After they came back from the store, Chris was still looking for trouble. "I got some matches," he told Lil Ronald.

"Let me see." Lil' Ronald stuck his gloved hand out.

Chris let Lil' Ronald see the matches, and said, "Let's go around back and set something on fire."

"Nah, Aunt Cristal can see us from her window, we gotta go behind the other building."

"Okay," Chris said. The boys went behind the very next building and began playing with the matches, trying to set trees on fire. They couldn't accomplish their goal. It was too cold outside. Chris came up with a better idea. "Let's set one of them old cars on fire," he said. Lil' Ronald looked at Chris like he said they should jump in front of a speeding train. "You scared?!" Chris challenged.

"I ain't scared of shit." Lil' Ronald's mouth was already foul, just like Chris'. "Come on, let's do it."

Like burglars, the boys snuck to the far side of the complex and found an old Ford with the doors unlocked. They went back and forth for a while about who would get inside and set the car on fire. Neither one really wanted to get inside the car. "I'll do it, you chicken," Chris said. He then got inside the back of the car and looked around while Lil' Ronald watched his back. Aside from an old lady down the walkway, there was no one outside where they were. Chris lit one match and dropped it on the floor of the dirty car. He then threw the rest of the book on the floor and jumped out, slamming the door behind him. "Let's go!" He and Lil' Ronald ran a safe distance away from the car and hid while they watched the flames inside the car grow.

As the flames grew out of control and smoke began to escape through the windows of the car, Lil' Ronald said, "Come on, let's go." He led the way back to Cristal's apartment. As soon as they bent the corner, they saw Cristal standing in front of the building with a belt in her hand. Keyona was standing right beside her.

"Get your little asses in the house!" Cristal hissed. "Y'all wanna hit little girls wit' snowballs?" she popped Chris in the back of the head as he walked by. Keyona smiled.

Later on as darkness fell, Frank and Baby Face, strapped with Uzis, sat across the street from Carole's Lounge in an old Cadillac with light tints on the windows. Patiently, they waited for more than an hour for their target to come out.

Frank and Baby Face had their murder charges dismissed for lack of evidence and were back in business. Frank had a new outlook on the streets and a new game plan as well.

"It's game time," Frank said, tapping Baby Face. They both hopped out the car in ski masks. Walking swiftly, they crossed the street against traffic and opened fire with the fully automatic weapons. They sprayed more than forty rounds in seconds and cut down three older men in fur coats, leaving them bloody and twisted on the snow-covered sidewalk. As Frank and Baby Face roared away in the Cadillac, Big Teddy and two of his men were left dead in front of the lounge.

Washington, D.C., Thursday, February 7, 1981

In life, many times, things were thrust upon a man by circumstances and forced him to play the hand he was dealt. Morris was such a man. He was a fifty two-year-old hustler and old school gangster that was the top man of what was left of The Black Widow's crew since Big Teddy had been murdered. Morris was sitting in the lounge surrounded by his bodyguards. The whole crew was on high alert since no one had an idea who murdered Big Teddy and his men.

The phone behind the bar rang and the bartender answered it. "It's for you," the bartender said to Morris, handing him the phone.

"Yeah," Morris said, sipping his drink.

"I always respected you, Moe," a deep voice said.

"Who the fuck is this?!" Morris snapped.

"Go somewhere where we can talk in private."

Morris went into the back office and picked up the phone. "Who the hell is this?"

"T-Bone."

Morris said nothing for a moment. He couldn't believe what he'd just put together. T-Bone was behind Big Teddy's murder; he'd reached out from federal prison and had Big Teddy hit. "Ty, what the hell is goin' on?"

"Niggas forgot about me, forgot that I'm family, momma's only boy."

"So, you uh ..." Morris knew he had to watch what he said on the phone. "So, you go against the grain?"

T-Bone huffed out a small laugh. "I never went against the grain, you know that. Somebody else went against the grain. I'm only correctin' a wrong. Dig?"

Morris and the rest of the crew knew that Big Teddy was wrong for the way he was carrying T-Bone, but nobody said anything about it. They didn't dare challenge Big Teddy, he was too strong amongst the crew and in the streets. Big Teddy was one of the men that dropped bodies in the streets for The Black Widow when he first came home from Lorton in the early seventies he rose through the ranks quickly and became the backbone of the crew after a while. When The Black Widow was murdered, he felt that it was only right for him to run the show. "Where do we go from here, Ty?"

"Here's what you do, go outside, only take two men, you'll see my peoples."

"How do I know it's not a hit?"

"I told you that I always respected you. If I felt otherwise, I wouldn't give you a heads up, you woulda been seen."

Morris thought about the situation for a second. He believed T-Bone. If T-Bone wanted him hit, he would've been hit with Big Teddy. "Okay, Ty."

"I'll call back in thirty minutes." T-Bone hung up.

When Morris got off the phone, he told his men what was going on. They thought he was crazy, but went along with the plan. Many of them were still loyal to The Black Widow and knew that T-Bone would be running the show if he were home. With two of his men, Morris stepped out into the cold night air. H Street was busy and full of nightlife.

Across the street from the lounge, Baby Face and Bennie leaned against an old Chevy. Bennie had beat his murder charge thanks to Frank for having the witnesses hit by Baby Face and his crew. Bennie was now down with their crew. Frank told him that he could get some real money if he got down with them.

Morris and his two men cautiously crossed the street with their eyes on the two youngsters. Everybody had their hands on their concealed weapons.

"Who's doin' the talkin'?" Morris eyed the two youngsters. He was certain they weren't in charge.

"I am." Fred stepped out of the Chevy.

Morris looked at Fred with a confused look on his face. He knew Fred from down Lorton. "You put this together?"

Morris asked.

"Nah, but I'm on the team. It's business, nothing more," Fred said. "Where can we talk?"

"Considering what's going on, we can talk out here."

"Cool," Fred said. He and Morris walked around the car, and stood alone on the sidewalk. Fred laid everything out as Frank said T-Bone wanted it. A block away with a car load of Valley Green killers, Frank watched the situation unfold. If anything went wrong, a lot of bodies were going to drop. Fred told Morris that T-Bone didn't want to have him hit, in fact, he wanted him calling the shots for the crew. However, T-Bone wanted Morris to know that it would really be him giving Morris the shots to call. T-Bone also wanted his woman and son taken care of. He wanted Frank and his crew put on with a heroin connect, just like the deal The Black Widow had going on with Frank.

"Damn, he want a lot, don't he?" Morris lit a Newport while watching his back like a fugitive.

"Just what he deserves, if he was home he would be runnin' things, you know that, Morris."

"If he was home his mother might still be alive, too," Morris said with a touch of sarcasm.

"Yeah, but that's neither here nor there. I told you how he wants shit now. You can take it or leave it."

"What if I leave it?"

Fred smiled. "You're a smart dude, use your imagination, but keep in mind that if it goes to another level that all those that are still loyal to The Black Widow will be loyal to her son. Think about that."

"I'm goin' back inside," Morris said.

"Later." Fred watched Morris and his men go back inside the lounge. Baby Face and Bennie gave him a look like, What's up? "He gon' do the right thing." Fred said to the youngsters as they all jumped in the car. "Morris always makes the smart move, he been like that for years."

A short while later, back inside the lounge, Morris was on the phone with T-Bone. "We'll work everything out when I come out there to see you," Morris said. He was going to fly out to Leavenworth to talk business with T-Bone.

"Moe."

"Yeah."

"You can trust me," T-Bone said.

Minimum Security, Wednesday, April 26, 1981

Scores of convicts filled the dorm, some laying around, others watching TV or playing cards, just doing time. G-Train sat on his bunk in the back reading the The Washington Post. The article was about the history of Lorton and how violent it had become. A lot of the information G-Train had never heard before.

In 1910, the U.S. Government acquired land along the Occoquan River in southeastern Fairfax County, Virginia. The Occoquan Workhouse was then built; it was later a place where D.C. sent its drunks, and after that it was a regular prison. When it was a workhouse for D.C. criminals of the early 1900s, it was believed that hard work would transform a convict into a model citizen. The convicts back then worked on a twelve hundred acre farm raising hogs, cattle and chickens; they also built many of the buildings on the land, including the dorms, chow hall, the old ice plant, and the hospital. On the very same land in 1913, the Hill was built, the Wall followed in the 1930s. In 1917, the Occoquan Workhouse, then a small prison housing only sixty convicts, became the center of a national controversy when a group of women—the notorious suffragists—were sent to the prison. The one hundred and seventy women had been arrested for protesting for women's right to vote. The protest was in front of the White House. The suffragists were beaten savagely, force-fed, made to live in filthy conditions, and much more for their struggle. News began to spread quickly about their horrible and inhumane treatment. Support for their cause began to grow as their struggle drew the line in the last phase of many struggles and protest that endured for decades, and resulted in women obtaining the right to vote in 1920, under the 19th Amendment of the U.S. Constitution. A historical marker was later placed on the prison grounds as a tribute to the sacrifice the women made for all American women, thus making Occoquan famous.

G-Train put the newspaper down and went to the bathroom to blow a bag of dope. He didn't have a worry in the world. Luck was on his side, it was always on his side. He'd beaten all of his murder charges, somehow. He was to do the few months he got for violating parole over Minimum, which was nothing. It was sweet, it had no walls or fence around it; he would be going home every day as a part of the work release program. As soon as he got out on work release, he planned to kill Frank and wash his hands of the whole situation.

After blowing the dope, G-Train called his new boy, Faggie Tony, into the stall. He bent the punk over and tried to tear open his asshole. The punk moaned loudly as if he were a real woman, telling G-Train to, "Fuck me harder."

G-Train returned to his bunk after getting a shot of ass. Laying back nodding off the dope, thoughts of Sarah came to mind. He missed her so much. She was the best thing he ever had. Before he knew it, he'd drifted off to sleep.

Hours later, around three fifteen A.M., a black Cadillac pulled up in the parking lot of the prison. Three masked gunmen got out and rushed toward the dorm under the cover of darkness. One was armed with a shotgun, the other with two with .44 revolvers. They burst through the front door of the dorm while the convicts were sleep and grabbed the two C.O.s by the door. "Don't try to be no fuckin' hero," the gunman with the shotgun said to the C.O.s as one of his partners flicked on the lights and ordered all the convicts against the wall at gunpoint. Slowly, the convicts got against the wall, not under-standing what was going on. "We lookin' for two snitches!" said the gunman with the shotgun. "Nobody move, nobody gets hurt!"

The two gunman with the .44s went down the line of convicts looking for their man. They didn't see him.

"G-Train, come on out. You can't hide!" said the gunman with the shotgun. G-Train knew the gunmen had come for him. He never thought they would come inside the prison to get him. It was unheard of. G-Train was hiding under a bunk as one of the gunmen began checking under all bunks. Knowing his time was running out, G-Train slid from under the bunk and tried to make a run for the door. The gunman with the shotgun caught him right in the chest with the first blast, taking G-Train off his feet and blowing him over a bunk. The two gunmen with the .44s ran over top of G-Train and pumped him full of bullets. Just like that, the gunmen were out of the door and running back to the Cadillac. They jumped inside the car where the getaway driver was waiting and disappeared into the night.

Miles away from the prison, the gunmen ditched the Cadillac and the weapons as they jumped into an old Chevy Nova and headed up I-95. Fred was behind the wheel with Frank riding shotgun, Bennie and Baby Face were in the back seat. "That's how you go get a muthafucka," Fred said. He was the one that came up with the idea to go inside the prison and kill G-Train.

Washington, D.C., Friday, April 28, 1981

G-Train's slaying inside a Lorton prison was big news and triggered an intensive investigation by the FBI and city officials who said the murder was the first prison "break-in" they could recall in the area. Officials in Fairfax County, where the minimum security facility was located, renewed their complaints about the risk to local residents due to the violence that came with the Lorton facility.

Meanwhile, Cristal was Uptown in the white part of Northwest shopping. She was working her credit card move. After breaking off Greater Washington's Diamonds for twenty thousand dollars in goods, Cristal headed across the Maryland line into Chevy Chase and went inside Saks Fifth Avenue dressed like a young businesswoman in her blue Burberry dress and black heels. Cristal mixed in with the uppity crowd. She set her sights on the Louis Vuitton bags, but something else caught her eye. Never one to forget a face, Cristal followed behind the woman until they ended up in the shoe section. Taking another look at the woman, Cristal knew her eyes weren't playing tricks on her. Anger boiled inside of her as memories of the little bitch came back to her. Cristal wanted to punch the little bitch in the face and rip her hair out right on the spot, but she was on a mission. She went back to what she was doing, but as she was looking over the Louis Vuitton bags her conscience began to bother her. She went to look for the woman. Ten minutes later, Cristal saw her in the fur section.

"Excuse me," Cristal said to the woman

"Do I know you?" The short woman looked Cristal up and down with attitude.

Cristal maintained her composure; she was trying hard to be the bigger woman. "I'm Ty's baby's mother."

Tonya Baker folded her arms and rolled her eyes as soon as she realized who Cristal was. Ms. Baker was also T-Bone's baby's mother. Her son was going on five-years-old; his name was Paul Baker. "What do you want?" She sucked her teeth.

"You had that baby, didn't you?"

"That's none of your damn business."

Cristal was getting fed up and about to blow. "Look, I don't want to get into no shit wit' you, but if you got a baby by Ty, the child got a right to know his father."

"Ty lost any say so about my son when he told me to get rid of him." Ms. Baker was still bitter.

"People make mistakes, you know that."

"What's your name again?" Ms. Baker asked.

"Cristal."

"Cristal, I respect where you're comin' from, but if Ty wants anything to do wit' his son, tell 'em to call me." She gave Cristal her phone number.

U.S.P. Leavenworth, Sumday, April 30, 1981

Inside the dangerous walls of the Hot House, as Leavenworth was called, there was twelve hundred or so hardcore convicts. Among them was a group of convicts that were in a class of their own, federal officials called them D.C. Blacks. Most of them were Lorton convicts that'd been sent to the feds. Ever since the 1930s, D.C. Blacks had been one of the most difficult groups to control in the feds. They were known to be convicts that didn't give a fuck and were willing to push everything to the limit. Most of the D.C. Blacks were strong-armers that made a living from "taking."

T-Bone was an exception to that rule. He was one of the few D.C. Blacks that was getting money in the Hot House on the strength of his drug connects on the outside. He was taking care of a lot of the homies in the feds, even though many of them were still living off the land through extortion and robbery. T-Bone had Morris under his thumb; he'd gotten him to put Frank on his feet with a kilo of heroin. On the strength of T-Bone, Morris was also paying for two buses to take visitors to Leavenworth twice a month so they could see their loved ones. Morris made sure T-Bone's family was taken care of as well.

T-Bone's status as a big dope man inside the Hot House had a lot of people unhappy, some were sending notes to the SIS—the jail-house version of the FBI—informing them about T-Bone's activities. He'd spent more than a few months in the hole behind those notes, but the SIS could never put anything on him. A lot of good came from the time he spent in the hole, T-Bone kicked his dope habit.

Back in population, T-Bone was in Cell Block B on the fifth tier. He and Wookie were cellies. They'd gotten cool through Ronald down Youth Center I. Wookie schooled T-Bone to what was what in the feds. He warned T-Bone that the racist C.O.s hated D.C. Blacks and saw them as unruly and deserving of harsh discipline. He also warned T-Bone about the Aryan Brotherhood—the ABs—that also hated D.C. Blacks, although they tried their best to avoid confrontation with the D.C. Blacks. Like all other Lorton convicts of his caliber, T-Bone caught on quick. If he could survive down Lorton, he could survive anywhere, in any penitentiary. Besides, he had some real soldiers on his team; in such an environment of hostility and tension, when D.C. Blacks attacked they came like a pack of wolves, taking the situation to the extreme. There was no other way to carry it when all odds were against them.

T-Bone passed Nate Bailey on the way to the phone. They gave each other five. T-Bone picked up the phone and dialed the number he had written on the little piece of paper in his hand. He had to try to correct his wrongs.

"Hello." A little boy answered the phone with a TV blasting in the background.

"Who is this?" A deep voice jumped on the phone.

"Ty, is Tonya home?" T-Bone sensed ill feelings.

"Hold on," the deep voice said with an attitude.

"Hello." Ms. Baker said in her little girl voice.

"What's up, Tonya?"

Ms. Baker paused for a moment. "I didn't think you'd call."

"You got the right to hate me..."

"Tell me about it."

"I done made a lot of mistakes in my life, I can't change that. I know I was wrong for how I carried things between us, but try to understand that I was just comin' to prison and still had a lot to learn then. I've grown a lot since then. We have a son together. I want to know him. I trust that you can open up your heart and try to understand that."

"I can't believe you. You sure know how to talk to a woman when you want something." Ms. Baker shook her head.

"It's not that. I know that I was wrong. I just want a chance to correct that wrong. I can't have a son out there and not know him. Can we work somethin' out?"

It took a lot of talking, but T-Bone got Ms. Baker to put her animosity to the side.

"I would never use my son against you. He deserves to know his father," Ms. Baker said.

"You gon' let him come see me?"

"I really don't want him comin' in no prison for real."

"I respect that, but there's no other way for me to see him right now."

"I ain't lettin no other woman bring him, either."

"You can bring him," T-Bone cracked.

"Please, I can't afford that. Where you at, Kansas?"

"Don't worry about the money. You won't even have to spend a dime. I got all that covered."

"Oh yeah, you still the man, huh?" She smiled to herself.

"You know me."

"I'll think about it. I'm sure we can work somethin' out."

Maximum Security, Monday, May 14, 1981

Things had gotten a little better behind the Wall since the riot. If men didn't stand for something, they'd fall for anything.

With most of the men that Ronald was close to gone to the feds, he had a lot of time to himself. He spent that time reading, working out, and teaching a youngster to box. Ronald's reading had drawn him to the study of Islam. He was attracted to the teachings of the Prophet Muhammad (PEACE

BE UPON HIM), just like Muhammad Ali, Malcolm X, and NBA great Kareem Abdul-Jabbar. At the time, Ronald was only studying the basics. He understood that the word "sunni," as in sunni muslim, was taken from the Arabic word sunnah which meant, "practice" or "way," but when used Islamicly, it meant the practice of Prophet Muhammad (PEACE BE UPON HIM).

"What's up, Ronnie?" Slide said as he stepped into Ronald's cell. "We goin' runnin'?"

Ronald sat his Qur'an down. "Yeah, I was waitin' on you."

Slide was the youngster Ronald was teaching how to box. Ronald took a liking to him; the youngster was thorough and reminded Ronald of himself when he first came to prison. Slide was a nineteen-year-old that had been sent behind the Wall for catching too many stabbings over Youth Center I in his first eighteen months. In fact, the youngster picked up the name Slide over the Center because of the way he stabbed his victims and slid away in a fashion that allowed him to get away with assault. The Youth Center I administration finally got hip to Slide and sent his young ass behind the Wall. By that time he'd stabbed seven niggas over the Center.

When Slide first got behind the Wall, a known butthole bandit tried to befriend him in hopes of tricking him out of the ass. Ronald was in the cell next to Slide and liked his style. Ronald hipped Slide to the butthole bandit's intentions one day after chow. Slide put the knife in the butthole bandit as soon as he got back to the block, stabbing him more than fifteen times. Ronald knew the youngster was about his business after that.

"Come on, let's hit the track," Ronald said as he led the way down the tier.

Later on after the four P.M. count, Ronald was headed for the butler building. The Moors had outside guest coming in to speak. Visitors were also coming.

Convicts and their visitors filled the large room as the

outside guest spoke about the strength of the Black race and all they'd been through in the world. Sitting in the back with Synthia, Ronald listened to the speaker closely. He was feeling every word. A few minutes later, Fly walked up behind Ronald and tapped him on the shoulder. He whispered in his ear, "Your turn."

Ronald and Synthia eased out of the room and down the hall to another room where convicts had set up a "hit spot"—a Wall version of a hotel. Boxes were stacked on top of each other, creating different sections for convicts to take their women for some "private" time. When Ronald and Synthia got in the room, there were already four other couples inside doing their thing. In the room next door there were four hookers taking whoever was sent their way.

Ronald's spot was already laid out with clean sheets and blankets. He quickly made a thick, comfortable pallet and laid Synthia down like they were at home, even though they only had twenty minutes. He began kissing her as he pulled up her skirt. She was wearing no panties. Breathing hard, Synthia said, "Come on, daddy, we ain't got all day." Ronald undid his pants and slid inside Synthia's tight wetness. "Aaaahhh, yeah, just like that, baby." She needed him inside her so bad. What she did for herself at home was nothing like the fullness she now felt with every deep stroke. Ronald slid one arm under her right leg and bent it back until her knee was touching her breast. "Sssss, oh yeah, daddy ... aaaaaahhhh." She wrapped her arms around his neck. "Oooooh ... I love you ... I love you ... I love you so mu ... oh yessssss ..." her eyes rolled back in her head as Ronald began digging deeper and harder, hitting all the right spots, making her moan as if they were alone in their bedroom. "Ahhhhhhh ... I'm ... I'm cummin'."

Chapter 14

U.S.P. Lewisburg, Friday, September 6, 1981

Ronald was sitting in the crowded library reading through the law books as he waited for Cadillac to meet him. The ball game was different now. He was in the feds.

Lorton's overcrowding was a dangerous problem dating back to the 1950s. The D.C. D.O.C. would have to send loads of convicts to the federal system to try to deal with the overcrowding. Aside from the overcrowding, politics played a major role in the loads being sent to the feds. Election time in Fairfax County, VA. was a time when Northern Virginia's politicians needed an easy target for their movements. Feuding with D.C. officials about the thirty five hundred acres of country land that the Lorton facilities sat on was always a topic in the local papers. Fairfax officials were pressing D.C. to clean up the lack of security and overcrowding of Lorton. A commissioned study by the Fairfax County government found that the Lorton complex was threatened by major security problems that made it "vulnerable to attack and takeover" by its convicts. The study also stated that "convicts run the place." G-Train's murder inside a Lorton facility was a big issue that Fairfax officials were pressing in order to accomplish their goal of having Lorton shut down.

The commissioned study came in the form of a one thousand, four hundred and sixty seven page report on public safety. The report mentioned the discoveries of hundreds of weapons inside Lorton. Behind the Wall, in a twelve month period, one hundred and twenty seven assaults—including three slayings—took place; out of the four hundred and fifty six weapons that'd been discovered in that time, one hundred and twenty four were manufactured outside of the prison's walls, including a .38 revolver and a .25 automatic. Drug discoveries came in at four hundred and ten. Finally, the report criticized sanitary conditions stating that stray cats roamed the prison from the surrounding community and wooded areas that may carry rabies. A Fairfax County Board Chairman made a public statement, "Chaos is right in our backyards. ... the District has dumped its trash at our back door and won't even watch over it. Inmates run the place like the Keystone Kops; the prison is dangerously understaffed, overcrowded, and grossly inadequate for convicts prone to such violence. I vow to put an end to the circus ..."

Under pressure, the D.C. D.O.C. made an attempt to clean up the thirty three percent overcrowding by sending loads of convicts to the feds. Out of the blue, around one A.M., convicts were herded onto buses and rushed off to places like Leavenworth, Terre Haute, and Atlanta.

On a bus load of forty, Ronald sat next to Slide as they headed up the highway to Lewisburg. They, along with the other Lorton convicts, rolled with the punches. Ronald and Slide spoke about all that they'd heard about the feds during the bus ride. They knew how much drama came with being labeled a D.C. Black. Ronald's mindset was to stay focused and to survive by all means. Slide's mindset was to kill anything that got in his way. He was for the home team all the way. He knew his homies were strong in the feds, even outnumbered and outgunned. Slide was ready to carry that torch; as far as he was concerned, if his homies were called D.C. Blacks, then that's what he was.

When Ronald, Slide, and the other Lorton convicts arrived at Lewisburg, they were stripped and ordered by the redneck C.O.s to open their mouths, stick out their tongues, lift up their dicks and balls, bend over, and spread their ass cheeks while the C.O.s looked on. Ronald hated entering prisons and going through the humiliation of strip searches. No matter how many times he'd been stripped searched over the years, he still hated it, but he had to deal with it. What was new for the Lorton convicts was the color of the C.O.s they had to deal with. They were used to dealing with black C.O.s coming from Lorton. The redneck Lewisburg C.O.s acted like they had a point to prove to the D.C. Blacks and stated that there would be no Lorton bullshit in "The Burg." Yeah, right! Intimidation was useless when it came to Lorton convicts.

Walking into the library, Cadillac saw Ronald sitting in the back reading a law book. He walked over and took a seat beside Ronald. "What's up, Ronnie?" Cadillac took a look around the library. There were three ABs in the far corner of the room talking business.

"Ain't too much up with me," Ronald said, following Cadillac's eyes over to the ABs. Cadillac was the first homie in the feds to school Ronald to how things went. His thing with the ABs was to keep them in their place. Cadillac didn't care who they were supposed to be. Just like George Jackson, Cadillac knew that in the face of death that a man could only die once. "Somethin' up wit' them ABs?" Ronald asked.

"Nah, I was just checkin' them out," Cadillac said, checking out their tattoos of white supremacy—daggers dripping with blood, naked women, and clover leaves with 666 on it.

"What did you want to holla at me about?" Ronald asked.

"Check this out." Cadillac leaned closer to Ronald and lowered his voice. "They brought a bus in from Marion last night. Marcel Perkins was on it. They got him in the hole right now, but they should be lettin' him out today. We need to talk to Slide and make sure we can get them to leave that situation alone while we up here. We gotta all be on the same team in this spot. It's us against the world."

Ronald sighed. He knew that Slide was down for the home team one hundred percent and was willing to stand on the front line. But, Slide was also the kind of nigga that refused to be rocked to sleep. He'd shot Marcel' s younger brother,— Allen, on the streets. Marcel had vowed to punish Slide whenever he caught him. Now, coming from Marion for a jailhouse murder, Marcel was sure to be a problem.

"I don't know if Slide gon' be comfortable wit' Marcel bein' on the same compound wit' him. You know he shot Allen," Ronald said. "Marcel done already let it be known that he gon' see Slide first chance he get."

"I understand all that, but we ain't got time to be goin' at each other up here, we got other shit to worry about. I'ma make sure Marcel leave that shit alone. You make sure Slide leave it alone. Okay?" Cadillac said.

"How you know Marcel gon' leave it alone?"

"He ain't got no choice, he ain't gon' come here and start no shit wit' the homies. He can get right back on a bus somewhere wit' that shit. Let me take care of Marcel. You take care of Slide, he got my word that that shit ain't gon' go nowhere."

"Let me talk to Slide first. I'll let you know what's up then. Cool?" Ronald said.

"Cool."

"We can go holla at shorty right now," Ronald said.

Cadillac and Ronald went back to the block to holla at Slide. Slide had a lot of respect for Cadillac, but Ronald seemed to do all the talking as the three of them sat in the cell that Ronald and Slide shared. Ronald stressed the importance of squashing the beef for the sake of being outnumbered in the feds.

Sitting on the bed, Slide said, "I respect the code and all that. I'm all about the homies, but this nigga been sendin' word about what he gon' do to me and all this other bullshit. I can't be on the same pound wit' him." Slide shook his head in disagreement.

Cadillac respected the stand Slide was taking, but still voiced his peace. "Slide, it ain't like he did somethin' to you. You shot his brother. His brother tried to rob you and you popped his ass, that's what you was supposed to do. I'ma make sure he leave the shit alone. If he don't want to leave it alone I'll take care of him myself. We don't need to be goin' at each other up here, we gotta stand together. That's what makes us strong."

It took a little talking, but Cadillac and Ronald got Slide to agree not to move on Marcel as long as Cadillac could assure him that Marcel wouldn't move on him.

"You got my word, Marcel ain't gon' move on you," Cadillac said to Slide before he left the cell.

U.S.P. Lewisburg, Saturday, September 14, 1981

Outside along with most of the D.C. Blacks, Ronald and Cadillac were watching the D.C. flag football team play the New York team. D.C. was up twenty one to fourteen on the bright sunny day. Bird, the quarterback for the D.C. team, dropped back and threw a forty-yard pass to his wide out. Touchdown! The D.C. Blacks on the sideline went off like they were at a Redskins game at R.F.K.

"What's up wit' Frank out there?" Cadillac asked Ronald.

"He doin' real good out there, he just sent me some pictures and a little bit of money."

"Yeah, he took some money over my woman's house the other day. But, I ain't been able to catch him on the phone." Cadillac watched a player for the New York team run a punt back to mid-field.

"Frank movin' fast as a speedin' bullet out there, but he takin' care of a lot of niggas that's in, though. He supposed to bring my woman and son up next week."

"That's alright. He a good nigga."

Meanwhile, Marcel was on the move. He'd agreed to leave the situation with Slide alone, he'd given Cadillac his word. Nevertheless, he planned to butcher Slide anyway. Couldn't nobody tell him what he could and couldn't do in the feds. He had ten years in the federal system under his belt, plus, two jailhouse murders. With a baseball cap pulled down tight on his head, Marcel slid into Slide's block and eased down the tier. He knew that most of the homies were outside watching the football game; he also knew that Slide was in the block sick from the flu. Under his jacket, Marcel carried a ten inch penitentiary dagger that could gut a bull. Looking inside the cell that Ronald and Slide shared, Marcel found it empty. He then looked around the deserted block. Two ABs were at the end of the tier watching him like a hawk. A punk dressed like a nasty hooker was folding his man's clothes in front of a cell at the other end of the tier. Marcel checked the TV room for Slide. It was empty as well.

In a nearby cell buying some tea from a Philly dude by the name of Muhammad that ran a jailhouse store, Slide saw Marcel creeping around the block. Sick and weak, Slide was in no position to defend himself; he was wearing shower shoes and had left his knife under his pillow.

"What's wrong, youngster?" Muhammad asked, seeing the concern on Slide's face.

Slide put Muhammad on point about what was up with Marcel and asked him for a knife and a pair of boots. Muhammad had to think twice about giving Slide a knife for a D.C. dude. Such an act could spark a bloody war between Muslims and D.C. Blacks, or Philly and D.C. Blacks. "It ain't gon' be no problem." Slide explained how Cadillac had assured him that if Marcel tried to move on him that he would be dealt with.

"Here you go." Muhammad gave Slide a mean knife.

Coming in the block, Cadillac and Ronald saw Marcel walking down the tier. He was way out of bounds, he'd never came in their block since he'd been on the compound. Ronald and Cadillac walked up on Marcel, who looked nervous. Tension was thick in the air.

"What you doin up in here? You don't never come over here," Cadillac said, glaring at Marcel.

"I was lookin' for the ticket man. He owe me some money," Marcel lied, looking from Cadillac to Ronald and back.

"Who the fuck you think you talkin' to? You think I just came to jail yesterday?!" Cadillac slapped the shit out of Marcel. "Huh?! Who the fuck you think you playin' wit'?!"

Marcel stumbled backward and pulled the huge knife.

"Nigga, I'ma make you eat that blade!" Cadillac and Ronald carefully approached Marcel. Marcel swung the murder metal, hitting Cadillac in the arm. It was his last swing. Ronald caught him with a left hook that knocked him backward, dazing him. Slide came out of nowhere and slammed six-inches of steel in Marcel's neck from the blind side. Warn! Warn! Warn! Slide hit him three more times, all in the neck. Blood was everywhere. Cadillac grabbed Marcel from behind and slammed him to the floor. Slide was dead on his ass, slamming steel into his chest.

"The law comin'!" a voice called out.

Ronald, Cadillac, and Slide left the bloody body and rushed downstairs to the first floor where they cleaned up and Slide got rid of the knife.

Twenty minutes later, the prison was locked down. The murder investigation began with body searches of all convicts in the block that Marcel was murdered in. Cadillac was the first to get locked down for the murder; he had a stab wound on his arm.

Ronald and Slide were laying in their bunks sweating bullets. They'd survived the body searches, but knew that they weren't home safe yet. The heat was sure to come down. All Ronald could think of was getting life without parole in the feds for a jailhouse murder. He had a chance of making parole within three years, and now he faced the thought of life without parole. His stomach was tied in knots. Although he would never admit it, Ronald was scared to death; thoughts of his family flooded his mind.

"I knew I shoulda moved on that nigga as soon as he got out the hole," Slide said out of the blue. He wasn't tripping off the threat of life without parole. He was mad at himself for letting Ronald and Cadillac talk him out of what his heart told him to do. He could've lost his life. "I knew he was goin' to try his hand."

"Yeah, you was right," Ronald said, not up for the conversation at all.

The sound of heavy prison keys, lots of them, could be heard coming down the tier. A squad of C.O.s and a lieutenant were coming down the tier; the lieutenant had two pictures in his hand. Ronald knew they were coming to get him and Slide. Backed by his officers, the tall white lieutenant stopped in front of Ronald's and Slide's cell. Ronald's heart pounded as if he was in a speeding car with his life flashing before his eyes moments before a fatal head-on collision.

"Cuff up fellas," said the lieutenant

U.S.P. Leavenworth, Wednesday, December 27, 1981

In prison, tension built and built until a violent eruption exploded like Mt. Vesuvius with volcanic devastation. For those who knew and understood the price of life and death, they enjoyed and cherished times of peace. But, once blood has been spilled, all bets were off.

Things inside the Hot House had gotten out of control.

D.C. Blacks and the ABs had had a run-in over a drug debt owed to the ABs. A convict from Lorton wasn't trying to pay his heroin bill to a white convict that was working for the ABs. The ABs stepped in to collect. The D.C. Blacks strapped up ready for war, letting it be known that nobody was going to do shit to anybody from D.C. After some intense politicing, T-Bone agreed to pay the debt for his homie to keep the peace in the Hot House. Five-hundred dollars was nothing to him.

Days later, a homemade bomb went off in the cell of a D.C. Black. The bomb was made out of thousands of tiny sulfur match-heads that'd been packed into a shampoo bottle and then wrapped with nails. The bomb was attached to the light in the cell of the D.C. Black. When the convict rushed into his cell and flipped on the light switch, the electric current from the light made the match-heads ignite. The bomb exploded like a real grenade, sending flying nails all over the cell and into the face of the convict. The convict survived, but lost his eye sight.

The prison was locked down for a couple of weeks while an investigation was conducted. The administration feared that the ABs had moved on the D.C. Blacks. That was wrong. The Mexican Mafia was behind the bombing. It was rumored that the attack was a favor for the ABs. As soon as the prison came off of lock down, D.C. Blacks went at members of the Mexican Mafia and the ABs. So much steel was slinging that outside help had to be brought inside the prison. Blood was everywhere, all over the walls, all over the floors. Four bodies dropped. Two Mexicans, one AB, and one D.C. Black. In the midst of the drama, T-Bone butchered one of the top ABs in the Hot House, although he didn't kill him.

Federal officials didn't know what to do, they began to pressure D.C. officials to take back their problem and move the D.C. Blacks back to Lorton. However, D.C. didn't have any space, even if they wanted to bring the Lorton convicts back. The feds were stuck with the problem and the war that was just beginning. Buses began rolling, sending D.C. Blacks all over the federal system, a lot of them were sent to U.S.P. Marion, which was the so-called "end of the line" for the "worst of the worst," according to the feds.

Even with all the transfers, the hole inside the Hot House was still packed as a slave ship. Three, and sometimes four, convicts were packed inside dungeon-like cells that were built in the early 1900s. T-Bone, Dave Ford, Dave Ashby, and Earl Coleman-BEY were in a cell together. Directly across from them in another four-man cell was Pearl Early, Joe James-BEY, Eddie Mathis, and Bird. Mail had just been passed out. Blocking out all the noise in the hole, T-Bone read the letter from Cristal:

12-27-81

Dear Ty,

I love you and miss you so much, baby, don't you ever forget that. I will always be here for you. No matter how hard it gets, I'm here for you. You are the only man I have ever loved. No one can ever take your place. Our love is worth whatever comes with it. I lay in the bed at night and the loneliness kills me, but I refuse to be with another. I knew what I was in store for when you first went down Lorton, but I swear to God, I never knew that it would hurt so bad to have you hundreds of miles away from me and Chris. But, like you always say, it gets greater later. I sure wish it was later!

Frank gave me $2,500 yesterday, I'm sending you $1,500 of that. He gives me money for you every time I see him. He's "the man" out here. If you only knew. They treat him like a movie star in this city.

Me and Synthia are doing okay, trying hard to raise these bad ass little boys. Ronald's brother,

Roland, comes to get them a lot; he takes them to the gym with him. They seem to love that. I had to tear their little asses up last week. They set their bedroom on fire. No one got hurt. I put out the fire myself.

Ronald, Slide, and Cadillac are on their way to Marion. Ronald said they are still under investigation for murder, but no charges have been filed. Synthia is worried to death. I feel her pain.

I love you. Be strong, keep your head up in there, and know that you are loved out here. We need you out here so bad.

Your Baby
Cristal

P.S. Don't let nobody see my pictures, either. They're just for you, Daddy. Something to think about. I got all this pussy just waiting for you.

T-Bone smiled and put the letter back in the envelope. Cristal would always be his baby. He lusted off the naked pictures of his baby for a second, and then told the homies the news about Ronald, Slide, and Cadillac being sent to the Southern Tip—Marion.

U.S.P. Marion, Sunday June 11, 1982

Marion was tucked away in a national refuge, surrounded by forests, lakes, and wildlife. Clusters of low level buildings dominated well kept lawns. Gun towers and chain-link fences with endless rolls of razor wire thrown between them were only a reminder of the dangerous convicts locked inside the prison. Racial tension suffocated Marion.

Ronald caught on quickly. Being from D.C., he had to, his life depended on it. Everyone was against him and his kind. He had to watch out for the ABs, the Mexican Mafia, and the racist, redneck C.O.s. Hate between blacks and whites was magnified tenfold inside of Marion. Nevertheless, Lorton had prepared Ronald and his comrades for anything the federal system had to offer. Marion was the host of countless escape attempts, group uprisings, convict-on-convict assaults, assaults on C.O.s, and murders; after all, Marion ended up replacing the notorious U.S.P. Alcatraz.

At the same time, although Lorton housed seven times as many convicts as Marion, the Lorton complex was the host of more than seventy murders between the years of 1974 and 1982. Between six and seven bodies dropped every year—true bill! One year alone there were twenty five physical escapes and one hundred and fourteen walkaways; in two separate incidents, convicts escaped by pulling C.O.s from their patrol vans and crashing them through the fence. No wonder the feds couldn't control D.C. Blacks. Maybe they should've checked with the Pentagon. In 1980, a management team from the Pentagon studied Lorton convicts under the auspices of collecting intelligence on what made them so aggressive and hostile. The program was called the Lorton Transformation Project. The Pentagon team concluded that Lorton held some of the most violent men in the country, men who were short-fused with poor attitudes. A "typical" convict, the report said, had no empathy, was impulsive, self-centered with no regard for others, and prone to violence. Lorton, as an institution, was said to be more responsible for crime in D.C. than anything else, it bred criminals. So much so that out of five hundred Lorton convicts, nine out of ten were repeat felons. To throw such men into Marion was to throw a stick of dynamite into a burning building.

Ronald, Slide, and Cadillac were sent to the Control Unit where the racial tension was burning like a forest fire. Ronald was put on C range along with Cadillac, Nate Bailey, Lue Lue, and two other D.C. Blacks that he didn't know from Lorton. Slide was sent on another range.

Laying in his small, one-man cell writing Synthia a letter, Ronald heard the steel gate open at the front of the range that separated the tier from where the C.O.s' station was. He heard the keys coming down the tier. Two white C.O.s stepped in front of his cell and told him he had a legal visit. They chained him up and took him to a small hearing room where he saw a tall white man in a cheap suit. Ronald knew the man had to be an FBI agent. "What the fuck is this all about?" Ronald looked at the two C.O.s, who now had smirks on their faces.

"Mr. Mays," the agent said, sitting behind an old metal desk. "I'm going to be straight with you..."

"Yeah, right." Ronald was still standing.

"You have a chance to go home in two years. I've read your file. You gotta bad break on the streets. You were a promising boxer before you came back to prison. You don't belong in prison. But, I'ma tell you, we're about to hand down indictments on that Lewisburg murder. If you're convicted of killing a convict inside a federal penitentiary, you can kiss your future good bye for good."

"Save it, you got the wrong man."

"Okay, have it your way. I'm giving you a chance to get out of Marion, maybe even go home early, but once you're indicted it'll be out of my hands. We know you didn't commit the murder. We want Cadillac Smith."

"Look, I done heard enough of this shit," Ronald said. He was then taken back to his cell.

Inside his cell, Ronald didn't feel like finishing his letter to Synthia. He was stressing. The FBI was really going to indict him, Cadillac, and Slide for murder. Ronald sighed. Life seemed to be an uphill struggle. Going on twenty five-years-old, Ronald was sitting in a cell in a unit of a prison that was a prison inside of prison. How bad could it get?

Marion's Control Unit, where Ronald had been housed for months, was a self-contained unit of the prison with four ranges of small one-man cells. In the Control Unit, there was another "prison inside of prison," it was called the box cars. The box cars were a group of cells behind a steel door that were separated from the rest of the Control Unit cells. When a convict was sent to the box cars that was the last stop, and the convict knew it as he sat in complete darkness behind an iron door with nothing in the cell with him. According to the feds, Marion's Control Unit was the most secure cell block the bureau had to offer. Yet and still, bodies kept dropping and wouldn't stop.

As Ronald laid in bed with his hands behind his head, all he could think about was his situation. He'd seen so much. The world was not a pretty place, not for a man that'd been through what he'd been through. Most couldn't imagine what he and his comrades had been through. In fact, the only people that he could even talk to about his present plight were his fellow comrades that had stood side-by-side with him on the front lines. No one else could understand where he was coming from. Ronald was a different man, but what bothered him the most was the fact that he was now numb to the effects on incarceration. The chains he was put in when leaving his cell didn't bother him anymore, neither did being confined in isolation. General population or the Control Unit was still prison, which part of the prison he did his time in didn't stop his time from running or make his time go faster. He felt that he was losing the part of his soul that made him human; compassion was being stripped from him with every second he spent in the Control Unit. On top of that, he and his comrades had to deal with their sworn enemies who shared the range with them—the ABs.

U.S.P. Marion, Saturday, July 25, 1982

The FBI was bluffing, trying to get somebody to talk and no one did. The Lewisburg murder investigation was dropped. That was a plus, but there were other problems on the home front for Ronald and the D.C. Blacks in the Southern Tip. They were in an "on sight" war with the ABs. It was hard to out right go to war in the Control Unit, so the warfare was taken to another level. An AB by the name of Conrad Tyler had thrown boiling hot coffee at Ronald from behind his cell bars as Ronald walked down the range going to the shower. The hot coffee missed Ronald's face, but burned the skin off his arm. Cadillac came out for rec right after Ronald and threw boiling piss on Conrad Tyler, telling him, "You fuckin' wit' the right ones, cracker."

"Fuck you, nigger." Tyler spat at Cadillac but missed. "You niggers ain't tough at all."

Days later, Cadillac threw a "shake bomb" in Conrad Tyler's cell. The bomb was a shampoo bottle filled with countless chemicals that would explode when shaken up thoroughly. The chemical explosion drew the attention of the C.O. behind the steel gate. A code was called and a number of redneck C.O.s rushed the range, taking Cadillac to the box cars in cuffs. Conrad Tyler was taken to the hospital. Cadillac and Tyler were right back on C range within the next two weeks.

Lue Lue, Ralph Walker, and Nate Bailey were on the front line as well, locking horns with the ABs.

Ronald got his hands on a broom stick and tied his knife to the end of it. He waited for an AB by the name of Peter Merriam to walk by his cell. When Merriam walked by the cell, Ronald harpooned Merriam, slamming the blade into Merriam's neck. Merriam didn't die and Ronald was locked down for the stabbing. After a short stay in the box cars, Ronald was returned to C range. Merriam was also returned to C range when he returned from the hospital. C range was out of control.

To add to the drama, the ABs had a C.O. working with them.

C.O. Bergman was a known Nazi.

After his eight A.M. hour in the rec cage, Ronald was

standing behind the bars of his cell keeping an eye on what was going on on the range. Two ABs, Tyler and Merriam, were in the rec cage working out. The rec cage sat on the other side of the tier, sealed off by wire mesh. Ronald heard a cell open down the range and saw another AB come out for his shower. The AB, Ivan Peabody, stopped in front of Ronald's cell and looked him in the eyes for a second. They glared at one another for what seemed like years. Deep hate was all that could be seen in their eyes. Peabody was 6 "3", two hundred and twenty pounds with a long Viking-like beard. "We gonna kill all you D.C. niggers before it's all over with," Peabody said in a calm voice.

Ronald spat in Peabody's face. "Fuck you, cracker!"

Slowly wiping the spit from his face with a smile as if he knew something Ronald did not, Peabody said, "You just watch." He then walked to the shower. Ronald could see his knife under his towel.

Forty minutes later, Ronald came out for his shower. Nate Bailey and Cadillac were in the box cars at the time for different kinds of assaults on the ABs. Ronald stopped at Lue Lue's cell for a minute and then headed for the shower, carefully passing every cell.

POW!

A gunshot went off. A "zip gun" had been fired from Conrad Tyler's cell. The bullet just missed Ronald's head and slammed into the shower. The "zip gun" was made of a makeshift pipe packed with a .32 caliber bullet and set off by electricity; it would only fire once. Ronald knew the "zip gun" would only fire once, but he didn't know how many ABs had one. Ronald carefully eased to the back of the range. Moments later, countless C.O.s rushed the range after hearing the gunshot. Ronald was cuffed and taken to the hearing room for questioning, but he had no information for the law. No bullets or "zip gun" was found.

Chapter 15

U.S.P. Marion, Wednesday, August 6, 1982

On D range in the Control Unit, Slide was in front of Big Naughty's cell. Big Naughty had just been sent to the Southern Tip from Lewisburg. Slide was telling him how things were going. The redneck C.O. that worked his range had already tried to set Slide up for the ABs by letting them out together by "accident." Slide was stabbed five times in the process. He really had to hold his own on D range until Big Naughty and Terry Trice were put on the range with him. "I ain't goin' for nothin' wit' these muthafuckin' crackers," Slide said.

"That's right, shorty. Them Aryan Brotherhood muthafuckas punks, that's why they move like they do. Don't get me wrong, they'll kill your ass if you let them catch your ass slippin'," said Big Naughty.

"That's why I'm tryin' to kill them muthafuckas every chance I get," Slide said. "Let me go holla at Terry real quick before my time up."

"I'll holla at you when I come out." Big Naughty sat back on his bed and cut on the black and white TV.

Slide went down the tier to holla at Terry Trice. Along the way he was called all kinds of stinking niggers by ABs and AB wannabes. He didn't pay it any attention. Talk was cheap,

Slide was trying to kill something. Opportunity popped up. An AB was sitting on his bed close to the bars nodding off of heroin while watching TV. Slide slid back down the tier to his cell and grabbed his spear—a broom stick with a knife on the end of it. I got this cracker mutherfucker, Slide thought. Slide eased back down the tier. Once in front of the AB's cell, in one swift motion, Slide jammed the spear through the bars and hit the AB in the heart. Yanking the spear from his chest, Slide slid back down the tier and went in his cell. His shower time was over. Locked in his cell, Slide could hear other ABs calling down the range checking on their brother. There was no answer, the AB was dead. Racist dog, Slide thought as he turned on his TV.

An AB by the name of Cobra came out for a shower a few minutes later. He was huge and looked like a pro wrestler with a tattoo across his forehead that read, Aryan Brotherhood. Another tattoo around his neck read, Nigger Killer. Cobra went to check on his brother. Once he saw that his brother was dead, Cobra walked back down the tier and stopped in front of Slide's cell. He saw Slide sitting on the bed with the bloody spear across his lap watching TV. "You niggers are cowards," Cobra hissed. Without a doubt, Cobra was dangerous. He'd killed a man with his bare hands in Leavenworth. "You can't win, you just don't know. All you D.C. niggers are gonna go home in body bags."

Slide got up and walked toward the cell door, spear at his side, and said, "If I ever get close to you you gon' go home in a body bag, but for right now, your brother will do just fine, cracker."

Looking like an angry Norseman, Cobra glared at the skinny, black youngster in front of him, and said, "The white man rules the earth, nigger. We always win. You niggers done got out of control, but you gon' learn. Watch." Cobra stepped off.

U.S.P. Marion, Thursday, September 27, 1982

Ronald woke up with a terrible feeling in his gut. Down the range, TVs and radios were blaring loudly. For the last week or so, the ABs and one of their Mexican buddies had been making it a habit to blast their TVs and radios all day and night. It was driving Ronald crazy. Nate Bailey had told Ronald to keep his eyes open at all times, they both felt that the reason the TVs and radios were blasting was because the ABs needed "cover" for something.

Ronald brushed his teeth and washed his face, getting ready for his day. He took off his T-shirt and admired himself, flexing a little. Hours of working out had him cut up like a Zulu warrior. He was a machine. The light color of the skin on his arm was a clear reminder of the war with the ABs. The hot coffee burn had left a lifetime scar. Ronald often looked at the scar as he worked out in his cell and used hate as a motivator. The wild thing about being in the Southern Tip was that Ronald was never a racist before he was sent to Marion, but once inside the place, his racism was born in the form of survival. It made him think of what Comrade George Jackson once said, "To determine how men will behave once they enter the prison it is of first importance to know that prison. Men are brutalized by their environment—not the reverse." Marion was a racial war zone, to say the least; racism was unchecked and encouraged by the redneck C.O.s that ran the place and armed the ABs against the D.C. Blacks. The Control Unit was eating at Ronald's mind, body, and soul, crushing the ability for him to see any good in the white race. Every face of his foes was white—Aryan Brotherhood. They shot at him, were trying to kill him, threw human waste at him and called him all kinds of niggers, all because he was a D.C. Black. For that alone, Ronald was dead-set on killing the first AB he got close to.

Pulling his books out for his morning studies, Ronald blocked out all the noise on the range. Being locked in a cell for twenty some hours a day didn't bother him at all, he used the time to educate himself. In the months he'd spent in the Control Unit, Ronald had transformed himself into a young scholar of sorts and had knowledge of topics far and wide. History and religion kept him up until dawn most nights. Besides, studying helped him deal with the pain of missing his family. He hadn't see Synthia and his son since he'd been sent to the Southern Tip; he told them not to come because he didn't want them to have to deal with the redneck C.O.s and he didn't want them to travel hundreds of miles to see him behind a glass. Ronald had came a long way from being a young convict that couldn't read down Youth Center I to being a walking encyclopedia.

Ronald's letters to his sister blew her mind. Diane was a diehard Christian. It wasn't like she went to church every Sunday or anything like that, but she would die believing what her mother taught her. Diane had a big problem with Ronald studying Islam. She began to push the Bible on him as much as she could. Ronald would come back in his letters with history and facts about many different things. He'd read the Bible from cover-to-cover four times and studied many aspects of the faith. It wasn't for him. Ronald didn't like the fact that Constantine, a Roman Emperor, had the final say so on the "Word of God." Constantine gave the order to canonize the four gospels in 325 C.E. at Nicaea. Out of fifty gospels, only four were selected by a vote of bishops. All other gospels were ordered to be burnt—like trash—by Constantine. At that time, all writings of Arius were to be burnt because out of the early followers of Jesus, Arius taught that Jesus was not God, but was created by God. Constantine ordered that anyone caught with any gospels other than the ones that he had canonized was to be put to death. The whole Constantine situation made Ronald look deeper into the history of the Bible; the things he found out drove him to look deeper into Islam.

Ronald opened his Qur'an to surah 3 ayat 185 and read,

"Every soul will taste death, and you will only be given your (full) compensation on the Day of Resurrection. So, he who is drawn away from the Fire and admitted to Paradise has attained (his desire). And, what is the life of this world except the enjoyment of delusion." Ronald drifted off into deep thought after reading the ayat; it made so much sense.

Rec began a short while later. By twos, convicts on C range got an hour in the rec cage that ran along the tier. Ronald and Nate Bailey were rec partners. They spent their time in the cage lifting weights.

"Man, Slide done jumped the moon," Ronald said.

Nate smiled and shook his head. "Yeah, he got out of here fast."

Slide had been sent back down Lorton.

"I like that youngster there, he cut from a different cloth," Nate said, looking through the bars at the front of the rec cage. C.O. Bergman, with his KKK ass, was watching the two convicts like a hawk; he always watched them closely.

"What's up wit' the dude Floyd-EL?" Ronald asked Nate. "He be actin' like he really ain't wit' us."

Floyd-EL was a big black dude out of Kansas that was on the range with Nate and Ronald. The ABs were trying to kill him when Nate first hit C range. D.C. Blacks extended him their protection on the strength that he was Black.

Nate shrugged. "Some of these brothers are naturally scared of the cracker. If it wasn't for us, these ABs would be out of control. Floyd-EL just tryin' to get by, but as long as I'm around I ain't gon' let them ABs get out on no Blacks. You can bet that."

"Yeah, I dig that. I feel the same way." Ronald nodded.

An hour later, Ronald and Nate Bailey were back in their cells as the day went on. Ronald came out for a shower a short while later. Carefully, he walked down to Cadillac's cell. To Ronald's surprise, no ABs said anything or threw anything at him. No attacks at all. Something was wrong. "What's up,

Cadillac?" Ronald found Cadillac on the floor in the corner of his cell sharpening a flat piece of steel.

"Just trying to finish this steel," Cadillac said. He just returned to C range after a trip to the box cars. When he was sent to the box cars, C.O. Bergman got the AB, Peter Merriam, to clean Cadillac's cell. Merriam found Cadillac's knife. Without question, he kept it.

Ronald spoke to Cadillac for a second, and then went to get in the shower. Locked behind the thick steel door that was shut by the C.O. at the control box, Ronald took his shower. Ten minutes later, he was let out of the shower and went back in his cell. As the cell door shut behind him, his day was over at ten fifteen A.M.

Hours passed without event. Meals were served. Mail came. Synthia wrote Ronald. Her letters made his day. Every time. They always smelled so good. He longed for her touch.

After reading her letter, Ronald sat down and wrote Synthia back:

9-27-82

Synthia,

Things in here are still complicated, but that is what comes with this side of the wall. I'm used to it now. Still no word on a transfer. They say stay out of trouble, but trouble is served as often as the food. Circumstances can only get better for me and the comrades here on the range with me. We have shared something here in the so-called worst-of-the-worst unit in the feds that just can't be put in words. We are all brothers here—one for all, all for one.

Tell Frank I said thanks for the money he sent me and Cadillac. Let him know we send our regards. I'm glad to see that he's staying out of jail. Smile! I hear T-Bone has been sent to Lewisburg, is that true?

Let Roland know that I thank him for looking after Little Ronald. That's what a big brother's supposed to do. Let him know that I love him.

I have found some gray in my hair. Yeah! Seriously. Time flies, but days here are packed with years of madness. I don't write about it because I don't think anyone outside of this place would ever believe me. I was told that I may be able to see the parole board early. My comrade, Bailey-EL, pulled my coat to a few things. I'll look into it and let you know.

I love you so much, baby. Tell Little Ronald that I love him and said to behave himself.

Love,
Ronnie

Cadillac came out for his shower a short while later.

"Frank sent me some pictures from Vegas," Cadillac said as he stopped in front of Ronald's cell and handed him the pictures. Frank, his father, Bennie, and Baby Face were surrounded by half naked women around a pool. "He doin' it, ain't he?"

"Yeah." Ronald smiled as he flipped through the pictures, thinking back to his fights out Vegas. Times had changed. Ronald tried to hand Cadillac the pictures back.

"I'll get 'em when I get out the shower."

"Did you finish that piece yet?"

"Almost, I'ma work on it when I go back in." Cadillac walked up the tier and told C.O. Bergman to let him in the shower. Bergman stood behind the steel gate, looking at Cadillac with contempt. Pulling the lever at the control box, Bergman let Cadillac in the shower. With another shift of the lever, he locked Cadillac in the shower.

TVs and radios were blaring on the range. Ronald stood at his cell door looking through the bars across the tier into the rec cage. Two ABs, Conrad Tyler and Peter Merriam, were in the cage, but they weren't lifting weights as they normally did. That was strange. Ronald stood at the cell door with his hands hanging out of the bars and watched the enemy.

Minutes later, well before Cadillac's shower time was up, Ronald heard C.O. Bergman yell onto the range and tell Cadillac that his shower time was up. Cadillac and Bergman began to argue.

Meanwhile, Ronald saw the two ABs in the rec cage head toward the back out of his sight.

Bergman gave in and told Cadillac to call for him when he was ready.

Moments later, Ronald saw a figure fly by his cell. Then another. Tyler and Merriam were on the tier; they'd found a way out of the rec cage. Nate Bailey began yelling down the tier to warn Cadillac that the ABs were on the tier.

"Don't come out the shower, Smith-EL!" Nate Bailey yelled.

Ronald got down on his hands and knees to look through the crack in the bars to see what was going on. "They right in front of the shower, Cadillac!" Ronald yelled. He knew Cadillac didn't have a knife with him.

Bergman, at the control box, also saw the ABs on the tier, but his actions proved that his KKK ass was really down with the move. He pulled the lever and opened the shower door. Ronald's heart dropped when he heard the steel door slide open. Other ABs on the range began to cheer on the attack from their cells as if their team was scoring the winning touchdown in the Super Bowl. Ronald's anger boiled to the max, hate began to fill his heart and pump through his veins like blood, tears of stone rolled from his eyes like huge boulders crashing down from moutain tops.

Merriam tried to rush into the shower, but Cadillac blasted him with a big right hand and grabbed him, trying to wrestle his knife from his hand as they tumbled out onto the tier. Tyler side stepped them and began stabbing Cadillac over and over as he wrestled Merriam. Repeatedly, Tyler stabbed him in vital spots with force. He was able to pick his shots. Finally, Tyler stopped stabbing Cadillac, he knew the damage was done. Merriam shoved Cadillac's dead body to the ground and in a frenzy of frustration began yelling and mutilating him. Merriam was enraged that he never got to stab Cadillac while he was alive. Even Bergman began to yell for Merriam to stop, telling him that enough was enough. Bergman squatted and reached through the gate, trying to pull Cadillac's body away from Merriam. Merriam yanked the body away from Bergman and continued his savage mutilation.

Ronald could watch no more. The pain he felt inside was something he had never felt before. The mixture of anger and a deep feeling of loss seemed to rob him of what little humanity he had left. Trapped behind thick iron bars, there was nothing he could do to help Cadillac; not being able to help his comrade made him feel helpless. He didn't notice that he was squeezing the bars so hard that he was bruising his hands.

Walking down the range making countless threats to D.C. Blacks, Conrad Tyler stopped in front of Ronald's cell. He was covered with blood from head to toe, his whole face and unkept beard were smeared with blood as if he were a cannibal. Dripping with blood at his side was a boning knife with an eight inch blade. It was a street knife. "You niggers gon' stay the fuck in your place now," Tyler hissed at Ronald.

Ronald said nothing. The only thing that could express his anger was murder.

Pointing his knife at Ronald and tapping the cell bars with it, Tyler said, "You're next, motherfucker." Tyler then walked down the tier.

Ronald stood at the bars, burning with rage; he hungered for vengeance.

Lorton Legends

U.S.P. Lewisburg, Tuesday, November 16, 1982

Cadillac's murder was felt far and wide. He would always be remembered in the hearts of his comrades. T-Bone, Harrison-EL, and other D.C. Blacks in Lewisburg had already plotted their move out. The ABs were fucking with the right ones.

T-Bone was up and ready to go to work at five A.M. He had butterflies in his stomach that would only go away once the drama kicked off.

"Take it easy, young buck," Harrison-EL said, sitting on the bed. He and T-Bone were cellies. "We gon' take care of business as soon as the doors pop."

An AB by the name of David Frost was in the same block as T-Bone and Harrison-EL. Frost was one of the top ABs in Lewisburg. He always got up early in the morning to watch the news in the TV room. Frost was supposed to be extremely dangerous; he and another AB by the name of Cobra were co-defendants on a murder in Leavenworth.

A short while later, the cells were popped and the convicts came out. Like clockwork, Frost headed for the TV room. T-Bone and Harrison-EL followed behind him. When they entered the TV room, Frost gave them a look of deep hate and pulled a gruesome knife.

"Come on, niggers!" he hissed. "I been waitin' on you."

T-Bone smiled. "That ain't gon' help your cracker ass." T-Bone rushed Frost, blocking his knife thrust with his towel-wrapped arm and then slamming his knife deep into his stomach as Harrison-EL came from the the other side with the deathblow to the jugular. They made quick work of Frost, and then sat his dead body in his chair. T-Bone put a pair of sun glasses on Frost and turned his body toward the TV.

Meanwhile, in another block, two D.C. Blacks caught another AB on the shitter. In seconds, they butchered him and were gone in a flash. In the same block in the laundry room,

229

two more D.C. Blacks butchered another AB and left his body hanging halfway out of the washer machine.

The whole prison was locked down just as breakfast was getting started. The feds had a war on its hands.

Chapter 16

Maximum Security, Friday, March 8, 1983

A crowd of convicts packed the gym watching two other convicts mix it up with the boxing gloves on. It was as if a title was on the line by the way the two fighters were working. Grunts and pops of the leather gloves along with cheers from bystanders were the only sounds in the gym. Tony Fortune was fighting a dude by the name of Patrick Nelson, who'd been talking a bunch of shit about fighting two pro fights on the streets. Nelson swore he was top of the line when it came to his hands. However, Tony Fortune was digging in his shit. A lot of money was riding on the fight—hundreds of dollars. Even C.O.s were betting, one way or another.

Ronald was watching the fight, standing beside Fly and Frog. Ronald respected Tony Fortune's fight game, they'd sparred before. It was no doubt in Ronald's mind about the outcome of the fight, Tony was going to knock his man out cold.

Being back down Lorton was like being home for Ronald, even though he was still locked up. The feds were still in an uproar. D.C. Blacks were terrorizing shit; they were in "overdrive" since the Cadillac murder. After the ABs were murdered in Lewisburg, the feds knew that a bloody war was on the rise. A number of D.C. Blacks were rounded up for a rash of violence and murders that followed the Cadillac murder. Most of them were sent to Marion's Control Unit. Ronald had left Big Naughty and Wild Man behind at Marion when he was sent back behind the Wall. T-Bone and Harrison-EL had been charged with the murder of an AB in Lewisburg and were about to start trial. D.C. Blacks in other federal prisons were also on a rampage. Christmas Day, 1982, in F.C.I. Petersburg, a C.O. was butchered to death. The feds began to send D.C. Blacks back to Lorton by the bus loads. Ronald was one of the few to make it out of the Southern Tip.

The crowd inside of the gym went off. Tony Fortune stopped Nelson with a hook to the body. Pissed off about losing their money, some convicts began smacking and kicking Nelson while calling him all kinds of bitch ass niggas. Ronald laughed and shook his head as he left the gym with Larry Williams and Fly.

On his way back to the block, Ronald ran into Slide. Slide was a different man after returning from the feds, he was dead serious at all times. He was more laid back, but one hundred times more dangerous and wouldn't think twice about killing anything that got in his way. Just like Ronald, Slide had seen and been through so much in the feds that his whole outlook on life was seen through the eyes of a man that had looked death in the face and feared nothing or no one. After being called so many niggers by people that hated them, Ronald and Slide no longer used the word, they didn't even let their comrades use the word around them.

"Tony stopped that joker, huh?" Slide said, leaning against the brick wall of 6 Block. It was a little chilly outside, but still felt good in the afternoon sun.

"Yeah, Tony ain't play no games wit' main man," Ronald said, watching two cats crawl under the fence at the end of the walk.

"You heard anything else about T-Bone and Harrison-

EL?" Slide lit a cigarette and put one foot on the wall he was leaning against.

"They about to start trial."

"You think they can beat that case?"

"I really don't know. The feds play real dirty. You know how it go. They can't stand when blacks kill whites." Ronald raised his eyebrow, having a flashback of how the redneck C.O. popped the shower door knowing the ABs were on the tier waiting to kill Cadillac. "I hope they come out on top, but ain't no tellin'."

"No bullshit, I'd hate to see them get trapped off like that."

"I hear that." Ronald shook his head. He had a parole hearing coming up at the end of the year. Thoughts of spending the rest of his life in prison crossed his mind and his heart went out to his comrades. As much as Ronald wanted to kill the ABs that murdered his man Cadillac, he knew that by being sent back to Lorton he had a chance to obtain his freedom once more. "I was thinkin' about T-Bone the other day. Me, him, Frank, and my man Blue went down the Center together as teenagers. We all grew up in prison. Blue lost his life in here. Prison made us the men we are. T-Bone, though, he ain't been on the streets a good six months since he was twelve-years-old. I hope him and Harrison-EL do beat that beef."

Washinton, D.C., Sunday April 26, 1983

It was a sunny spring day around Valley Green when a blue Corvette with gleaming chrome rims pulled up and parked in front of building 3930. The smooth sounds of Curtis Mayfield had everybody's attention, they were checking out the new car with the paper tags. Frank stepped out of the driver's side in a red, white, and blue Fila sweat suit. He wore a pair of dark Gucci shades, a thick gold chain, and a gold Rolex. It was clear that he was the "man." Little kids ran up to him like he was a super star. Frank pulled a huge knot of cash from his pocket and handed out more than one hundred dollars in ones to the little ones. They ran off with the money talking about what they were going to get from the store.

Frank was living large by all means. He had the best dope on the south side; it was called Magnum. Frank's father, Fred, was the master mind behind the operation, but word on the streets was that Frank was the man to see if a nigga was trying to get some real money.

Frank walked up on Baby Face, Bennie, and a few other dudes that were standing in front of the building. He gave them all five and asked how things were going. Baby Face let Frank know that all was well and that the workers were bringing the money in with no shorts.

Looking at the new Corvette, Baby Face said to Frank, "You hurtin' 'em wit' that thing right there." He pointed at the car.

"I had to treat myself to somethin' nice," Frank said, seeing Cookie coming out of the building in skin-tight blue jeans. She was the baddest dark skinned honey around the Valley. Thick thighs, phat ass, huge, sexy lips, cute around-the-way-girl face, and street smarts. Frank was burning the pussy up at will, but didn't claim Cookie as his "woman."

"Here come your peoples." Bennie laughed, counting a handful of cash. He and Baby Face were the real "muscle" of the crew, they made sure the money was collected and they pulled the triggers if something needed to be dealt with. Frank still pulled triggers as well, even though his father kept telling him that he needed to leave that part of the game to others in the crew.

"Frank," Cookie called, standing on the sidewalk with her hands on her wide hips. At twenty six, Cookie still had the voice of a little girl.

"What's up, baby girl?" Frank said as he walked in her direction, checking her body out. He gave her a hug and kissed her on the lips.

"I'm trying to go to Atlantic City wit' my cousin. Can you slide my a few dollars?"

"Yeah, I can do that for you, you know that." Frank smiled and then told one of the dudes that were in front of the building to go get him some money. The dude brought Frank a brown paper bag full of cash. Frank looked inside and rounded off that it was close to three thousand dollars. He handed the bag to Cookie. "That'll hold you for a second."

She gave Frank a kiss. "Thanks, Frank."

"I gotta take care of some business. I'll see you a little later," Frank said, watching Cookie walk away throwing that ass.

Fred pulled up in a silver Benz. Frank went to holla at his pops for a second. "What's up, old man?" Frank stood outside of the driver's side window.

"I'm on top of business," Fred said, looking like new money in his Hugo Boss gear. Since he'd checked out of rehab, Fred was his old self again. "Your mother said she need you to have somebody look at her car." Fred turned the Maze tape down.

"I got that. I'm goin' to see her later on. I bought her one of those big floor model TVs." Frank looked at his Rolex, and said, "I gotta make a run. I'll catch you later."

Twenty minutes later, Frank was knocking on the door of the apartment that Synthia and Cristal shared. Synthia answered the door in jeans and a T-shirt. "I'm glad you here," she said as she closed the door behind Frank. "I'm 'bout to kill these little knuckle heads."

Frank laughed as he sat on the sofa. "Why you wanna do that? You know if you cross my little men I'ma have to see you about that."

Synthia put her hands on her hips and rolled her eyes. "Whatever, your little men were just fighting over the TV."

Lil' Ronald and Chris ran into the living room and

attacked Frank with punches to the body.

Synthia laughed. "Their all yours." She went back to her room shaking her head.

Moments later, Cristal came out of the bathroom in a purple Fila sweat suit and saw Frank beating up the boys on the sofa; they'd taken his beeper and gold chain. "That's what you get." Cristal laughed. "You let them get away wit' murder."

Putting both boys in a headlock, Frank smiled and said, "They little boys, I just let them be they self around me." He then stopped playing and told the boys to go get their jackets. When they left the room, Frank asked Cristal what was up. She looked stressed out.

"I'm okay, just been worried about Ty's case." Cristal sighed, she really wasn't trying to talk about the situation. T-Bone was only a few years away from seeing the parole board and now he was facing life without parole.

"T gon' be okay. I got him the best lawyer for the job. Things gon' work themselves out," Frank said as the boys came running back into the room. Pulling some money from his pocket, Frank handed it to Cristal. "I'll see you when I bring them back."

An hour later, Frank and the boys were flying around the go-cart track. Frank, being the big kid that he was, was trying to chase Chris down. Chris was leading the pack around the corner. Flying around the next bend, Lil' Ronald took the inside and shot in front of the pack, finishing first.

The three of them spent hours racing and didn't leave until close to ten P.M. Frank loved hanging out with his comrades' sons; he felt that since their fathers were locked up it was his duty to look out for them. As they all walked back to Frank's Benz, Frank's beeper went off. It was Baby Face. Frank called the number back from the pay phone in the front of the parking lot as the boys sat in the car.

"Hello." Baby Face sounded like something was wrong.

"What's up, man?" Frank watched people head to their

cars. The wind was blowing, making the night chilly.

"It's Fred, get over here right now."

Frank hung up the phone and shot Uptown to drop the boys off. His heart was pounding and his mind was racing. He feared the worst, but really didn't know what to fear.

A short while later, Frank was inside Baby Face's apartment sitting around the dining room table under a dim light with Baby Face and Bennie. Cigarette smoke filled the air as an old TV set played in the background. Baby Face put Frank on point about the situation. Baby Face had gotten a call from a dude saying that he had snatched Fred and wanted two hundred and fifty thousand dollars or Fred's body would be floating in the Potomac River in the morning. The caller said he'd call back at midnight.

"How much money we got in the safe?" Frank asked Baby Face.

"A little over eighty Gs here."

Frank's face began to turn flaming red. He looked at his gold Rolex, it was almost midnight. "I gotta run out Maryland to get the money. When the muthafucka call back, tell 'em we got the money. I'll be back in twenty minutes." Frank headed for the door. "We gon' find out who did this shit. Believe that!"

When Frank returned to Baby Face's apartment with the gym bag full of money, Baby Face told him that the kidnapper had called back. "He said drop the money off at ..." Baby Face looked down at a piece of paper in his hand and read the address. "That's an apartment building Uptown with an underground garage. It's gon' be a brown 280 ZX wit' Virginia tags, the joker say we can't miss it. We gotta put the money in and leave."

"How we gon' know where my father at?" Frank snapped.

"The nigga say he gon' call back."

"Bullshit!" Frank barked and sat on the old sofa.

"We gotta roll wit" it right now, or they gon' kill Fred," Baby Face added with a shrug.

"We can try to follow the money," Bennie said, eating Chinese food.

"Nah, if they catch us trying to follow them they gon' kill Pops off the top." Frank rubbed his temple and sighed, shaking his head. Frank couldn't believe niggas were trying him. However, he was making more money than Ronald Reagan. For the right price, somebody would talk and he would find out who snatched his father. "Let's go. We gon' drop the bank off and roll wit' it from there."

Frank, Baby Face, and Bennie got in Bennie's new Cadillac and headed Uptown to 16th Street. They dropped the money off as they were told and then headed back to Valley Green. During the ride, there was little talking. Everyone was worried about Fred; he was like a father to them all.

Inside the apartment, the phone rang and Frank answered. "Yeah."

"R.F.K. parking lot. Gray Ford," a voice said before the line went dead.

"Let's go." Frank led the way out the door. They jumped back in the car and headed to R.F.K. Stadium in Northeast. When they pulled into the dark, empty parking lot, the gray Ford was the only car in sight. Frank pulled up and parked beside it. Looking around carefully, Frank and his men got out. In the cool morning air, they searched the car and found the keys. Frank popped the trunk and found his father handcuffed and gagged. He was still alive. They pulled Fred from the trunk and snatched the duct tape from his mouth. Bennie picked the handcuffs with a paper clip. "You okay?" Frank asked his father.

"Yeah, I'm cool." Fred stretched. He was sore from spending hours in the trunk. "Let's get out of here."

On the way back to the south side, Fred told the crew what had went down. He was coming out of his apartment when two masked gunmen came out of nowhere and smacked him in the head with a pistol. He went out cold and woke up in the back seat of a car. All he could remember was that one of the gunmen had blue eyes.

"Blue eyes?!" Frank asked in disbelief. "You tellin' me that some white muthafucka just got us for two fifty?"

"Yeah, I'm tellin' you he had blue eyes." Fred was rubbing his sore wrist. "We gon' have to tighten up and stay on point." He lit a cigarette and blew smoke in the air. "We been havin' a nice run, but the word on the streets is that we gettin' paid. The hounds 'bout to be at our doorstep, from here on out we deal wit' all situations on the spot. No more buyin' all them pretty cars and flashy chains, at least for a while. We'll find out who was behind the move."

"Yeah, no doubt, bodies 'bout to drop, too," Frank added.

Washington, D.C., Friday, May 1, 1983

Just after three P.M. when school let out, the sound of afternoon traffic and young kids filled the air. A group of kids were grouped up behind Tubman Elementary in a circle. Two little boys were inside the circle fighting like pit bulls. The bigger of the two boys was wrestling and not really throwing a lot of punches. Another little boy pulled the wrestler off of his man. "Fight! Stop grabbin' him, nigga!" Lil' Ronald said to the bigger boy. Chris wasted no time punching the bigger boy right in the eye as soon as Lil' Ronald pulled him off of him. The bigger boy grabbed Chris again, that time he tried to throw Chris to ground. Lil' Ronald jumped in it and he and Chris jumped the "bully." The bully had touched a little girl's butt by the name of Keyona. Keyona was supposed to be Chris' girlfriend, the same little girl that Chris used to hate.

Seeing the group of kids, a teacher ran to the scene. One of the kids alerted the others that a teacher was coming. All the kids ran like the police were coming. Lil' Ronald and Chris took off across Kenyon Street, Northwest, and ran into the alley. Down the small alley they ran into the back of Diane's house.

"What y'all done got into now?" Diane asked, seeing the look on the boys faces. Plus, they were out of breath. They assured her that nothing was wrong and then ran down the basement to watch cartoons. "There's some tuna fish for y'all in the fridge."

The boys watched TV for a while before getting bored.

"Let's go outside, man," Lil' Ronald said.

"Okay, let me use the bathroom first," Chris said.

Minutes later, they were on their Mongooses riding up 14th Street. They hooked up with two other boys and headed toward the National Zoo.

Maximum Security, Monday, July 18, 1983

A. group of convicts sat in the back of 6 Block drinking liquor, smoking weed, and eating crabs by the bushel while listening to Earth, Wind, & Fire. It was Larry Williams' birthday and Fly had put a little something together for the men.

Cracking open a crab, T-Bone felt good to be back down Lorton. He and Harrison-EL had been sent back to Lorton a week ago from Marion after beating their murder beef. Their lawyers filed motions to the courts about them being sent to Marion even though they were found not guilty at trial.

"T, you tryin' to use the phone?" Fly said, coming back from up front with the straight out phone.

"Yeah, let me get that." T-Bone got the phone and called Cristal.

"What's up, baby?" Cristal said with a big smile on her face. She was the happiest woman in the world when she found out that T-Bone had beat his murder beef. He would be home in no time.

"I'm okay, down here eatin' some crabs and just relaxin', it's my man Larry's birthday," T-Bone said.

"I'll be down there tomorrow, I can't wait to see you."

"I can't wait to see you, either, I got somethin' to tell you."

"What?!"

"I'll tell you when I see you."

"Boy, don't play wit' me."

"I'll tell you when I see you," T-Bone said.

"Play games if you want to. You gon' want some pussy when I come down there."

"And, you gon' give it to me, too."

"Come on, Ty, stop playin', tell me what you talkin' "bout."

"No, I want to tell you face-to-face."

"You make me sick." Cristal sucked her teeth."

"I love you, too." T-Bone laughed.

After T-Bone got off the phone with Cristal, he went to holla at Ronald and found him in the cell looking at some old pictures.

"Them pictures old as shit," T-Bone said, seeing the old Youth Center I picture Ronald was looking at.

"Yeah, man, we been in prison since we was kids. It's time to get out of here," Ronald said, looking at another picture with Fray and Eddie Mathis in it at a Youth Center go-go.

"No bullshit, it's time to hit the streets. We got kids out there." T-Bone lit a Newport.

"Did you tell Cristal how you feel?" Ronald smiled.

"Nah, I'ma ask her to marry me when she come down here tomorrow." T-Bone smiled.

Washington, D.C., Saturday, July 30, 1983

The summer sun was in the clear blue sky all alone making the day a beautiful one to be outside. Cars crossed the 14th Street Bridge, overlooking the Potomac River. Frank, in his Corvette with the top down, raced across the bridge and back into the city. He hated crossing the bridge, he didn't like being over top of the big body of water. He was coming from seeing Ronald and T-Bone; he'd taken them a thousand dollars each. He'd also told them that he'd put money down on a nice house Uptown for Synthia and Cristal. The way he saw it, the money was coming in by the truck loads, so he was in a position to spread the love.

As Frank made his way through the D.C. streets heading for 8th and H Street, Northeast, he thought about what was going on in the streets. A number of big dope boys had been kidnapped for money in the past few months. None of them had been murdered after the money was dropped off. However, the snatch moves were always the same, two gunmen, one with blue eyes.

Frank parked on H Street and got out. People were all over the place. Cars were back and forth up and down the street. The honeys outside had on next to nothing. Frank's curly hair was cut low, his linen short set by Armani flapped in the wind as he walked up the street behind Armani shades in Armani loafers with no socks. His holstered 9mm wasn't visible. He stopped to holla at a few honeys along the way and then went inside Carole's Lounge to holla at Morris.

Upstairs, the office that was out like a scene from The Godfather with thick leather chairs, an old oak desk, thick carpet, and two book shelves filled with all kinds of books. The room was dim and thick curtains blocked out the sun. Frank and Morris sat on the sofa and discussed business. The blue-eyed kidnapper had snatched one of Morris' partners, but that time a mistake was made: The kidnapper did too much talking. While in the back seat of the car with the kidnappers, Morris' partner constantly heard the blue-eyed kidnapper refer to the ransom money as "taxes." He would say, "Such and such owe taxes and they would pay up with no problem."

"My partner says he knows who the kidnappers are, or at least he's got an idea," Morris said, sipping on Coke and rum.

242

"What makes your partner think he knows who's doin' the snatchin'?" Frank didn't trust Morris, they could never be friends; their relationship was only business.

Morris gave Frank the rundown. A vice cop out of 7D had been extorting a few old timers with long money. The blue-eyed kidnapper was an ex-marine by the name of Cowboy. "I'm certain this is our man," Morris said.

Frank gave it a little thought. He'd been hit for two hundred and fifty thousand dollars when his father had been kidnapped. Morris paid five hundred thousand dollars for his partner's life. "Let me ask you this here." Frank rubbed his chin. "If this Cowboy joker is the same blue-eyed muthafucka that's snatchin' niggas for money, why you ain't get him touched yet?" Frank raised his eyebrows. "He hit you for five-hundred strong, right?"

Morris smiled. "That's why I like you, you get to the point."

"That's how it goes."

"Here's the deal. Cowboy is a cop. If we move on him it's gon' bring too much heat. Aside from that, he's got a crew of ex-marines on the force that's down with the lick. Most of the old timers know Cowboy's a problem, but they don't want to go to war with the cops. It's bad for business.

"Where do I come in? You still ain't told me nothin'." Frank knew exactly what Morris was getting at, but he wanted Morris to spell it out.

"I been checkin' you out, you still got that young spunk, that fire burnin' inside you. You can get rid of the problem ..."

Frank laughed. He was flattered. "What makes you think I'd risk my ass to get rid of this problem? Like you said, we talkin' 'bout a cop. Killin' a police ain't like killin' no average joe. What's in it for me, and why should I do it? I know you got somebody else for the job."

"There's money in it for you."

"I ain't pressed for money right now."

243

"To be honest, I'm too old for this kind of thing. I went to war with the pigs in the sixties, I don't have another street battle in me. I paid my dues and I'm still here to talk about it, but I'm old now. I'm not cut out for what needs to be done. You know how the game goes. My name's gettin' me by right now. What I did when The Black Widow was around is where my respect comes from. Nevertheless, you are out here right now, doing your thing. The streets respect you. You got what it takes to deal with a situation like this here. And, you can get paid for it. You can take care of Cowboy."

"I can get paid like what?" Frank asked.

"Who knows, maybe a hundred grand, maybe two. Niggas will give that money up to get rid of Cowboy," Morris said.

"Give me a few days to think about it." Frank got up and left.

Frank headed over Southeast, he needed to holla at his father about the move. Killing Cowboy would be taking things to another level; Frank was sure he could pull the move off and get away with it.

An hour later, Frank and his father were sitting in the living room of Frank's six-bedroom house out Maryland. They discussed the Cowboy situation. Fred didn't like the move, but he knew that it could be pulled off if it was thought out well.

"I think we should hire somebody else to do the dirty work," Fred said.

"Yeah, I thought about that, too, but I don't want nobody to be able to connect us to the hit," Frank said.

"This is gonna bring a lot of heat, you know that, right?"

"I already thought about that, but we can stand the aftermath."

"I'm wit' it." Fred nodded in his Hugo Boss gear.

"The way I see it, we get the money back we lost and we make our position in the streets stronger. Cowboy deserve a good killin'. I'll be damned if I let a cracker extort me."

"We need to plan this out," Fred said.
"I'm all ears." Frank smiled.

Washington, D.C., Thursday, August 11, 1983

Fred had done his homework on Cowboy and his crew, he knew where they all laid their heads. To kill some heat that would come with the hit, Fred wanted to hit Cowboy while he was off duty.

Sitting in a green Chevy Caprice parked on a dark residential street in Georgetown where the whites lived free of inner-city dangers that plagued the D.C. streets, Frank and Fred watched a house that they'd followed Cowboy to. Fred had learned that Cowboy was having an affair with a female officer that lived in the house that they were watching. They'd been watching the house for over an hour when Frank said, "The pussy must be good."

"Must be," Fred said, toying with the silencer on the .22 automatic in his hand. "It better be the best pussy he ever had 'cause it's gon' be the last piece he gon' get."

Twenty feet or so away from the Caprice Frank and Fred were sitting in, an ex-marine was crawling through the dark front yard of a house surrounded with short hedges. He had a clear shot at Fred's head, but wanted to get closer to make sure he got the job done. He was hunting Frank and Fred with a small assault weapon. Cowboy had spotted Frank following him and had called his partner to flank his pursuers from the blind side. The ex-marine double checked the silencer on his weapon, sprang up outside of the passenger side window of the Caprice, and sprayed Fred in the side of the head. The rapid coughing sound of the silenced fully automatic weapon and the sound of breaking glass was all that could be heard as more than twenty bullets flew through the car, flying by Frank's head. Frank jumped out of the car with an Uzi and began spraying. His weapon sounded off with a loud string of fully automatic bursts of flames. The ex-marine ducked behind the car, but Frank never stopped firing as he ran around the car. The ex-marine thought Frank was taking flight, but Frank kept spraying as he rounded the car, hitting the ex-marine in the back close to fifteen times. The ex-marine fell to the ground coughing up blood; Frank stood over him and sent five more bullets into his head. Nosy white people began to look out of their windows as police sirens hit the air. Two police cars with blaring sirens and flashing lights skidded around the corner and began flying in Frank's direction. Frank took off running into the night. It sounded like police were everywhere, but Frank kept running. He refused to go back to prison. Through yards and dark alleys he ran, cutting through wooded areas and across more dark streets and through more alleys, Frank was at top speed. As a helicopter flew over head lighting up the dark alley with its powerful lights, Frank hid in the backyard of a small house off of 35th Street. He was trying to catch his breath. A white woman in her mid thirties opened her back door to see what was going on. Behind his ski mask, Frank quickly forced his way into the house at gunpoint.

"Please, don't hurt me, I'll give you anything you want," the woman said, wearing nothing but a night gown. She eased down to the floor and balled up as if Frank was going to shoot her.

"I'm not goin' to hurt you," Frank said. Visions of his father's brains being blown all over the car flooded his mind. With his black driving gloves on, Frank shut the back door. Looking at the petrified woman, he said, "Who's here wit' you?"

The woman could barely speak she was so scared. "Uh ... uh ... I'm ... I'm here alone, by myself." She began to sob loudly, covering her face. "Please, don't kill me, I have kids. Please, don't hurt me ... please..."

Frank looked out the window, and then picked the trembling woman up by her arm.

"Please!" she yelled. "What are you doing? Please, don't hurt me." She feared that she was about to be raped.

"Look, I'm not gonna hurt you. I just need to check the house. After that, I'm gone." Frank led her through the house with the Uzi in hand and checked every room and corner there was from top to bottom. The house was empty. Frank then made the woman sit on the sofa in the living room while he looked out onto Foxhall Road. Police sirens were still all over the place. A serious manhunt was taking place. Police cars were riding up and down the street shining spotlights everywhere. Frank didn't know how he was going to get out of the area. His heart was pounding. He looked down at his assault weapon and told himself that he was never going back to prison alive, not with four extra clips in his pockets. Frank couldn't believe how Cowboy had been ready for them; it was clear that he was dealing with an ex-marine.

An hour later, police activity had died down some, but patrol cars were still riding by every few minutes. Frank looked at the crying woman, and said, "I need your car keys."

"They're in my coat pocket. Take them, my BMW is out front. Just don't hurt me, please!"

"Get the keys," Frank ordered.

With the keys to the woman's BMW in hand, Frank thought about what he should do with her. He didn't have to kill her, she couldn't identify him. However, he needed time to get out of the area before she could call the police.

The woman looked at Frank and the Uzi he held—the long clip put the fear of God in her. She could tell he was deciding her fate. "Look, please, sir. Don't kill me. I ... I ..."

"Grab your coat," Frank ordered. He made the woman drive him to the Maryland line at gunpoint. "Sorry for everything," Frank said as he jumped out the car and ran into the shadows of the night

Chapter 17

Bethesda, MD, Saturday, August 13, 1983

"Ahhhhh!" Screams of pain and agony filled the basement of an old warehouse. Morris was being beaten savagely for information. Cowboy and two of his cohorts had kidnapped Morris in hopes of finding out where Frank was laying his head. Cowboy knew Frank had been paid to take him out; he got the information from another old timer that was close to Morris, who was now dead from a .45 slug right between the eyes.

"Fuck you, cracker!" Morris yelled, covered in his own blood. His left eye was the size of a softball; he was beyond recognition. However, he wouldn't give up any information about Frank. He'd been taking the vicious punishment for close to an hour and had suffered broken ribs as well as a broken leg. "Ahhhgggrrraahhhh, muthafucka!" Morris yelled as the iron pipe crashed down on his leg, making a cracking sound. "Frank gon' kill you! He gon' hunt you down and kill your cracker ass! You can only kill me once, bitch!"

"You right, dirtbag." Cowboy popped Morris in the head twice with a .357 magnum. "Stinkin' nigger."

Lorton Legends

Washington, D.C., Wednesday August 17, 1983

When someone was gunned down in the ghetto it was the norm. Rarely did it stay on the news more than a few seconds in passing. However, the murder of Fred and an ex-marine in an all-out gunfight in the heart of Georgetown was all over the news for days. A public outcry was calling for "justice." Frank wasn't on the run; he'd had some of The Black Widow's people look into the situation. Cowboy had no intentions on arresting Frank, he wanted to kill him. Cowboy and his crew of dirty vice cops were pressing all street level dealers trying to find out where Frank was. Word on the streets was that Cowboy wasn't going to let anybody make a dime until he found Frank. No one gave up any information; the hood loved Frank.

The sun was bright and blazing on the D.C. streets. People were out and about everywhere. Just after three P.M., all the drug spots on the south side were in full swing. Cowboy and his crew were jumping out left and right, making it clear that they were dead serious about nobody making a dime until someone gave up information about Frank's whereabouts.

Jumping out on Valley Avenue, Cowboy and his crew ran down on street dealers. They caught only one. Standing over the street dealer with his gun to the back of his head, Cowboy slammed his knee into the young man's back, and said, "You dirty?"

"Nah, man! I ain't got shit on me," the young man said with his face smashed into the sidewalk.

Cowboy smiled, looking like Burt Reynolds in his blue jeans and white T-shirt. "Why you runnin' then?" Cowboy began to search the young man. "I know you know Frank Thompson, right?"

"Never heard of him," the young man lied. The pressure of Cowboy's knee in his back was killing him.

Cowboy smacked the young man in the back of the head with a loud pop. A forming crowd began to protest, but

249

Cowboy's crew kept them at bay while Cowboy continued to rough the young man up. After getting nothing out of the young man, he let him go.

The crew of dirty vice cops jumped back in their car and left. As they rode through the streets of Southeast, Cowboy spoke to his cohorts from the front passenger seat as they all kept an eye on what was going on on Alabama Avenue. "We'll catch this little nigger before it's all over. Bet that."

"Let's pay his mother a visit," Kirklen said from the back seat.

"I don't want to shake up his peoples. I only want him, but if we have to go that way then we will," Cowboy said as they stopped at a 7-Eleven. All four men went inside and bought chilli dogs. They ate in the big, red Lincoln as they continued to prowl the streets. Stopping at a traffic light on South Capitol Street, a big Ford pickup truck smashed into the driver's side of the Lincoln with a loud crashing sound. Cowboy and his crew were shaken up real bad. A black van pulled up right behind the pickup and skidded to a stop.

"It's a hit!" Cowboy yelled. All four vice cops went for their guns. The two on the passenger side tried to get out, but the force of the pickup truck had slammed the Lincoln into a parked car. On the driver's side, the pickup had the Lincoln's doors pent shut. The hood of the Lincoln was smoking and it looked like it was about to blow. A man jumped out of the pickup with a pistol in hand. He was dressed in a white gown and hood as if he was a KKK memeber. The KKK look alike began firing shots into the Lincoln at close range. The vice cops returned fire. Fully automatic fire hit the air. Two more KKK look alikes jumped out of the van firing M-16s. People in the area began running and screaming. Cars sped away with screaming tires. Gunfire seemed to be nonstop in broad daylight. The vice cops were sitting ducks. The KKK look alikes with the assault rifles swiss-cheesed the Lincoln in seconds; they then ran up on it and sprayed it with one last wave of fully automatic fire to make sure everybody inside was dead. The KKK look alike with the pistol lit the cloth of a Molotov cocktail and tossed it in Cowboy's lap. The inside of the Lincoln went up in flames. All three KKK look alikes jumped into the van and sped off with screaming tires, leaving behind four dead dirty cops, countless shells, and a scene of death and destruction. It all went down in under a minute, even though it seemed like hours.

Hours later, the shooting was all over the news, TV, and radio. No one had an answer for the KKK look alikes. The FBI was sure the KKK had nothing to do with the murder of four vice cops. The FBI's investigation was focused on organized crime.

In a small motel room not far from Andrew's Air Force Base, Frank, Baby Face, and Bennie were about to go their separate ways for a while. They were each hitting the road with one hundred and fifty thousand dollars. Frank made sure Cowboy and his crew paid for Fred's death. Nothing would bring his father back, but he had to move forward. Frank made sure he left his mother enough money to take care of herself while he was laying low down south.

"Lay as low as possible. No matter what," Frank said to Baby Face and Bennie as he grabbed the duffel bag full of money off the floor. "Don't go back to the city for shit until the new year come in. We gon' disappear for a good little while, but when we come back, we gon' be set. I already got it all laid out." Frank gave his comrades five. They had proven that they had no picks and were willing to go all the way with him. Anybody could get it.

In his Corvette on 1-95 South, Frank thought about the move he and his men had pulled off. He smiled. That was some gangster shit, he thought. Frank thought about his father. Hell of a nigga!

Chapter 18

Central Facility, Wednesday, May 14, 1986

18 Dorm was alive and full of action, in and out traffic was in full swing. Heroin was in the dorm. T-Bone slept in 18 Dorm; he had his hands in everything moving. At thirty-years-old, he'd seen a lot and understood prison politics as well as anyone on the Hill.

T-Bone also controlled a lot of things that were going on in the streets. After Morris was murdered, most of the old timers from The Black Widow's crew called it quits and washed their hands of the dope game. They left the game to the next generation. T-Bone was still plugged into the New York heroin connect and he plugged Frank into that connect when he returned to D.C. T-Bone was a major factor in Frank's position in the streets. Frank had one of the strongest crews in D.C. and was taking the city by storm. T-Bone controlled Carole's Lounge; he turned it into a night club and changed the name to The Black Widow. The club was one of the top night clubs in D.C. Cristal and Synthia ran The Black Widow; Frank made sure they had no problems whatsoever. T-Bone married Cristal, she was the woman of his dreams and they were meant to be. The only thing that was in the way of them being together in the free world was T-Bone's prison record. The parole board gave him a two year set off in '83 and an eighteen month set off in '85. Nevertheless, T-Bone kept pushing forward, rolling with the punches. He made sure his family and his kids were straight and wanted for nothing. Chris was always in trouble, T-Bone saw it as growing pains and felt that it would pass. T-Bone's other son, Paul, was a good kid that lived out Maryland. Paul was doing good in school and sports and his mother was playing fair, letting Paul see T-Bone.

"T-Bone." Slide called out as he walked into the dorm. "It's a dude outside sellin' a gold chain for a woman, I know how you is about your woman." Slide smiled.

"What the dude want for the chain?" T-Bone walked to the door with Slide.

"A bag of blow."

T-Bone and Slide stepped outside into the cool evening air.

There was an orange haze in the sky as the sun set. Convicts were everywhere. The foot traffic outside of the dorm was like that of the downtown area of a busy city during Munch hour. T-Bone bought the gold chain with a twenty dollar bill; he never walked around with heroin on him.

After buying the chain and watching the dude step off to get high, T-Bone looked at Slide, and said, "You seen Ronald?"

"I left him over the gym liftin' weights."

"I'm 'bout to go holla at him real quick, what you 'bout to do?"

"I got some K.F.C. in the dorm, I'm "bout to go eat. I'll catch you later. I'll have that money for you then, too."

"Cool." T-Bone gave Slide five and then headed for the gym. T-Bone always had to go find Ronald to holla at him. Ronald didn't like coming down the Hollow to see T-Bone. The Hollow was too much like the streets for Ronald, who was focused on getting out of prison. Ronald always said the Hollow reminded him of 14th Street.

Going on twenty nine-years-old, Ronald had had enough of prison, but like T-Bone, Ronald's prison record was a thorn in his side. The parole board did him the same way they did T-Bone. Ronald didn't let the parole set offs get him down; he knew his time would come as long as he stayed focused. Ronald worked hard on making himself a better man day in and day out. He was now Muslim and practiced Islam with all of his heart.

Ronald was dealt a painful blow when Diane died in '84 from a brain aneurysm after being in a coma for a short time. The death of his sister crushed Ronald; she was like a mother to him. However, Ronald didn't lose focus of the future.

Ronald and Roland were tight as brothers should always be. Roland was by Ronald's side every step of the way, doing all that Ronald needed him to do.

Ronald was also in college on the Hill taking up business management and criminal justice. He was trying do something with himself. If he had to be locked up he wanted it to work for him.

Ronald was also a married man. Synthia loved him and respected him and his religion, but she was afraid of Islam. Synthia grew up going to church and didn't want to turn her back on what her parents had taught her. Ronald respected that, although he still taught her about Islam in bits and pieces.

Lil' Ronald was doing well in school, and was outstanding in boxing and football. Roland was training Lil' Ronald and Chris, it was his way of keeping them out of trouble.

Coming out of the gym tired and sweaty with a towel around his neck, Ronald smiled when he saw T-Bone walking his way. Checking T-Bone out, Ronald laughed and shook his head: T-Bone attracted a crowd even when he walked alone, he was a star on the Hill. Having dope on the compound made T-Bone a very important man. Shaking the small crowd, T-Bone slid up on Ronald and gave him five. "What's up, Ronnie?"

"Just gettin' a little shake out in," Ronald said as he and T-Bone made their way down the crowded walk. They stopped in front of Ronald's dorm—7 Dorm.

"I talked to Frank today," T-Bone said as he lit a Newport. "I caught him up the club, him and Fray was hangin' out."

"Oh yeah," Ronald said, watching a punk and his man come out the dorm; the punk looked just like a woman.

"Frank told me to tell you to call him tonight after nine, he said he gon' be waitin' for your call." T-Bone blew smoke in the air. "He said he got all the stuff you asked for for your box, too. He gon' mail the joint off in the mornin'."

"Cool, I'll call him after I come back from prayer." Ronald rubbed his chin and thought about how much of a true comrade Frank was. Frank was a man of his word; he always did what he said he was going to do. Everybody loved Frank; he was taking care of countless men in prison and their families on the streets. "I meant to ask you about this situation Frank got wit' this dude Roy Evans, what's up wit' that?" Ronald asked with concern.

Roy Evans was a dude T-Bone went to school with when he was young. Roy was also a new player in the upcoming crack game that was taking over the streets. Somehow, Roy had slipped into the drug game on a banana pill and bumped into a big coke connect at a fight in Atlantic City. Most of the coke that came into D.C. came through Roy Evans' hands; he was blowing up and blowing everyone out of the water with his coke prices. A lot of proven street dudes in the drug game that had paid their dues didn't respect Roy nor his choke hold on the game. Frank couldn't stand the nigga Roy, but didn't want to take him out because a lot of men were eating because of the nigga. Frank had a lot of pull in the city. Everybody knew it. The broad daylight killing of Cowboy and his crew had earned Frank a lot of respect in the streets. Frank's crew and Roy's crew had bumped heads a few times in the last few months, but no blood had been spilled. However, animosity between the two crews was brewing. Word on the streets was that Frank was jealous of Roy, but that was far from the truth. Frank saw Roy as a punk and in Frank's book, punks had no place in the game. Only the strong survived.

"The dude Roy Evans ain't even on Frank's level in the streets. He got a lot of money, but Frank is too strong city-wide for a nigga like Roy. The nigga don't want to fuck wit' Frank and his crew. I think the shit is goin' to blow over. You know how it is when a new comer gets in the game."

"I just want Frank to watch his back. I been hearin' a lot about him and this joker Roy."

"Don't trip off it, Frank gon' always be on top of his game." T-Bone patted Ronald on the shoulder.

Washington, D.C., Wednesday, May 28, 1986

"We just got twenty-five keys from the airport," Baby Face said to Frank, standing outside the driver's side window of Frank's white 1986 BMW 735i.

"Cool, you and Bennie know what to do. I'll catch y'all later, I gotta run Uptown and take care of a few things." Frank gave Baby Face five and pulled off.

Heading Uptown with Fray in the passenger seat of the BMW, Frank got on his car phone, called, one of his weight customers, and told him in code that he could holla at Baby Face. The coke game was still new to Frank, but he caught on quickly. It was Baby Face's idea to get involved with cocaine; Frank was still in love with the dope money. However, Frank had to admit that the cocaine money came fast and around the clock like nothing he'd ever seen. It just came with too many problems for him. Nevertheless, Frank was a player in the new game.

"Frank, you know the dude Roy Evans pulled up on me in front of the Madness Shop. He want me to holla at you to make sure y'all ain't got no problems," Fray said, counting a handful of cash.

"Man, I ain't even thinkin' 'bout that chump." Frank sighed. "I'm tired of that scared nigga, anyway. I don't know why he so worried about me. If I wanted to do somethin' to him he would be hit by now."

Fray laughed. "He know that. Don't worry about him, though. For real, you should be tryin" to squeeze that nigga for that connect he got. He want a reason to say y'all cool, anyway."

"Fuck that nigga. I don't need him. I'm cool wit' what I'm workin' wit'."

"Yeah, but if you can get that nigga to plug you in wit" that connect he got, it would open up a lot of doors. All you got to do is have a little talk wit' the nigga, tell him you tryin' to clear the air and that y'all can get some money together. He gon' go for it."

"I don't know, Horse Collar, I gotta think about that move there." Frank said.

Stopping at a traffic light on Georgia Avenue, Frank said, "I'll be right back." He got out the car and jogged toward the 7-Eleven. Fray looked out the window wondering what the hell was going on. He saw Frank jog around the side of the 7-Eleven to the parking lot. Moments later, Frank returned to the car with a young boy.

Back inside the car with young boy in the back seat, Frank made a U-turn and headed back toward the Maryland line. Adjusting the rear-view mirror so he could look at the young boy in the back seat, Frank said, "I don't want to catch you cuttin' school no more. You hear me?"

The young boy frowned.

"I don't care nothin' 'bout your little attitude," Frank said.

"You not my father!" Chris snapped. Going on ten-years-old, he and a few older boys had cut school. Lil' Ronald wasn't with them; he didn't do anything to risk going to the gym with

Roland.

"It don't matter if I'm your father or not, I'm your uncle, little nigga. I'm takin' you back to school, and if you keep running your mouth, I'ma tell your mother I caught you cuttin' school." Frank turned off of Georgia Avenue and headed for Takoma School.

"That's T-Bone's son?" Fray asked with a smirk on his face.

"Yeah, shorty swear he grown." Frank pulled up in front of the school and turned to Chris. "You got money in your pocket?"

Still frowning, Chris shook his head no. Frank gave him twenty dollars and reminded him about their deal, Chris and Lil Ronald got a hundred dollars for every A they got on their report cards. Frank walked Chris inside the school and back to class.

Central Facility, Thursday, May 29, 1986

The visiting hall was packed. Ronald, Synthia, and Lil' Ronald were sitting a few seats away from T-Bone, Cristal, and Chris. Ronald was talking to Lil' Ronald about his progress in school and sports; he was proud of his son. Lil' Ronald had showed Ronald some of his new combinations that Roland had taught him.

"So you think you sharp, huh?" Ronald smiled, throwing a punch at Lil Ronald, who weaved it.

"I'm on top of my game, young." Lil' Ronald made both of his parents laugh. "I'ma be just like you when I grow up." Lil Ronald had seen tapes of his father's fights; he watched them over and over. He was obsessed with the fact that his father was a pro boxer before he went to prison. Ronald was Lil' Ronald's role model.

"You wanna be like me, huh?" Ronald smiled.

"Yeah."

"I hope that don't mean you gon' come to prison like me." Ronald shot back at his son, just to see where his mind was at.

"Nah, I'ma be a fighter like you." Lil' Ronald punched his father in the chest.

"Just wanted to make sure you still thinkin' like the man of the house," Ronald joked.

"Why you keep tellin' him that? I'm the man of the house until you come home." Synthia playfully rolled her eyes. She was looking good in her huge bamboo earrings, gray Polo sweat suit, and her around-the-way-girl hairdo.

"You can't be the man of the house, ma. You a woman," Lil' Ronald said, looking just like his father.

Ronald laughed. Looking at Synthia, he said, "He got a point, baby. You can't be the man, you gotta be the first lady." He leaned over and kissed his wife.

T-Bone was getting on Chris for getting back-to-back bad report cards. "You think all this is a joke." T-Bone looked his son in the eyes and waved his hand around the visiting hall. "You think it's cool to keep getting in trouble?" T-Bone didn't raise his voice, but it was clear that he was very serious.

Chris shrugged. "I don't know." He looked down at the floor; he hated when his father got on him. Although he respected his mother to the utmost, his father was the only one that could grab his attention and keep it.

"Your mother told me you been sneakin' out the house. What's up wit' that?" T-Bone asked.

"Ma don't be tryin' to let me hang out wit' my friends. Now that Lil' Ronald be goin' to the gym wit' Roland everyday, it be borin' in the house."

"Why you don't go to the gym wit' Roland and Lil' Ronald no more?"

"I do sometimes, but not everyday. Roland be makin' us do push-ups and sit-ups. I just want to get in the ring and put the gloves on. I don't be feelin' like workin' out everyday."

T-Bone laughed. "You don't want to get big and strong

while you learn how to box?"

"I know how to box, dad. I don't need to do all those push-ups and stuff."

"He want to hang out wit' all those older boys," Cristal said. She was looking good, too, dressed in a Guess jean outfit and a pair of red Gucci tennis shoes. "Them boys up Georgia Avenue like thirteen or fourten. Chris ain't got no business hanging out wit' them."

"I don't hang out wit' them, that's Markelle and them. I be wit' Eyone and them. They my age."

"Look here, big man. I don't want you sneakin' out the house no more. If you wanna go outside ask your mother. That ain't hard," T-Bone said.

Central Facility, Wednesday, July 10, 1986

Smoke filled the sky over the Hill as fires burned out of control. Gray skies filled with clouds threatened to rain as the evening grew old. Police and National Guards had the prison surrounded with shotguns and rifles; they had already fired shotguns and tear gas at the rioting convicts around noon, which was about three hours after convicts had attacked C.O.s and began to set fires. The problem came as a result of different changes concerning visits and packages from home. Lorton had been run one way for so long that any changes would never be taken lightly. Unlike other group uprisings, that one exploded out of the blue due to a build up of frustration, overcrowding, and summer heat.

Amongst a number of convicts tearing through the prison destroying everything in their way was T-Bone. He was smashing windows with a baseball bat. Other convicts were doing the same. They headed for the administration building. Once there, they forced their way inside. No one was inside. The warden and his staff was outside of the fence. A few C.O.s were trapped inside the prison. T-Bone and Slide broke into the records office; they planned to find their records and destroy them. "Set all this shit on fire!" T-Bone yelled as he snatched prison records from the metal file cabinets and set them on fire. As flames grew, he and Slide ran back outside and mixed in with the crowd of convicts that were running by the building. Gunfire thundered from behind them. D.C. and VA police were shooting at the convicts through the fence. No one was hit as the mob of convicts disappeared into the smoke and destruction.

Ronald was in no mood for the riot or what was to follow. His focus was on going home. However, when the National Guards began firing tear gas and shotguns, Ronald was forced to take cover. He and a group of convicts had taken a stand on the ball field.

"Here they come!" a convict yelled. The National Guard were entering the front gate in riot gear with German shepherds. The convicts headed for the burning dorms seeking refuge as the tear gas began hitting the air again. Jogging through a cut between two dorms, Ronald could hardly see due to the thick smoke. The thick smoke was burning his nose, eyes, and throat, even with a T-shirt wrapped around his face. As he came out on the other side of the dorm he saw a bloody body stretched out on the walk. A few feet away, there was a C.O. laying stretched out in the middle of the street who'd been stabbed repeatedly. Ronald kept moving toward the Hollow.

A short while later, the National Guard had the convicts surrounded. They moved in quick, cracking heads. Within two hours, they had regained control of the Hill. More than five hundred convicts were shipped out before nightfall. Ronald, T-Bone, and Slide were among the convicts that were sent behind the Wall.

Maximum Security, Wednesday, July 10, 1986

The convicts that were sent behind the Wall were beaten

with clubs and sprayed with mace while they were still chained up. They were then left in holding cells in R-N-D, packed like sardines. T-Bone was still bleeding with his eyes and throat burning from the mace. T-Bone was pissed off and in a murderous rage. He knew and would never forget the lieutenant that smacked him in the face with a walkie talkie and sprayed him in the face at point blank range.

"I swear to God, I'ma kill that cracker!" T-Bone hissed, his eyes were burning so bad he thought he was going blind. "Watch!"

Angry as a raging bull, banged up, and bleeding, Ronald sat on the floor beside T-Bone. From the pain in his side, Ronald thought that his ribs may have been broken when he was stomped out by five C.O.s. He felt just like T-Bone.

"I'ma put that knife in that punk ass lieutenant first chance I getl" T-Bone said as tears of burning anger rolled down his cheeks.

Maximum Security, Friday, August 9, 1986

3 Block was loud, live, and hot—too hot! Even the walls were sweating from the summer heat. The block was for "cut up" convicts; dangerous -men.

Standing behind the bars of his small, one-man cell with his arm through the bars holding a small plastic mirror looking into the cell next to his talking to Slide, Ronald laughed as Slide told him how he had robbed a dude without a gun one time at a crap game in Southwest. There was a terribly unbearable smell in the air at the time that the convicts had to deal with. Mad about not being let out of his cell for a shower, a convict on the bottom tier had thrown shit and piss in the face of the C.O. that was running the block. The human waste was still on the tier, almost cooking because of the intense heat. An old, six-foot fan in front of Ronald's cell on the catwalk was blowing the foul smell around, making things worst. Even with a towel around his face, the smell was still getting to Ronald.

Downstairs, convicts were banging and yelling for the C.O. to let somebody out to clean up the waste. Threats were made to set fires and flood the block if something was not done about the waste.

Fifteen minutes later, convicts on the top and bottom tier were burning sheets and newspaper on the tier. The block filled with thick gray smoke in no time. The sound of men coughing and choking only added to the confusion. Three C.O.s came with fire extinguishers and put out the fires. Detail men were let out of their cells to clean up the block.

Hours later, the block was running smooth. Convicts were being let out for recreation. Ronald and Slide had finished their one thousand push-ups in their cells and were back at the bars kicking it, waiting to come out for their showers. Ronald was schooling Slide to a few things about Islam.

"I didn't know Muslims believe in Jesus," Slide said.

Ronald laughed. "Cut it out."

"No bullshit."

"Muslims believe in all prophets, man. We just don't believe Jesus is God nor the son of God. We believe he is a created man that was a great prophet, born to a virgin mother."

"I can't go for that virgin mother stuff, either, Ronnie." Slide laughed and shook his head. "I don't believe no woman can have a baby without a man. That's too much right there."

"How you think we got here?"

"I believe in God and all that, I just don't believe Mary ain't have sex wit' a dude. I just can't buy that one."

"How you think the first man got here? He ain't need a mother or a father. The first man was created by Allah, so why can't Allah, as a sign, create a situation where a woman has a baby without havin' sex? The first man, Adam, is proof that Allah can create whatever He wants to."

Slide gave up a skeptical look. "I see what you sayin', but it's still hard to believe, for me, anyway."

"I ain't gon' force it on you. I'm just givin' you somethin' to think about," Ronald said.

A little while later, mail was passed out. Ronald got a letter from Synthia and Slide got one from his cousin, Wayne Perry, who was over Youth Center I.

Back at the bars with Slide, Ronald said, "You know Eddie Mathis got that murder beef overturned."

"Oh yeah, that's alright."

"Yeah man, E.J. said he was gon' give that time back, he got them peoples. I know they mad as I don't know what about that." Ronald smiled; it was always good to hear that one of his comrades had beat the system. "Who wrote you?" Ronald asked Slide.

"My cousin, Wayne. He sent a picture." Slide handed Ronald the picture through the bars. There was about ten dudes in the picture at a Youth Center go-go.

Ronald looked at the picture, it reminded him of his Youth Center days. He knew a few men in the picture: Wayne Perry, Gator, Sop Sop, Titus, Mario, Rome, and Wendell. "They over there funnin' ain't they?" Ronald smiled as he handed Slide the picture.

"Yeah, no bullshit. The Center was sweet." Slide looked at the picture again.

"Do Wayne still be playin' baseball?" Ronald asked Slide. "He was one of the baddest baseball players I ever seen."

"Man, Silk ain't thinkin' 'bout no baseball no more. He on his gangster shit."

Ronald laughed. "Yeah, Silk always been wild. I remember when he beat the baseball coach with a bat down Randall, that was in the seventies."

"Tier wet!" a convict yelled from downstairs. "White shirt in the house!" All convicts in the block understood that a lieutenant was making his rounds on the bottom tier.

T-Bone came out for rec and walked by Ronald's cell without speaking to him or Slide. T-Bone never did that.

"What's up wit' T?" Slide asked Ronald.

"I don't know." Ronald frowned, flipping his mirror the other way to see what the hell was up with T-Bone. All of a sudden, a light came on in Ronald's head and he began calling T-Bone. "T! T! Let me holla at you!" Ronald had to call T-Bone a few times.

"What's up, Ronnie?" T-Bone's eyes had that old fire in them.

"Don't do it, man. It ain't worth it," Ronald said.

"Fuck that. I'ma punish this cracker." T-Bone stepped off and walked down the tier toward the shower area.

Ronald called T-Bone a few times, but T-Bone wasn't trying to be talked out of what he planned to do. T-Bone and the lieutenant that had smacked him in the face had bumped heads a few times since T-Bone had been in 3 Block, but T-Bone was always behind bars. Now, T-Bone could catch him on the tier.

Looking down the narrow tier with their mirrors, Ronald and Slide had bad feelings in their stomachs; they knew how T-Bone was when he had his mind made up. There was no way for them to stop him from stabbing the lieutenant By no means was Ronald among the broken men, but he didn't want to see T-Bone throw his life away by killing a lieutenant. Ronald called T-Bone a few more times. No response. T-Bone was hiding in the shower with his knife.

The back gate to the top tier popped open and Lieutenant Brinkley strolled onto the tier. "Top tier wet! Soaking wet, from the back!" a convict yelled. Smoking a Newport, Lieutenant Brinkley walked up the tier looking into the cells along the way. He was a tall, white man with a huge belly. In his mid forties, the lieutenant had worked behind the Wall for close to twenty years and was one of the so-called "tough cops."

Ronald's heart pounded as Lieutenant Brinkley walked by his cell. T-Bone stepped out of the shower, knife in hand, and began walking in the lieutenant's direction. Watching the whole thing through his mirror, Ronald gritted his teeth and shook his head. T-Bone always did what he said he was going to do, no matter what the cost. Lieutenant Brinkley dropped his Newport and took off running back down the tier when he saw T-Bone, but the back gate was locked. The C.O. at the control box didn't understand what was going on at that point. The lieutenant tried to grab his walkie talkie to call for help, but T-Bone was already on his ass. "Come here, muthafucka!" T-Bone hissed as he grabbed the lieutenant and slammed his knife into his chest with the force of a powerful right hook. The lieutenant screamed for help and dropped his walkie talkie. T-Bone stabbed him repeatedly and slammed him against the catwalk gate. "Don't get scared now, cracker muthafucka!" The lieutenant tried to fight T-Bone off of him but there was no use, T-Bone was all over him, turning his white shirt red. Seconds later, ten C.O.s ran onto the tier and sacked T-Bone, but not before he stabbed the shit out of one of them. They commenced to beating the life out of T-Bone. More C.O.s ran onto the tier and joined in the beating of T-Bone. Convicts in the cells went off, yelling and throwing things at the C.O.s.

Lieutenant Brinkley was dragged off the tier covered with his own blood, clinging to life. After more beating, T-Bone was also dragged off the tier, unconscious.

Ronald dropped his head and felt a deep sense of regret for not being able to stop his comrade from stabbing the lieutenant Thoughts of Cristal and Chris flooded Ronald's mind. "Damn!" Ronald snapped.

Chapter 19

Washington, D.C., Wednesday, February 25, 1987

It was cold outside. The skies were white with thick clouds all over that blocked out the sun. Snow covered the ground from three days ago. The streets of D.C. were now held hostage by the crack epidemic. Eric B. & Rakim's Paid in Full was coming through the speakers of the D.O.C. van as it headed into the Northeast section of town. Ronald sat in the back of the van nodding his head to the rap music. He had made parole and was on his way to the halfway house on G Street. During the whole ride up 1-95 from Lorton, the C.O. that was driving kept asking Ronald if he would ever box again. Boxing was the last thing on Ronald's mind as he headed toward freedom once again. He'd done seven years and some change, and had made it back to the streets alive. Ronald's goal was to stay out of prison, and be a father to his son and a good husband to his wife. He wanted no parts of the fast money that came with the crack era.

"I know you messed up about your man T-Bone," the C.O. said. "That's fucked up how he got caught up at the end of his bid like that. He could be takin' this ride wit' you."

"T-Bone man enough to deal wit' his situation," Ronald said, taking up for his man even though he knew the C.O. was right. "Sometimes, a man gotta do what he gotta do. One thing for sure, slim ain't gon' cry about his situation, he gon' do his time like a man wit' his head held high."

The C.O. sighed. "I don't see how y'all do it." He turned the radio down. "I couldn't do no twelve years and then get twenty more at the end of the road."

T-Bone took a cop to twenty years in the feds for the murder of the lieutenant He had no win in court; if he would have went to trial he would have gotten life without parole.

"I respect T-Bone, one thing I can say about him is that he ain't goin' for shit. He damn sure a legend, they gon' be talkin' 'bout how he killed old Brinkley for years."

"Yeah, I'm hip." Ronald sighed and looked out the window. A legend? What did that really mean to T-Bone, who was going to have to spend twenty more years away from his wife and son? T-Bone put that knife in the lieutenant because the lieutenant crossed a line with the wrong nigga. T-Bone was one of the many men that left nothing behind, nothing unchecked. T-Bone didn't care about the price he had to pay for correcting a wrong; if he was ever crossed there would always be hell to pay. Ronald felt sorry for his comrade, but knew that T-Bone wouldn't want pity. All T-Bone wanted from Ronald was his realness. Ronald would give his man that without asking.

Community Correctional Center 3 at 1430 G Street was Ronald's first step back into the free world. He was processed and assigned a bunk in a room with other ex-cons. The room was set up like a Lorton dorm. Ronald knew most of the dudes in the half-way house; he'd done time with them down Lorton and in the feds. After Ronald got himself together, he found a place to pray. He praised Allah and thanked Him for seeing him through all of his struggles. Ronald then got on the phone and called Synthia to let her know that he'd touched down; she assured him that she was on her way to bring him all the things he needed.

After getting off the phone, Ronald went to the bathroom. There was a funny smell inside. A dude was under the vent smoking crack. Ronald shook his head and left. Welcome home, huh? he thought. Ronald knew times had changed.

Big Floyd saw Ronald coming out of the bathroom arid gave him five. "What's up, Ronnie. Somebody told me you was here."

"Yeah, just got here a few minutes ago. I was tryin' to use the bathroom, but some joker up in there hittin' the pipe." Ronald nodded toward the bathroom.

"That's the thing out here. You'd be shocked to find out who on the pipe. That crack shit is like the devil in a bottle. Everybody got they hands in that shit some kinda way. All the bad bitches I knew before I went down Lorton smoke that shit now; they'll do anything for a rock, too. I get my dick sucked every time I leave out for work."

Ronald shook his head. "I don't want no parts of that there."

Floyd sat on Ronald's bunk and brought him up to speed with all that was going on in the streets. By the way Floyd spoke, Ronald could tell that Floyd was impressed by what Frank had going on in the streets. Floyd told Ronald that Frank was the "man."

"Ronald, somebody outside for you," another dude said as he came in the room.

Ronald went out front to get his belongings from Synthia. She was sitting in her silver '86 Volkswagen Jetta. Ronald jumped in the car. He hugged and kissed his wife like it would be the last time. She questioned him about a few things regarding his stay at the half-way house.

"When can I get you alone?" Synthia rubbed his crotch with a wicked smiled.

"In a day or two." He smiled. "Believe me, you gon' know when it's time." He leaned over and kissed her again. Synthia couldn't stop smiling. Her man was home! They sat in the warm car for a good twenty minutes before someone from the halfway house told Ronald he had to come back inside. "I love you, baby. I'll call you later." He kissed her again.

Back inside the halfway house, Ronald could hear gunshots in the distance. Although the gunshots were blocks away, they were a strong reminder of the violence that had a stronghold on the streets. He and Floyd continued to talk.

"I'm messed up about ole T-Bone," Floyd said.

"Yeah, me too. Slim did what he felt he had to do, though." Ronald slid on a pair of brand new Timberlands. "You know how T is."

"He been like that since we was young," Floyd said. He and T-Bone had found out that an old timer from Uptown was riding around with twenty thousand dollars in cash in his Cadillac; they ended up robbing the old timer and when they were done, the old timer promised them that they would pay with their lives. The old timer then spat in T-Bone's face. T-Bone didn't think twice, he put seven bullets in the old timer's head. "T-Bone one of them dudes that just don't take no shit. Good man, though."

Ronald didn't really want to talk about T-Bone anymore, it was bringing him down. "T gon' be alright, though."

Floyd understood that Ronald was trying to cut the conversation about T-Bone. "So, what you gon' do wit' yourself out here?"

"I ain't sure yet, but I ain't playin' no games. I'ma get a job and chill out." Ronald glanced over at the TV and saw that there was some big shooting on the news.

"You ain't gon' try to get back in the ring?" Floyd lit a Newport. "You ain't too old."

"Everybody been askin' me that. It really ain't in my heart no more, for real. But, I won't say no. I'm just tryin' to get used to bein' back in the streets, dig where I'm coming from? Besides, I'm gettin' old, I'll be thirty this year. Boxin' takes up a lot of time. I got a family. I'm tryin' to make up for lost time wit' my wife and son." Ronald pulled a Polo sweatshirt out of the bag Synthia brought to him. Pulling the shirt over his head, he said, "What's up wit' you, though? You been out here for two months now. What you been up to?"

Floyd pulled a knot of cash from his Guess jeans and flipped through it, showing Ronald the big bills. "I'm fuckin' wit' the dude Roy. He got shit sewed up wit' that crack shit. He hit me off wit' a whole key of powder as soon as I touched down, told me to get on my feet. You know me, him, and T-Bone used to go to school together, right?"

"Yeah, T told me."

"Roy a good nigga. He wanna see real niggas get money. If you just comin' home and your name ringin', he gon' holla at you." Floyd respected Roy Evans.

"You just gon' sneak back in town and don't holla at your man or nothin', huh?" a voice said from the bedroom door.

Ronald looked up and saw Frank in a huge black Polo winter coat, holding a duffel bag full of clothes and other things. Ronald smiled as he got up to hug Frank. "How you get in here?" Ronald asked.

"I run the city. I do what I want out here." Frank smiled.

"There you go wit' that Godfather stuff, I keep tellin' you..."

"I'm just playin'. I know the dude at the door. He buy coke from one of my little men. Anyway, I brought you some fresh gear and stuff. Synthia told me you was up here. I had to slide through." Frank looked at Floyd and gave him a nod. Floyd did the same as he left the room.

Frank and Ronald went down to the rec room where a few dudes were shooting pool. Ronald and Frank grabbed a pair of chairs and got a spot in the back. Under the sound of go-go music that was coming from a boom box, Ronald and Frank spoke for a while. Frank knew Ronald wanted nothing to do with the drug game, so the subject never came up. Most of their conversation was about T-Bone and Ronald's plans for the future. Frank was still hurt about T-Bone's situation. "It ain't like he can't do twenty, though," Frank said, trying to find a bright side to a dark situation.

"I guess that's one way to look at it. Nevertheless, that's gon' be thirty-some years in prison for T. His kids gon' be grown when he get out, if he ever get out. We both know how his temper is."

"No bullshit." Frank sighed.

A short while into their conversation, Frank's beeper vibrated. He went to call the number back and found out that Bennie and three others had been murdered in the big shooting that was on the news a while ago. Frank told Ronald about the news. Ronald just shook his head; the streets took no prisoners.

"I know what you thinkin', you don't even have to say it," Frank said. He and Ronald wrapped up their conversation and Frank left; he had to go deal with what was going on in the streets. Bennie was part of his crew and Frank had to make sure somebody answered for what had happened.

Later on as Ronald laid in the bed listening to slow music that was playing from someone's radio, the distant sound of police sirens made him think of how blessed he was to be crime-free. He was grateful to be out of prison and he planned to never return. After facing death, life without parole, and all the other struggles of prison life, Ronald felt like he was now out of the woods, so to speak. He said a quick prayer and thanked Allah again for seeing him through. Slowly, Ronald fell asleep.

Washington, D.C., Monday, March 9, 1987

For an ex-con, finding work was hard, but Ronald did it. He got a job working as a youth counselor in a group home for troubled youth. Frank had a number of jobs lined up for Ronald, but he didn't want anything to do with the dudes that owned the businesses where the jobs were. However, Ronald did accept the car Frank bought him, a white 1987 Nissan 300 ZX.

Ronald's good friend, Wilfred Walker, was trying to talk him into getting back into the ring, but Ronald wasn't ready to dedicate himself to boxing, even though he felt he could get in the ring with Spinks or Tyson.

Stepping out of the group home on Kennedy Street, Ronald saw one of the youngsters that was in the group home coming down the street smoking a cigarette. Ronald smiled and shook his head. "Creek, come on, lil' man, you know you can't be walkin' down the street smoking like that," Ronald said. "Ms. Perry gon' take your home visits for that."

Creek smiled and plucked his Newport into the busy street; he respected Ronald. At seventeen-years-old, Creek was grown and didn't pay any adults any attention, however, Ronald was like a big brother to him. "I'm gettin' tired of all these damn rules, joe." Creek shook his head as he gave Ronald five.

"You only got two months left, you can suck it up for that long, right?" Ronald said, watching the passing cars fly up and down Kennedy Street.

"Yeah, I guess so." Creek sighed. He'd done eighteen months down Oak Hill and had to do six more months in a group home to finish up the time he got for being caught with a Tec-9 at fifteen-years-old.

"I'm 'bout roll out. You keep your head up. I'll see you tomorrow." Ronald gave Creek five and headed for his car as Creek went inside the group home.

It was sunny and cool outside with clear skies. Ronald slipped on his Gucci shades as he stuck the keys in his car door. A gold Benz with tinted windows pulled up right beside him. Ronald eyed the suspicious car. A touch of fear attacked Ronald, but he kept his cool. The passenger side window dropped smoothly. Junk Yard Band could be heard coming from the speakers. Ronald locked eyes with a brown-skinned dude that looked like a young Isiah Thomas in a Hugo Boss sweat suit with a thick gold chain around his neck.

"What's up, home team?" the brown-skinned dude said with a bright smile.

"Do I know you from somewhere?" Ronald asked the dude.

"Come on now, you gotta know who I am." The dude spoke with a tone of surprise that Ronald didn't know who he was. He was almost arrogant. "Everybody know me, like everybody know you, Ronald Mays. I bet a lot of money on you before you went to jail. You had one of the best left hooks I ever seen."

"I don't know you," Ronald said flatly.

"I'm Roy."

It all came together for Ronald.

"Oh yeah, I heard about you," Ronald said, ready to get on about his business. He and Roy Evans had nothing to talk about.

"I heard a lot about you, if you need anything out here you can holla at me. I know you just comin" home."

"Thanks, but no thanks. I'm cool." Ronald didn't like Roy and he had just met him face-to-face.

"Okay, I was just showin' a little respect to a good man. I'm a big fan of yours. You gon' get back in the ring? I'd put my money on you any day."

"I really don't know, I'm just tryin' to get a feel for the streets right now."

"Yeah, no doubt. I can dig that. I'ma let you go, but if you ever want what's due to a man of your caliber, holla at me." Roy's Benz pulled off.

Ronald shook his head and got in his car, rubbed the wrong way.

Later on inside The Black Widow, Ronald and Synthia sat in the upstairs lounge just talking and enjoying the time they had together before Ronald had to return to the halfway house. While they were talking, the phone rang. Synthia got it, it was T-Bone. She spoke to T-Bone for a second and gave the phone to Ronald.

"What's up, slim?" Ronald said.

T-Bone was still behind the Wall waiting to be sent back to the feds. "I'm holdin' on down here," he said.

Ronald could tell something was wrong with his man just by the sound of his voice. "You sound like somethin' wrong, what's up?"

"I was just arguin' wit' Cristal. She beefin', talkin' 'bout I don't love her and Chris. She say if I loved them I wouldna done nothin' to make me stay in prison." T-Bone explained the whole conversation. "I got a lot of time to do, Ronnie. I'm thinkin' about tellin' her to go head on wit' her life."

" I wouldn't move that fast." Ronald knew T-Bone and Cristal were going to start having issues as a result of the fresh twenty years T-Bone had to do. "You don't gotta push the hand of fate, what's meant to be is gon' be. Cristal just hurtin'' right now. She love you, that's her emotions talkin'."

"Yeah, I know." T-Bone thought about his situation; he had no one to blame but himself. He knew he lost all control when he was mad. "You know what? I ain't never been one to cry over my yesterdays and I ain't gon' start now, but ever since I punished that lieutenant in 3 Block and you told me not to do it, I been wishin' I let that shit go. I ... I couldn't, though. I couldn't let that shit go. I been like that all my life. I just blank out and it costs me every time. I know Cristal can't do twenty more years wit' me and I don't expect her to. On the strength, I know I ain't never gon' get out of prison. I ain't like you, Ronnie. I can't rationalize when I'm pissed off. I just go, slim. Picture me doin' twenty years in the feds."

"T, look here. You a fighter—mind, body, and soul—and fighters don't never give up! They never lay down! You talkin' crazy. Yeah, you got a dub to do. You could be doin' life, you still don't lay down or give up. You don't talk about you ain't never gon' come home. You do what you gotta do and then let the pieces fall where they gon' fall. We done been through too much, we done seen too many dudes do twenty or thirty years and make it back home. Don't nobody wanna do that much time, but it can be done. As long as I'm alive, I'm here for you, your wife, and kids. Y'all my family. I'm gon' make sure they okay. Shit ain't gon' be sweet, life is full of hardships, but dudes like us make a way. Even when it ain't no way. No matter what. That's what makes us different. You know that. Our principles and what we stand for make us real men and can't nothin' or nobody take that from us. If we gotta do one hundred years, we do it wit' our head held high. It is what it is. We can't change that. You dig?"

"Yeah, slim ... you right. You one hundred percent right. I gotta get off this horn. I love you, slim, you one of the realest dudes I ever met. We gon' always be family."

"Always."

"Holla at Cristal for me."

"No problem."

When Ronald got off the phone, he told Synthia that he'd be back, he had to go holla at Cristal for T-Bone. He went upstairs and found Cristal in the office crying with her face in her hands as she sat on the sofa. Cristal looked up when she heard the door open, she tried to wipe away her tears.

"We family, girl. You ain't gotta hide your feelings from me." Ronald sat beside her and put a brotherly arm around her. She needed it; she began to cry with her face in his chest.

"I can't do it no more." Cristal sobbed. "I can't take it, I can't do it no more, Ronald."

Ronald patted her on the back. "I understand..."

"No, you don't!" Cristal vented. "You'll never understand what I go through, you'll never understand what me and Synthia went through all these damn years! We been doin' time, too!" She continued to sob. "I been doin' time wit' Ty since I was fourteen, I done did time! I always been there for him! I done broke the law for him and everything, Ronald! He don't think about me and Chris when he be livin' by the jail codes, he don't care about us! What the fuck am I supposed to do?! Sit back and wait another twenty fuckin' years! I just did twelve years waitin' on him. I can't do it no more!" Cristal broke down into more sobs. Ronald let her get it all out. "And, I feel like shit! I feel like I'm the bad guy! I feel like I'm the one that's bein' the sell out! I'm breakin' our bond! It was supposed to be me and him for life, but I can't do twenty more years! I just can't do it!"

Ronald gently lifted her chin and looked into her sad eyes. "You ain't the bad guy." His words were smooth and soothing. "You just bein' real wit' yourself, most women would be in the wind by now ... shh ... most women would've been in the wind a long time ago, but you are still here and you are still here because you love Ty. Love is not always a good feelin'. Love hurts sometimes. We are all human, it hurts when the one we love is away from us. But, you know like I know that there is no one else for you but your soul mate. One day at a time, that's all we can do. T feels like yo..."

"How?! How can he feel like me?! I would never do anything to take me away from him and Chris for twenty years."

"Come on, you know he don't want to be away from you and Chris, but in the world he lives in everything is different. It's a world where disrespect is damn near like sin, and it has to be dealt with in a certain way. Men like me and Ty, that have been in prison all of our lives, we only know how to deal wit' those situations in one way. That's what makes us different, that same thing is what makes T the man you love. His situation is one of struggle, you are right, but when one of us hurt we all hurt. We are family, a team, a whole unit. Things are not always perfect, but we do the best we can. That's all we can do. That's all T will ever ask of you, just for you to do the best you can do. Don't just walk away, that's not your style.

Just do the best you can do, that's all."

Synthia walked in and told Ronald that Frank was downstairs looking for him. Ronald left Synthia to comfort Cristal and went to holla at Frank.

Downstairs, Ronald found Frank at the bar eating fried chicken. Frank was wearing a black Fila sweat suit and a pair of black Gucci tennis shoes. "What's up, Frank?" Ronald sat on the bar stool next to Frank.

"Shit done hit the fans, Ronnie," Frank said in a slow, even tone. He didn't even look up from his food. Ronald was alert and all ears. "Word is that the nigga Roy Evans had Bennie hit. He got him hit Uptown to try to put the shit on Tim-Tim since Bennie and Tim-Tim had some issues. Roy thought I would go right at Tim-Tim and them 14th Street niggas, but I looked into it. I knew Tim-Tim wouldn't move on me without checkin' wit' Fray. Roy must think I'm stupid, like I was just goin' to go straight to war and let him get all the money. He done fucked up now. Can't nobody talk me out of gettin' him hit now. I might do it myself."

"Why would the dude Roy get Bennie hit and not just get you hit? That would take care of it all, right?" Ronald raised his eyebrows. "Somethin' is missin'."

"That's the wild part. He put money on my head, too. He want me out the way. The nigga scared of me for real."

Ronald sighed deeply. He'd only been home for a hot second and too much drama was coming too close to home. "How you know he put money on your head?"

"I found out who hit Bennie and his men Uptown." Frank ordered a drink. "Baby Face and a few of my homies took care of that already. Baby Face got word on who's supposed to hit me."

"Who, man?!"

"The dude Willie Porter," Frank said.

Ronald gave Frank a look of disgust/disbelief. "Willie Porter?" Ronald couldn't believe it. Willie Porter was a cold-blooded chump down Lorton. Frank had stopped dudes from robbing Willie more than once when they were down Youth Center I and behind the Wall. "Cut it out, Frank."

"I ain't playin' no games. Baby Face got the info from a dude that's real close to the dude Roy," Frank said.

"Since when did Willie start takin' hits?" Ronald asked.

Frank told Ronald how the dude Willie came home from Lorton and started acting like all the Lorton gorillas he dreaded when he was locked up. Overnight, Willie came home and started dropping bodies for money; he'd killed two big names in the drug game. Roy Evans had paid for the murder of every dude Willie had hit. It was amazing how much heart a gun gave a coward. "The funny thing about the whole situation is that I was the one that put the bitch nigga, Willie, on his feet when he first came home." Frank sighed.

"The game done changed so much. It ain't no honor among men." Ronald shook his head. It was no way he was ever going to get back into a life of crime. "I saw the dude Roy today. He act like he known me for years." Ronald told Frank about the run-in with Roy. "He know you my man, so all that crap he was kickin'" was for show. He had to be tryin' to feel me out.

"Hell yeah, that scared ass nigga was tryin' to feel you out. But, he gon' learn that it's more to this game than makin' money. He don't know what he done got himself into, fuckin' wit' me."

A thought popped into Ronald's head. "The dude Roy only know me through what he done heard about me, he might think I'ma do somethin' if you get hit." Ronald didn't feel safe going back to the halfway house.

"If somethin' went wrong and things got out of hand, but you ain't gotta trip off that. His number gon' get bucked tonight, right along wit' that bitch nigga Willie's."

Nightfall covered the city and The Black Widow was packed. Fray and Greg Royster had rented the spot out to throw a party. Everybody that was somebody came through at one point or another throughout night. Drinks were on the house. Tons of the baddest women the city had to offer were all over the place. Eric B. & Rakim, and L.L. Cool J. were in the spot. D.C.'s own, Rare Essence, and Chuck Brown had the party moving in that Chocolate City way. Outside of the club, traffic was backed up and around the block. The police were making people move along. People who weren't invited to the party were trying to buy their way in.

Sitting at the bar talking to Roy Evans like there was nothing in the air, Frank sipped his drink without a worry in the world. Music blasted throughout the club as people crowded the spot. Roy knew Frank would be in the spot, but for Roy not to show his face in the place would be a sign of guilt that he had something to do with Bennie's murder. A deadly game of mental chess was being played.

"Fray and Greg done put together a nice get together here," Roy yelled over the go-go music as he sipped his drink, waiting for his chance to leave. He'd shown his face in the place for a good hour and had been seen having a friendly conversation with Frank out in the open.

"Yeah, they put it together wit' class." Frank smiled. Mike Blackwell walked by and spoke to Frank.

"I ran into your man Ronald today." Roy leaned close to Frank's ear.

"Yeah, he was tellin' me." Frank looked down at his Gucci watch. It was twelve forty one A.M.

"Ronald act like he don't want none of this money out here."

"Yeah, that ain't his thing. He don't mess around." Frank didn't like the fact that Roy even had Ronald on his mind.

"Well, I gotta run, baby boy. You be safe." Roy gave Frank five and a hug before leaving The Black Widow.

Outside The Black Widow, there was still a lot of people trying to get inside. Flashy cars and blasting music were everywhere. A police car turned on the flashing red and blue lights and pulled up behind a white Benz 190 E. A female officer got out and walked up to the driver's side window of the Benz. She asked for the driver's license and registration. The young hustler went with the program.

"Why do you keep driving around the block?" the officer questioned as her partner walked up on the passenger side, flashing a light inside the Benz.

"I'm tryin' to pick up a female," the young hustler said. The officer ran his name and told him to keep it moving. The police got back in their car and continued to patrol the area.

Around the corner on a dark residential side street, Roy Evans and his hired gun, Lil' Knuckles, walked to the Benz they rode to the party in. A few other people on the street were heading for their cars. Inside the Benz, Lil' Knuckles pulled his Mac-10 submachine gun from his leather jacket and sat it on his lap.

"That nigga Frank don't even know what's 'bout to hit him," Roy said, feeling confident that Frank was rocked to sleep and would never know what hit him. With Frank dead, Roy could really spread his wings in the streets with no one to get in his way.

"You shoulda let me hit his ass right in the club," Lil' Knuckles said as they rode down 8th Street.

"Nah." Roy smiled. "That would bring too much heat. I got it all mapped out. By this time tomorrow Frank won't be around no more. I think we should send somebody at his man Ronald just in case he want to do somethin' about Frank's murder."

Lil' Knuckles felt his palms begin to sweat. It wasn't normal for him to be nervous during times of drama. "Yeah, that's a must. I can go up in the halfway house and hit that nigga tonight, for real." He looked around as they stopped at a stop sign. They seemed to be the only souls out on the streets.

Out of nowhere, a burst of loud fully-automatic fire

exploded at close range. Blood and brains flew all over the driver's side window as Roy's lifeless body slumped forward behind the wheel. Lil' Knuckles jumped out of the car and ran around to the driver's side. He snatched the door open and shoved Roy's bloody body over to the passenger seat and jumped behind the wheel. With the smoking Mac-10 on his lap, Lil' Knuckles pulled off smoothly and disappeared into the night to get rid of Roy's body and burn the Benz.

The first part of Frank's plan was executed perfectly. He had been working on turning Lil' Knuckles for some time. Frank found out that Roy was spoon feeding the twenty one-year-old Lil' Knuckles. Two bricks of powder coke and a little coaching was all it took for Frank to get Lil' Knuckles to blow Roy's brains out.

An hour later, the body of Willie Porter was dumped in the woods along 1-95; he'd been shot in the back of the head five times.

Chapter 20

Washington, D.C., Sunday July 26, 1987

The summer heat was punishing everything outside as Ronald jogged through Rock Creek Park with Lil' Ronald and Chris behind him on their bikes. He was back in training, he couldn't resist getting back in the ring. Ronald had a fight coming up. Nothing big, just something to get him back in the ring. Wilfred Walker had pulled a few strings and put some hype on Ronald's "come-back." The press in the D.C. area were making a big deal out of the come-back of a home town hero. Even Ronald's parole officer was encouraging him to get back in the ring for another run.

Forty-five minutes later, dripping with sweat, Ronald took a seat on some rocks overlooking the flowing creek as water rushed over a small five-foot waterfall. The smell of the woods was strong and the sounds of passing cars flew by on the road behind him. Lil' Ronald gave his father a bottle of water to cool him off.

Both boys were looking more and more like their fathers. Lil' Ronald was light-skinned and slim with a medium build. Chris was dark and tall.

"Ronnie," Chris said. "We gon' go get my brother before you go to work?" Chris was real close with his brother Paul.

Ronald made sure he got all three boys together at least once a week.

"Yeah, we gon' go get Paul as soon as we leave," Ronald said, pouring a little water on his head.

Chris nodded and began throwing rocks into the creek. Moments later, he was thinking about his father. He was still hurt about his father's situation.

Right after T-Bone got the twenty years for killing the lieutenant Cristal took Chris to see his father. T-Bone came to the control center visiting room chained up like Harry Houdini. He got straight to the point. T-Bone had always made it a point to talk to his sons as if they were men.

"I got some bad news." T-Bone sat right in front of Chris.

Off to the side with tears in her eyes, Cristal looked at the floor with her arms folded.

At ten-years-old, Chris could tell something was wrong. "What's wrong, daddy?"

"Remember when I was tellin' you about your attitude, tellin' you how my attitude always kept me in places like this?"

Chris nodded.

"Well ... since I ain't learned how to control my attitude and temper, I done got into trouble again and I got to stay here longer."

"How much longer?"

"A long time."

"What's a long time?"

"Twenty years."

Chris was stunned. Quickly, he did the math. He would be thirty years old in twenty years. He felt like "hope" was being ripped away from him. Tears swelled up in his eyes. "Twenty years?! Why?!" He began to cry.

T-Bone understood that his son was still young, but he wanted to give it to him in the raw, to teach him a lesson about life. "This is what happens when men do things they shouldn't do."

"Why would you do something you shouldn't do if they gon' keep you here for twenty more years?" Chris wiped tears from his face.

"I really can't answer that question. I messed up, Chris. That's all I can say. Prison changes a man sometimes. At times, this place can make a man blow. That's what I did, I blew. I need for you to be strong for me and be a better man than I have been. Always know that I love you," T-Bone said.

That day down Lorton stayed with Chris and would never leave his heart. Looking at Ronald, Chris said, "Ronnie, you 'bout start boxin' again, so we gon' be rich, right?"

Ronald laughed a little bit. "Nah, we ain't gon' be rich, baby boy. We gon' have a little extra cash, though. We ain't gon' be rich unless I get some big fights. Why you ask me that, though?"

"'Cause Lil' Ronald said that when you start boxin' again that we gon' be rich and then we can bail my father out of jail."

Ronald felt the child's pain and wished he could bail T-Bone out of prison with money, but he couldn't. Rubbing Chris on the top of the head, Ronald said, "It don't work like that, if it did we would have your father out here wit' us right now."

Chris was tough. Tougher than most eleven-year-olds. He had accepted the fact that his father would be locked up for twenty years, which seemed like forever to him. Without a trace of emotion on his face, Chris said, "I told Lil' Ronald that."

Washington, D.C., Saturday, August 8, 1987

Ronald walked in the house just after six in the evening and Synthia told him that Chris had been arrested all the way out Rockville, MD with a group of older boys in a stolen car. Ronald sighed, he could see that he was going to have a hard time keeping Chris out of trouble. "Where Chris at?" Ronald asked Synthia.

"He upstairs in his room. Cristal tore the skin off his ass."

"I'ma go talk to him."

"You need to."

Ronald went to holla at Chris, who was alone in his room. Chris was still fired up from the beating his mother put on him. However, Ronald got Chris to open up to him.

"What's going on, Chris?" Ronald said. "What you thinkin' about?"

"I don't know."

"Come on now, you gotta do better than that, lil' man."

"I didn't know the car was stolen."

Ronald put his arm around Chris' shoulder. "Look here, you not like the young dudes that you hang wit'. You see what me and your father been through, right?"

Chris nodded.

"Do you want to go through that same stuff?"

"No."

"Prison is real, Chris. I went to prison for bein' hard headed and hangin' wit' the wrong crowd. I'm not goin' to let you and Lil' Ronald go through that mess. No matter what I gotta do. Now, me and you can be the best of friends or we can be beefin', but I'm not goin' to let you go down the same road me and your father went down. That's not for you. You dig?"

Chris nodded.

"From now on, you hangin' wit' me. Wherever I go, you go. Got that?"

"Yeah."

Later on, sitting on the porch with Chris' white pit bull, K-9, Ronald stared out at the dark field across the street from his house. The only sounds that could be heard were the sounds of the wind blowing and the chirping of crickets. It was peaceful. Ronald had just finished praying outside and was now sitting back thinking about the brothers he left behind in the system. He often thought about them to keep himself focused and grateful.

Synthia came outside and sat beside Ronald. She gave him a kiss and commended him for the way he dealt with Chris.

Synthia was Muslim now. Ronald didn't force it on her; she loved to read, so he began sliding her stuff to read and the rest was history. She took to Islam almost overnight.

"I was readin' the History of Islam book today," Synthia said. "Why does it always say A.H. after the dates?"

"That's how the Islamic calendar is dated. It means anno Hegirae in English, it's the start of the calendar from the date the Prophet Muhammad (PEACE BE UPON HIM) made his migration from Makkah to Madinah. So, when you see A.H. just think of the Hijrah and remember that the word means migration."

"Oh, I see. Like the regular calendar says A.D., the Islamic calendar says A.H."

"Somewhat." Ronald leaned forward. "There is no 'regular' calendar, as we sometimes say. The calendar that people call regular is really the Julian calendar, named after the joker Julius Caesar. So, when we say this is such and such month of '87, we are really sayin' it's 1987 A.D. and A.D. stands for anno Domini, which comes from Medieval Latin, meanin' in the year of our Lord. See where I'm comin' from?"

Synthia smiled. It amazed her how smart Ronald was after spending so much of his life in prison. It seemed like it was nothing he didn't know. Things he would just spit off the top of his head were things she had never heard of unless it came from him.

"Why you smiling?" Ronald asked.

"You're so smart. How do you remember all that stuff?"

"A prison cell is not always a bad place. If you are forced to be in one you gotta make the joint work for you. That's what I did."

"Let me ask you this, you said we use the Julian calendar, right? Well ... what did people use before that?" Synthia asked.

287

"Wow, that's a serious question. Let me put it like this. Since the beginning of time, as far as recorded history, people have used different ways to keep track of time. Some use the seasons, like the end of winter, some people used the moon. The oldest and most reliable calendars of all time are the lunar calendars. The Islamic calendar is a lunar calendar. The Julian calendar is a solar one. Then, you had the people of Egypt that at one time kept up with time based on the flooding of the Nile during the rainy season. It was different ways. When Rome came along with all their superstitions and complicated everything because they believed that even numbers were unlucky, they changed certain months, that's why we have months with 31 days. In fact, at one point, they even added a whole extra month to the calendar, it was called Mercedonius. I could go on and on about them Roman jokers, but we'll be here all night. But, that's how we get the calendar we use. The Romans changed everything, the calendar, the days of the week, even the Bible and the Sabbath day. They changed the Sabbath day from the seventh day of the week to Sunday—the day they worshiped their sun god. As a matter of fact, look at the days of the week. The days used to be based on seven celestial bodies. The Sun, Moon, Mars, Mercury, Jupiter, Venus, and Saturn. The seven day week came from ancient Mesopotamia, but were made a part of the Roman calendar in 321 A.D., then the Romans changed that, too. Mars was changed to Tiw's Day, Tiw is their god of war. Tiw's Day is what we call Tuesday. Mercury was changed to Woden's Day, Woden is their god of wisdom. That's how we get Wednesday. Jupiter was changed to Thor's Day, Thor is their god of thunder. That's how we get Thursday. Venus was changed to Frigg's Day, Frigg is their goddess of love. That's how we get Friday." Ronald raised his eyebrows. "You see what kind of games they be playin'? If we don't do our homework, we'll go for anything. I read a book while I was in Marion by Cater G. Woodson, it was called The Miseducation of the Negro. It was deep. The brother said that the best education we can ever get is the one we give ourselves. I never forgot that piece there. That's why I'm like I am and that's why I be makin' Lil Ronald and Chris read, they gotta have somethin' upstairs."

Synthia nodded. "I agree. I've learned so much readin' all them books you got upstairs."

Meanwhile, Frank and Baby Face were pulling up in the parking lot of a Landover, MD apartment complex. Frank used one of the apartments as a stash house. Frank and Baby Face got out of Frank's BMW and went inside the apartment building. Frank got ten bricks of powder cocaine out of the gun safe and placed them in a gym bag. He handed the bag to Baby Face. "That's more than enough to set up shop," Frank said, looking down at his beeper.

"Yeah, no doubt," Baby Face said. He was on his way down North Carolina to open up shop. He had a man that had already made the trip down 95 and swore to Baby Face that NC was a gold mine.

"How long you plan to stay down there?" Frank asked.

"'Bout two weeks, I want to see if it's like Sop Sop said it was. If everything work out, I'm just gon' start sendin' shit down the highway."

"Cool," Frank said. "Let's get outta here."

Frank and Baby Face headed out of the building into the cool darkness of the night.

"Don't move, muthafucka!" a voice hissed from behind them.

Frank and Baby Face found themselves at gunpoint. A masked gunman had been laying on the stash house for weeks.

"Drop the bag! Don't be a fool!" the gunman ordered, waving a .45 automatic.

Baby Face's face turned red with anger. He wanted to reach for his pistol.

"Give 'em the bag, slim," Frank said to Baby Face, knowing what was on his cousin's mind.

"Yeah, give me the bag, chump!" the gunman said. He then smacked Baby Face in the face hard with the heavy pistol, opening a nasty gash over Baby Face's eye. Enraged, Baby Face rushed the gunman, swinging punches. BOOM! BOOM! BOOM! The .45 knocked Baby Face to the ground. Frank went for his 9mm, but was hit with five rounds from the .45. As he fell to the ground, he heard the .45 continue to blast until everything went black.

The gunman grabbed the gym bag and took off running, not knowing that there was forty more bricks of cocaine and two hundred and sixty five thousand dollars inside the apartment.

Washington, D.C., Wednesday, August 19, 1987

The beeping sounds of the life support machines filled the small hospital room. Frank had all kinds of tubes running from his body as he laid in the white hospital gown wrapped up like a mummy. Nine .45 slugs had tore through his body with no mercy and left him clinging to life. He awakened from a coma three days ago and still remembered everything that went down. In his weak and painful state, the first thing he asked about was what happened to Baby Face. Ronald had to be the one to tell Frank that Baby Face was dead. The .45 slugs that Baby Face took to the head killed him instantly.

Sitting by Frank's side, Ronald couldn't stand to see his man in such a state. Weakly and painfully, Frank eased his head to the side to look at Ronald and forced a smile. The two bullets that grazed Frank's head had his head wrapped up as well. "This is what it's all about, huh, slim?" Frank didn't feel sorry for himself; he felt sorry for Baby Face, Bennie, and Fred, not to mention all the others that had died in the game. Life was short. Frank suffered a painful cough that snatched the smile off his face. He still cracked a joke. Sounding like Mike from The Godfather, Frank said, "Just when I think I'm out, they pull me right back in."

Ronald smiled and shook his head. "Stop playin', man. Shit is serious."

"Yeah, you right." Frank looked out of the window. It was a bright day outside. Without looking at Ronald, Frank said, "Whoever did this is gon' pay. You hear me? They gon' pay big."

"Don't worry about that right now. Just worry about gettin' better right now." Ronald squeezed Frank's hand. "Every dog has its day."

Washinfton, D.C., Thursday, September 3, 1987

Frank put up one hundred thousand dollars to find out who had robbed him and killed Baby Face. Money talked. Always. Within two days, Frank had learned that Big Floyd was the gunman that had crossed him. Big Floyd had turn to robbery after Roy Evans was murdered. He had murdered Lil' Knuckles a week before he moved on Frank and Baby Face after hearing that Lil' Knuckles had killed Roy.

Frank was in no shape to be out hunting for Big Floyd, so he stepped to somebody that he knew would do the job the way he wanted it done. He paid Wayne Perry fifty thousand dollars and two bricks of powder coke to get rid of Big Floyd. Wayne got right on it.

Georgia Avenue was alive and busy with traffic. People were everywhere. A group of dudes were standing in front of the Madness Shop talking shit and rapping to honeys that were walking by. A black Benz 300 E pulled up and double parked. Big Floyd got out like a movie star and spoke to a few old timers that he knew from down Lorton.

"Where that money at you owe me, nigga?" Floyd joked with his man, Patrick.

"I got you, nigga," Patrick said.

"Don't got me, get me, nigga," Big Floyd said.

While Big Floyd and Patrick were talking, a black Nissan Pathfinder with tinted windows pulled up nice and smooth. Wayne got out in a gray Hugo Boss sweat suit, a black Madness hat, and a pair of Gucci shades. He walked up to Big Floyd, and said, "Floyd, what's up, man?"

"Damn, ain't shit, Wayne." Big Floyd gave Wayne five. "When you get out?"

"Just got out last month," Wayne said.

"You need anything?" Big Floyd asked.

"Your life!" Wayne pulled out a .44 Mag and blew Big Floyd's brains out in front of everybody in broad daylight. As Big Floyd slumped to the ground in a pool of blood, Wayne looked around at the bystanders, and said, "Ain't nobody seen shit, right?"

Everybody was frozen with fear.

"That's what I thought." Wayne smiled as he walked back to the Pathfinder and rolled out.

Annapolis, MD, Sunday, September 27, 1987

The Jamerson Center was packed for the fights. Ronald was on the way to the ring with his team. Marvin Gaye's Let's Get it On played on the loud speakers. Ronald's whole team wore black Madness T-shirts with a picture of T-Bone on them. The words on the shirt read, Struggle Is a Way of Life! Lil' Ronald and Chris led the pack to the ring. By the way people were calling Ronald's name, it was clear that he had attracted a nice following. He felt that old magic again and was ready to go to work. There was no doubt about it, he was in good shape at a solid two hundred and five pounds. His opponent was a twenty five-year-old, two hundred and thirteen pound slugger that was up-and-coming. Wilfred Walker had picked the young slugger by the name of Louis Sparks to show the fans that at thirty-years-old, Ronald could still stand firm against young bulls.

After the fighters were introduced, Roland gave Ronald some last minute instructions. "This is it, baby boy. It's all about you. Keep in mind that you know more about the game than the youngster. You thirty now, it's about bein' smart and boxin'. Got me?"

"I got you," Ronald said, looking across the ring at Sparks. The bright lights and crowd had Ronald in a zone already.

The fight started. The first two rounds went by in a flash. Ronald was feeling out Sparks' speed; he'd taken Sparks' best shot and shook it off. Ronald's left hook was still deadly, but hidden well behind his long jab.

Round three was a great display of power and boxing. Sparks caught Ronald with a hook to the body that felt like a horse kick and followed that up with a four piece combination that brought the crowd to its feet. Ronald answered that with a flurry of ten punches followed by a crushing left hook that hurt Sparks and staggered him. Ronald then closed in with big lefts and rights from all directions. He forced Sparks into the corner and never allowed him to get himself back together. After a good five unanswered blows to the head of Sparks, the ref jumped in and stopped the fight. Ronald raised his arms and walked to his corner. Roland, Frank, and the rest of Team Ronald Mays rushed into the ring.

"That's what I'm talking about!" Frank hugged Ronald. Frank was much smaller after getting shot, but he had healed well. "You the man, slim."

Ronald smiled. He felt good about his performance. He was ready for another run in the boxing game.

Later on, on the phone with T-Bone who was calling from Marion, Ronald told his man how he had put that work in in the ring.

"They say you showed off." T-Bone smiled.

"Yeah, I brought that Lorton game out, you know how that go, slim."

"I'm proud of you. Out of all of us, you was the one that really understood what it takes to be a man, a real man. You never gave up. I respect that. Always did."

Ronald was honored. "We cut from the same cloth, we come up together. If one shine, we all shine. Ain't that how it go?"

"Yeah, you right, but dudes done forgot that part of the game."

"Not me."

"Ronnie ..."

"What's up, T?"

"Make sure you raise our sons to be men. Protect them from what we been through. Keep doin' the right thing out there and protect our sons. Let them see that it's another way."

"You got my word, T. They gon' get the chance they deserve," Ronald said.

Chapter 21

Silver Spring, MD, Saturday, May 10, 1993

Scarface's Money and the Power was pumping through the speakers of the black '91 Volvo 740 turbo as it headed up Georgia Avenue.

"Put that Chronic in," Chris said to Lil' Ronald, who was behind the wheel. They were on their way to City Place Mall.

Going on seventeen-years-old, Chris and Lil' Ronald were young men. Chris was over six feet tall and still growing. He was a younger looking version of T-Bone. In the eleventh grade at Coolidge High School making good grades, Chris was one of the best shooting guards in the D.C. area and had led his school to two city championships. He also held the record for most points scored in a quarter of a championship game— twenty seven points in the fourth quarter; he finished the game with forty three points. Lil' Ronald was 5" 11", one hundred and sixty three pounds, and was running through Golden Gloves opponents like a young Marvin Hagler. Lil' Ronald was also in the eleventh grade at Coolidge High School. He was at the top of his class, and he stayed in the sports section of The Washington Post. Big Ronald was the driving force in the lives of both young men.

Inside the mall, Lil' Ronald and Chris headed toward the

eatery, pulling up on a few honeys along the way.

"Chris! Ronald!" a voice called out.

Lil' Ronald and Chris turned around and saw Paul mixed in with the crowd that was coming in the door to the mall.

Paul was totally different than Lil' Ronald and Chris. At sixteen-years-old, the streets had a strong grip on Paul. He was already selling coke and carrying guns. He'd been down Oak Hill twice for coke charges. Word on the streets was that he fired that pistol, too. Ronald tried his best to keep Paul out of trouble, but being as though Paul lived out Maryland with his mother, there was only so much he could do to help the youngster. Paul had an older cousin from 1st and Kennedy Street, Northwest that he looked up to and hung out with all the time. His cousin was the one that had the most say so in his life.

"What's up wit' y'all niggas?" Paul walked up, and gave Lil' Ronald and Chris five. He was dressed in all black with a black bandanna around his head.

"We 'bout to grab some of them new Jordans," Chris said.

"Y'all niggas stay fly." Paul looked down and checked his beeper. He was still very close to Chris and Lil' Ronald; they were all brothers and that would never change.

"What's up wit' you, joe?" Lil' Ronald asked Paul as a group of young honeys walked by, they all had on skin tight jeans. The three teenagers had to check the honeys out. One of the honey winked at Chris, who returned the wink.

"I came up here to grab a few outfits real quick. Me and my cousin, Kobi 'bout to go up New York," Paul said.

Chris, Lil' Ronald, and Paul hung out for a while. They bought the new Jordans and a few outfits. Then, Chris saw the same bad little honey that had winked at him earlier; she looked like a young Lisa Bonet. Chris was tired of the winking and flirting from afar. He stepped to the honey.

"How you doin'?" Chris said with a smooth smile as he walked up on the honey.

She smiled. "I'm okay, what's up wit' you?" she said, looking Chris up and down, checking out his gray Polo sweat suit.

"I'm chillin'. What's your name, pretty lady."

"Shawnna, what's yours?"

"Chris."

"You go to Coolidge, right?"

"Yeah."

"I saw you do your thing at the Wilson game." Shawnna saw Chris score forty nine points in that game.

"Oh yeah?" He smiled. "You like basketball?"

"Hell yeah. I love it. I play for Wilson."

Chris and Shawnna kicked it for a few minutes. Chris was feeling her. As they were talking, more like flirting, a group of young dudes bent the corner wearing all black. They looked like street thugs. The one wearing the L.A. Kings cap walked up to Shawnna, and said, "Fake ass bitch! You just in everybody's face, huh?"

Chris' face twisted up with anger. He felt disrespected.

"Get out my face, Kelvin," Shawnna snapped. She used to mess with Kelvin, but had cut him off after he fucked her cousin.

"You know this nigga?" Chris asked Shawnna, he was ready to fuck the nigga up.

"Why you wanna know all that, main man?" Kelvin asked with aggression. His four homies made it clear they had his back.

Paul and Lil' Ronald slid up beside Chris. They had his back.

"I asked her that 'cause if she don't know you I'ma knock your bitch ass slam out." Chris got in Kelvin's face. Kelvin swung a wild punch. Chris slipped the punch and fired two hard blows right down the pipe, staggering Kelvin, who would have hit the ground if his homies didn't catch him.

"You always startin' shit!" Shawnna yelled at Kelvin.

"Act like you want some work!" Lil' Ronald glared at Kelvin and his homies. They looked like they wanted to jump Chris.

"What the fuck you niggas wanna do?" Paul whipped out a Glock 19.

Kelvin and his homies got some "act right" real quick and piped down.

"You niggas betta get the fuck on somewhere 'fore I let these hot ones go." Paul mugged.

Kelvin and his homies took off running.

"Punk ass niggas." Paul put the gun back in his waistband and looked at Chris. "You cool?"

"Yeah, I'm cool. Them niggas was fakin' for real," Chris said. He then turned to Shawnna, and said, "You okay? That nigga ain't gon' fuck wit' you, is he?"

"No." Shawnna told Chris who Kelvin was. "This some way to meet, huh?" She was embarrassed.

"Don't trip. I'm glad we met. Why don't you let me give you a ride home."

"I'm wit' my girlfriend."

"She can come, too."

"Let me go get her." Shawnna stepped off.

"You know them niggas?" Paul asked Chris.

"Nan, the nigga was fucked up 'cause he saw me talkin' to shorty."

"Y'all niggas gon' be cool?" Paul asked. "I need to get out of here, somebody had to see me pull this burner."

"We cool," Lil' Ronald said. "Go 'head and roll just in case."

Paul gave Lil Ronald and Chris five and then left the mall.

As Shawnna and her friend approached, Lil' Ronald looked at Chris, and said, "I'm feelin' her friend."

Forty minutes later, the Volvo that Big Ronald had let Chris and Lil' Ronald drive was sitting in front of Shawnna's house on 16th Street, Northwest. They were in a very nice part of D.C. Shawnna's peoples had a little money.

Chris walked Shawnna up the walkway to her door and left Lil' Ronald in the car with the other girl, Yevon. Lil' Ronald had Yevon smiling and laughing for the whole ride to Shawnna's house. Yevon was a cute light skinned girl with long black hair. She was well built and thick as she could be at seventeen-years-old.

"I know you got a girl, smooth as you is." Yevon smiled, showing even white teeth as she and Lil' Ronald sat in the back seat.

"Nah, I just broke up wit' somebody."

"Yeah right. I guess you would say that while you tryin' to holla at me."

Lil' Ronald smiled. "For real, I had a girl I was messin' wit' for 'bout a year and a half, but we broke up. She said I wasn't spendin' enough time wit' her."

Yevon smiled. "Why you wasn't spendin' time wit' her? What, you run the streets?"

"Nah, I box. I stay in the gym all the time."

"Oh yeah, you can fight?" That was a turn on for her.

"Yeah." He smiled. "I been boxin' since I was a kid. You ever heard of Ronald Mays?"

"No, I don't think so." Yevon wasn't into boxing.

"That's my father, he's a pro boxer. He had me boxin' since I was old enough to walk."

"For real?" She was impressed.

"Yeah, he's about to fight for the heavyweight title. You ever heard of Ricky Bowling? He's the champ."

"Nah, I never heard of him, either, but your pops sounds big time."

"He tight, but I'ma bring home the bacon." Lil Ronald smiled

"Why you say that?"

"My pops gon' be thirty six this year, he only planned to

fight until he was thirty five, but last year he lost a close decision to Ervin Holinsfield in their title fight. That was his first title shot. He wanna give it one more shot. Holinsfield lost the title to Bowling, so my pops gon' try his hand wit' him, and he gon' win, but when he hangs his gloves up it's all about me." Lil' Ronald smiled, he really believed in himself and his fight game.

"Sounds like you got it made," Yevon said, thinking that Lil' Ronald came from a rich family.

Lil' Ronald laughed. "I'm okay, but I'm still from the hood, I ain't got it made yet. I done been through some hard times. My pops done fought hard to get where he at, he fought hard for me and my brother, and the rest of our family." Lil' Ronald gave Yevon a quick rundown on his father, telling her about the prison time Big Ronald had done, how he could have been one of the best fighters of his time but he went back to prison on a fluke beef in his twenties.

Hearing Lil' Ronald talk about his father, Yevon could tell that he looked up to him.

"Damn, your father been down Lorton and now he 'bout to fight the heavyweight champion of the world. That's like a rags to riches type story," Yevon said, impressed.

U.S.P. Lewisburg, Saturday, June 27, 1993

On his hands and knees down in prostration, T-Bone offered his morning prayer, thanking Allah for guiding him to Islam and away from his old ways. While locked down in Marion, Ronald kept sending T-Bone Islamic books to read. For three years T-Bone studied Islam and a number of other things. He was now Muslim, going on thirty eight-years-old. His path to peace and truth had been filled with hardships and struggles, but T-Bone believed that it was a divine force behind everything that happened in life. T-Bone used to think Ronald was tripping when he first became Muslim, but now T-Bone understood.

After praying, T-Bone jumped in the shower and got ready for his visit. Cristal was coming up to see him with Chris and Paul. Times had been more than hard for T-Bone and Cristal, but they were still together. They had their spells of beefin', but at the end of the day they were meant to be; they were soul mates.

T-Bone looked at his watch and decided to try to catch Frank early. He knew Frank was a busy man, so he had to catch him before he left out the house. Frank ran a promotion company, among other things. Frank's promotion company was called Toe-to-Toe Promotion; Ronald was the biggest fighter being promoted by Toe-to-Toe. However, some good up-and-coming fighters out of D.C. and Philly were making names for themselves on the under card of Ronald's fights. Wilfred Walker was on board, bringing years of experience to Toe-to-Toe Promotions. Things were working well for Frank in the business world. He'd stacked close to five million dollars in the drug game and washed his hands of the fast lane.

"Hello." Frank answered the phone sounding like he was just waking up.

"What's up, Frank?" T-Bone said.

"Man, what time is it?"

"Seven fifteen."

"What's up wit' you, T?" Frank rolled out of bed, waking Cookie up. He had two sons by Cookie, Frank Jr. who was five, and Fred who was three. "I'm glad you called, anyway, I got a meetin' wit them Ring magazine peoples at ten this mornin'."

"Yeah, you need to get up out that bed then," T-Bone joked. "I wanted to remind you to call the dude's son that owns the renovation company. He waitin' for your call." T-Bone had met an older black dude from Philly who's family owned a construction and renovation company; T-Bone and the dude were in the same cell block. The dude told T-Bone that he'd get his son to renovate The Black Widow for a good price. T-Bone had Cristal buy the space next door to the club so they could expand the size of The Black Widow. Frank was overseeing the project for T-Bone.

"I'll call the dude today. I'll have it all worked out by the end of the week, slim."

"Good lookin' out, homes."

"Oh yeah, before I forget, tell Sop Sop I said I took that money over his mother's house," Frank said.

"I'll tell him as soon I come back off my visit," T-Bone said.

A short while later, T-Bone walked into the visiting hall and saw Cristal and Chris waiting for him. The sight of them put a huge smile on his face, although he wondered where Paul was. Cristal was still looking good and hadn't aged one bit.

"What's up, baby?" T-Bone hugged Cristal and gave her ass a subtle squeeze as he kissed her.

Squeezing his rock hard body tight, Cristal said, "Damn, you smell good, baby."

Turning to Chris, T-Bone hugged his son. "You taller than me youngster."

"And, still growin'," Chris joked.

T-Bone, Cristal, and Chris took their seats.

"What happened to Paul?" T-Bone asked.

"I called him last night and told him to be ready when I came to get him. This mornin' his mother said he didn't come in the house last night," Cristal said. "He grown now, he be hangin' on Kennedy Street wit' his cousin."

T-Bone sighed. He always thought Chris was going to give him the most trouble. "I know one thing," T-Bone said, "a hard head make a soft ass. I just hope and pray Paul don't end up like me. I pray he don't have to learn the hard way. Them said. peoples givin' up too much time nowadays."

"He just goin' through that stage right now," Cristal

"I hope so, but I can't blame nobody but myself."

"Paul gon' be cool, pops," Chris said.

"Hope so." T-Bone rubbed his chin and gave Moose a nod as he walked into the visiting hall. Looking back at Chris, T-Bone said, "So, what basketball camp you gon' go to?"

"Arizona is too far for me, so I'ma go to North Carolina, that's where I wanna go to school, anyway," Chris said. He was a big Mike Jordan fan; he'd been wearing number twenty three since he was thirteen-years-old.

"I like that." T-Bone smiled and gave his son five. "You thinkin' for the future. That's part of bein' a man, slim. I always knew you was goin' to be a thorough young man."

Chris smiled with honor; his father's words meant the world to him.

"You thought about what you wanna study in school?" T-Bone asked. "You know the NBA ain't a given for everybody."

"I wanna study law. If I don't go pro, I wanna be a lawyer," Chris said with a serious face.

T-Bone smiled and glanced at Cristal. She smiled also with a shrug. If their son wanted to be a lawyer, who was to say that he couldn't be one?

"That's right, slim. You can be whatever you wanna be in life," T-Bone said to his son.

Laurel, MD, Wednesday, August 4,

Surrounded by the press inside his gym, Ronald answered questions about his upcoming fight with Ricky Bowling in Las Vegas.

"People are saying that Bowling is going to be too much for you. After all, Bowling did destroy Holinsfield. How will you overcome Bowling's punishing attack?" a sports writer for The Washington Post asked Ronald.

Standing beside Frank and Wilfred Walker, Ronald smiled, and said, "I'm comin' to box and I'm goin' to leave everything I have in the ring. You can bet that."

A female writer cut in, and said, "Mr. Mays, you just turned thirty six, do you think this will affect your fight game?"

"Look at Ali and Louis, two of the greats, they were still champs at thirty five, so if Allah wills, I'll do well at thirty six."

"You once told us that you were done boxing. What's your limit now?" another writer asked.

"Let's just focus on this fight right now."

"What if you lose?" asked another writer.

Ronald looked at Frank and smiled. "Come wit' me. I want you all to see somethin'." Ronald led the press to the back of the gym where Lil' Ronald was in the ring with Roland throwing lightning fast combinations at the mitts on Roland's hands. "If I don't win this upcoming fight, my son is the future." He pointed at Lil Ronald with pride. "That's the future right there." Ronald smiled.

Las Vegas, NV, Saturday, August 28, 1993

Synthia woke up in her hotel suite and found Ronald watching tapes of Bowling's fights. It was eight eleven A.M. "I see you are up early," she said as she rubbed Ronald's back.

He smiled, sitting at the foot of the huge bed with the remote in his hand. "This is it, it's all or nothin' tonight, baby."

"Baby you gon' be just fine." Synthia raised up. "After all you've been through in life, you walk away a winner no matter what, insha Allah. For us to even be here in this position is more than what most people ever expected. Allah has blessed us. You fought your way from the bottom to the top, I saw it wit' my own eyes. I'm proud of you, baby. Everyone is proud of you. You are more than I could have ever dreamed of in a husband. Insha Allah, you'll win tonight. You trained hard, you gon' knock the bamma slam out."

Ronald laughed. "Is that right?"

"You know it."

"Since you callin' money, what round will he go to sleep in?"

"No more than five, you'll put him to sleep in less than five rounds." Synthia pointed at the TV. "He all big and fat, anyway, he don't even look like he in shape."

"I'm goin' for a knock out in five then, just for you." Ronald rubbed his wife's smooth leg.

Hours later, Ronald was sitting on the balcony of his suite looking out over the city of sin. Lil' Ronald and Chris were on the balcony chillin' with him. Ronald loved spending time with the two young men that he had helped raise; they were headed in the right direction and Ronald was proud of that. He would give every dime he'd ever made from boxing to insure that Lil' Ronald and Chris made something of themselves in life.

Paul came out onto the balcony squinting his eyes due to the bright sun in the clear blue sky. "Today is your day, Ronnie." Paul patted Ronald on the back. He had a lot of respect for Ronald and looked up to him, even though the way he carried it in the streets said something different. Paul was hard-headed. "You already the champ as far as I'm concerned." Paul sat down beside Ronald. "They should go ahead and give you the belt right now, joe."

Ronald laughed. "Is that right?"

"Come on, young, everybody know you beat Holinsfield the last fight, you banged him out the whole fight. I watched it over and over again wit' Lil' Ronald," Paul said, sliding on his Versace shades.

"Yeah, well, I'ma let it all hang out tonight. That's for sure." Ronald winked at Paul.

Cristal stuck her head out of the balcony door, and said, "Ronald, Frank said he need to see you in his suite. He said it's important."

Ronald went to see what was up and found Frank and Wilfred Walker talking to a big-shot fight promoter from New

Eyone Williams

York.

"What's up, men?" Ronald said as he took a seat next to Frank.

Wilfred told Ronald that Erik Ruiz had come down with food poisoning and couldn't get out of the bed. Ruiz was one of the super middleweights that was supposed to fight on Ronald's under card. Frank, Wilfred, and the big-shot New York promoter stood to lose a lot of money since Ruiz couldn't fight.

"Okay, so now what?" Ronald knew that his twelve million dollar pay day was safe no matter what.

"We need to find another fighter to fill in for Ruiz." Ronald told Lil' Ronald about the situation. The seventeen-year-old was fearless. Lil' Ronald told his father that he would destroy the nineteen-year-old Santos. Synthia, on the other hand, wasn't comfortable with the idea, however, she left the decision up to father and son.

"Pops, I can do it. I'm tellin' you," Lil Ronald said, trying to get his father to say yes. "I'm in great shape. I train like I got a fight comin' everyday. You know I do. Let me do it. We can make history together, pops."

"He can do it, Ronnie," Roland said to his brother. "Santos gon' be scared to death of Lil' Ronald. Let him do it, slim."

Ronald looked at his wife, then his brother, and then his son. He took a deep breath, and said, "Okay, but you better fight your gloves off, Lil' Ronald." He pointed at his son.

Ronald went back to Frank's suite and told them that he'd let Lil' Ronald fight. They were pleased and the stage was set. Dave King made a few phone calls and sealed the deal.

Lil Ronald's fight was the first of the night. He and Santos were both 5' 11", one hundred and sixty five pounds, and they both had mean jabs that allowed them to do other things in the ring with their skills and power. The crowd was pleased to be a part of history in the making; they showed a lot of love. It was a good night for boxing. After the introductions, it was fight time. Lil' Ronald was a little nervous in his corner as he listened to Roland. "You gon' smash this joker. You did it before," Roland said.

"I'ma smash him again, too," Lil' Ronald said.

The bell rang. Both fighters came out dancing and jabbing with a lot of head movement. Santos landed the first punch. A left hook. Lil' Ronald came right back with one of his blazing combinations and ended it with a double uppercut. The crowd went off.

In his dressing room, Ronald was impressed while he watched the fight on the big screen as he got his hands wrapped.

Lil' Ronald and Santos battled through the first two rounds giving the fans what they paid their good money to see. Trading punches in round three, Lil' Ronald landed a big over-hand right that hurt Santos. Santos grabbed Lil' Ronald in hopes of slowing him down.

The ref separated them. Lil' Ronald attacked Santos' body, and then went upstairs with a crushing hook that sent Santos against the ropes like a drunk driver. Lil' Ronald had been taught well by Roland, he put the pressure on, but Santos fought through the round.

"You got this joker, shorty," Roland yelled into Lil' Ronald's face as he sat in the corner. "Work the body. You hurtin' his ass to the body!"

The bell rang for round four. The fighters came out swinging. Lil' Ronald popped a long jab and then dug to the body twice. Santos frowned and grunted in pain. Lil' Ronald weaved a hook and went hard to the body again. Santos rocked Lil' Ronald with a quick three piece to the face area. Lil' Ronald covered up and took the flurry of punches on the arms and gloves. Out of nowhere, Lil' Ronald sidestepped Santos and threw a short uppercut that snapped Santos' head back like he'd been hit by a shotgun. Santos fell and slid backward. Lil' Ronald watched as the ref began the count. When the count got to eight, Lil' Ronald raised his arms and began jumping up and down. He'd put his work in. His people rushed the ring and crowded around him in celebration.

"You did it! I knew you could do!" Roland yelled as he picked Lil' Ronald up in the air. Lil' Ronald had never felt so proud in his life. His first fight was in Vegas and he'd knocked his man out in four rounds. Looking at the camera, Lil' Ronald said, "Get ready, Ronald Mays, heavyweight champion of the world!"

A short while later in Ronald's dressing room, the only voice that could be heard was Roland's. "It's all about you, baby boy!" Roland was fired up. Team Ronald Mays was about to march to the ring. "Tonight is our night! We 'bout to take this thing back to Chocolate City! Work ain't hard!"

Scarface's Money and the Power played as Ronald's team made their way to the ring in black Madness T-shirts with T-Bone's face on them. Under T-Bone's picture were the words, Death Before Dishonor. Team Ronald Mays entered the ring close to fifteen deep. Ricky Bowling made his grand entrance moments later. He was a big, brown skinned huge man at 6' 4", two hundred and forty pounds. His fighting style was all about power punching and constant pressure. He could end a fight with either hand. At 5' 11", two hundred and ten pounds, what Ronald lacked in size he made up for in heart and skill.

The announcer began. "In the blue and white trunks at twenty eight and zero with twenty four knockouts, we have the WBA and IBF heavyweight champion of the world!" The announcer then dragged his deep voice and conttinued. "Ricky 'Big Dynamite' Bowling!" The crowd went off.

"And, from the nation's capital, in the black trunks at thirty four and one, with twenty seven knockouts, we have Ronald 'Razor' Mays!" The crowd went off again. The rules were given again and the fighters headed for their corners.

"Remember the game plan," Roland said to Ronald. "No matter what happens, your defense and speed will get you to the promised land."

The bell rang and Ronald took a deep breath as he headed for center ring with his guards up. The cheering crowd had him in a zone. A surge of energy flowed through Ronald's body. Bowling swung a murderous left hook off the top followed by a shotgun blast of a right hand. Ronald stepped out of the way with ease and fired back-to-back stinging jabs as he circled the bigger fighter. The first real exchange of championship blows came next. Bowling worked his long jab and then caught Ronald with a loud overhand right. Ronald felt the punch throughout his whole body, but answered it with a body-head attack that came in the flash of red gloves. Ronald grabbed Bowling, showing a lot of strength, and slung him behind him. Bowling became enraged and spent around with a strong left and right hook. Ronald slipped them both and peppered the champ with a three piece to the head. Another heavy exchange of blows ensued with loud and powerful force followed by a roar from the crowd. Suffering from a crushing uppercut, Ronald found himself against the ropes taking a number of blows to the gloves and arms. Although he was well protected, Ronald felt the champ's power. The bell rang and the round ended.

In his corner, Ronald listened to more instructions from Roland, who wanted more boxing out of Ronald and less brawling.

Ronald came out for round two and got down to business. He gave the champ different looks and continued to blast him with his long jab, frustrating him. "Fight!" the champ grunted. "Fight like a man! Stop running!" Ronald answered the request with more jabs followed by a few powerful left hooks every time the champ rushed him. Ronald clearly out-boxed the champ for the rest of the round.

For the next five rounds, Ronald stuck to his game plan, but the champ changed his and began rushing and trying to strong-arm Ronald. He pushed Ronald around, hit him with low blows and elbows, all out of sight of the ref.

Ronald came out smoking in round eight. Halfway through the round, the two fighters were tearing into each other like fighting lions until Ronald slipped a Mike Tyson-like uppercut into the mix. The champ took a long fall and hit the canvas with a hard bounce.

A loud gasp came from the crowd.

"Four ... five ... six ..." The ref stood over the champ flagging his hand in his face as he counted.

Ronald and his team watched with their hopes up. Ronald could almost taste the title.

"Seven ... eight ..." the ref continued, but the champ was climbing off the canvas. "Fight!" the ref said, getting out of the way. Ronald went straight to work, throwing another chopping combination that staggered the champ. The champ grabbed Ronald and held him until the round was over.

In round nine, the champ had his legs back under him and was landing hard blows. Ronald changed the tone of the fight after throwing a deadly flurry of punches to the champ's head, and then backing out of danger with a popping jab. The champ launched a powerful assault, rushing Ronald, who took his defense game to the level of an art form as he positioned himself in one spot of the ring and slipped every punch thrown by the champ, driving him crazy.

Rounds ten and eleven came with more action than the crowd could've asked for. Bowling got more aggressive, sensing that he needed a knockout. Ronald put more footwork into effect and went into his long range assault with textbook precision. Both fighters showed that they had the heart of a champion and steel chins that could stand the test of time in the ring.

In his corner before the final round, Ronald took in deep breaths as Roland coached him. "You got this fight, you got the only knock down of the fight. Just box and bring it home. It's in the bag."

The bell rang and both fighters came out for the moment of truth. The champ wasted no time, he took the fight to Ronald. At one point while he had Ronald on the ropes, it looked like his fire was burning at full flame, but Ronald slid from under him and pushed him into the ropes. Back in the center of the ring, Ronald went back to his long range fight game. The champ began chasing Ronald. Ronald ducked a wild hook and came back with a left hook to the body and head of the champ. The crowd went off. The champ tried to grab Ronald, but found himself slung into the corner. As the final seconds of the fight ticked away, the two fighters let it all hang out, throwing every punch in the book. The bell rang and they were still throwing punches. The ref jumped in and broke it up. Ronald walked to his corner with his arms raised.

Moments later, both fighters were in the center of the ring as the decision was read. Synthia and Cristal were in the front row hoping and praying that Ronald had made it clear that he was the champ. "... and your winner by unanimous decision ..."

Synthia closed her eyes, she couldn't take the excitement.

"...and new heavyweight champion of the world, Ronald "Razor" Mays!"

Synthia and Cristal went off ghetto style, and rushed the ring, yelling and screaming.

The feeling was like no other for Ronald as he was given the WBA and IBF belts. He was mobbed by his peoples and camera crews from HBO and other sports networks. Surrounded by Synthia and the rest of his peoples, Ronald addressed the press. "I want to give all praised to Allah for giving me the strength to do what people said I would never be able to do. I want to thank my family and friends for standing by me every step of the way. I gotta thank my brother and comrade, who's still down Lorton, Harrison-EL for first training me when I was still young and wild. Thank you to everybody that ever stood by my side." Ronald was still breathing hard as he put his arm around Synthia and kissed her for all of the world to see.

"Mr. Mays," the anchorman for HBO said. "What's next for you? Will you defend the title? You have always claimed that thirty five was your limit."

Ronald smiled as Frank walked up and hugged him. "I'm goin' to give Bowling his rematch, then I'm gon' give Holinsfield a shot. If all goes well after that, which will be within the next year or so, I'm goin' to call it quits and pass the torch to my son. You got to see what he can do tonight. Things look good for the home team."

"People say that you have had an easy fight to the top since most of the greats are gone," the anchorman said.

Ronald looked at Frank. They both laughed. "People that say that ain't been where I been , seen what I seen, or been through what I been through as a man. They ain't from where I come from. I don't pay that kind of talk no attention. To stand here wit' my family wearin' these belts is more than a blessin' for me and I've worked hard for this. Can't nobody take that from me. I'm the champ. I earned it."

The night went down as one of the best times of Ronald's life. A celebration was due.

Aftermath

Denver, CO, Sunday, February 13, 2005

People from all over the country made their way to Denver for the NBA All-Star Game. Hotels were booked up for miles. Stars of all kinds—rappers, boxers, ball players, actors, and street legends were on hand. The parties were nothing but the truth. It was just after ten in the morning when Philadelphia 76er guard, Allen Iverson, and his crew came through the luxurious lobby of the Four Seasons hotel.

"A.I." A female fan with blond hair and blue eyes ran up and asked if she could take a picture with Iverson. He fulfilled her wish and kept it moving. The white girl went crazy as she ran back over to her friends with the camera. Her whole crew was college students. Moments later, they got to take pictures with Will Smith and Kobe Bryant. Their morning was going well.

"Oh my God! There's Ronald Mays Jr.!" one of the girls yelled, rushing over to get a picture with the super middleweight champion of the world. Unlike his father, Lil' Ronald was a popular champ. The ladies loved him. At twenty eight-years-old, he was thirty two and zero with twenty nine knockouts. He'd brought new life to a division that he'd ruled since he was twenty two when he unified the world title. At 6'

3", one hundred and sixty eight pounds, Lil' Ronald came with a full assault kit. Excellent upper-body strength, sturdy legs, stamina that could last twenty rounds, and a body attack that had caused internal bleeding more than once. The quality of his opposition was beyond question; he had fought every big name that wanted to see him. He was planning on stepping up to light heavyweight and doing some damage in the near future.

"What's up, baby." Lil Ronald smiled as he put an arm around his young female fan and took the picture with her and her friends. The young white girls couldn't stop smiling and asking Lil Ronald different questions. He gave them what they wanted; he was good at dealing with attention from the fans.

After taking a few pictures with the fans, Lil' Ronald headed upstairs to his suite. He'd just returned from a good work-out at the hotel gym. Inside the suite, he found Chris and Tracy McGrady playing NBA Live 2005 on Play Station 2. Chris was playing with the 76ers and McGrady was playing with the Rockets.

Chris ended up going to Georgetown where he cut up and played big for four years. He was drafted by the 76ers in the second round of the '98 NBA College Draft as a power forward that scored an average of twenty five points a game. He was also an all-star every year since then. He was a 6' 10", two hundred and twenty five pound forward with ball handling skills like a point guard.

"What's up wit' y'all?" Lil' Ronald sat on the bed with the two all-stars. They spoke, but were deep into the game as they leaned toward the TV smashing away at the controllers rapidly. The game was in overtime with the 76ers down three. Lil' Ronald watched as the two all-stars battled back and forth for a few minutes. As the last seconds ticked away, the 76ers were down by one. Chris used Allen Iverson to throw the ball up over the rim for Chris' video game image of himself to grab it and slam it down hard for the win.

"That's what I'm talkin' 'bout, slim!" Chris dropped the

controller on the floor and raised his arms triumphantly. "Hit
the floor!"

McGrady knocked out a quick one hundred push-ups
straight, jumped back up, and said, "Run it back."

"Let's work!" Chris reset the game.

A knock at the door grabbed Lil' Ronald's attention. He
opened the door and let the dude in. The dude walked over to
Chris and tried to snatch the controller out of his hand, but
Chris quickly pulled it away. "How can you sit there and play
that stuff for hours like that?"

"Come on, pops, you messin' me up," Chris said to his
father without taking his eyes off the TV.

T-Bone smiled. At forty nine-years-old, he didn't look a
year older than thirty five. Prison had kept his appearance
looking good. He worked out hard and ate right. His dark skin
had a serious glow. Light traces of gray in his hair didn't stand
out at all. His 6" 4" frame was packed with two hundred and
thirty five pounds of penitentiary muscle—Cristal called it
love-making muscle. She never left T-Bone; she did close to
thirty years with her man. When T-Bone touched down and
tasted the outside world, it was like he'd been transferred to
another world. He'd wanted for nothing in prison, but seeing
and feeling all the wealth and success his family had been
blessed with blew his mind. Million dollar homes, top of the
line cars, businesses, and more was a dream come true. Ronald
had put the whole family on his back and built something
priceless. T-Bone thanked Allah for having a comrade and
brother like Ronald.

Later on at the hotel restaurant, the men all sat around a
round table eating and joking. The restaurant was top of the
line, it was full of big names and everyone seemed to be in the
spot for lunch. Ronald, Lil' Ronald, Roland, T-Bone, Chris,
and Paul enjoyed their lunch and hung out at the hotel for a
few hours before going to the all-star game.

Paul took a while to wake up, but after a few trips

through the juvenile system and one trip down Youth Center I, he got himself together. He had a job running one of Frank's many night clubs.

The evening came quickly. While Chris, Lil' Ronald, Paul, and Roland headed to the Pepsi Center for the all-star game, Ronald and T-Bone were in a rented big-body Benz on their way to the airport. Ronald was behind the wheel. He and T-Bone joked about old times.

At forty eight, Ronald had done more with his life than he'd ever dreamed of. After winning the heavyweight title, the city of D.C. threw a parade for him that went down Georgia Avenue. He was proud. As promised, he fought Ricky Bowling again and knocked him out the second time around; the fight only went three rounds. He then fought Ervin Holinsfield five months later and knocked him out as well in the ninth round. Ronald called it quits after that and put all of his energy into Lil' Ronald.

The airport was busy. Pulling up behind a cab, Ronald and T-Bone watched as people came out through the sliding doors. Frank came out into the cold evening air, rushed to the car, and jumped in the back. On the way to the all-star game, Frank told Ronald and T-Bone about his trip to Vegas where he'd met with Dave King and some other men from the Nevada Boxing Commission. Everything was looking good for a June title fight for Lil' Ronald and a boxer by the name of Anthony Porter.

Ronald, Frank, and T-Bone got to the Pepsi Center a short while later and made their way to their court-side seats. The game got under way and was full of NBA excitement. T-Bone couldn't believe he was really watching his son post up Kevin Garnett and dunk on Tim Duncan. T-Bone stayed on his feet yelling for Chris to dog whoever tried to check him. Everybody went off when Allen Iverson and Chris ran the floor on a fast break, and Iverson threw the ball off the backboard and Chris caught it high in the air, did a three sixty and slammed it with two hands. The whole Pepsi Center jumped to their feet yelling and screaming.

As the evening came to an end, the East won one hundred and fifteen to one hundred and thirteen. Chris finished with nineteen points, fifteen rebounds, and four blocked shots.

"Can't get no better than that." Ronald smiled as he, T-Bone, and Frank headed for the car.

LORTON LEGENDS

About The Author

Eyone Williams was born and raised in Washington, D.C. He is a publisher (Fast Lane Entertainment), author, rapper and actor representing urban life in a way that is uniquely his. Known for hard-core, gritty novels, Eyone made the Don Diva best-seller list with his first novel, Fast Lane (Fast Lane Publications). He followed up his debut novel with Hell Razor Honeys 1 and 2 (Cartel Publications). He then delivered his readers a short story entitled The Cross (DC Bookdiva Publications). He's also a staff writer for Don Diva Magazine , his most notable work is featured in Don Diva's issue 30, The Good, The Bad, and The Ugly, where he outlined the rise and fall of D.C. street legends Michael "Fray" Salters and Wayne Perry. Eyone's first acting role was in the forthcoming movie Dark City (District Hustle). His latest mixtape, A Killer'z Ambition, is a sound track to the novel, A Killer'z Ambition (DC Bookdiva Publications) by Nathan Welch.

For more information about Eyone Williams visit his Facebook page: facebook.com/eyone.williams

Order Form

DC Bookdiva Publications
#245 4401-A Connecticut Avenue, NW
Washington, DC 20008
dcbookdiva.com

Name: _____

Inmate ID _____

Address: _____

City/State: _____ **Zip:** _____

QUANTITY	TITLES	PRICE	TOTAL
	Up The Way, Ben	15.00	
	Dynasty By Dutch	15.00	
	Dynasty 2 By Dutch	15.00	
	Trina, Darrell Debrew	15.00	
	A Killer'z Ambition, Nathan Welch	15.00	
	Lorton Legends, Eyone Williams	15.00	
	Coming Soon		
	The Hustle	15.00	
	A Beautiful Satan	15.00	
	A Hustler's Daughter	15.00	
	Q, Dutch	15.00	

Sub-Total $_____

Shipping/Handling (Via US Media Mail) $3.95 1-2 Books, $7.95 1-3 Books, 4 or more titles-Free Shipping

Shipping $_____
Total Enclosed $_____

Certified or government issued checks and money orders, all mail in orders take 5-7 Business days to be delivered. Books can also be purchased on our website at dcbookdiva.com and by credit card at 1866-928-9990. Incarcerated readers receive 25% discount. Please pay $11.25 per book and apply the same shipping terms as stated above.